Shakespeare and the Triple Play

The Face of Shakespeare, by Cao Wenhan.

Shakespeare and the Triple Play

From Study to Stage to Classroom

EDITED BY
Sidney Homan

Lewisburg
Bucknell University Press
London and Toronto: Associated University Presses

Associated University Presses
440 Forsgate Drive
Cranbury, NJ 08512

Associated University Presses
25 Sicilian Avenue
London WC1A 2QH, England

Associated University Presses
P.O. Box 488, Port Credit
Mississauga, Ontario
Canada L5G 4M2

The paper used in this publication meets the requirements of the American National Standard for Permanence of Paper for Printed Library Materials Z39.48-1984.

Library of Congress Cataloging-in-Publication Data

Shakespeare and the triple play.

Includes bibliographies and index.
1. Shakespeare, William, 1564–1616—Criticism and interpretation. 2. Shakespeare, William, 1564–1616—Study and teaching. 3. Shakespeare, William, 1564–1616—Dramatic production. I. Homan, Sidney, 1938–
PR2976.S33734 1988 822.3'3 86-73239
ISBN 0-8387-5122-9 (alk. paper)

PRINTED IN THE UNITED STATES OF AMERICA

Contents

Part III: The Classroom

To my beloved friend, Zhang Siyang,
and the Shakespeare Society of Jilin Province,
the People's Republic of China

爱逢河畔小布衣
伦敦城郊大手筆
身逢聖世勤模創
根源民间知寒飢

喜悲映史鑄诗剧
美善和真入主题
深情妙喻辞如海
推陈出新今勝昔

光夺群星有众誉
功亚上帝无人疑
琼弥贊颂題遺篇
馬恩景仰树藝旗

文采長留照天地
神州传颂猶杜李

Thinking Afar of the World's Beloved Dramatic Poet, William Shakespeare, upon the 416th Anniversary of His Birth

From Avon's banks up to the bustling suburbs of London,
Industrious WILL, a country youth, you went to be the Poets' King;
As in the Spring, a bud fresh fast bloomed golden.
You thrived among the masses, ever sharing their suffering.
All comedies, tragedies, and histories of yours are poems
unsurpassed;
Fair, kind, and true is the whole of your treasured argument.
Alive with images and feelings, your language seems an ocean vast;
Renewing things extant or past, you've built yourself a monument.
No wonder that none but you could the multitude of stars outshine,
And, next to God, create most with all your fervent heart.
Not only did young Milton follow Jonson to praise you line by line,
But later Marx and Engels worshipped your living art.
Far brighter now your volume's light illumes the earth and sky.
You are as much loved in China as our own Du Fu and Li Bai.

Zhang Huaiqing

Introduction: Play Ball

SIDNEY HOMAN

THIS COLLECTION OF ESSAYS WAS BORN IN MY HOMETOWN, PHILADELPHIA, traveled to the People's Republic of China, and returned to Bucknell University and Lewisburg by way of Gainesville, Florida. Allow me to explain.

i

Two years ago, Michael Payne, the chairman of Bucknell's English department, asked if I would organize a Shakespeare session for the College English Association's national conference to be held in Philadelphia in April 1986. Not much of a conference goer myself, indeed a wallflower of the worst order at the few I have attended, I agreed immediately, glad to satisfy my friend's request. Since I work both on campus and in the theater, I picked as the inevitable topic for that session the interplay among the Shakespearean's work in the study, the theater, and the classroom. I did not, however, intend to limit participation only to scholars who work as actors or directors—far from it. Therefore, the middle term, "work in the theater," included being a member of the audience, for as I have suggested in a recent book, *Shakespeare's Theater of Presence*, and as Bert States argues much more eloquently in his *Great Reckonings in Little Rooms*, the spectator offstage is surely no less vital to the performance than the actor onstage: a production, properly, represents an enactment of the playwright's text as it is received, *ratified* by the audience. A baseball fan of long standing, I chose the triple play as the metaphor for the title of my session, not to imply that this link among study, theater, and classroom occurs infrequently, as does the triple play, but rather that whenever it occurs it, like the triple play, is "rare" in the sense of being wondrous, something that enhances the lives of all its participants.

To be sure, Shakespeare's text may be construed as literature, or read as autobiography, or as a window to the mentality of his age. It can even be deconstructed. There are many ways of skinning this cat. My concern, however, was performance, and how thinking about Shakespeare influences both that performance as well as one's perspective as a spectator, and—no less—how the influence flows in the opposite direction. In my first year out of graduate school I met a distinguished Shakespearean who boasted that he had never been to the theater, that for him no performance of Shakespeare could ever equal the play as constructed in his own mind. How unfortunate, I thought then. Yet Sherman Hawkins, who writes in this collection on his experience playing Prospero and who was—coincidentally—my teacher in the first class I took at Princeton University some thirty years ago, reminded me, his student, in a recent letter that the scholar who teaches Shakespeare—who teaches him effectively, with conviction—is no less an actor, for in inhabiting Shakespeare's dramatic world as he or she perceives it, and in conveying to the students that personal world, thus interpreted, as a model of thinking and feeling, the scholar-teacher "experiences" the play in a way no less intense, albeit different, than does the actor. "Theater" is a very large term, inclusive and generous.

The December before the CEA convention, I dutifully sent out a "call for papers" to some two hundred English departments. The response was overwhelming, and I found myself incapable of limiting my choice to just four papers for the CEA's two-hour session on Friday. The program chairperson agreed that I could have a second session on Saturday. The essays here of Philip McGuire (in a somewhat revised form), Robert Hapgood, Barbara Rosen, and Sherman Hawkins (also in revised form) were delivered at the "Shakespeare and the Triple Play" session, and those of Roger Geimer, Suzanne Burr, and Ronald Shafer at the "Teaching Shakespeare" session the following day.

Payne and I had plans to publish all seven papers, along with mine on directing *The Comedy of Errors*, in the *CEA Critic*, but then, just before I left for the People's Republic of China for a summer of teaching Shakespeare at Jilin University and directing *The Merry Wives of Windsor* in Changchun City, he asked if, instead, I would expand the collection for the new annual book-length format of *Bucknell Review*. After forcing my friend to "pay me back" by contributing a piece on *The Tempest*, I solicited essays from James Calderwood, Harvey Birenbaum, Laura Keyes, Marvin Rosenberg, June Schlueter, and James Lusardi, besides asking my colleague Norman Holland to do an "Afterword." When I returned from China in the fall, my experience there had—predictably—very much altered the way I thought about Shakespeare, the theater, and my own role in performing this triple play. My director's notes for *The Merry Wives of Windsor* that will be produced this spring in Changchun City displaced the piece I had planned on *The Comedy of Errors*. I also added to the collection essays by Zhang Siyang, the distinguished Shakespearean at Jilin University and my host during my stay in the People's Republic, and by his son Zhang Xiaoyang. Added too was "Thinking Afar of the World's Beloved Dramatic Poet, William Shakespeare," by the well-known Chinese poet Zhang Huaiquing; and on the book-jacket and the frontispiece is reproduced a portrait of Shakespeare by the gifted artist Cao Wenhan, a present to me from the Shakespeare Society of Jilin Province.

Now in its second year, that organization, comprising scholars, actors, directors, political officials, and townspeople, is the first provincial Shakespeare society in China and plays a vital role in the cultural life of the country's northern province. I owe that Society "a thousand thanks"—as my Chinese friends would say—for making my stay so exciting, so productive; in dedicating this book to them I express a gratitude deeper than did ever plummet sound. For all times, for all peoples, Shakespeare and his stage are, of course, very large. The collection itself was becoming very large, in fact too large for the space limitations of the *Bucknell Review*, and hence it is here published by the press of that excellent university.

ii

I divide the essays into the three areas of the book's subtitle: Study, Stage, and Classroom. But like Bottom's wall in *Pyramus and Thisby*, the walls here, I assure you, are more "down" than up. Thus the "scholarly" essays of the first section are really individual "stagings" of the text, where perspectives range from metadramatic to psychoanalytical, stagings to which the author is simultaneously his or her own metacritical audience. In the second section the actors, directors, playwrights, and spectators commenting on performance, both historical and present, are also scholars whose readings of their experience is inevitably colored by work in the study—and colors, in turn, their work in the classroom. In section three, fellow teachers concentrating on the challenge of bringing Shakespeare to students have first considered such issues as what options the text offers to directors, the alarming way that the visual in *King Lear* drains the language of its metaphoric flexibility, or how attendance at a performance loosens the authoritarian stage of the classroom. If the walls between the three sections, then, are collapsible by design, the triple-play metaphor, even when not directly stated, is implied by each essay's position in the collection. For the movement of this volume itself is from the fairly formal prose of section one, where the posture of the writer is that of the scholar encountering Shakespeare's text, to the first-person accounts of experience in the theater and the performance criticism of the second section, to the increasingly informal essays in the third section whose focus is on strategies for the classroom and actual encounters with students.

I have also tried in each section to place the essays in a sequence that is itself evolutionary. Part I, "The Study," opens with James Calderwood's "Immortal Money: *The Merchant of Venice*." From his first book, *Shakespearean Metadrama*, to his latest, *If It Were Done: "Macbeth" and Tragic Action*, Calderwood has, I believe, entertained an increasingly catholic definition of metadrama. If his earlier work focused on the theater's self-reflexive nature, its own metacritical commentary, this latest essay first considers money from the perspective of economics, theology, psychology, and mythology before invoking its paradoxical function as the dominant image in the play. A material surrogate for god, it bonds the enemies Antonio and Shylock in a sterile symbiosis built on the Venetian's guilt and the Jew's envy; a false god, a deceptive image, when adopted only for itself, money, conversely, can symbolize true value when it is used for love, for a communal good. By the end of his essay, Calderwood has converted these seemingly extradramatic and thematic issues to metadramatic ones: words become Shakespeare's own money, his medium of exchanging something concrete for something otherwise ineffable. The playwright uses such linguistic currency to earn interest, to establish the "circular exchanges of meaning" that constitute the play *The Merchant of Venice*.

Michael Payne examines the text of *The Tempest*, particularly from the perspective of the audience who, unlike the characters, witness the "full extent" of Prospero's powers, as he responds to the recent polarization in the play's criticism where the liberal tradition celebrating Prospero's benevolent magic has been challenged by political readings that find Shakespeare promoting a "self-deceptive psychology of colonization." Like the playwright's own art, Payne's approach is itself multilayered. He examines the age's divided attitude toward transitive magic, used to manipulate others, and subjective magic, directed inward to the control of oneself; then he turns to the play's own political focus on the self as "a repertoire of externally, socially interactive roles, which clothe or encase a vulnerable inner core of being." At length he looks at the political circumstances attending the court performance of *The Tempest* and the three general but conflicting views of the natural man in the Renaissance. Not a synthesis of polarized critical views, Payne's reading appeals to the modern audience asked to see Shakespeare's art reflecting both his time and our own, and to experience the playwright's compelling blend of realism and romanticism in which magic and politics are linked, indeed "not only need but also require each other."

In "Between the Mirror and the Face: Symbolic Reality in *Richard II*," Harvey Birenbaum's initial concern is the desposed king's symbolic consciousness, the way his self-generated, and therefore idiosyncratic, world view, based on the faith in divine right, invariably conflicts with Bolingbroke's own social realism, his literalism. By definition setting up Richard for defeat, fragile as the ego itself, imparting meaning to the individual's existence even as he hastens toward suffering, nihilism, and the concomitant yearning not to exist, this symbolic consciousness at once forces Richard to see the tragic isolation of the self even as it enables him to be sentient, to understand the basis and the necessity of his own tragedy. In his postscript, Birenbaum extends Richard's vision to Shakespeare's: *Richard II* represents the playwright's encounter with the real world and his reflection on the symbolic medium of his theater. Birenbaum takes one more step. Our response as audience—or, I might add, as teacher—duplicates that of playwright and his character, for the tragedy is "rich with human presence and urgent with a sense of our own needs."

I have taken an editor's liberty in chapter 4 of abridging somewhat Mason Wang's translations of "Hamlet's Melancholy" by Zhang Siyang and "Shakespeare and the Idea of Nature in the Renaissance" by Zhang Xiaoyang. In part I did so to highlight those features of each essay which I thought would be of special interest to readers in the West, and in part so that I could juxtapose in a single chapter essays that so complement each other: Zhang Siyang was also his son's teacher during his graduate years at Jilin University. As the father delves into the cause and, no less, the social significance of Hamlet's psychological state and the son assesses the conflict between old and new concepts of nature in the Renaissance as manifested in Shakespeare's plays, their writing will, I suspect, appear sometimes familiar, sometimes less so to readers in this half of the world, perhaps even old-fashioned or "Bradleyan" at times and at other times deeply personal, even political to a degree beyond what we normally experience in scholarly prose. Both are staging their individual Shakespeares for a country that has known the playwright for some time but, only in the more immediate past, has intensified its study of his plays. And their performance: in April 1986 there was a massive Shakespeare festival in Beijing, where over half of his plays were staged by numerous companies ranging from the traditional to the very modern. Yet if this full-scale interest in Shakespeare is of recent vintage, the fact is that both Zhangs write from a theatrical tradition predating Shakespeare by several thousand years, and in a country whose theater has as its first concern the character in the context of his society, and of its public needs.

Laura Keyes's "Hamlet Fat" serves as a transition between Part I and its successor, "The Stage." She starts with Gertrude's description of her son as "fat and scant of breath." Does the mother mean that Hamlet is overweight, paunchy? Keyes examines other references to fat in the play, along with images based on eating, overeating, and excess, before reviewing arguments of whether we place "solid" or "sullied"—or even "sallied"—before Hamlet's "flesh." Speculating on the anguished responses of critics and actors to the possibility of Hamlet's being fat, she then asks the reader: what would be the value of having as a tragic hero a prince who, on the surface, looked most unheroic—fat? Could Hamlet, as a scapegoat, be the fatted calf fit for sacrifice, or might he be fat like a woman, a mother nurturing her sick child Denmark? Is his fleshy exterior and lean, intellectual interior an instance of dissimulation in a play built on deception? In suggesting that by resisting the notion of a fat Hamlet, we only define our ideal hero, Keyes would have us ask our students to reconsider their own preconceptions about *Hamlet,* to entertain a reading of the play they might unconsciously want to deny.

The actor first takes "The Stage" in Part II as Sherman Hawkins recalls how in playing Prospero he was exposed to the "symbiotic interplay between criticism and performance." Hawkins establishes a series of equations. The character Prospero, like the actor playing him, must use the power of words to win centrality to himself; the productive comradeship that Prospero learns to establish with his fellow humans parallels the ensemble playing that actors must cultivate for the good of the production. The fairly equal division in Prospero's part between his longish speech to Miranda in the second scene and his reappearance after act 4 echoes the tonal split in the play between storm and music that G. Wilson Knight spotted years ago. And as the concept of wonder evolves from magical effects to human relationships, from the artificial to the natural, the actor playing Prospero himself moves from being an illusory stage figure to a fellow human who in his "Please you draw near" addresses those offstage no less than onstage.

The student, properly, follows his teacher as I offer a "Director's Notebook" for a production of *The Merry Wives of Windsor.* In advising the two Chinese companies who will perform that play on my concept for *Wives,* and then on the specifics of set, lighting, costumes, music, acting styles, as well as a suggested blocking for the play's first two scenes, I am very aware, as any author should be, of just what has influenced these notes. For me, that influence ranges from the writings of two fellow scholars, William Carroll and Barbara Freedman, to my own feminist politics and metadramatic bias, which, in recent years, have in turn influenced both my writing and teaching. No less my experience with modern Chinese drama, where the community takes precedence over the individual, and where the audience itself becomes a "player" in the performance, shaped my reading of *Wives,* even as I adapted the play for a theater based on ritual and symbolic stage blocking, a theater valuing the suggestive, or "magic," over realism. To the same production, I add my own notion of the characters' inner lives, a subtext reflecting not only the practice of current American theater but a recent personal interest in psychology.

A playwright and actor himself, not to mention being the author of those several *Masks of* . . . studies which document the various options directors and actors have taken over the centuries in staging Shakespeare's major tragedies, Marvin Rosenberg looks at the various and seemingly contradictory ways that the Macbeths have been played. In particular, he charts the changing relationship between husband and wife, the way both Shakespeare's open text and the cultural norms of the age, our sense of conscience that alternately encourages and prohibits behavior, can encourage a cruel or an appealing Macbeth, a domineering or a soft-natured Lady Macbeth. That today actors and scholars tend to see each of the two central figures as possessing contradictory human traits may reflect our own modern sense of relativity. As directors and actors discover the play's wide range of tones, its "polyphony," they bring us—and we can bring our students—closer "to the full experience of complexity and depth in Shakespeare's characters."

As a stage historian, Rosenberg traces *Macbeth*'s history from the eighteenth century to the present. In "The Camera in Gertrude's Closet" the performance critics, June Schlueter and James Lusardi, move from a literary reading of act 3, scene 4, to an identification of the signals the text provides for staging, to a detailed re-creation of the scene as enacted in the 1948 Olivier film and then in Rodney Bennett's 1980 BBC production. Was Gertrude an accomplice in her husband's death? When she says that Hamlet has "cleft" her heart, is she repentant of her crime or anguished over her son's madness? Why does the Ghost appear when he does? Later, when Gertrude tells Claudius that Hamlet is mad, is she preserving his secret (that he was merely "mad in craft") or expressing her honest conviction? What does her cry, "Help, ho!" signify—guilt, fear, or what Alan Dessen has called a "larger shared effect"? In carefully providing answers but not *an* answer to each of these questions—and more—Schlueter and Lusardi show how a scholar's reading of the scene coupled with an account of two very different productions demonstrates the options for interpretation available to the teacher and student, no less than to those enacting Shakespeare on stage or in the study's quieter stage.

In Part III, "The Classroom," Philip McGuire's "Intentions, Options, and Greatness: An Example from *A Midsummer Night's Dream*" also looks back to Part II because, like Rosenberg, Schlueter, and Lusardi, he is interested in directorial options. McGuire asks how, in what mood, and when precisely does Egeus exit in act 4, scene 1 after Theseus has overruled the father when he insists that the law of Athens be brought to bear on Hermia? Further, if Egeus is present in the final scene (the Folio, but not the Quarto, specifies that he is), what is his mood here: is he resentful, resigned, or happily reconciled to the marriage of Hermia and Lysander? The Folio gives Egeus dialogue in the final scene that the Quarto assigns to Philostrate. One option for the director, then, is to have Egeus depart sullenly in act 4, scene 1, never to return to Athens, with the actor who had played Egeus now doubling as Philostrate in act 5. Hermia and Lysander are present in the final scene but do not speak to Egeus, nor, in the Folio version, does he speak to the newlyweds. What decision does the director make, indeed *must* make, with such "open silences" (a subject McGuire explores at greater length in his recent *Speechless Dialect*)? In choosing among such options present in the text, the director or actor only continues a process that Shakespeare initiates. In turn, the teacher needs to show the student that fixity, the notion that there is a single right way of interpreting Shakespeare, goes against the playwright's own intent.

Barbara Rosen in her essay "Actualizing the Metaphor" is more concerned with students' "seeing" Shakespeare. An actress herself, she means not just attending productions—valuable as that is—but also realizing that there is a constant, productive tension in the plays between language and vision, between Shakespeare's poetry and its actualization in what we observe onstage. After a "preface" where she shows how descriptions of Malvolio are activated onstage when he appears wearing cross-gartered yellow stockings that suggest his own insecurity and dated sexuality, she turns to *King Lear* where the stage picture often brings the poetry preceding it to a horrifying visual close. Edgar's optimistic "The worst returns to laughter" is cruelly qualified when he sees his blind father; even the villain Edmund's courtly "yours in the ranks of death" receives a bitter enactment when the bodies of Goneril and Regan are born onstage. For Rosen, *Lear* underscores the "willed failure of rhetoric." At best the play simultaneously affirms and discredits man's picture-making ability: Edgar's description for Gloucester of the fiend atop Dover Cliffs resembles a "child's grotesque," is a patent lie, and yet moves the father to believe in the fairy tale. At the end of the play, the visual has drained language in those lines, "Speak what we feel, not what we ought to say"—whoever speaks them. For Rosen, then, it is essential in class, no less than at performance, to teach our students how "to see" a play whose "text" is visual no less than poetic.

Robert Hapgood, Roger Geimer, and Suzanne Burr concentrate even more directly on their experience with students. Hapgood outlines the stages of a class exercise, using Hamlet's soliloquy "O that this too, too sullied [or "solid," or "sallied"] flesh would melt," wherein he asks students to identify the various emotions in the speech before choosing the most dominant one. If students in the "old days" sought one right answer, Hapgood observes that these days they tend to be too relative, too generous in accepting different views; thus the exercise at once appeals to the students' modern mind set even as it asks them to make a choice. The exercise itself is followed by viewing various actors doing the soliloquy, from a rather passive Jacoby to a superactive Burton. Concerned that the students see how the text leaves "generous room" for interpretation, Hapgood asks that students—and those in the profession—entertain the notion that not all views are valid and that some are to be preferred to others equally valid.

Roger Geimer plays the role of his own student as he records his reactions to three versions of the second scene of *The Taming of the Shrew* where Petruchio beats Grumio after the servant puns on his order that he "knock [him] here" on Hortensio's door. As Geimer examines the Zeffirelli film, Jonathan Miller's BBC production, and Wilford Leach's televised version of a live performance from Joseph Papp's "Shakespeare in the Park" series, he raises such questions as: how compatible is physical farce with a more human portrait of Petruchio's relation with his witty servant? how does the director's decision about that relationship influence Petruchio's character as it later engages with Kate's? what influence does the medium (film and television, particularly) have on the directorial concept? if the essence of farce is to deny any serious consequence of action, is farce, as so understood, the most productive way of reading this scene? In responding to the three versions, and in preferring one, Geimer performs, in essence, the role he hopes his students will learn: coming to a personal reading of the play. At the end of his essay he recounts the students' own reactions to his classroom experiment.

A beginning teacher, Suzanne Burr found herself confronted by her students' absolutist views of the playwright. There must be a single right way of understanding Shakespeare. The teacher holds the key to that truth. Once one "does" Shakespeare in class, the subject is closed. Her recourse was to make a detour around what her students saw as an authoritarian classroom, where they assumed that she would provide them with a single, right interpretation of the "institutionalized" playwright, and take them to see a performance of *Macbeth* that was, for a variety of reasons, clearly an artistic failure. As her students properly objected to the director's choice of incongruous costumes, or the no less jarring presence of natural and declamatory acting styles, they became intensely aware of "production values," the decisions, some right, some terribly wrong, that are made in the theater, decisions that reflect, whether right or wrong, the same creative choices described by other writers in this collection. Seeing the enacted text as an instance of taking risks, realizing that some interpretations of Shakespeare could fail onstage, that complementary readings are all that we can or should expect, Burr's students began to take the initial step toward that day when, for her, they "will be able to supplant their teachers . . . and to make Shakespeare their own." Hers, I think, is an especially poignant essay, for she reminds us of our own continuing obligation to our subject and our students.

The final essay in Part III is Ronald Shafer's account of an NEH-sponsored Shakespeare Institute that he headed. Designed to increase the scholarly and classroom abilities of high-school English teachers, his program was itself based on a triple-play metaphor: Phase 1, in which the teacher-students were exposed to lectures, concerts, and exhibits on Shakespeare and his age, did research on designated topics, pooled their own knowledge, and recorded their experience in diaries; Phase 2, when they attended performances of Shakespeare in a variety of theaters, as well as seminars where Shakespeareans, theater historians, actors, and directors met on their common subject; and Phase 3, where the teachers planned classroom units together and discussed how to implement in their own courses what they had learned at the Institute. Shafer's exuberant prose reveals his own high pleasure in this enterprise that, for those of us who teach at the university level, may also serve as a reminder: we are the beneficiaries of our colleagues whose teaching is closer to the front lines.

iii

I will not comment on the "Afterword" by Norman Holland, except to say that it is there. To say more about his essay, speculating on and then extrapolating from the other essays in this collection, would be to create a hall of mirrors: Homan reading Holland reading seventeen essayists reading Shakespeare who, it can be assumed, read both life and the theatrical world that for him was its mirror.

Nor will our finest practitioner of reader-response theory have the last word here. For I can imagine a "conventional" triple play making its way from a line-drive catch near third base, to a tag of the runner streaking from second to third, and finally a doubling-up of the player desperately trying to get back to first. That first base is the classroom, the place where a "mere" double play is converted, or can be converted to that wondrous triple play. For me, the classroom is not only first base, but also "first," the object of our work in the study and in the theater. The statement of principle of the College English Association puts it effectively: "Recognizing that scholars must teach to live, these men and women [who founded the CEA] wanted to effect a more substantial nexus between teaching and scholarship than economic necessity." Surely, this final out can best be made by the readers of these essays.

I have almost worn to the ground the baseball metaphor informing this collection. Now, as its editor or, in baseball parlance, the umpire, I can only say to the contributors and their readers the very words with which the real-life umpire opens each and every game—"Play Ball!"

N.B. I decided not to impose a single text of Shakespeare's plays on this collection, but rather to allow each author to use the text he or she prefers—probably the very text carried from the study to the classroom.

Shakespeare and the Triple Play

PART I
The Study

1

Immortal Money: *The Merchant of Venice*

JAMES L. CALDERWOOD

Gold and the Devil

THE MERCHANT OF VENICE AMPLY SUPPORTS THE CONTENTION OF MOST OF Shakespeare's villains and fools that the road to immortality is paved with gold. Gold is the god men worship, and the Exchange is their church. If, as this implies, the content of your purse is sacred stuff, then all you need do is to put money in it again and again, as Iago advises Roderigo, and you can purchase the secular equivalent of immortality in Venice, the divine Desdemona.

In *Twelfth Night* Feste fools with the divinity of money when he amuses the Duke Orsino by making gold migrate from the Duke's pockets to his own:

> *Duke.* Thou shalt not be the worse for me. There's gold.
> *Clown.* But that it would be double-dealing, sir, I would you could make it another.
> *Duke.* O, you give me ill counsel.
> *Clown.* Put your grace in your pocket, sir, for this once, and let your flesh and blood obey it.
> *Duke.* Well, I will be so much a sinner, to be a double-dealer. There's another.
>
> (5.1)

And of course Feste tries for a third but is put off. Here, then, we find religious and aristocratic grace played off against the sinful flesh and its hankerings after gold. Feste's "put your grace in your pocket" means for

---

This essay, which appears in James L. Calderwood's book *Shakespeare and the Denial of Death*, is reprinted here through the kindness of the University of Massachusetts Press.

his Grace to put his hand in his pocket but also for his ethereal "grace" to disappear and for gold to materialize in its stead. In the religion of aristocracy practiced by dukes like Orsino, divine grace quite naturally incarnates itself in the shape of *his* Grace; but in Feste's religion of postlapsarian flesh and blood it should descend one step further and become coins for clowns.

Feste's substitution of gold coins for grace forecasts Timon's labeling gold a "visible god" (5.2). According to Kenneth Burke, gold and money have an air of divinity about them because they substitute for God as a common denominator of human motives. A common deistic faith once dissolved cultural and international differences: God represented "the universal substance in which all human diversity of motives was grounded."[1] Money can compete with such a faith because it too serves "as a universal symbol, the unitary ground for all action." Antonio and Shylock can scarcely speak to each other across the barrier dividing Christian from Jew, but one is a merchant and the other a usurer, and so for both of them money talks.

But according to Luther it talks with a diabolic accent. For him, money does not substitute for God directly; the devil does that. Money is simply the medium of the devil, and capitalism is his creation. "Money," Luther declares, "is the word of the Devil through which he creates all things the way God created through the true word."[2] If gold is a visible god, the god is not God but the devil; and he who worships gold worships the devil:

> Usury lives securely and rages, as if he were God and lord in all lands . . . There is therefore no worse enemy of mankind on earth, next to the Devil himself, than the covetous man and the usurer, for he wishes to become God over all men.[3]

Covetous men like Shylock are bound by money into the devil's cult. For that matter, most economies are bound together by money, especially that of Venice. Business activities like buying and selling, loaning and borrowing, bring men together as members of a common society. However appalling the bond between Antonio and Shylock, it does bind them despite their hatred, just as their common language binds them even when they use it to "trade" insults.

In fact one might argue that precisely because he lends money for interest, Shylock is more bound into Venetian society than the Christian Antonio, who lends money gratis and conducts his trade abroad. For the same reason, the philanthropic Timon is as alienated from Athenian society as the misanthropic Timon he later becomes. He does not loan but gives money, and in the spirit of Aristotelian magnanimity he espouses pure giving with no expectation of repayment. This idealistic one-way practice militates against "bonds," the essential feature of which is reciprocation. Thus when Timon's money runs out and he looks to his friends for relief, he makes the unhappy discovery that pure giving creates pure receiving—receiving devoid of a sense of moral indebtedness—and this discovery sends him into the wilderness where he digs up gold and identifies it as a visible god, a god that cannot "redeem" or atone mankind but can circulate the diseases that will bind men in their common mortality.

In *The Merchant of Venice* at any rate, money binds not merely the devilish Jews into a tribe but the Christians as well. Antonio's unholy bond to Shylock must be honored because the law will have it so; but the law itself is bound to higher masters, as even Antonio acknowledges:

> The Duke cannot deny the course of law;
> For the commodity that strangers have
> With us in Venice, if it be denied,
> Will much impeach the justice of the state,
> Since that the trade and profit of the city
> Consisteth of all nations.
>
> (3.3)

With trade and profit enthroned over all, the boundaries between Christian and Jew begin to blur, and Luther's fears about the threat of capitalism to religion appear to have some basis, at least in Venice where Christianity seems little more than a social shibboleth. Where, after all, are the other magnanimous Christian merchants when Bassanio goes forth to "try what [Antonio's] credit can in Venice do"? Of course Shakespeare has got to get Antonio indebted to Shylock, but he does not even trouble to suggest a reason for Bassanio's failure to try the Christians first. Ducats are ducats; they weigh as much in the Jew's pocket as in the Christian's.

Because money binds men in such unholy alliances, capitalism for Luther is a thoroughly devilish business. And devilish business is for him fecal business. As Norman O. Brown says,

> the anal character of the Devil is sensuously perceived and sensuously recorded by Luther (in his *Table-Talk*) with a gross concreteness that latter-day Protestantism cannot imagine and would not tolerate.[4]

Let us forego the illustrations and merely agree that from Luther's point of view money is both fecal and devilish. As such it becomes, like the devil, the visible god of a degraded materialistic world.

This Lutheran equation, though often endorsed by psychoanalysts, does not appear in Shakespeare, so far as I can tell, except on one significant occasion in *King Lear.*[5] Instead he would seem to side with those who argue that money represents a reaction formation to the unfortunate presence of feces in humans. Norman O. Brown and Ernest Becker, for instance, say that "money is god" because it "negotiates immortality"—because it symbolizes, not feces, but "the denial of feces" and what it represents, "physicalness, animality, decay, and death."[6] In other words, if the body in its material repellence betrays us to death, and if the most repellent feature of the body is feces, then one way to transcend both is to accumulate gold and buy our way to greatness.[7] The compulsion to deny death and the body acts as a philosopher's stone to transmute base feces into the gold that can purchase immortality.

Money is especially conducive to these high-flying aspirations because it generates disembodied desire. That is, purely bodily needs can be satisfied, at least temporarily. We can eat and drink our fill, engage in sex, sleep, get warm or cool off. But the desire for money compounds like interest itself, more begetting more.[8] Like the mystic yearning for the City of God with its streets paved with spiritual gold, the capitalist dreams of an El Dorado forever situated just beyond the horizon. If we run a little faster, work a little harder, get a little luckier, then grace will come to us as it does to Feste. But, alas, we can never get our fill of the sacred stuff. The insatiate trafficker in gold, Luther complained, will not content himself until he has become "God over all men." And to become a god is to become immortal. Let the Dow-Jones average rise just one more point and I can buy all the indulgences I will need for the sin of possessing an animal body.

One great virtue of money as a means of denying death is, as Timon noted, its visibility. As an external recognizable sign for elusive internal qualities, it quantifies our worth, for our own benefit as well as for others. Terms of value like value, dearness, worth, price, estimate, wealth, and so on are indispensable, but even they lack the measurable precision of money, which can tell me to the penny how much more I am worth than Jones and how much I need to catch up to Smith. In this respect money has the additional virtue of being hierarchically ordered, ranging upward from pennies to crowns and sovereigns, and therefore reflects and reinforces the hierarchical gradations and degrees in the socioeconomic chain of being.[9] A penny will make you a pauper, but crowns may make you a queen; at least they will buy you country estates and servants and all the livery of wealth. Which is to say that in the immortality market God, being invisible, finds it hard to compete with the devilishly visible god whose pockets jingle with sovereigns and crowns and nobles by the score. Divine signifieds are merely so much celestial vapor without signifiers of highly visible substance. It is names, icons, churches, and rituals that keep the pews full. And that means dealing in the devil's coin. For great cathedrals betoken not only great spiritual worth but also lots of tithes. So too with people. Who can spot a Joan of Arc, an Albert Schweitzer, or a Martin Luther King on the boulevard? and who can miss Midas, the Aga Khan, or a Rajneesh with his ninety Rolls Royces? For that matter, who can miss Portia, the wealthy heiress of Belmont?

Midas and Portia

Before turning to Portia, let us take a look at Midas, the very symbol and personification of wealth. He came by his golden touch by doing Dionysus a service and getting his choice of a reward. In choosing gold it is as though he said to Dionysus "If you can't immortalize me as a god, do the next best thing: make me the richest of men." But Midas's fate reveals that an obsession with symbolic immortality may lead to the very death it seeks to transcend. Men deny their bodily nature at their peril, as Ovid makes clear when he tells us how Midas's pleasures take a painful turn:

> Then whither his hand did towch the bread, the bread was massy gold,
> Or whither he chawde with hungry teeth his meate, yee might behold
> The peece of meate betweene his jawes a plate of gold too bee.[10]

The attempt to satisfy the spirit, it appears, is inimical to the satisfaction of the body; if the soul surfeits, the belly must fast. This is evidenced by the fact that the distinction between Midas's own body and spirit is paralleled by that between gold as metal and gold as money. For in his hunger for the symbolic value of gold, its sacred power, Midas unwisely ignores its material nature. His fate foretells the fate of all immortality projects: a demystifying return to the body and death.

To elaborate: the Midas story illuminates the difference between gold and silver metals and gold and silver money. The metals in themselves are as useless as dog's teeth, beads, shells, currency, cheques, and so forth. "In money," Marx says, "the value of the things is separated from their substance."[11] Of course, as malleable metals gold and silver can be transformed into artifacts, but even then they exist primarily as works of art, better for disinterested contemplation than for hard service over time. The wise king will use gold for his crown, not for his helmet, and silver for his scepter, not for his sword. And the wise suitor for

Portia's hand in *The Merchant of Venice* will distinguish between Portia's symbolic commercial value as a woman of wealth and her human value as a woman of beauty and virtue—the kind of distinction she herself makes in assuring the Prince of Morocco that his black exterior is irrelevant to his inner worth (2.1).

Portia's first two suitors should have taken instruction from Portia and Marx, since in choosing the gold and silver caskets they both misvalue the lady and misunderstand money. If gold and silver are to graduate from useless metal to precious money, they must be assigned an arbitrary value, and in this play that suggests a kind of lie or presumptuous superficiality of which the precious metals are guilty and lead is innocent. Lead is a good honest metal; it takes on no glittering airs but appears as plain and valueless as in fact it is. It is therefore an appropriate stand-in for the virtuous Portia, who exhibits a leadlike maidenly modesty in saying "You see me, Lord Bassanio, where I stand, / Such as I am" (3.2).

Thus before Bassanio rejects the gold and silver caskets he muses at some length about false appearances and true realities, and exhibits an awareness of the distinctions Midas could not grasp. In fact, he turns from the golden casket murmuring "gaudy gold, / Hard food for Midas, I will none of thee" (3.2). He chooses metal instead of money, material object instead of symbol, and Portia such as she is instead of Portia as she appears in the eyes of the avaricious world. In doing so he escapes the "carrion Death" that lies within the gold casket (2.7).

Bassanio's conception of human worth runs counter to that of Shylock. Later, when Bassanio proposes that Shylock loan Antonio a thousand ducats, the noncommittal Jew observes that Antonio is "a good man" (1.3). Bassanio replies haughtily "Have you heard any imputation to the contrary?" and Shylock hastily corrects him: "Ho, no, no, no, no! my meaning in saying he is a good man is to have you understand me that he is sufficient" (1.3). For the usurer it is not moral worth but collateral that counts. Besides, what evidence has the Jew had of Antonio's moral or simply human goodness? Antonio's mode of valuation is no more attractive. "Many a time," Shylock says, "and oft / In the Rialto you have *rated* me" (2.1). "You call me misbeliever, cut-throat dog, / And spit upon my gaberdine," and Antonio replies that he is like to do so again if the opportunity presents itself (1.3). The "dog" epithet makes it clear that Antonio's sense of his own personal worth derives largely from the superiority of the "human" Christian to the "animal" Jew and, as he (and everyone else) says again and again, to the "devil" Jew. From the perspective of the Christians, Shylock more than qualifies as Luther's diabolical money-god seeking to rule over a manure-heap world.

Denying Death by Choosing Death

Let me pause at this point and return briefly to the "Theme of the Three Caskets." In an article of this title,[12] Freud associates the lead casket with death because of its dumbness—that silence which moves Bassanio "more than eloquence"—which he says often represents death in myth and the unconscious. This view is somewhat misleading because the play specifically associates the gold casket with death when Morocco opens it and discovers a skull within—"O hell! What have we here? / A carrion Death" (2.7). Still, Freud's instincts are right. Actually all three caskets can be said to represent potential death, even the lead one. Caskets, after all, are caskets—that is, coffinlike—and Portia tells Bassanio, "I am locked in one of them" in the form of a picture that is her "shadow." Moreover, for Bassanio to "give and hazard all he hath" on the lead casket clearly implies a willingness to risk his life. In making such a choice, Freud suggests, Bassanio "chooses" death and transcends it at the same time. For to choose potential death is to reverse the natural scheme of things in which death chooses us. Bassanio's choice represents the ultimate in wish fulfillment, an occasion on which we triumph over our mortal victimage and transform death into Portia—into life and love, not to mention a substantial dowry.

In any event, as Bassanio gathers himself for the choice, both he and Portia insist that they are liminally poised between death and life. Let me choose quickly, he says, "for as I am, I live upon the rack"; and Portia declares "I stand for sacrifice" and hopes that Bassanio can rescue her from imminent death as Alcides did Hesione when she stood for sacrifice before the sea monster. "Live thou, I live," she says, as though he, and she as well, confronted death. Of course Christians have always maintained that the way to everlasting life is by choosing death, by dying to the world. Bassanio and Portia do not risk death to attain eternal life but to attain the symbolic immortality offered by a love that conquers death—or, in this trade-dominated play, a love that bargains with death and wins life.

Portia as Apportioner

In a recent article on *The Merchant of Venice* Lars Engle perceptively notes that Portia's name implies the "portion" that an Elizabethan bride brought with her into marriage, a portion that Bassanio can employ to relieve his debts.[13] This certainly helps account for what Portia *is*—a prize. I wonder if a supplement to this symbolism might also help account for what she *does*. I have in mind the fact that the Greek concept of fate, Moira, is expressed in terms which imply that human lives are allotted, shared out, or, in our present context, apportioned. Clotho (the spinner), Lachesis (the apportioner), and Atropos (the inflexible) combine to distribute shares of life to humans as though they were dividing the spoils of a victory or portioning out food for a meal. It is not we who choose our lots but the Moirai who assign them to us.[14] That Shakespeare may have had this or a similar notion in mind is suggested when Portia associates "lot" and "destiny" in telling Morocco

> In terms of choice I am not solely led
> By nice direction of a maiden's eyes;
> Besides, the *lott'ry of my destiny*
> Bars me the right of voluntary choosing.
>
> (2.1)

Although Shakespeare probably did not have the Moirai in mind, Tyche (or Ananke), the mother of the Moirai, is equivalent in Roman religion to Fortuna, a goddess Shakespeare was quite familiar with and likely to associate with this lottery of life and life's goods.

If we think of Portia as being not only a portion in her own right but also an apportioner, then she would appear to fulfill her destiny by insisting on a strict accounting of the portion of Antonio due Shylock:

> If thou tak'st more
> Or less than a just pound, be it but so much
> As makes it light or heavy in the substance
> Or the division of the twentieth part
> Of one poor scruple, nay, if the scale do turn
> But in the estimation of a hair,
> Thou diest, and all thy goods are confiscate.
>
> (4.1)

Shylock's lot—his life and all his goods—depends on his taking no more than his just share of Antonio's flesh; and needless to say, Antonio's lot hangs in the same balance, in the scales of Fortune.

Fortune unfortunately is fickle and unfair. She spins out more life from her wheel of fortune to some than to others, and pours forth more goods, health, and happiness from her cornucopia of plenty to some than to others. Because of these discrepancies in physical, social, economic, and mortal status, some men envy others, and the others are often apprehensive of being envied. It is part of the business of culture to foster systems of belief that will reduce envy or justify it and hence reconcile men to their unequal lots—by creating, for instance, myths that make goddesses like Tyche and Fortuna responsible for the discrepancies, or by calling on the spurious analogies of social Darwinism to legitimize having and not-having as the inevitable consequences of natural selection.[15]

Surely the envy generated by inequality plays a powerful role in *The Merchant of Venice*. In an Iago-like speech Shylock says he cannot or will not explain his insistence on his bond—

> So can I give no reason, nor I will not,
> More than a lodged hate and a certain loathing
> I bear Antonio.
>
> (4.1)

That tells us next to nothing. Gratiano seems closer to the mark when he observes Shylock whetting his knife:

> Not on thy sole, but on thy soul, harsh Jew,
> Thou mak'st thy knife keen; but no metal can,
> No, not the hangman's axe, bear half the keenness
> Of thy sharp envy.
>
> (4.1)

Helmut Schoeck points out that no society seems immune to envy, certainly no Western one, and yet envy is almost always repressed as a motive.

> It is remarkable how seldom the vernacular forms of different languages permit one to say directly to another person: "Don't do that. It will make me envious!" Instead, we tend to talk in abstract terms of justice, saying that something or other is intolerable or unfair, or we relapse into sour and bitter silence.[16]

That seems an apt description of Shylock, who prefers to cite an unmotivated hatred and loathing than to admit that he envies the Christian merchant whose lot in Venice is so much more fortunate than his own.

Might this not have some bearing on Antonio's mysterious sadness? The ethic of the New Testament is designed to protect Christians against the envy and hostility built up by social and economic inequalities. It insists that we should love our neighbor as ourself, expunging all envy, that in the eyes of God we are all spiritual equals, that the poor inherit the earth while the rich are stuck like camels in the eye of the needle, and so on. But since even Christian societies retain discrepancies in status, particularly those as devoted to commerce as Venice, the handsome, the brilliant, the powerful, and perhaps especially the wealthy must be made to carry a burden of guilt for being so favored by Fortune. If you envy me, it is my fault, not yours. If I am greatly fortunate, then I am greatly at fault. Everyone I pass who is less fortunate than I stares back at me with the evil eye. They hate and revile me. I must do something to ward off the evil eye, to rid myself of guilt, to atone for my being so favored. "Guilt-engendered activity," writes the psychoanalyst Gerhart Piers, "is at best *restitution* (sacrifice, propitiation, atonement) which rarely frees, but brings with it resentment and frustration rage, which in turn feed new guilt into the system."[17]

Perhaps Antonio's unaccountable sadness is a symbolic product of Shylock's unaccountable hatred and loathing, his secret envy. If so, if Antonio feels mysteriously guilty, then he is by the logic of metaphor in debt. This metaphorical debt owed the despised Jew by the Christian is as it were taken literally by Shakespeare, who quickly converts it into monetary debt and then bodily debt. It would be in keeping with such a view that when his bond falls due Antonio accepts its consequences with resignation and patience, as though some part of him welcomes the opportunity to pay the debt and hence to atone for his criminal superiority. Having had more than his fair share of Fortune's gifts, he yields to the Jew who will gladly take more than his fair share of vengeance. Only Balthazar the apportioner can rescue him by pointing out that the law of Venice measures the financial transactions of its citizens with scrupulous exactitude, however unequally their lots in life may weigh in Fortuna's scales.

Metaphoric Trade

As Sigurd Burckhardt first observed, the patriarchal "law" that governs Portia in Belmont is as harsh as the (equally patriarchal) law that governs Antonio in Venice.[18] Both laws appear to prescribe death, Venetian law literally, Belmontian law figuratively; both, properly interpreted, make apparent death yield life; and both are subordinate to a higher law, Trade. As Antonio's lines quoted above indicate, the law in Venice must be upheld for the sake of Venetian trade. By the same token, the paternal law in Belmont must be upheld for the sake of a marital and sexual trade—vows and bodies—that is also grounded in money (Portia's) and debt (Bassanio's). Both laws, in other words, must function in such a manner as to promote exchanges, whether of money, goods, or love.

Thus despite the differences between Belmont and Venice the two laws are metaphorically interchangeable. Which suggests that if money is the principal medium of exchange in Venice, metaphor is the principal medium of exchange in Shakespeare's play. As such, metaphor closes gaps and dissolves differences. Metaphor is Shakespeare's money.

Who for instance could be more different and antagonistic than Antonio and Shylock? Yet Shakespeare takes pains to dissolve the differences between the two men. Each invests his immortality overtly in his religion—where else should immortality come from?—and yet, as we have seen, their common god is money. After all, Antonio expects from his oceanic ventures a "return / Of thrice three times the value of this bond" (1.3). And the point of his accumulating these sacred ducats is to deny death and the body. Hence by substituting a pound of flesh for ducats, Shylock demystifies the money-god, demonstrating just what it is that the money they share and the religions they do not share repress and transcend. That is part of the driving force behind Shylock's most famous speech,

> I am a Jew. Hath not a Jew eyes? Hath not a Jew hands, organs, dimensions, senses, affections, passions; fed with the same food, hurt with the same weapons, subject to the same diseases, healed by the same means, warmed and cooled by the same winter and summer, as a Christian is?
>
> (3.1)

As Shylock has demonstrated, the religious differences between Jew and Christian are bridged not only by money, their shared immortality symbol, but also by the body, their shared mortality symbol. No wonder Shylock can make money and flesh interchangeable, substituting the one for the other in his bond with Antonio. And no wonder Portia-as-Balthazar asks on entering the courtroom "Which is the merchant here, and which the Jew?" (4.1). Like Portia's erring suitors, the two financial venturers are misled by the glitter of religious and social symbolism into regarding one another merely as stereotypes of those hateful abstractions, the Christian and the Jew, when the symbolism of the play itself suggests that they should present themselves to one another as Portia presents herself to Bassanio: "You see me . . . where I stand, / Such as I am."

But Shakespeare is not so naive as to think the Jew and the Christian can divest themselves of their culture. That sort of thing is proper to Belmont and romance, not to Venice and materialism. Hence the abstract money-dealings of the two men devolve into a murderous bodily bond, just as Midas's greed for sacred power led back toward death. Even more obviously than, say, honor or patriotism or kingship, money is exposed as a form of false immortality, the god that always fails. And yet in *The Merchant of Venice* money metaphorically points the way to what Shakespeare regards as a true or at least a more humanly satisfying immortality. It is a matter of breeding.

As Shakespeare presents it, the artificial symbolic value that converts gold from metal to money is a kind of interest or "use." As Aristotle said, as the laws against usury said, and as Antonio says, gold and silver, like lead, are "barren metal" (1.3).[19] On being converted into money, however, they acquire a capacity to breed and multiply: money makes money whether through usury or mere trade. By that account Portia's wealth, her symbolic value, is an inherited product of her father's use of money to make money. But it is just that kind of use which the casket scheme rejects. Of the three equally barren metals, Bassanio chooses the one that modestly presents itself as it is, and thus he wins Portia as she is. But as she is, apart from her wealth, Portia, far from being barren, derives her greatest value from her natural ability to breed. Not to breed money, like Shylock's "use," but offspring, like Laban's "ewes." Such as it is, the human solution to death is for Bassanio and Portia to "get the ring upon [Bassanio's] finger that never will come off," as the phallic riddle in *All's Well* puts it, and to show "a child begotten of [Portia's] body" (3.2).

Thus as Marc Shell has shown,[20] the procreativity of Belmont stands in opposition to the barrenness of Venice, where the mysteriously sad Antonio is by his own denomination a "tainted wether" (4.1)—that is, castrated ram—and where Shylock metaphorically suffers the same fate when Jessica makes off with his money, including "two sealed bags of ducats / Of double ducats . . . / And jewels—two stones, two rich and precious stones" (2.5). Bereft of his "two stones"—the "family jewels," as the familiar pun aptly puts it—Shylock, like Antonio, is gelded and reduced to the human equivalent of barren metal. Money and the body are metaphors for one another in this play, but to take the metaphor literally, as Shylock does, is to take a great risk. For in losing ducats and jewels he also loses both his body's ability to increase (the stones) and indeed his body's increase (Jessica herself). As a result the infertility represented by his and Antonio's commercialism points to the fertilities of Belmont as a truer medium of immortality.

At the same time, we have to admit that Shylock is not entirely barren. Unlike Antonio he has married Leah, he has begotten Jessica, he makes money breed money, and he makes language breed meanings. The essence of his verbal style is metaphor, the medium through which words and meanings are exchanged. The fact that his metaphors beget most of the truly eloquent speeches in the play suggests that we should not dismiss him or his values out of hand, for he may tell us something about Shakespeare's sense of verbal value in this play.

For words, after all, are Shakespeare's money. Like Portia's wealth, they are as good in Venice as in Belmont, as "sufficient" as Antonio's collateral, as binding as Shylock's bond, as all-governing as the will of Portia's father or the law of Venice. Words are not only Shakespeare's money but his bonding agent, and metaphor is his special medium of exchange. By virtue of the playwright's penchant for metaphoric trading, money, the body, guilt and innocence, religion, law, and sexuality circulate here and there throughout *The Merchant of Venice*, assembling all of the play's different themes in the marketplace of art.

Before Bassanio chooses the lead casket he launches into a long speech repudiating the silver and gold caskets for their deceptiveness. They are ornamental, superficial, and dangerously seductive—the visual equivalent to the gilded Ciceronian style of Shakespeare's day. The equivalent, indeed, to Shakespeare's own style in a play like *Love's Labour's Lost:* self-consciously playful, verbose, full of fire-new sesquipedalian phrases and sentences that turn obediently inside-out like cheveril gloves. Unfortunately for the scholars, such a style proves "useless" inasmuch as it fails to generate a bond, a "world-without-end bargain," between them and the French ladies. Therefore, in penance, Berowne vows to tailor his language more simply in the future, discarding "taffeta phrases [and] silken terms precise" in favor of "russet yeas and honest kersey noes."

In *The Merchant of Venice* Shakespeare makes good as it were on Berowne's promise. Like Bassanio he chooses the lead casket and the plain style. Not of course that he now writes a leaden style or one in which words are as literally exact as those of the Venetian law, but that he employs the plain style procreatively, to multiply meanings, to promote metaphoric trading, to create finer verbal bonds. Even the lead casket, after all, is not just barren metal but a visual metaphor for sincerity, honesty, and modesty—and, as we are arguing, for a literary style that embodies these qualities. If it illustrates the Puritan precept that "every man," as Stephen Gosson claimed, "must show him selfe outwardly to be such as in deed he is,"[21] still it also violates that precept by being figurative, by being more than it appears to be. In this respect the lead casket, the metallic parallel to Portia's modest virtues, forecasts her later figuration, or transfiguration, of herself as Balthazar. That is, if we think of Balthazar as the vehicle of a metaphor whose tenor is Portia, and think of this exchange of identity as part of a geographical metaphor in which her journey to rescue Antonio carries the meaning of Belmont to the signifier Venice, then it is by means of these metaphoric exchanges that the two otherwise discrete worlds of Shakespeare's play are beneficently bound together.[22]

Because of its network of metaphors, then, *The Merchant of Venice* brings about marriages not merely among its characters but among its own parts. The result is a denial of artistic death analogous to the denial of actual death by the marriages of the lovers. We can phrase it in ringlike terms. Portia rebukes Bassanio for losing the ring, which was "a thing stuck on with oaths upon your finger, / And so riveted with faith unto your flesh" (5.1). The faithful riveting of flesh to ring bawdily metaphorizes the sexual fidelity of husband and wife. To give the ring to another, as Bassanio does, is to become guilty of wantonness. Thus Portia-as-Balthazar performs a ring-trick analogous to the bed-tricks performed in *Measure for Measure* and *All's Well* later. When the rings are revealed to be in the proper feminine keeping, and go back on the proper masculine fingers, the jeopardized bond is sealed. The promiscuity of Venice is thus redeemed by the chastity of Belmont.

Inasmuch as the ring represents the womb, it is a source of life. From such a ring Bassanio and Portia will take new life in the form of the children in whose veins their blood runs. From such metaphors Shakespeare's play takes new life also. If Venice is redeemed by Belmont, the lovers will be redeemed by children. Children are the "use" of sex, the interest earned by a faithful keeping of the marital bond. This multiplication of meaning is likewise the interest earned by Shakespeare's richly metaphoric but more than ornamental use of language. Bodies breed like ewes, ewes breed like interest, interest breeds like metaphor, and metaphor breeds like bodies. Such circular exchanges of meaning bond *The Merchant of Venice* into a ringlike shape, a magic circle enclosing a wealth of meaning, and capable of keeping such envious devils as time and death outside its circumference.

Notes

1. Kenneth Burke, *A Grammar of Motives and A Rhetoric of Motives* (Cleveland and New York: Meridian Books, 1962), p. 111.

2. Cited by Norman O. Brown, *Life against Death* (New York: Vintage Books, 1959), p. 221.

3. Cited by Brown in *Life against Death*, p. 224.

4. Ibid., p. 208. Brown sums up by saying: "Hence Luther expresses his readiness to depart this world in the formula, 'I am the ripe shard and the world is the gaping anus.' The world's anus is the Devil's anus" (p. 226).

5. See *King Lear*, 3.4.33–35: "Take physic, pomp, / Expose thyself to feel what wretches feel, / That thou mayst shake the superflux to them." As regards the anal theory of money, see *The Psychoanalysis of Money*, ed. Ernest Borneman (New York: Urizen Books, 1976), esp. part 1.

6. See Ernest Becker, *Escape from Evil* (New York: The Free Press, 1974), pp. 82–83. Since an understanding of money develops about the same time as an understanding of death, an armchair psychologist might wonder if money comes to symbolize immortality for the child in compensation for the shock of knowing it will die.

7. This transformative process would be abetted by the sense of guilt the child feels for producing and possessing feces. After all, he is rewarded with praise when he gets rid of it properly, so it (and he or she) must be bad; yet because it is also a means of acquiring approval, it is also a source of power, the coin of a kind of primitive economic exchange: the child gives, the mother

praises. From this standpoint feces is valuable and can be associated with money. On the other hand, if it is thought of as bad and the child as guilty, the guilt can be assuaged by a reaction formation in which the repellant is transformed by sublimation into the desirable, feces into money. There is an analogy in the Protestant condemnation of the body and the consequent feelings of guilt about inhabiting such a vile structure. The way to assuage such feelings is to condemn oneself to hard labor, to adopt the Protestant work ethic. Work is tiring and painful, as repellant as feces, but because of that it is also sacred and purificatory, a daily sacrificial ritual designed to please the gods and ameliorate one's sense of worthlessness: "No rest for the wicked." The principle of the scapegoat operates in both cases to generate virtue out of pollution—that is, the scapegoat is repellant because full of sin but also a source of sacred power because its sacrifice will prove redemptive.

8. As a matter of fact, it has been argued that the capitalist has a right to earn interest on his capital because he might have achieved maximum pleasure and satisfaction by spending it all at once—see Schilder, "Psychoanalysis of Economics" in *The Psychoanalysis of Money*, p. 300. According to this view, then, usury and profit-taking represent a form of deferred gratification, a restraint on desire that sustains desire. Such an argument fails to take account of the symbolic value of money, which makes possessing it gratifying in itself, quite apart from what it can purchase. The dedicated capitalist does not want to obtain instant and total gratification at the cost of yielding his money; he wants the money itself to keep multiplying toward an infinitely desirable but also undesirable (because terminal) state of financial fulfillment.

9. As Fernand Braudel mentions somewhere (though I cannot find where) in *The Wheels of Commerce*, vol. 2. trans. Siân Reynolds (New York: Harper and Row, 1982).

10. *Shakespeare's Ovid: Arthur Golding's Translation of the Metamorphoses*, ed. W. H. D. Rouse (New York: W. W. Norton, 1961), book 11, p. 221.

11. Karl Marx, *Grundrisse zur Kritik der Politschen Okonomie*, cited by Michael Schneider in *Neurosis and Civilization*, trans. Michael Roloff (New York: Seabury Press, 1975), p. 128. The abstract process whereby gold becomes money is the same as that whereby acreage becomes land, workers become labor, and properties become capital. As Robert B. Heilbroner points out in *The Worldly Philosophers*, 4th ed. (New York: Simon and Shuster, 1972), pp. 23–28, the concept of gain itself did not appear until roughly the sixteenth century because land and capital were not constantly for sale or workers constantly for hire until then. The profit motive had not been institutionalized.

Moreover, money could not transcend the body symbolically until use-value, which is geared to practical needs for bodily survival, was supplemented by exchange-value, which, like interest rates, is arbitrarily established. The importance of exchange-value in what he calls "The Repression of Use-Value" is stressed by Schneider, "Psychoanalysis of Economics," pp. 125–30. Exchange-value transcends the material (the realm of use-value) much as symbolic immortality transcends the expectation of bodily death. Thus Schneider says "Exchange-value consciousness is indifferent, even blind to the sensuous-concrete quality and diversity of the use-value; it 'transcends' constantly the sensuous-qualitative world of useful things so as to discover on their invisible ground their 'essence,' that is, their 'value.' For an exchange-value consciousness each thing is only the physical husk of its 'value substance' " (pp. 126–27).

Interestingly enough in regard to the money-religion, the commercialization of land owed much to the redistribution of monastic estates by Henry VIII, which inspired land-jobbers to buy and sell again as speculation—see L. C. Knights, *Drama and Society in the Age of Jonson* (New York: W. W. Norton, 1968; first published 1937), pp. 100–103.

12. Sigmund Freud, "The Theme of the Three Caskets," trans. C. J. M. Hubback, in *Collected Papers: Papers on Metapsychology, Papers on Applied Psychoanalysis*, vol. 4 (London: Hogarth Press and the Institute of Psychoanalysis, 1956), pp. 244–56.

13. Lars Engle, " 'Thrift is Blessing': Exchange and Explanation in *The Merchant of Venice*," *Shakespeare Quarterly* 37 (1986): 32–33.

14. In *The Republic*, however, Plato uses the Moirai as a way of claiming that humans are responsible for their own fortunes because they have chosen their lot—see William Chase Greene, *Moira* (New York: Harper and Row, 1944), pp. 315–16.

15. This general thesis is maintained by Helmut Schoeck in *Envy: A Theory of Social Behaviour*, trans. Michael Glenny and Betty Ross (New York: Harcourt, Brace & World, 1969; first published in 1966 as *Der Neid*).

16. Ibid., p. 10.

17. Gerhard Piers and M. B. Singer, *Shame and Guilt: A Psychoanalytic and Cultural Study* (Springfield, Ill.: Thomas, 1953), pp. 28 ff.

18. Sigurd Burckhardt, *Shakespearean Meanings* (Princeton: Princeton University Press, 1968), pp. 215–16. Burckhardt's chapter on the play is typically brilliant despite, it seems to me, a reductive (and fanciful) tendency to treat it as an allegory of Shakespeare's attempt to free himself from his literary sources. I should add in connection with "laws" a reference also to Lawrence Danson's study of the play in terms of the old and new law of Judaism and Christianity in his excellent book *The Harmonies of "The Merchant of Venice"* (New Haven and London: Yale University Press, 1978), especially chaps. 2 and 3 on divine law and on law and language.

19. See Lawrence Danson's account of attitudes toward usury in Tudor England in *The Harmonies*, pp. 141–48.

20. Mark Shell, *Money, Language, and Thought* (Berkeley and Los Angeles: University of California Press, 1982), pp. 61–64. See also on love, language, and usury, John Russell Brown, *Shakespeare and his Comedies* (London: Methuen, 1957), pp. 45–81; Burckhardt, *Shakespearean Meanings*, pp. 26–36; Danson, *The Harmonies;* William C. Carroll, *The Metamorphoses of Shakespearean Comedy* (Princeton: Princeton University Press, 1985), pp. 117–26; and, with special emphasis on business exchanges, Lars Engle, " 'Thrift is Blessing.' "

21. Stephen Gosson, *Plays Confuted*, cited by Jonas Barish, *The Anti-Theatrical Prejudice* (Berkeley and Los Angeles: University of California Press, 1982), p. 94.

22. An analogous way of looking at it is from the perspective of metamorphosis, as Carroll does in his brilliant study *The Metamorphoses of Shakespearean Comedy;* see pp. 117–26 regarding Portia's metamorphoses.

2

Magic and Politics in *The Tempest*

MICHAEL PAYNE

RECENT CRITICAL INTERPRETATION OF *THE TEMPEST*, PERHAPS MORE THAN that of any other of Shakespeare's plays, has become thoroughly polarized. Those who have concentrated their attention on Prospero's magic and the traditions it reflects have, with rare exception, seen the play as the crowning glory of Shakespeare's achievement and Prospero as a character who grows in power and moral stature to a height unmatched by any other of the playwright's creations. This view of the play has come to be strongly supported by a series of studies emanating from the Warburg Institute that have reconstructed the traditions of natural and spiritual magic, which Shakespeare carefully draws upon. These interwoven traditions extend from Ficino's complex network of Neoplatonism, hermeticism, and occult philosophy—whose goal is the attainment of knowledge and wisdom—through the more pragmatic teachings of Agrippa and Paracelsus—who would give the magician not only the power to attract but also to control good and evil spirits—on to the tradition's fulfillment in Bruno and Dee—who establish the tradition firmly in England just before its precipitous decline.[1]

Confidently asserting the magician's power to transcend the earth for the sake of "far other worlds and other seas," Bruno expands on the idea of man's ability to ascend in thought to a state almost divine that Pico mentions in a famous passage in his *Oration on the Dignity of Man*: "It will be within your power to rise, through your own choice, to the superior orders of divine life." John Dee encourages the occult philosopher to take a further step. In his *Preface to Euclid* he instructs the magical polymath to return from heaven to the world of nature and to practice his occult art there:

> Thus can the mathematical mind deal speculatively in his own art and by good means mount above the clouds and stars; . . . he can [then] by order descend, to frame natural things to wonderful uses; and when he list, retire home into his own center and there prepare

> more means to ascend or descend by; and all to the glory of God and our honest delectation in earth.[2]

When Prospero is considered in light of this magical history, it is not surprising that he is seen either as Shakespeare's recapitulation of occult tradition or more specifically as the reenactment on the stage of John Dee's career.[3] Prospero confesses to having neglected worldly ends in Milan for the improvement of his mind (1.2.89–90)[4] and appears in the course of the play to follow Dee's directive "to frame natural things to wonderful uses." His motive for creating the tempest is not revenge but primarily the attempt to regenerate his former enemies; thus, he declares,

> Though with their high wrongs I am struck to th' quick,
> Yet with my nobler reason 'gainst my fury
> Do I take part: the rarer action is
> In virtue than in vengeance: they being penitent,
> The sole drift of my purpose doth extend
> Not a frown further.
>
> (5.1.25–30)

The storm is not only a means of bringing those who wronged Prospero to the island, but also an occasion for the display of his extensive magical powers, which give him command of both the worlds of nature and of spirits. It is, however, only retrospectively that the audience is informed, along with Miranda, of Prospero's beneficent control over the tempest. Throughout most of the play we mainly witness his ability to command spirits, while the other characters are restricted to seeing displays of Prospero's artistic or dramatic virtuosity. Indeed, as an ultimate indication of his self-confidence and artistic control, Prospero conceals his magical and artistic powers. Finally, with those powers at their height, he gives them up entirely in order to resume his common humanity and to allow others the freedom to "be themselves" (5.1.32), which includes his brother's freedom to reject regeneration.

In explicit opposition to this affirmative view of Prospero is a rapidly growing body of revolutionary, polemical commentary that condemns not only Prospero but also the play and Shakespeare himself for promoting a self-deceptive psychology of colonization. Although this view of *The Tempest* has a complex history that reaches back at least as far as Renan's *Caliban* (1878), the case against Prospero has been most powerfully made in two important studies published in 1985.[5] Paul Brown's essay in *Political Shakespeare: New Essays in Cultural Materialism* goes beyond earlier polemical studies in arguing that the play does not simply reflect colonialist practices but is itself "an intervention in an ambivalent and often contradictory discourse" promoting a colonialist political psychology. *The Tempest*'s "powerful and pleasurable narrative" tries but fails, in Brown's view, to harmonize or transcend the irreconcilable internal contradictions of colonialist discourse.[6] Francis Barker and Peter Hulme, in an essay in *Alternative Shakespeares*, develop a similar argument. They believe that Shakespeare today is made to participate in the construction of a false English past "which is picturesque, familiar and untroubled." But in *The Tempest* the usual opposition between the autotelic text and its historically problematic context actually invades the text of the play itself. This invasion can now be properly understood, they argue, because of the displacement of the old critical paradigm of liberal humanism by the poststructuralist emphasis on intertextuality. An important consequence of such an emphasis, they conclude, is to see the play as two irreconcilable dramas that undermine or deconstruct each other. Prospero's play is preoccupied with his attempts to legitimate his power by securing recognition of his claim to Milan; in Caliban's play Prospero suppresses a reenactment of the original usurpation of his kingdom when he puts down Caliban's mutiny, which allows him (in the words of Barker and Hulme) "to annul the memory of his failure to prevent his expulsion from the dukedom."[7] Both of these essays find the play—and by extension Shakespeare himself—guilty of being controlled by a political unconscious that awaits, not criticism, but a critique powerful enough to make the play's latent politics fully manifest. The essays claim to offer such a critique of the play and its use by generations of critics and performers, who have, perhaps unwittingly, promoted liberal humanism and Western imperialism by accepting *The Tempest*'s politics without question.[8]

The evidence offered to support such a negative view of the play includes Prospero's need, in scene 2, to establish his own version of the past, which no one (least of all Miranda) is able to question. Furthermore, his usurpation of the native authority of Caliban; his need to make both Caliban and Ariel his slaves; his suppression of the matriarchal magical order of Caliban's mother Sycorax; his dualistic categorization of others as virgins or rapists, friends or foes; his insisting on regulating his daughter's sexuality; his division of the shipwrecked travelers into two clear groups of aristocrats and plebians—all lend considerable support to a polemical deconstruction of the play in an effort to expose its place in a Shakespearean hegemony.

Rather than being necessarily exclusive of each other, the two views of the play I have summarized—the one emphasizing the tradition of magic and Prospero's personal growth and the other emphasizing politics and Caliban's enslavement—not only need but also require each other. To suggest, however, the complementarity of magic and politics is to confess resistance to recent attempts to displace a liberal, humanistic tradition of history. The editor of *Alternative Shakespeares* warns his readers that "'historical' and, in certain cases, historicist, accounts of Shakespearean texts, pluralist in emphasis and liberal in their capacity to assimilate revisionist, or even radical, challenges, have become a staple of Shakespeare criticism."[9] To this, one may respond simply that Shakespeare himself may be the model for such pluralistic assimilation, especially in the all-encompassing ecumenicism of the dramatic romances.[10]

Magic and politics are linked throughout *The Tempest*. In the narrative past Prospero neglected politics for magic. In the dramatic present he uses magic as a means to achieve specific political ends. The reclaiming of his dukedom, establishing a line of succession through Miranda and Ferdinand, creating amity between Milan and Naples, controlling the conspiracies against Alonso and himself, regenerating his enemies in preparation for the return to Italy, and restoring Caliban to authority over the island are all political accomplishments of his magical art. In the future, to which the Epilogue points, Prospero will lack the authority he has drawn from magic; yet in choosing vulnerable weakness, he displays his greatest strength and highest art. By the end of the play he has made a complete transition from what D. P. Walker has called transitive magic, used to manipulate others, to subjective magic, directed inward to the control of himself.[11] In aesthetic terms this is an achievement of an artistic style of such subtlety and refinement that it hides itself, transferring power from playwright, director, and actor to the audience. In religious terms it is the attainment of the state of grace, a willing suspension of presumed self-sufficiency that makes one receptive to an act of mercy. Prospero combines in his Epilogue the religious, aesthetic, political, and magical significance of his chosen weakness:

Now my charms are all o'erthrown,
And what strength I have's mine own,
Which is most faint: now, 'tis true,
I must be here confin'd by you,
Or sent to Naples. Let me not,
Since I have my dukedom got,
And pardon'd the deceiver, dwell
In this bare island by your spell.
. . . Now I want
Spirits to enforce, Art to enchant;
And my ending is despair,
Unless I be reliev'd by prayer,

Which pierces so, that it assaults
Mercy itself, and frees all faults. . . .
(Epil. 1–8, 13–18)

Prospero's salvation requires the audience's mercy that is made possible by a full imaginative identification with his desire for freedom and absolution.

The complementary relationship between magic and politics is diffused throughout the action of the play. It shapes the characterization of Prospero, whose control over the action is greater than that of any of Shakespeare's other creations, and it determines an important part of the audience's perspective on the play. The action of the play may be thought of as consisting of three tempests, each one manifest in a different form. The first is the visual spectacle of the storm itself that occupies the first scene and is the most dazzling display of Prospero's magical powers. In his account of how he brought about the storm at Prospero's command, Ariel suggests that what he did was to play upon the visual perceptions of the voyagers, enflaming their imaginations:

I flam'd amazement: sometime I'd divide,
And burn in many places; on the topmast,
The yards and boresprit, would I flame distinctly,
Then meet and join. Jove's lightnings, the precursors
O'th' dreadful thunder-claps, more momentary
And sight-outrunning were not: the fire and cracks
Of sulphurous roaring the most mighty Neptune
Seem to besiege, and make his bold waves tremble,
Yea, his dread trident shake. . . . Not a soul
But felt a fever of the mad, and play'd
Some tricks of desperation. All but mariners
Plung'd in the foaming brine, and quit the vessel,
Then all afire with me.
(1.2.198–206, 208–12)

Ariel concludes his account by insisting that the effect of their ordeal by water and fire was to make the voyagers fresher than before, as Prospero had specifically commanded:

Not a hair perish'd;
On their sustaining garments not a blemish,
But fresher than before: and, as thou bad'st me.
(1.2.217–19)

These words reinforce Prospero's earlier assurances to Miranda and firmly establish his intent to regenerate and restore his former enemies rather than avenge himself upon them.

Immediately following the visual spectacle of the storm but preceeding Ariel's account of his role in creating it is Prospero's narrative of the tempestuous series of events occurring before the play begins—his neglect of his responsibilities as Duke of Milan, his entrusting the dukedom to his brother Antonio, and his own banishment following Antonio's usurpation—all caused by Prospero's apparently selfish absorption in the inactive and purely bookish delights of "the liberal Arts" and "secret studies" (1.2.73, 77). Rather than condemning Prospero's attraction to magic, the play emphasizes his error in choosing between the political world and the magical, an error that he has had twelve years to contemplate and now the opportunity to rectify. Thus, Shakespeare would seem to be supporting Dee's advocacy of the active use of magic by a sage who may have first mounted "above the clouds and stars" in pursuit of spiritual truth but who at last retires "home into his own center," applying his knowledge to the affairs of the world.

Following the spectacular tempest of the play's first scene and Prospero's narrative of his stormy past in scene two, the dramatic action of the play itself unfolds, joining the consequences of Prospero's past with his new redemptive purpose. The main action includes Prospero's bringing his tutelage of Miranda to an end by preparing her to return to Italy with a new husband, Ferdinand. Just as he gives his daughter her freedom, so also does Prospero end his control over the lives of Ariel and Caliban. In the midst of these affairs he also attempts to regenerate the usurpers of his dukedom by allowing them the freedom to reenact their crimes against him in the plot to supplant Alonso. In restraining his power over Miranda, Ariel, Caliban, and the voyagers, Prospero exhibits his own self-regenerative control that is also a manifestation of the highest refinement of the art he practices. His abjuration of magic is no second abdication. Rather it is a confident expression of Prospero's self-realization, of his belief in the powers of freedom and self-determination, and of his artistic style that conceals itself by encouraging the recreative participation of his audience, first the several audiences of the masques within the play and then the larger audience of *The Tempest* to whom Prospero finally—in the Epilogue—entrusts himself. This main action may be seen as moving through a complete revolution: from Prospero's self-indulgence in the magical arts with its political cost, to his using art for the purpose of regenerating himself and others; from the bondage of Miranda, Ariel, and Caliban, to their liberation to "be themselves"; from Prospero's "neglecting worldly ends," to his abjuring "rough magic" and reassuming a common humanity.

In bringing Prospero's tempestuous past to bear on the present action of the play, Shakespeare simultaneously divides up the characters into significant groups and arranges those groups and the individuals within them in a hierarchy of discrepant awarenesses, further strengthening the link between magic and politics. The principal division initially lies between those who are on the island from the beginning of the play—Prospero, Ariel, Miranda, and Caliban—and those who are shipwrecked there by the storm. The second group is further subdivided into three: Ferdinand; the royal party (Alonso, Gonzalo, Antonio, and Sebastian); and the clowns Stephano and Trinculo. Although the manipulations or "practices" of one character upon another leading to different degrees of knowledge is a basic ingredient in Shakespeare's dramatic art, *The Tempest* is unique in placing Prospero on a pinnacle of awareness that allows him to tower, however briefly, even over the audience.[12] Beneath him, from Miranda to Stephano and Trinculo, the characters occupy different positions of varying ironic limitation in a pattern that is recapitulated even within the royal party, as Antonio and Sebastian scheme to overthrow Alonso in an act of treachery that would parallel the original usurpation of Prospero's dukedom. As though to undermine any static sense of hierarchy in these groupings, having once established them, Shakespeare meshes the islanders with the shipwrecked voyagers, bringing Ferdinand and Miranda together, Ariel into a position of control over the royal party, and Caliban into contact with the clowns, while Prospero interacts with them all. The continuum from Prospero to the clowns represents a range of regenerative possibility, from Prospero's radical reorientation to the world and his power over it to Antonio's final, stubborn silence and the clowns' punishment. Prospero's magical power, conducted through his agent Ariel, controls all of these groups and maintains the advantage for the islanders. Even Caliban finally rises above the mindless scheming of the clowns.

The minidramas set within each of these groups are essentially political. The meeting of Ferdinand and Miranda establishes the order of rightful succession in Milan, as well as the union of two Italian states; and in terms of sexual politics it insures the equality of husband and wife, as the chess game with its accompanying wit combat between the lovers suggests. Sebastian's and Antonio's intrigue recapitulates the political treachery of Shakespeare's tragedies: brother conspires against brother and against rightful heirs in a manner that shatters the utopian illusions of Gonzalo. Thinking themselves masterless men, Stephano and Trinculo would replace the only authority they believe remains and substitute their own debauched tyranny for it. Despite all these acts of rebellion (even Miranda believes she is defying her father in loving Ferdinand), none of these characters finally realizes how much Prospero's magic controls them. Instead, they see an effacement of his magic in the four entertainments that he produces for their enlightenment. For the court party the disappearing banquet (3.3.18 ff.) exposes the appetite for illusory power; for Miranda and Ferdinand the wedding masque (4.1.60 ff.) captures their prospect for harmonious love and fruitful marriage that has the potential of renewing their soon to be united kingdoms; for Stephano and Trinculo their being hunted and hounded (4.1.255) is a means of singling them out for punishment because of their incapacity for regeneration, or what Henri Bergson would have called their mechanical inelasticity; and for Alonso and the royal party the scene of Ferdinand and Miranda at chess (5.1.172) is both an occasion for reunion of father and son and a forecast of a greater union to come of Prospero's and Alonso's states.

All of these internal dramas contribute to the triumph of Prospero's "rarer action" that ultimately manifests itself rather "in virtue than in vengeance" (5.1.27–28) and that makes possible through his art the restoration of all of the characters to their own true selves, as well as the restoration of the play's several political worlds. Alonso facilitates the return of Prospero's dukedom, Prospero provides for the union of their dynasties, the rebellions against both of them are exposed, and Caliban regains his island kingdom. Prospero's magic, thus, provides the world of the play with the security and pleasurable resolution of the romantic comedies, which typically move from a state of bondage to an old law or a dark past to a new and liberated society based on love, "natural perspective," and the promise of new life. The shipwrecked voyagers, on the other hand, bring to the island all the dangers of violence, evil, death, and lost identity that permeate the tragedies. In Prospero, Shakespeare creates a protagonist who has grown and developed out of a past marked by many of the same losses suffered by Lear—indeed, Bradley notes how *The Tempest* in effect continues Lear's story[13]—yet Prospero is also complete from the beginning of the play, as his unusual autobiographical narrative in the second scene reveals.

In defining Prospero's character, Shakespeare further develops in this play a dramatic psychology that conceives of the self as consisting of a repertoire of external, socially interactive roles, which clothe or encase a vulnerable inner core of being. The recurring metaphor for this psychology throughout Shakespeare's works equates the roles with the parts an actor plays—these are further called "spirits" in Prospero's revels speech (4.1.149)—and the inner being is equated with the actor's true personality, which is what remains of Prospero after he ceases to play the magician's part. Each role is a means of relating to others and can be terminated at will. The core of being is given at birth, like Antonio's "evil nature," but it can change and develop through experience or be hidden by the roles one plays.

Prospero's roles as father and teacher that have occupied him for the past twelve years are brought to an end in the course of the play. Indeed, Prospero implies that there is a logic of self-effacement in both roles: the father invites his child to assert her own will as a necessary consequence of her maturing independence that he has fostered, and the teacher's authority must finally give way to the student's need to test what she has learned against her experience of the world. As magician, on the other hand, Prospero's achievements have been absolute and cosmic in scope, as he recalls in his speech on abjuring magic. Addressing the daemons who have assisted him, he recalls,

> I have bedimm'd
> The noontide sun, call'd forth the mutinous winds,
> And 'twixt the green sea and the azur'd vault
> Set roaring war: to the dread rattling thunder
> Have I given fire, and rifted Jove's stout oak
> With his own bolt; the strong-bas'd promontory
> Have I made shake, and by the spurs pluck'd up
> The pine and cedar: graves at my command
> Have wak'd their sleepers, op'd, and let'em forth
> By my so potent Art.
>
> (5.1.33–50)

Indeed as he looks back on his magical career, Prospero claims as achievements the very powers Marlowe's Faustus longed to possess:

> Emperors and kings
> Are but obey'd in their several provinces:
> Nor can they raise the wind, or rend the clouds:
> But his dominion that exceeds in this,
> Stretcheth as far as doth the mind of man.
> A sound magician is a mighty god.
>
> (*Doctor Faustus,* ll. 85–90)

Unlike Faustus, however, Prospero serves a moral purpose with his magic. He uses it to bring others to a full realization of themselves by first working "upon their senses" (5.1.53) until "their understanding / Begins to swell," flooding their "foul and muddy" minds with reason (79–82).

Although his final rejection of magical power forms the dramatic climax of the play, Prospero acts principally as a magician in all that we see him do. His fatherly care of Miranda and his instruction of her and Caliban are in the past, while the resumption of his political role is projected into the future. Indeed it would seem that whereas magic costs Faustus his soul, it is the means by which Prospero regains his and restores those who come under his influence. According to the familiar distinction, Faustus practices goetic magic, calling up evil spirits and commercing with the devil, while Prospero practices theurgic magic, commanding planetary spirits in order to turn loss into restoration. Despite Gonzalo's irrepressible enthusiasm, which has inspired the stage convention of depicting him as a complete fool, he does see clearly the dominant pattern of loss and restoration that extends from Prospero's exile and the marriage of Alonso's daughter Claribel to the concluding action of *The Tempest:*

> Was Milan thrust from Milan, that his issue
> Should become Kings of Naples? O, rejoice
> Beyond a common joy! and set it down
> With gold on lasting pillars: in one voyage
> Did Claribel her husband find at Tunis,
> And Ferdinand, her brother, found a wife
> Where he himself was lost, Prospero his dukedom
> In a poor isle, and all of us ourselves
> When no man was his own.
>
> (5.1.205–13)

Gonzalo does not see Prospero's magical agency creating this pattern because Prospero presents himself to the royal party not as the magician he has been but as Duke of Milan. Immediately after breaking his staff and drowning his book, Prospero directs Ariel to attire him in his princely garb:

> Fetch me the hat and rapier in my cell:
> I will discase me, and myself present
> As I was sometime Milan.
>
> (5.1.84–86)

The audience alone has witnessed the full extent of Prospero's power.

This unique role of the audience in the play makes the circumstances of *The Tempest*'s earliest performances especially significant, adding as well another political dimension to the play. The Revels Accounts list the presentation of *The Tempest* at Court by Shakespeare's company in 1611, which is its first recorded performance. In the winter of 1612–13 it was played again as part of the Court entertainments between the betrothal and marriage of the Elector to Princess Elizabeth, both of whom are specifically mentioned in the record of payment to the King's Men. It is not surprising, therefore, that *The Tempest* abounds in themes and details that mirror concerns and interests of the royal family: the politics of succession, the desire to unify two kingdoms, interest in New World exploration, the study of magic and demonology, the rights of kingship, the theatrical role of the monarch, even Prince Henry's fascination with ships are all reflected in the play and can easily be imagined to have been a powerful part of the royal audience's apparent pleasure at its first performance. Alonso's situation throughout much of *The Tempest* parallels James's when he saw the play for a second time in 1613.[14] Just as Alonso's daughter Claribel is married to the sovereign of faraway Tunis and his son Ferdinand presumed by him to be drowned, so within four months had James's son Prince Henry died of typhoid and his daughter Elizabeth become the "Winter Queen" of Bohemia. Such parallels create an almost irresistible temptation to resort to various forms of topical reductionism or historical determinism in interpreting the play. Recent studies of Shakespearean mimesis by Jonathan Goldberg, Howard Felperin, and David Bergeron, however, have emphasized the ways in which Shakespeare mediates by "re-presentation" all of the sources that can now be identified.[15] In re-presenting the traditions of magic, the interests of the royal family, and his identifiable written sources, it is Shakespeare's transubstantiation of those sources rather than his duplication of them that is most important for an understanding of his art.

In his re-presentation of the traditions of magic, Shakespeare gives Prospero a sense of his magical power that is close to John Dee's; but unlike Dee, Prospero chooses art, theater, and specifically the masque as the means of exercising that power. In reflecting the contemporary political preoccupations of the Jacobean Court, Shakespeare embodies those topical concerns more specifically in the Alonso subplot than in his account of Prospero, thus invoking those concerns but not allowing them to dominate the play. Despite *The Tempest*'s thematic preoccupations with politics and Prospero's manifesting his magic in the creation of masques, Shakespeare specifically avoids using the masque to flatter James's illusions of imperial power.[16] Instead, either Ariel or Prospero offer sufficient commentary on each of the masques to transform them into moral allegories. Shakespeare's transformation of his written sources is an even more telling instance of his art of re-presentation. Unlike the sources for most of his other plays, those for *The Tempest* do not provide Shakespeare with a narrative. The Bermuda pamphlets and Montaigne's essay "Of Cannibals" instead offer points of view on the contact between Europe and the New World, which Shakespeare weaves into his depiction of the relationship between Caliban and Prospero.

Samuel Purchas's travel books, though they contain the first published version of William Strachey's *True Repertory of the Wrack*, which was written and privately circulated in 1610, carefully surround the reporting of new facts about foreign exploration with accounts of classical voyages and an apology for colonization based on religious and moral ideas. Drake, for example, is typologized as a Christian Moses who brings the law to savages. Montaigne, on the other hand, argues that the New World is a place of natural virtue, free of the corruption of civilization. In the Indians, he writes, "are the true and most profitable vertues, and naturall properties most lively and vigorous, which in these we have bastardized, applying them to the pleasure of our corrupted taste."[17] The authors of the Bermuda pamphlets generally maintain the high moral tone of those, like Purchas, who rationalized colonization; but when Strachey and Jourdain describe the islands and the life they found there, the point of view they adopt, based on personal experience, approaches Montaigne's naturalism. Strachey confronts the issue directly:

> . . . I hope to deliver the world from a foule and generall errour: it being counted of most, that they can be no habitation for Men, but rather given over to Devils and wicked Spirits; whereas indeed wee find them now by experience, to be as habitable and commodius as most Countries of the same climate and situation. . . . Men ought not to deny every thing which is not subject to their owne sense. . . .[18]

When he created Caliban, Shakespeare had available to him these three views of natural man: that he was wild and immoral, in need of the virtuous instruction and saving grace of Christianity; that he exhibited natural virtues and enviable vitality that civilized man is ready to corrupt; and that he is like other men and can be understood by anyone who takes the trouble to cut through propaganda and see native life for oneself.[19]

Rather than choosing to follow one of his sources and to reject the others, Shakespeare blends in Caliban all three views of natural man, combining in effect Strachey and Montaigne. Caliban recalls that when Prospero first came to the island, the relationship between them was one of affection, mutual care, and love:

> When thou cam'st first,
> Thou strok'st me, and made much of me; wouldst give me
> Water with berries in 't; and teach me how
> To name the bigger light, and how the less,
> That burn by day and night: and then I lov'd thee,
> And show'd thee all the qualities o' th' isle,
> The fresh springs, brine-pits, barren place and fertile.
> (1.2.334–40)

That initial relationship, like that of father and child, was shattered by Caliban's attempt to violate Miranda, which Caliban recalls in terms of Montaignean biological growth—"Thou didst prevent me; I had peopled else / This isle with Calibans" (1.2.352–55)—but which Prospero and Miranda understandably consider in moral terms:

> Abhorred slave,
> Which any print of goodness wilt not take,
> Being capable of all ill!
>
> (1.2.353–55)

Throughout the play, however, Caliban identifies himself with the minute details of natural life on the island. He offers to take Stephano and Trinculo where crabs grow, to dig them pig-nuts, to show them a jay's nest, to instruct them in snaring the marmoset, and to provide them with filberts and sea birds (2.2.166–72). This aspect of Caliban reflects the humane interest among some sixteenth- and seventeenth-century explorers in careful observation of life in the New World that led to the level of achievement in ethnographic art found in John White's drawings of American Indians.[20] These drawings pose a sharp contrast to the physical deformity of Caliban, which is apparently the result of his unnatural birth from the union of the devil and a witch (1.2.321). Finally, however, Caliban is redeemed. His being duped by Stephano and Trinculo not only makes him willing to return to Prospero's service but also leads him to wisdom and the desire for grace (5.1.294–95). In this repentance Caliban rises in moral stature above Antonio. In exchange for the final act of service to Prospero in preparing his cell to receive the royal party, Caliban can look forward to the pardon and freedom he desires. Caliban's life, thus, recapitulates the view of natural man to be found in Shakespeare's sources: Strachey denies that the Bermudas are "given over to Devils and wicked Spirits," which Shakespeare identifies with the birth of Caliban and the worship of his mother's god Setebos (1.2.375). From the time of Prospero's arrival on the island until the end of the play, Caliban is the natural historian of the island, intimately acquainted as he is with its flora and fauna. By the end of the play he moves into the moral and theological order that Prospero himself has commanded since his exile. In Caliban, Prospero's magic and the politics of the play come fully together: his theurgic art of self-realization is defined in contrast to the goetic practices of Caliban's mother Sycorax, and his commitment to the freedom of self-determination arising out of service leads him simultaneously to abjure that magic and to allow others to be themselves.

The polarization of recent critical commentary on the play was anticipated by Oscar Wilde in the Preface to *The Picture of Dorian Gray:*

> The nineteenth century dislike of Realism is the rage of Caliban seeing his own face in a glass.

> The nineteenth century dislike of Romanticism is the
> rage of Caliban not seeing his own face in a glass.[21]

The Tempest, like all of Shakespeare's works, invites us to see his art as reflecting both his time and our own—"the very shape and body of the time, his form and pressure," as Hamlet calls it. It invites us as well to see our own image reflected back to us. A dislike of either Shakespeare's realism or his romanticism, Wilde suggests, turns us into raging Calibans, unredeemed by the art of Prospero and Shakespeare.

Notes

1. The best recent study of this tradition is Barbara Howard Traister, *Heavenly Necromancers: The Magician in English Renaissance Drama* (Columbia: University of Missouri Press, 1984), pp. 1–32.

2. "Preface to Euclid," sig. Ciii^{v}. Bruno's views are conveniently available in *Giordano Bruno: His Life and Thought*, ed. and trans. Dorothea Woley Singer (New York: Abelard-Schulman, 1950), esp. p. 249. The passage from Pico appears in *Renaissance Philosophy I: The Italian Philosophers*, ed. and trans. Arturo B. Fallico and Herman Shapiro (New York: Modern Library, 1967), p. 144.

3. This is the view of Frances Yates in *Shakespeare's Last Plays: A New Approach* (London: Routledge and Kegan Paul, 1975) and *The Occult Philosophy in the Elizabethan Age* (London: Routledge and Kegan Paul, 1979). For a comprehensive study of Dee's life and thought, see Peter French, *The World of an Elizabethan Magus* (London: Routledge and Kegan Paul, 1972).

4. Quotations from *The Tempest* are from the Arden edition, ed. Frank Kermode (London: Methuen, 1962).

5. The earlier studies are summarized by Philip Mason in *Prospero's Magic* (London: Oxford University Press, 1962), pp. 75–97.

6. Paul Brown, " 'This thing of darkness I acknowledge mine': *The Tempest* and the Discourse of Colonialism," in Jonathan Dollimore and Alan Sinfield, eds., *Political Shakespeare: New Essays in Cultural Materialism* (Ithaca: Cornell University Press, 1985), p. 48.

7. Francis Barker and Peter Hulme, "Nymphs and Reapers Heavily Vanish: The Discursive Con-texts of *The Tempest*," in John Drakakis, ed., *Alternative Shakespeares* (London: Methuen, 1985), p. 201.

8. Terry Eagleton, *William Shakespeare* (Oxford: Basil Blackwell, 1986), pp. 90–96, and Terence Hawkes, *That Shakespeherian Rag* (London: Methuen, 1986), pp. 1–25, 51–71, develop a similar argument. Eagleton and Hawkes stress Shakespeare's identification with "the retiring magus" to the point of seeing them both as capitalists who inhumanly create unemployment by the policy of land enclosure (Hawkes) or as practitioners of "oppressive patriarchalism" and a "colonialism which signals the imminent victory of the exploitative, 'inorganic' mercantile bourgeoise" (Eagleton). Eagleton's earlier study of *The Tempest* sees Prospero as a positive and sympathetic figure (*Shakespeare and Society* [New York: Schocken Books, 1967], p. 168).

9. Barker and Hulme, "Nymphs and Reapers," p. 17.

10. Cf. Northrop Frye, *The Secular Scripture: A Study of the Structure of Romance* (Cambridge: Harvard University Press, 1976), p. 53.

11. *Spiritual and Demonic Magic from Ficino to Campanella* (London: The Warburg Institute, 1958), pp. 82–83.

12. Bertrand Evans, *Shakespeare's Comedies* (Oxford: The Clarendon Press, 1960), p. 332.

13. A. C. Bradley, *Shakespearean Tragedy* (London: Macmillan, 1905), pp. 328–330.

14. For a detailed discussion of the parallels, see David M. Bergeron, *Shakespeare's Romances and the Royal Family* (Lawrence: University Press of Kansas, 1985), pp. 182–87.

15. Jonathan Goldberg, *James I and the Politics of Literature: Jonson, Shakespeare, Donne and Their Contemporaries* (Baltimore: Johns Hopkins University Press, 1983); Howard Felperin, *Shakespearean Representation: Mimesis and Modernity in Elizabethan Tragedy* (Princeton: Princeton University Press, 1977); David Bergeron, *Shakespeare's Romances and the Royal Family.*

16. See Stephen Orgel, *The Illusion of Power: Political Theatre in the English Renaissance* (Berkeley: University of California Press, 1975).

17. Florio translation, reprinted in *The Tempest*, ed. Kermode, p. xxxv.

18. Reprinted in ibid., p. 137.

19. For an excellent history of the wild man, see Hayden White, "The Forms of Wildness: Archaeology of an Idea," in Edward Dudley and Maximillian Novak, eds. *The Wild Man Within: An Image in Western Thought from the Renaissance to Romanticism* (Pittsburgh: Pittsburgh University Press, 1972), esp. pp. 20–21. White slights the third view, however.

20. See Paul Hulton, *America 1585: The Complete Drawings of John White* (London: British Museum Publications, 1984), esp.p. 9.

21. *Complete Works of Oscar Wilde* (London: Collins, 1966), p. 17.

3

Between the Mirror and the Face: Symbolic Reality in *Richard II*

HARVEY BIRENBAUM

SHAKESPEARE'S PLAYS, LIKE ALL LITERATURE, ARE SYMBOLIC FORMS MADE of language. However, they often derive special power and penetration from a consciousness of their own symbolic nature. In both comic and tragic modes, the playwright's imagination is drawn over and over again to the relation between consciousness and the symbolic world that the mind inhabits—the world, or rather worlds, of symbolic values, symbolic institutions, symbolic representations of the self, symbolic bonds between people, and the symbolic mesh of language that establishes, contemplates, and confirms all this. In the comedies, the mind achieves a freedom from its symbols *through* them. Through the subterfuge of disguises, freed from identity in a spirit of play, Self eludes the conventional traps that stagnate society. In tragedy, the self observes in horror its symbolic world disintegrating. All the customary means of interpreting experience fail until consciousness is completely isolated, forced to know its own bare forked being.

This theme—the impact of symbolic reality on consciousness—is bound to be universal and profound, because it reflects the structure of all values, all cultures, all personalities. It strikes the modern reader with its existential force. It was, also, a natural expression of Shakespeare's times, still deeply committed to the Christian-feudal culture yet disturbed and changed for good by the modern realism. According to the old sense of things, all of creation, all social institutions, and all personal acts could be known as symbolic emanations of an ultimate reality;[1] according to the new, experience was immediate and primary, distinct in essence from what images might represent it. Shakespeare's consciousness, in other words, is simultaneously *intra*symbolic—contained within the coherent symbolic world, the living logos—and *extra*-symbolic—regarding the symbols from outside *as symbols:* as mere words, accoutrements, or sentiments, as means of experiencing something else. The result is a split allegiance that not only stimulates keen tension throughout his plays but also raises profound challenges to the understanding of life, challenges that he met, of course, with an extraordinary justice.

This conflict often centers upon an issue that we can call *symbolic integrity:* the impression that life's coherence depends upon a real continuity between image and meaning, between subject and object, between self and the world experienced. A later dictum of Coleridge would be taken quite literally: "The symbol partakes of the reality which it renders intelligible." In fact, the symbol is a spiritual or imaginative presence real in its own right, reflecting the way spirit exists in the universe. For life to be meaningful, symbols must be meaningful. A central Shakespearean question, accordingly, is whether what *must* be true *can* be true.

When, early in *Macbeth,* Duncan observes:

> There's no art
> To find the mind's construction in the face,

he is not merely moralizing about human dissembling, he is noting a basic discontinuity between symbol and significance. When Cleopatra whips a messenger for representing bad news, she assumes that her royal world has symbolic integrity; but when she asks, "Can Fulvia die?," she is struck with wonder that the symbol that had such power over her can be mere woman. When Hamlet frets over "words, words, words" or Lear recoils at the bleak power of the word "Nothing," the symbolic integrity of the world is bursting at the seams.

i

The testing out of symbolic reality is especially important in *Richard II,* where it centers upon the theme of the king's divine right. The theme has been studied thoroughly in terms of archaic political theory,[2] but it is usually explained away, either as an unfortunate superstition Shakespeare shared or, more likely, as a self-deception of Richard's for which he is justly punished. The scholar is in a peculiar position here. If he justifies the notion in an historical context, he opposes the drift of the play and of history, for Richard, who claims he *cannot* be overthrown, is indeed stripped of his rights. If he interprets it as Richard's fallacy, rejected by Shakespeare, much of the play's foreshadowing and sense of imminent disaster will seem like shallow dramatic trickery. The concept of divine right does contribute, however, somehow, to the power and the significance of the play. It seems to express some feeling within the tragic complex that the play communicates. The question should be, then, not whether it is valid but in what sense it is valid.

John of Gaunt provides one perspective on the king's divinity when he refuses to help his sister-in-law, the Duke of Gloucester's widow, seek just vengeance for her husband's death (1.2.37–41). He believes Richard responsible yet he assumes the king cannot be challenged except by God Himself, since he rules as "God's substitute." From his point of view, then, the whole present play can be interpreted as the righting of God's quarrel with His own deputy. Richard is punished through Bolingbroke for misusing his ministry. Yet such a reading does not seem to strike the tone of the play at all. Richard's grief is too compelling, his complaint too challenging, for a crime-and-punishment reading.

The sympathetic theme of England's special glory is carried further by Richard himself when he returns to his kingdom from Ireland and addresses the soil directly, personalizing his relationship with it mythopoeically (3.2.4–11). Richard is not speaking as Gaunt was, in "This royal throne of Kings," as a mere lover of his native land, albeit "a prophet new inspired." Rather, he speaks as the divinely sanctioned bearer of the land's sanctity, as the symbolic embodiment, in fact, of the land's nature. His sense of such a bond with the land lies behind his complete assurance of Bolingbroke's impotence. "Not all the water in the rough rude sea / Can wash the balm off from an anointed king" (ll.54–55).[3] The extravagance of Richard's language suggests some basic misconception, but he feels intensely what he says. When it does appear that an advance can indeed be made against him in spite of his absolute confidence, he collapses immediately, and the result may seem bathetic. The realist will say that now Richard should try to understand his kingship in a new light and start to behave like an ordinary human being. But Richard has to be right. You are involved in a miracle or you are not. There is no middle ground, no time for transition, so Richard knows that his position is nothing if it is not absolute. "Ay, no; no, ay; for I must nothing be" (4.1.201). Just before Richard's deposition in Westminster Hall, Bolingbroke ascends the throne "in God's name." The Bishop of Carlisle resists passionately.

> My Lord of Herford here, whom you call king,
> Is a foul traitor to proud Herford's king,
> And if you crown him, let me prophesy—
> The blood of English shall manure the ground,
> And future ages groan for this foul act,
> Peace shall go sleep with Turks and infidels,
> And, in this seat of peace, tumultuous wars
> Shall kin with kin, and kind with kind, confound.
> (ll.134–41)

Carlisle's courage in denouncing the king on the instant of his ascent to the throne is dramatically very imposing, and his eloquence makes us shudder for him. Later Henry spares Carlisle's life (5.6.25–30), but at the moment we sense the tragedy of history itself: the impotence of good intentions enmeshed in the inevitable struggles for power, the transition from resistance to triumph to tyranny. But there is something more ironic about Carlisle's prophecy: his point will be borne out. The efficient violation of Richard's divine right splits the land disastrously.

We have a paradox, then, and it is no accident but the importantly tragic paradox of Richard's predicament. Richard does rule by divine right, yet he deceives himself by believing in that right. His conviction of a secure and lofty role in the universe is justified; all the same, he is destroyed by others who do not share that conviction. What, then, does this archaic doctrine express symbolically when we read the play? What version of divine right, the invalid absolute, has universal value?

It helps if we emphasize an essential similarity between Richard and other tragic figures. He is destroyed, in the tragic manner, by his own personal flair for being himself and by the totality of his faith that he belongs to a coherent world. Like *Macbeth, Othello,* and *King Lear, Richard II* records the disintegration of an ego through an intense, precisely realized process of humiliation. Experienced from within, as we are obliged to experience tragedy, this means the breakdown of an entire universe. It is not a matter of having made a mistake, of realizing one should not have done something or other, or of having a particular personality trait too many. It is identity that has to go, and with it one's total sense of truth. Richard's divine right is the right to the only understanding of life the self *can* have until challenged by cataclysm and shattered to elements.

The intensity with which the tragic character resists his fate—the intensity, that is, of his hubris—measures his stature, what Aristotle calls his magnitude. It is also the measure of what he is up against. The harder he fights his destiny, the more dreadful his destiny seems. It is appropriate, when Richard's understanding of his identity is challenged, that the impact be devastating, for the prospect is the prospect of chaos. If I abandon my defenses against outrageous fortune, my vulnerability will be unutterable. Though I live literally, I shall be a dead person. For we have, as it were, a divine right that the fragments of our world cohere even though they are *merely* symbolic. We have a right that all our achievements have some substance that cannot be erased. And the height of absurdity: since we find ourselves existing, and with some semblance of meaning, we have a divine right to go on existing indefinitely.

The "divine right" of hubris is a right beyond law—beyond the laws of society and the laws of physics both—and it is mine because I, and I alone, am myself. Since there seems to be all the difference in the world between the vitality of my *feelings* and the facticity of others' actions, between being a self and merely *being*, as a self I must have a freedom of expression that others do not need. The total and uncontained universe of subjectivity can understand no principles from beyond, and it is through this universe that I must know myself. When Richard flaunts his royal powers, in ways that are cruelly and flippantly selfish, he is testing to the hilt these assumptions of selfhood. If Bolingbroke can tread with violent forces on Richard's holy soil, there can be no King Richard. Chaos *will* come again. Every tragic hero has the utterly useless and patently ridiculous divine right to his hubris. That is what it comes down to. Our rights are as vulnerable as we are. Our kingship is the vaguest fantasy. The tragedy is that we are trapped only if we have the integrity, only if we care, only if we insist on the terms of a desperately fantastic contract.

ii

The sense of "symbolic integrity" is essential to Richard's reality. It also adds substance to the point about his apparent love of poetry and theatrical effect that critics have talked so much about, for it bears upon the symbolic reality of the play itself. Peter Ure rehearses some of the points that have been asserted and provides a sober reply:

> Richard . . . longs for other roles than that which fate constrains him to play:
>
> Thus play I in one person many people,
> And none contented.
>
> But it is quite another thing to claim that because Richard "thinks in images," Shakespeare therefore wished us to think of him as a poet, or even as a bad poet because his images sometimes misfire, with the corollary that "Richard's fall is due . . . to his preference for words over deeds." . . . The poetry which he speaks . . . is Shakespeare's medium, which he uses to show—and by means of images to show as lustrously as possible—what is going on in Richard's mind and heart.[4]

Ure's solution, however, retains a rhetorical conception of medium, by which the "poetry" is only a means toward an end. The argument must be circular. The poetry creates the consciousness of Richard, and in it we sense a self taking pleasure in his own articulate sensuousness. In poetry, his experience is, naturally, *of* poetry. The medium provides the metaphor beautifully in itself. When, for example, at the beginning of the play, Richard is about to confront Mowbray and Bolingbroke and have them confront each other, he summons them "face to face, / And frowning brow to brow . . . " (1.1.15ff.) We can say that these phrases, pragmatically superfluous, belong to an elevated style appropriate to a king operating in a formal situation, but what is the meaning and effect of this elevation? It sets apart and aloft the consciousness (and the consciousness of power) of the royal self. There is and should be a significant disjunction between the mind thinking and speaking these lines, pitched aesthetically, and the personally very serious concerns of the men to whom they refer. Suffused with its own enlivening pleasure, the self does not need and cannot use the experience of others. The first part of the play dramatizes this disjunction keenly, climaxing in the scene of Gaunt's death. In these earlier lines we, as audience, are prepared for the tragic pain of being split against ourselves as we sense through Richard the imaginative force that wields both words and men.

Richard's "theatricality" also expresses a self-consciousness inherent in the tragic ordeal, a quality related to that "stoical" self-consciousness which disturbed T. S. Eliot[5] but which has to be seen in terms of the whole experiential structure of tragedy. Richard is the playwright-director-star trapped now in Bolingbroke's play, the heroic lead, in fact, cast as a villain. It is as though one were to discover that one really is the image in another man's dream, an effect potentially Kafkaesque. "It is the contrast between what Richard has to do with the way he does it that brings out the shocking paradox of the helpless king, the king who must."[6] This last phrase is perfect, and Ure returns to it later. As tragedy, the play focuses upon the selfhood's realization of its otherness, and this is tragic not because a man in power ought to behave more sensibly but because the realm of selfhood actually is at once so completely self-generating and self-sufficient, so lavish with its promises of fulfillment, and so disastrously, shamefully helpless.

Richard D. Altick has pointed out the awareness by characters in this play that "words are mere conventional sound moulded by the tongue, and reality is something else again."[7] M. M. Mahood has argued further that to "doubt the real relationship between name and nominee, between a word and the thing it signified, was to shake the whole structure of Elizabethan thought and society."[8] In Professor Mahood's reading, "Richard . . . has always been deceived by the seeming power of words," while for Bolingbroke "the *value* of words . . . lies only in the actuality of the things they signify."[9] Thus the play moves toward Richard's discovery of what his supplanter has always assumed: that words "cannot blow out facts."[10] In the great speech in Wales, "sad stories of the deaths of Kings," Richard, I think, is only testing out, with some horror, the inescapable proposition that must not be true: that his anointed self is merely mortal. Bolingbroke does actuate a side of the truth that Richard must face and integrate, but it is not the ultimate truth of the play. To the extent that he *is* right—that words must yield to action—we may feel that it is tragic he is right. And we do not realize this point as a tragic one unless we have first recognized a kind of necessity, the "divine right," that it not be so.

Henry Bolingbroke's positivism is the naive security of a prosperous man. It will break down when he comes to feel trapped by Richard's death (having wished but not willed it)—in *Henry IV* rather clearly and by hint perhaps in the last speech of this play. However, when Richard sits upon the ground to tell sad stories, he moves in the direction of Shakespeare the playwright, by the mirror-trick of infinite regression. The image is essentially a play-within-a-play, for Richard is projecting his own story as a living fiction, so that he can comprehend it. Language and imagination provide the media of this experience, the body, so to speak, to which experience is the soul. As Professor Mahood does indeed conclude, beautifully, about *Hamlet, Lear,* and *Othello:*

> When the seeming truth of things is found to be fiction, fiction may be the only way to truth. Hamlet's use of the players points to a discovery Shakespeare was making about his own art. The consolation of a Shakespearean tragedy is ultimately to be found, not in any explicit statement that all is best, nor yet in the events of the play, but in the existence of the play itself.[11]

The point applies well to *Richard II,* but again, the medium is itself a symbol for immediate reality. The consolation for tragedy is the experience of tragedy, so long as life is an apprenticehood to grief.

iii

The symbolic reality of language is an issue earlier in the play. In the first act, Richard attempts to maneuver the two combatants, Mowbray and Bolingbroke, out of their own realities, and there follows a significant analysis of how words exist. When, to gratify Gaunt, the King reduces Bolingbroke's exile from ten to six years, Bolingbroke remarks:

> How long a time lies in one little word!
> Four lagging winters and four wanton springs
> End in a word: such is the breath of kings.
>
> (1.3.213–15)

What follows shows, I think, that he is too absorbed in his own sorrow at this point, too busy being the victim now of history, to entertain the king's power for himself. For me, the tone here is poised, curiously, between bitterness and a reluctant sense of wonder. He is not concerned with his own possibilities, but he *is* awakened to *something*. It is a subtle dimension of reality that has to be understated because it is concerned precisely with the tenuousness of causes and the enormity of effects. Time lies in a word, where we would not have thought to look for it, the human extremes of both "lagging winters" and "wanton springs" encompassed by what has seemed so negligible and arbitrary. Words are only breath, yet breath is life. So what is utterly insubstantial is also the essence of our nature. The breath of kings is the living will, irrational, perhaps perverse, but miraculous nonetheless. Bolingbroke is touched with awe in spite of himself, I think.

The living wield vast power over life, but not total power. Gaunt's development of the theme places it tragically.

> *Richard.* Why, uncle, thou hast many years to live.
> *Gaunt.* But not a minute, king, that thou canst give:
> Shorten my days thou canst with sullen sorrow,
> And pluck nights from me, but not lend a morrow;
> Thou canst help time to furrow me with age,
> But stop no wrinkle in his pilgrimage;
> Thy word is current with him for my death,
> But dead, thy kingdom cannot buy my breath.
>
> (225–32)

On this level, at which the will deals directly with life, its powers must be ultimately destructive ones. We can help time only to have a stop. At the end, this king of mighty words becomes nothing but a clock watching its own motion.

> I wasted time, and now doth time waste me;
> For now hath time made me his numb'ring clock;
> My thoughts are minutes, and with sighs they jar
> Their watches on unto mine eyes, the outward watch,
> Whereto my finger, like a dial's point,
> Is pointing still, in cleansing them from tears.
>
> (5.5.49–54)

Here just before he is murdered, Richard meditates on the mind's need for its own projections. A man alone in prison, accustomed to continual activity for his mind, has nothing to think about but the mind itself.

> I have been studying how I may compare
> This prison where I live unto the world;
> And, for because the world is populous

And here is not a creature but myself,
I cannot do it. Yet I'll hammer it out.

(1–5)

Richard's exercise succeeds: the structure he develops is microcosmic, but what he succeeds in creating is the pattern of inevitable failure.

And these same thoughts people this little world,
In humours like the people of this world;
For no thought is contented.

(9–11)

Thought and discontent are inextricable, for the mind's activity is a desperate restlessness. Even the transcendent compendium of symbols, the Bible, which draws man's mind to God's, sets words at war.

The better sort,
As thoughts of things divine, are intermix'd
With scruples, and do set the word itself
Against the word,
As thus: "Come, little ones"; and then again
"It is as hard to come as for a camel
To thread the postern of a small needle's eye."

(11–17)

Thoughts of doubt—the sense, that is, of our hopeless mortality—humble our aspirations, making the salvation that in itself sounds so simple impossibly problematic. In ordinary life, the prison of the world, "thoughts tending to ambition" (18–22) and "thoughts tending to content" (23–30) deceive us alike into doomed illusions. The conclusion is a general picture of a self that can achieve many identities, all futile, with no stability of its own. "Thus play I in one person many people, and none contented" (30–31). In such a mixture of memory and fantasy, bound to frustration, Richard relives and probes his own "sad story." As king he must depend upon potential traitors; as beggar he must yearn for relief. The contrary fantasies cancel each other out, for discontent would seem to be the human condition and the basis of identity, since to be human, truly, is to be conscious. Of course we cannot be content with that; we can be relieved only by becoming what we fear—nothing, for we can neither tolerate the prospect of our nothingness nor put our trust in any gratification that tries to alleviate it.

. . . whate'er I be,
Nor I, nor any man that but man is,

With nothing shall be pleas'd, till he be eas'd
With being nothing.

(38–41)

Short of that ultimate transformation, the tragic vision must yield to the mechanism of self-defeat and the rhythm of frustration.

iv

Historical fact challenges this "symbolic truth," but symbolism also tests history. We would oversimplify the theme to treat it as a contrast between "appearance and reality," the Bradleyan theme, because what the realist regards as mere appearance has its own cogent truth and power as a symbolic force active in the heart and mind. The sense of "symbolic integrity" is an awareness that consciousness is real and an insistence that the mind aware does reflect—if not create—the world it inhabits. Upon those axioms rests the conviction that one's personal identity is substantial, capable of valid commitment.

Symbolic integrity is one of the usual marks of the Shakespearean tragic self, who has thereby not only an intimate relation with the world (like the sacrificial king with his land, in myth and ritual) but also a passionate concern for that relation, to cherish and comprehend it. In tragedy, this symbolic consciousness admits the challenge of "reality" and faces disintegration so that it can reconstitute itself on a paradoxical and therefore solidly inclusive basis. Richard finds this new basis by recognizing the paradox directly: together with the agony of being reduced to nothing, there is also the relief. The chaos is so much clearer. Our apprenticehood through grief teaches us nothing more than to be journeymen to grief, but we have learned something, after all. Nothing satisfies us, so we have the satisfaction of becoming nothing and feeling our misery. Thus the symbol achieves a new kind of integrity by encompassing itself. If nothing is all, so is the grief of knowing this nothingness. The original assumption that one's experience is substantial is proven by redefinition, through the *real* experience of insubstantiality.

It is not Richard alone, therefore, with his divine right, who depends upon symbols in the world of the play. The first scene brings us into a culture that has always been built of symbolic coherence. The medieval trial by combat, which will determine a man's guilt or innocence by his fate in a joust, is presented naturally as a symbolic reality. Its form is assumed to embody living meaning. When, in refusing the king's command to avoid combat, Mowbray offers his life before his "name" (167), we all realize that "name" is far more than a word. It is defined, quite traditionally and perhaps automatically, by the humiliation that is its alternative (166–73). "Mine honour is my life, both grow in one, / Take honour from me, and my life is done" (182ff.). Bolingbroke is the pragmatist opposing Richard, but he is also the child of his age. He challenges Mowbray "by the glorious worth of my descent" (107). When he returns to England, it is to claim the possessions that are his right but also the name that is his identity. Thus the stable order he overthrows is the assurance of his own significance. When Richard violated Bolingbroke's right of inheritance, York interpreted the act with full awareness of its awesome meaning:

> Take Herford's rights away, and take from time
> His charters, and his customary rights;
> Let not to-morrow then ensue to-day:
> Be not thyself. For how art thou a king
> But by fair sequence and succession?
>
> (2.1.195–99)

The rights of both men are as absolute as time itself, over which men have only negative power, as old Gaunt has remarked. They can take from time, "but not lend a morrow."

Shakespearean reality always retains or returns to a conventional basis in symbolic integrity—often through the ideals of honor and reputation. A good example is the ascent of Fortinbras to the throne of Denmark, his main qualification, perhaps, being the rather thin symbolic integrity that enables him to sacrifice "two thousand souls and twenty thousand ducats" for a patch of worthless land "when honour's at the stake." Hamlet regards the prospect, extrasymbolically, with realistic incredulity yet envies him and, in the end, gives him his blessing for the succession. Hamlet himself dies with his thoughts on his reputation and the integrity of his story, the drama we have, in fact, been watching. Symbolic integrity is manifest commonly in portents, prophecies, the meteorological reverberations of "sympathetic nature," ghosts, hallucinations, and the like. In *Richard II* the royal gardener's famous lecture provides a symbolic center of reality, not only a political but an ontological norm as well. At such a moment the density of the medium itself becomes more apparent and develops its own thematic significance.

Only through the tragic order, however, is this symbolic reality fully tested, because only there is it argued with the clarity of hubris. As he endures his downfall, Richard probes the paradox of his situation through a series of concrete myths, all of which are images and more than images, gestures and more than gestures: his very personal salute to the earth of England upon returning from Ireland; his visualization of the hollow crown; his explicit descent into the "base court" of Flint Castle after appearing upon the walls as (in Bolingbroke's words) "the blushing discontented sun"; his climactic self-immolation with the mirror.

The king's cry, as he musters the force within him, "Arm, arm, my name!" (3.2.86), epitomizes the hubris of symbolic integrity, for it is as necessary as it is absurd. He must summon his royalty into action, yet it is hardly *there* to respond. It is himself and it is only a word. This motif of the king's name, which spirals through the play, brings into focus the problem of how self and symbol relate to make up one's identity, an issue that reaches an agonizing climax in the deposition. When Richard appears at Westminster to let himself be made mere mortal, he asks a question the answer to which he knows but cannot really comprehend:

> Alack, why am I sent for to a king
> Before I have shook off the regal thoughts
> Wherewith I reign'd?
>
> (4.1.162–64)

His predicament is that he cannot comprehend his predicament. His thoughts, his kingly consciousness, are a tangible reality for him. They constitute a garment that is more substantial, in fact, than his cloak or his crown, because they are harder to displace. At least, they are more intimately part of himself, belonging more truly to his self than clothes belong to the body. The rebels have denied, in effect, the reality of spirit. It is for this reason—not just the divine-right doctrine in itself—that he is like the betrayed Christ (l.170). He is, in fact, more desolately alone than Christ: "He, in twelve, / Found truth in all but one; I, in twelve thousand, none" (170–71). He has, moreover, no identity that can be recognized or acknowledged:

> I have no name, no title:
> No, not that name was given me at the font,
> But 'tis usurp'd. Alack the heavy day,
> That I have worn so many winters out,
> And know not now what name to call myself!
>
> (4.1.255–59)

Clearly his name is more than a word, just as his crown is more than a token of his social role.

Richard calls for a mirror to watch himself as his life dissolves. This is an epitome of self-consciousness, yet it is not vanity. Richard is struggling to examine himself as he yields to join the treason against his own reality, for in yielding he finds himself doing something he knows to be impossible. The mirror is a book and in it, on the image of his face, are written his sins, acts that are himself (273–75). In the structure of his overlapping metaphors lies the sense of living continuity, and therein too lies the agony.

It is this sense of life's coherence being violated, then, that gives full weight to Richard's feeling of being crucified. It is not that he is being made by the playwright to symbolize Christ, but that he (together with his Father the playwright) is invoking Christ as a symbol of his situation. Richard's own ordeal suggests Christ's Passion because both manifest the pattern of life: confronting tragic truth is crucifixion. The comparison has further significance, however, for through it Richard calls attention to his own symbolic nature. Behold the symbol, he is saying, see its majesty and its absurdity at once. What is most basic to Richard's sense of himself is that he is, alas, neither mere substance nor mere image—in either possibility "a mockery king of snow" who could melt "before the sun of Bolingbroke." In order to exist humanly, he must exist symbolically, actual and virtual at once, with significance that can be felt and known. In other words, he is the king of symbolism—the king of ceremony and divine right. But that means he is also the king of consciousness, for symbols do have their value only in the mind and reflect our awareness of them. Now, facing the inexorable king of fact, he is caught between his existence and his awareness of existence, between the mirror and the face. The symbolism by which he must be aware is itself the crucifying process.

When Richard smashes the mirror, he acts as though he were shattering the face with the image of it, in order to emphasize by "this sport" the absurdity of the whole ritualistic drama:

> For there it is, crack'd in an hundred shivers.
> Mark, silent king, the moral of this sport—
> How soon my sorrow hath destroy'd my face.
>
> (289–91)

Henry's simplistic lesson in response justifies the ritual in the terms that make political choice and action possible, terms that distinguish objectively between internal and external realities. It is exactly the purpose of such rituals, as Richard realizes, to disconnect actions from a personal context so that public realities can be sustained. Henry's argument shows him the source of his own misery more profoundly than he has yet expressed it himself:

> I thank thee, king,
> For thy great bounty, that not only giv'st

Me cause to wail, but teachest me the way
How to lament the cause.

(299–302)

Yet Henry's realistic separation of image from reality presupposes a self content with mortality, "a king of infinite space" though "bounded in a nutshell." When Hamlet speaks this phrase, he too sighs hopelessly for such an ideal, restrained as he is by the "bad dreams" of being conscious.

The reflection that Richard sees has a very complex and elusive truthfulness for him. Through it, however, he tests the reality of symbols in general and his own reality in relation to them. On one level his reflection is not really a symbol at all. Ontologically, it is closer to his own nature, an extension of himself that is as mortal as he is, as spontaneous and as insubstantial. Hence, he is disappointed that it does not reveal the severity of his torment. Like a symbol, the reflection exists beyond him, to be held in awareness and to proclaim his truth. Yet it will vanish when he dies, or even when he turns away from himself; and it has no great value for anyone but him.

A mirror image is, as Hans-Georg Gadamer says, only a copy (as opposed to a representation, such as a picture); and as a copy, it has "its real function . . . in pointing . . . to what is copied," then "cancels itself out . . . when it reaches its goal."[12] But it is more than that as well. It has meaning beyond its function and it has being in its meaning. Our reflection gives us more than information about wrinkles or the part in our hair. For instance, it reminds us of our aging, our "deposition" from the past. Richard's response shows in fact how poignantly it represents for us, emblematically, the insubstantiality of life. Without flesh, it is more mortal than flesh. And it drives home the tragic miracle: what is insubstantial yet *is;* we are actually *here* facing death.

Our reflection then shows *how we are* because it is *as we are.* It is reassurance of our being. It is a private symbol, little more than a thought in our minds, but it is for us a very heavily charged presence in itself—not only because it is so perfectly responsive to both form and spirit, not only because we are fixed to it with vanity, self-hate, and anxiety—our strongest feelings about ourselves—but because it is also us beyond ourselves, ourselves beyond our being. It is the self as other. It has, at the same time, the elusiveness of the self: not even we can touch our reflection. It lives in a world beyond the mirror. It is bound to the mirror's mediation, but it does not belong to the glass. To kill it, Richard must destroy more than his image and less, the glass that is nothing like the image, a mere impersonal thing, totally innocent, yet totally responsible, for it is its own nature to reflect.

For the same reasons that it "reflects" life, the mirror image can symbolize symbolism. Even as it shares with proper symbols the extension of our presence, it makes us especially aware of both our continuity with them and our hopeless difference, their confirmation of our being and their helplessness to save. For the symbol is *of* us in both senses at once: it is *about* us and it is made *from* us.

When Richard calls for the mirror, therefore, it is to confront not just his appearance but his nature in being. Earlier, when he first glimpsed the doom before him, his impulse was as a dying king to tell stories of the deaths of kings, to envelop himself in his symbolic aura. That too was looking in the mirror, but now the image is more immediate. It was a moment of infinite regression, like Prospero's vision-within-a-vision, but now the reading is unavoidably finite.

Richard is purporting to smash his divinity. He feels he is smashing his life. Actually, he is smashing the paradox that the two are one—spirit and symbol, self and significance, the divine right and the human—for the facts of life, Bolingbroke's pragmatism, history, will not tolerate it. His ritual is not entirely ironical, however. It makes the deposition something that now he is doing in part himself, acting in his own style at least, for his own understanding. Seeing in his image "No deeper wrinkles yet" (l. 277), he notes the discontinuity between physical and emotional realities, and with a mixture of surprise, disgust, and heartbreak, he acknowledges the limits of symbolic integrity.

Yet, as he goes through the emotional process of abandoning his identity, Richard also reveals the impossibility of doing so. It is only, as Henry rationally observes, the shadow of his face that he can destroy. Richard responds with irony that is painful because he knows that Henry is logically right even as he misses the point. One cannot get to the real self because that is what one *is*. We are such stuff as shadows are made on too. Neither the reflection nor the face is oneself. The only truly human reality is that event between face and mirror, the phenomenon of consciousness, which struggles to maintain the world in which it knows itself.[13]

In his last meeting with the Queen, Richard offers her consolation that is not condescending, since he speaks as one who has himself been suffering and who knows that consciousness leads to suffering:

Learn, good soul,
To think our former state a happy dream;
From which awak'd, the truth of what we are
Shows us but this.

(5.1.17–20)

Then he speaks with the strength of a new commitment:

> I am sworn brother, sweet,
> To grim Necessity; and he and I
> Will keep a league till death.
>
> (20–22)

In this half-realized figure of Necessity—at once completely abstract and unavoidably tangible, more immediate than "Fate," "Destiny," or "Fortune," more clearly our own while more clearly our opposite—come together all the play's terms of mortality: the tread of time, the ego's greed, the limits of will and authority, the need for a divine right *and* its uselessness, the constant grin of the hollow fellow in the crown who is hollowly both king and jester beyond our talents, the alternate movement of pails in the well and the separation of selves that it signifies, the insubstantiality of role-playing, and the ultimate substantiality of "nothing." It is with a fine tone of courage that Richard takes on this new commitment, embracing what he cannot avoid and need not love, in painful sweetness.

Postscript

We have seen in Richard's divine right a psychological principle basic to tragic experience and an essential feature of symbolic reality. We have seen in his mirror reflection a symbol that tests the relation between his own reality and the reality of his symbolic world. How do these two factors relate in turn to the symbolic world that includes Richard—the symbolic form created by William Shakespeare, his play of Richard?

If the mirror of the play reveals as much to us as Richard's mirror reveals to him, then Hamlet's comparison becomes more subtle than it may seem in itself. But just as there was an ontological difference between a proper symbol and a mirror image, so there is certainly one between these two mirrors—between our experience of Richard and Richard's experience of his reflection. Let us think of the difference between the king's role and the author's. The king, the tragic self, annihilates himself in his agonizing symbolic dismemberment until he finds that his truth rests upon Nothing. Shakespeare, the tragic playwright, composes his play and leaves behind a vital image of Nothing's place in the scheme of things. The king is wrenched apart within the symbolic world that human culture has given him. The artist gives the world a symbolic vision it did not have before, re-creating culture on a new level. But such giving is not likely to be a painless donation. The artist's mirror is also an ontological probe, through which he tests out, we may well presume, his own relation to the reality of his experience and the reality of his figments. We may further presume that he does so with suffering enough, probably with vanity enough. We may also presume that he does so with an aesthetic elation to which he has his own kind of divine right, a kind that can achieve appropriate fulfillment. It may not save him from death and misunderstanding, but it is an elevation that he can transmit to the rest of us so that it can instill in us all the will to probe our being.

If we think of the Renaissance as the emergence of extrasymbolic consciousness (with an energy capable of revitalizing the culture's old symbols in a new spirit), then we can see that it is the Renaissance artist who finds out the solution to the medieval king's dilemma—although it is a dilemma as the artist sees it looking backward. Through the powerful new secular art, he partakes of the king's agony from within while he portrays it scrupulously from without. The symbolic aura of divine right is reinvented as dramatic and poetic symbolism. While he annihilates the king's divinity, he creates it. Together with other conceptions like the honor of one's name, such symbolic objects as the crown, such symbolic acts as the crucifixion, and such symbolic presences as the soil of one's country, the theme of divine right becomes part of the symbolic "work" that can transcend its historical context to achieve power within beauty and the grace of the emotions, which is power for all time. Still, it is a power rooted in symbolic integrity, in the reality of the world within symbols and the capacity of symbols to partake of our being. With its foundation in archetypal form, Shakespeare's art appreciates the symbolic forms of ritual, re-creating a sacred king's ordeal in a world now grown skeptical of myth, even of art, and even of the human spirit. And it extends its truth to us because of the way it exists in itself, rich with human presence and urgent with a sense of our needs.

Notes

1. See H. Flanders Dunbar, *Symbolism in Medieval Thought and Its Consummation in the Divine Comedy* (New Haven: Yale University Press, 1929).

2. Particularly suggestive and particularly influential has been Ernst Kantorowicz's treatment of the play in his *The King's Two Bodies: A Study in Medieval Political Theology* (Princeton: Princeton University Press, 1957). The discussion of *Richard II* is reprinted in *Four Centuries of Shakespeare Criticism*, ed. Frank Kermode (New York: Avon Books, 1965). Germane to my discussion is Kantorowicz's account of "a curious change in Richard's attitude—as it were, a metamorphosis from 'Realism to Nominalism'. . . ." (Kermode, p. 315). James L. Calderwood provides a thorough and astute commentary on the shift from Richard's "essentially medieval, sacramental, and poetic" conception of language and of symbols to Bolingbroke's, which is

"modern, utilitarian, and scientific" (*Shakespearean Metadrama* [Minneapolis: University of Minnesota Press, 1971], p. 162). I think Calderwood gives Richard's sense of symbolism the credit it deserves: "Richard covets symbol and ceremony . . . because he believes that they participate in facts, realities, deeds" (p. 178).

3. All quotations are from *King Richard II*, New Arden edition, ed. Peter Ure (Cambridge: Harvard University Press, 1956).

4. "Introduction" to the Arden edition, p. lxxi. In this passage Ure quotes or paraphrases W. Clemen, C. H. Herford, and R. D. Altick. Discussions of this matter usually refer back, as Ure's does, to Mark Van Doren's chapter on the play in *Shakespeare* (New York: H. Holt and Co., 1939).

5. In the essay "Shakespere and the Stoicism of Seneca," *Elizabethan Essays* (London: Faber and Faber, 1934).

6. Ure, Arden edition, p. lxxxi.

7. "Symphonic Imagery in *Richard II*," *PMLA* 62 (1947), reprinted in Nicholas Brooke, ed., *Richard II*, Casebook Series (London: Macmillan, 1973), p. 112.

8. M. M. Mahood, *Shakespeare's Wordplay* (London: Methuen, 1968), p. 73. The chapter on *Richard II* is also in Brooke.

9. Mahood, *Wordplay*, p. 78. In an excellent discussion of the Pomfret soliloquy, Calderwood observes: "What [Richard] experiences is a concrete version of the whole Renaissance and modern process by which the primordial marriage of word and thing, symbol and symbolized, was put asunder and man's thought divorced from his world" (p. 173).

10. Mahood, *Wordplay*, p. 85.

11. Ibid., p, 184.

12. *Truth and Method*, trans. ed. by Garret Barden and John Cumming (New York: Seabury Press, 1975), pp. 123, 122f.

13. Shakespeare's imaginative response to the symbolic ontology of such theatrical images as crown and mirror is a natural extension of the play-as-a-world trope. See Anne Righter, *Shakespeare and the Idea of the Play* (Baltimore: Penguin Books, 1967), p. 73f. As Righter's book demonstrates throughout, the ultimate virtuosity of Shakespeare and his actors was to make the consciousness of their own skill the profoundest subject of communication.

4

(a)

Hamlet's Melancholy

ZHANG SIYANG

HAMLET HAS SUFFERED THE UTMOST AFFLICTIONS, THE MOST MISERABLE fate in life. His honorable father was murdered, his mother stained, his inherited throne usurped, his beloved alienated—such miseries as few people could endure. But Hamlet does not yield. From personal misfortunes he has learned of the adversity of life precipitated by an irrational society: "The time is out of joint" (1.5.196),[1] the world "a goodly [prison]" (2.2.245).

To "set it right" (1.5.197) he must wage a life-or-death war against reactionary forces. Linking the hero's personal misfortune with the destiny of humankind is, intellectually, the play's claim on immortality. Yet because of the limitations of historical conditions and circumstances, Hamlet's eventual triumph is only a moralistic, not a real victory *in* life. He perishes with his enemies; his person, family, love, career are all destroyed. Even the rule of the kingdom falls into a stranger's hands.

The character of Hamlet has been the primary problem in studies of the play. What kind of man is he? Cowardly weak-minded or dauntlessly determined? Indecisive or stubbornly resolute? A mere babbler or man of action? Fanciful or pragmatic? Hungry for power or an unswerving fighter for justice? A pessimistic misanthrope or optimistic go-getter? Faced with these questions, we may add still more, about his melancholy and depression, his love or lack of love for Ophelia, and the reasons for his procrastinations.

Originally published in Chinese in *Wenke zhiyou* [*Companion to the Humanities*] no. 2 (1983): 19–22. Translated and edited by Mason Y. H. Wang.

Hamlet's ideology and sustaining interest are both congregated in the prince; the playwright's intent also finds its expression through him. His first appearance on stage is as a melancholy soul, woebegone, silent, depressed, and deeply reflective. Surely he must once have been an open-minded, agile, and witty man, for his humorous side frequently manifests itself, even in moments of utmost suffering. But man changes with the changes in his environment. Returning from the University of Wittenberg, Hamlet cannot but feel saddened with righteous anger at a marriage any humanist would consider not only heartless and unjust, without moral principle, a violation of holy matrimony, but also an act of shameless, destructive incest. Moreover, the man Gertrude marries is loutish, ugly of soul, and offensive in appearance. Educated in the university's humanistic tradition, idealizing everything, endowed with new ways of thinking and, as a consequence, new moral principles, Hamlet has to be affected emotionally and intellectually when he confronts the disparity between his environment and his vision of life. This disparity causes an aversion to and, consequently, a skepticism about humanity, life, and the world. Hamlet can find no other outlet than letting his suffering and melancholy gnaw at his heart.

Melancholy is therefore the mark of his character. Indeed, stripped of melancholy, Hamlet would not be Hamlet. Marx once observed, "And the Empire with the victories of the Empire reminds one of the adaptation of Shakespeare's *Hamlet* which not only lacks the melancholy of the Prince of Denmark but also the Prince himself."[2] Elsewhere he called this kind of melancholy a "Hamletlike expression."[3] Hamlet's melancholy, though, is not merely an exhibition of his personal despair; it involves a compassion for humanity and deep concern for his kingdom and its people; and it is inseparable from the procrastination and despondency precipitated by his search for a course of action. Nor can melancholy leave Hamlet, since he cannot transcend "this harsh world" (5.2.353) until the very moment before his death.

Not inborn with him, this melancholy is fostered by the realities of his environment, by the deep wounds inflicted upon him by life's indifferent whips, and by the burden gnawing at his heart. Aware of the tremendous responsibilities imposed upon him, he is in an isolated position, prevented from resorting to outside help, incapacitated in confronting his arch-enemy. A witness to the suffering people, corroding bureaucracy, and deteriorating morality, he cannot help but fall into a state of burning anxiety. If Hamlet were an ordinary man, he could be blind to what he saw, turn a deaf ear to what he heard, and simply await his position on the throne. But Hamlet is not this sort of man. He despises such a way of life: "If [man's] chief good and market of his time / Be but to sleep and feed?" (4.4.34–35). Possessed with a vision of perfection for humankind, Hamlet nevertheless cannot find a way toward its realization. He is thus inevitably baffled by an intense conflict between reality and vision.

Closely associated with his melancholy are his world-weariness, feeling of loss, his sense of life's impermanence and futility, the notion of this world as being like a dream. Less significant than his melancholy, such sentiments are occasioned by chance encounters with unexpected situations, and may be regarded as the outpourings of a warrior's sufferings, his sense of negation stirred up by special circumstances. Hamlet's feelings are like those expressed by the poet in Sonnet 66: "Tired with all these, for restful death I cry." No matter how strong-willed or courageous Hamlet is, he is powerless to resist such onslaughts, and this causes his fiery, revolutionary spirit to sink into a state of melancholic contemplation and puzzling vacillation. In accord with the law of human conduct, it is quite natural for a man like Hamlet to appear psychologically contradictory, unpredictably changeable in his emotions, and self-destructive in his desires. All these chance encounters, these unexpected situations, however, do not diminish the hero's ideological struggle. Instead, he has been constantly undergoing self-criticism to overcome these negations and transform them into positive pursuits.

Beclouded in melancholy, Hamlet is still not dumbfounded, idling with nothing to do, sucking melancholy for its own sake. Quite the contrary, his mind under stress has quickened and is activated even more than usual. He cannot help questioning the evils of the world, as they embrace body and soul, phenomenon and essence, individuals, families, society, nations, humankind. Moral standards, human relationships, exemplary human behavior, love, life and death, ideals, heaven and hell, time and eternity—such are the issues that swarm in his mind; the whole universe seems to have squeezed itself into his head. Hamlet's strength does not reside in being able to solve the world's problems but in his recognition that in an irrational society the good, the noble-minded, become victimized by the power of evil. This awakening has pushed his melancholy to an ultimate point.

"The time is out of joint. O cursed spite, / That ever I was born to set it right" (1.5.196–97)—Hamlet's exclamation, as pointed out by many critics, is the crux to the evolvement of the play's plot as well as the development of his character. Earlier, Hamlet was merely in a melancholy frame of mind—depressed, sorrowful, suspicious. But when the Ghost reveals to Hamlet the cause of his death, and demands that his son "revenge his foul and most unnatural murder" (1.5.25) through a private vengeance, Hamlet extends the evil of his father's death to the whole of society, moving from personal to public grievance. His determination to bring fairness, justice, even happiness to all humanity is indeed a tremendous task, and Hamlet is fully aware of its difficulty and complexity. He is also aware of his limited personal strength. When he can find no way to carry out the undertaking, he only intensifies his melancholy.

Hamlet's repeated delays in carrying out his revenge have been attributed by some critics to his inborn cowardice or weakness in character, his regression to empty daydreaming. Such claims, I believe, are unfounded, nor are they in conformity with Hamlet's character. We need to be concerned not just with what Hamlet ought to do but with his environment, one that prohibits him from action. It is true that Hamlet is at times indulgent in his fantasizing, is highly sensitive, and lacks resolution; but he is certainly not an idle man. At the critical moment, facing the choice between right and wrong, he engages in struggles. Let us remember how he bitterly castigates the wicked; how with a sharp tongue he taunts the Queen; how relentlessly he pushes his former school acquaintances to the corners; the arrogance he daringly exhibits toward Claudius, whose crime Hamlet had bravely enacted on the stage; and how courageously Hamlet proves himself in the fencing match with Laertes. All these show that Hamlet is not by nature a weakling. He is quite brave and resolute, capable of transforming words into action.

If there is a flaw in Hamlet's character, it is in the abundance of his heart. Only a man with such innate goodness could become so intensely melancholy. Such a man could not imagine that the harsh realities he faces would turn out to be even worse; nor could he suspect that his fencing match with Laertes would be a trap for his destruction. Claudius takes advantage of this noble quality of Hamlet, as he reminds Laertes that Hamlet has a heart "most generous, and free from all contriving" (4.7.134). Oftentimes a man of such goodness cannot appraise adequately what a wicked man would do, and in this regard Hamlet's kind heart lacks imagination. Hamlet's very decency strengthens the wicked and, in turn, inflicts a fatal blow on himself. Shakespeare through Adam in *As You Like It* has said, "to some kind of men / Their graces serve them but as enemies" (2.3.10–11). Hamlet's character has such tragic contradictions.

What we see in Hamlet cannot be easily stated. He undergoes changes of a most complex and contradictory nature: he is at once gentle and brash, loving and full of hate, selfish and magnanimous, rational and emotional, prattling and eager for action, cold-heartedly cruel and full of warm feelings, indecisive and resolute, dispirited and full of energy, at times scrupulous and then reckless, reserved and impulsive, sometimes mad and at other times clear-headed, depressed and hateful of life and yet unwilling to die; scholar and soldier, prince and commoner, childishly naive and highly sophisticated. These characteristics seem to intermingle in a most complicated way, constantly changing, coming to the surface in fashions seemingly incomprehensible, eluding our grasp. Tolstoy, who was madly against Shakespeare's art, has noted that "one moment [Hamlet] is awestruck at his father's ghost, another moment he begins to chafe at it, calling it 'old mole'; one moment he loves Ophelia, another moment he teases her, and so forth. There is no possibility of finding any explanation whatever of Hamlet's actions or words, and therefore no possibility of attributing any character to him."[4] The fact, however, is that the contradictions in Hamlet's character must be regarded as the labyrinth he himself establishes in his search for truth, indeed are a microcosm of human history. From time immemorial, how often have human ideals of happiness been truly realized? How many fluctuations and repetitions must history go through before one step can be advanced? And how heavy and slow our step is! Hamlet's character embodies the very principles of Shakespeare's theater: to "hold . . . the mirror up to nature" (3.2.22); to show "the very age and body of the time his form and pressure" (3.2.23–24); to be "the abstract and brief chronicles of the time" (2.2.520).

Hamlet *is* a mystery. A man's character is so complex, so hidden, so difficult to grasp. This is true of any man in real life. Everyone is a mystery. A man is a world. And Hamlet's complexities are those of his world. Because of the limitations of historical realities, he has not been able to explore and find the revolutionary truth and way. At the time of his death, Denmark is still a "harsh world." This is the greatest tragedy in Hamlet's life, one necessitated by historical determinism.

Related to Hamlet by their former love, Ophelia naturally has a deep and thorough understanding of him. Her words of immeasurable sorrow and pity may supplement my own thoughts:

> O, what a noble mind is here o'erthrown!
> The courtier's, soldier's, scholar's, eye, tongue, sword,
> Th' expectancy and rose of the fair state,
> The glass of fashion and the mould of form,
> Th' observ'd of all observers, quite, quite down
> . . . .
> Now see that noble and most sovereign reason
> Like sweet bells jangled out of tune and harsh,
> That unmatch'd form and feature of blown youth
> Blasted with ecstasy.
>
> (3.1.152–56, 159–62)

Had Hamlet been a man in real life, how would we mourn his destruction? How the world, past and present, would mourn him! Alas, what a pity!

Notes

1. All citations from *Hamlet* are from the New Arden edition, edited by Harold Jenkins (London: Methuen, 1982).

2. Karl Marx and Frederick Engels, *Collected Works* (New York: International, 1980), 14: 297.

3. Ibid., 17: 116.

4. Leo Tolstoy, "Shakespeare and the Drama," in *Shakespeare in Europe*, ed. Oswald LeWinter (Cleveland: World, 1963), p. 259.

(b)

Shakespeare and the Idea of Nature in the Renaissance

ZHANG XIAOYANG

IN SHAKESPEARE'S AGE, NATURE AS CREATED BY GOD WAS AT FIRST PERceived as harmonious and orderly, serving as a model for human society. The idea is basically similar to ancient China's notion of *Tiandao* (the way of nature) in its relation to *Rendao* (the way of human being). The Christian conception of the creation of the universe, and its development, was expounded on the basis of direct perception from the senses and the imagination, and, besides putting an end to the chaos caused by the rivalry among the polytheists, revealed the people's ardent desire to define the essence of the world. The principal characters in Shakespeare's plays are, accordingly, no longer the stilted, ignorant people of the Middle Ages, but passionate, intelligent, sound in mind and body—exemplary prototypes of character in the Renaissance. In *The Taming of the Shrew* Tranio advises his master Lucentio:

> Balk logic with acquaintance that you have
> And practice rhetoric in your common talk.
> Music and poesy use to quicken you.
> The mathematics and the metaphysics,
> Fall to them as you find your stomach serves you.
> (1.1.34–38)[1]

People were tired of the trivial inquiries advanced by scholasticism; nominalism and realism opened up the battle between the new philosophy and theology.

Along with uninterrupted development in medicine, commerce, navigation, and astronomy, there was also a shift of interest from cultural

Originally published in Chinese in *Jilin daxue shehui kexue xuebao [Journal of Jilin University*, Social Sciences edition] no. 1 (1986): 53–60. Translated and edited by Mason Y. H. Wang.

arts to scientific technology. Shakespeare's contemporary, the Cambridge-educated Gabriel Harvey, "was urging young wits in 1593 to leave poetry for studies of more 'effectual use.'"[2] Harvey also urged people to go adventuring, seafaring, and mining. Shakespeare's characters do not live in a divine environment of inexplicable abstraction; assimilated to Nature, they roam over the wide expanse of the earth. In *The Taming of the Shrew* Petruchio has "heard the sea, puffed up with winds, / Rage like an angry boar chafed with sweat" (1.2.200–201). Here are reflected man's desire for adventurous journeyings, for experiencing the mysteries of Nature. Othello recounts for Desdemona and Brabantio his battles with "the Anthropophagi," those "men whose heads / Grew beneath their shoulders" (1.3.143–44). Shakespeare himself seems adept in astronomy, navigation, handicraft, flora, medicine, architecture, zoology, geography, and custom. Indeed, as Goethe put it, in Shakespeare's plays, "Art and Science, Commerce and Industry, all bear him their gifts. Shakespeare's poems are a great animated fair."[3]

Despite theology's reign of terror, natural scientists and philosophers such as Nicholas of Cusa (Nicolaus Cusanus), Leonardo da Vinci, Nicholas Copernicus, Giordano Bruno, and Francis Bacon, in particular, argued that in expounding "The First Cause" and "The Final Cause" religion had only specified the creation of the world and its ultimate ideal state as yet to be reached, but had itself no relevance to our present existence. Walter Raleigh complained about our ignorance of "how second [physical] causes should have any proportion with their effects."[4] In *2 Henry VI* one character calls the new knowledge "the wing wherewith we fly to heaven" (4.7.75). Even the pseudosciences showed man's desire for probing into the mysteries of the cosmic world. Astrology had elements of astronomy; and alchemy was the predecessor of chemistry, though lacking its scientific basis and methodology. For most humanists, the distinction between science and pseudoscience remained opaque.

Still, in the Renaissance, science did not gain real independence,and its tender shoot was quite weak. The Christian view of cosmology, based on the biblical notion of genesis and Ptolemaic geocentric theory, prevailed. Ulysses's famous speech on order, according to Theodore Spencer, "sums up nearly everything the Elizabethans felt about the matter."[5] Commenting on the significance of the idea of the "Great Chain of Being," Christopher Gillie has observed, "it [the 'Great Chain of Being'] was useful in giving a sense of order amid the otherwise bewildering proliferation of natural phenomena . . . [and] in the hundred years between 1650 and 1750 it was not only found useful in new ways, but it was found inspiring."[6]

There was actually no direct conflict in the belief of humanists with these traditional concepts; they simply focused their attention on the relationship between man and Nature. In fact, many of the religious reformers and humanists did not understand the new concept of Nature as science's representative; some were even antagonistic toward it. Thus, in Shakespeare's comedies there are many references to Nature as orderly, kind, a reflection of a benevolent God. Man's music, for example, "is / The patroness of heavenly harmony" (*Shrew,* 3.1.4–5), a conceit also found in ancient China. Harmony in Nature parallels social concord; disorder anticipates chaos in human society.

In Shakespeare's tragedies, however, Nature is no longer endowed with manifest tenderness; instead, it is dark, violent, and terror-stricken. Strange events or phenomena are often used as progenitors of chaos to come. In *Macbeth,* for example, we hear that "The night has been unruly. Where we lay, / Our chimneys were blown down . . . / Lamentings heard i' th' air, strange screams of death, / And prophesying with accents terrible / Of dire combustion and confused events / New hatched to th' woeful time" (2.3.54–59).

Though similar on the surface to the orthodox concept of the Christian church, Shakespeare's humanistic idea is quite distinct in substance. If the church argued that to imitate Nature is tantamount to yielding to the power of the church, humanists, including the playwrights, were concerned not with orderliness as barbarically enforced by the church but with principles of social harmony that might be deduced from the study of the world about them. In Hamlet's poem to Ophelia—"Doubt thou the stars are fire, / Doubt that the sun doth move . . ." (2.2.116–17)—Shakespeare expresses the heliocentric theory advocated by Copernicus and Bruno in their misgivings about, indeed opposition to, the geocentric theory of the Ptolemaic system. The new learning inevitably led men to seek behavior norms from Nature. Wanting to take advantage of Justice Shallow, Falstaff concludes: "If the young dace be a bait for the old pike, I see no reason in the law of nature but I may snap at him" (*2 Henry IV,* 3.2.335–36).

However, when no longer regarded as a model of harmonious coexistence, Nature could become a cruel arena where men competed for survival. Such a view surfaces in *Timon of Athens:*

> If thou wert the lion, the fox would beguile thee. If thou wert the lamb, the fox would eat thee. . . . What beast couldst thou be that were not subject to a beast? (4.3.327–29, 342–43)

Relegating man to the same level as other species, the new attitude exposed a reality that had long existed between different classes in society, from ancient times to the Middle Ages.

An even more "radical" attitude was to place self above Nature. Like

Shakespeare's other bastard characters, Edmund is a destroyer of the old order; traditional ideas exercise no effect of restraint on him:

This is the excellent foppery of the world . . . as if we were villains on necessity; fools by heavenly compulsion. . . .

(1.2.121, 124–25)

Professor Danby has made some keen observations on this new idea represented by Edmund: "It is significant that in the figure of Edmund the sense of separation from nature and superiority to it goes with a sense of the individual's separation from the community and a feeling of superiority to his fellows. As Nature goes dead, community becomes competition, and man a nexus of appetites."[7]

A more positive expression of Edmund's secular humanism was found in pantheism. Deriving their philosophy from Plato's notion of Ideas, Plotinus and the Neoplatonists believed that the psyche exists in all Nature's created beings according to their status of hierarchy in a descending scale, and thus they laid the theoretical foundation for pantheism, a doctrine that people in Shakespeare's day found more suitable than Aristotelian scholasticism to meet the needs of the time. The dialogue between Lorenzo and Jessica, as they look into the starry sky in *The Merchant of Venice,* reflects this extension of Renaissance thought:

Look how the floor of heaven
Is thick inlaid with patens of bright gold.
There's not the smallest orb which thou behold'st
But in his motion like an angel sings,
Still quiring to the young-eyed cherubins. . . .

(5.1.58–62)

Two of Shakespeare's plays, *A Midsummer Night's Dream* and *The Tempest* (particularly the latter), according to most critics, give fuller expression to such pantheism. Walter Clyde Curry has argued that "*Macbeth* is medieval and Christian. On the contrary, *The Tempest* is found to be formalized by traditional Neo-Platonic conceptions and may be considered, therefore, as being essentially classical and pagan in spirit."[8] In Prospero, hero of *The Tempest,* one may detect man's relationship with various sprites representing the power of Nature—Ariel, Caliban, and the pagan deities. In *A Midsummer Night's Dream* Shakespeare enacts the concord between men and gods. Weakening Christianity's control over ideology, pantheism enabled people to look into the reality of their world, thereby strengthening those efforts to probe into nature conducive to intellectual emancipation. From an even higher philosophical perspective, pantheism realized the gradual restoration of the essence of Nature formerly alienated by religion, transforming a personified God to a naturalized one. It became at once a powerful weapon to abolish the cruel reign of monotheism, a process in democratizing religious ideology, a bridge leading to atheism, and a vision enabling humanity and Nature to join for the emancipation of the self. As Goethe put it, "Shakespeare associates himself with the World-Spirit. . . . The inanimate insists upon speaking; the elements, the phenomena of sky, earth, and sea, thunder and lightning, wild animals, lift their voices. . . ."[9]

This pantheism was in turn linked with the new interest in causation. As a methodology, the law of causation serves as a key to recognizing and observing nature, and thereby improving upon it; causation itself opposed the scholastic view that movement and changes are divinely directed. Leonardo da Vinci regarded causality as permanent in nature. Bruno, on the other hand, lay emphasis on the *causa sui* in the cosmos. In Shakespeare's plays Nature and society are linked by a chain of causation, emphasizing the relationship of cause and effect. Petruchio, for example, cries out to Kate and Hortensio, "Well, forward, forward! Thus the bowl should run / And not unluckily against the bias" (4.5.24–25). Man's behavior and motivations are similarly tied, as Warwick observes in *2 Henry IV:*

> There is a history in all men's lives,
> Figuring the nature of the times deceased,
> The which observed, a man may prophesy,
> With a near aim, of the main chance of things
> As yet not come to life, who in their seeds
> And weak beginning lie intreasured.
>
> (3.1.80–85)

Indeed, as E. M. W. Tillyard has pointed out, "As powerful as the theme of order in the tetralogy is the continual insistence on cause and effect in the unfolding of history."[10] E. E. Stoll expressed a similar view: ". . . the causal connection is observed and recognized; and in this tragedy *[King Lear]* too, once the situation is attained, character becomes its own destiny."[11]

This notion of causation is inseparable from that of dialectics. Nicholas of Cusa saw the unity of opposites in things. Bruno considered everything capable of transformation, such as straight lines and curves, love and hate, fortune and disaster. In Shakespeare's works we find a kaleidoscopic world full of changing movements, a world with wide horizons and multiple colors and contradictions. Hugo might be cited here: "Shakespeare is all in antithesis. . . . Nature is the eternal bifrons. . . . The antithesis of Shakespeare is the universal antithesis, present always and everywhere; it is the ubiquity of opposites,—life and death, cold and heat . . self and not-self, objective and subjective . . . This endless ebb and flow from this perpetual yes and no, from this irreconcilable opposition, from this vast, permanent antagonism. . . ."[12] Not only did Shakespeare find contradictions in things, he also allowed for their mutual transformations, a special stage generated by the struggles between contradictions. In *Romeo and Juliet,* for example, the Friar notes: "Nor aught so good but, strained from that fair use, / Revolts from true birth, stumbling on abuse. / Virtue itself turns vice, being misapplied, / And vice sometime by action dignified" (2.3.19–22). *Hamlet* reveals the absolute inevitability for such transformation from an earlier stage: "And nothing is at a like goodness still, / For goodness, growing to a plurisy, / Dies in his own too-much" (4.7.116–18). The process could also be from the quantitative to the qualitative: "To climb steep hills / Requires slow pace at first . . . Heat not a furnace for your foe so hot / That it do singe yourself" (*Henry VIII,* 1.1.131–32, 140–41). In the presence of such changes, Shakespeare insists upon exercising the proper "limit": "The sweetest honey / Is loathesome in his own deliciousness / And in the taste confounds the appetite. / Therefore love moderately: long love doth so; / Too swift arrives as tardy as too slow" (*Romeo and Juliet,* 2.6.11–15). No less, he was sensitive to the possibility that extreme change could lead to negation. In *Julius Caesar,* Brutus expresses this concern:

> There is a tide in the affairs of men
> Which, taken at the flood, leads on to fortune;
> Omitted, all the voyage of their life
> Is bound in shallows and in miseries.
>
> (4.3.215–18)

Development in things is not a straight line, and man must accommodate himself to this fact.

For me, then, at the heart of Shakespeare's "Nature" is his recognition of the fact that the essence of anything must be seen through the phenomenon itself. Content is a determinate factor, though form cannot be neglected. Unity of meaning and form is the ideal of Shakespeare's aesthetics.

Notes

1. All quotations from Shakespeare are from Sylvan Barnet, gen. ed., *The Complete Signet Classic Shakespeare* (New York: Harcourt, 1972).
2. L. G. Salingar, "The Social Setting," *The Age of Shakespeare,* vol. 2 of *The New Pelican Guide to English Literature,* ed. Boris Ford (Harmondsworth: Penguin, 1982), p. 25.

3. Johann Wolfgang von Goethe, "Shakespeare ad Infinitum," in *Shakespeare in Europe*, ed. Oswald LeWinter (Cleveland: World, 1963), p. 60.
4. Cited in Salingar, *Age of Shakespeare*, p. 26.
5. *Shakespeare and the Nature of Man*, 2d ed. (New York: Collier, 1966), p. 21.
6. *A Companion to British Literature* (Detroit: Grand River Books, 1977), p. 156.
7. John F. Danby, *Shakespeare's Doctrine of Nature: A Study of "King Lear"* (London: Faber, 1958), p. 38.
8. W. C. Curry, *Shakespeare's Philosophical Patterns*, 2d ed. (Baton Rouge: Louisiana State University Press, 1959), p. ix.
9. Goethe, "Shakespeare ad Infinitum," pp. 59–60.
10. "The First Tetralogy," *Shakespeare Criticism: 1935–60*, ed. Anne Ridler (London: Oxford University Press, 1963), p. 80.
11. "Art and Artifice in Shakespeare," *Shakespeare Criticism: 1919–1935*, ed. Anne Ridler (London: Oxford University Press, 1936), p. 76.
12. Victor Hugo, *William Shakespeare*, trans. Melville B. Anderson (Chicago: McClurg, 1887), pp. 204–15.

5

Hamlet's Fat

LAURA KEYES

> Be not griedie in all delites, and be not to hastie upon all meates. For excesse of meates bringeth sichenes, and glotonie cometh into choliricke diseases. By surfet have manie perished: but he that dieteth him self, prolongeth his life.
>
> —Ecclesiasticus 37:28–30 [Bishops Bible]

WAS HAMLET FAT? THAT IS THE WORD GERTRUDE USES DURING THE LAST scene: "He's fat and scant of breath."[1] Her comment on Hamlet's physical condition has prompted much throwing about of brains. Some critics have defended the integrity of the text; some have ingeniously modified it. Others, echoing the popular opinion that fat is a comic, not a tragic flaw, have deleted the line in stage productions or explained it away in textual commentaries. The controversy over Hamlet's fat mirrors the play's contrariety, uncertainty, inclusiveness, and humor; in the classroom, it can provide a window for understanding how readers, critics, and actors adapt Shakespeare's Hamlet for their own purposes and their own times. This essay will examine Hamlets both of the theater and the "mind's eye" to suggest a shape for the Hamlet of the late twentieth century—a Hamlet embodying romantic conceptions of the hero but reflecting a disquietingly timely cynicism about the possibility of heroism outside the traits and behaviors comporting with survival.

Among the commentators content to take Gertrude's word for a thousand pound, interpreting Shakespeare's line literally, was Goethe. Having first carefully noted that he himself did not resemble Shakespeare's hero, the German poet opined that Hamlet's inactivity, melancholy, and "perpetual vacillation" are indeed more typical of a plump blonde than a muscular brunette.[2] An anonymous English commentator of 1830 concurred in a fashion Goethe might have resented, saying of Hamlet, "He is by birth a German; and from indulging in the inactive habits of that deep-thinking nation, he has become 'fat and scant of breath,' as the Queen says."[3]

Thomas Wade, in a lecture delivered to the Jersey Mechanics Institute, waxed eloquent on the subject: Hamlet has "degenerated" into a man "Fat, and scant o' breath." At "but thirty years old," he is, through "heavy-headed revels" and "constitutional inactivity," well on his way to becoming "aldermanic and asthmatic!"[4] Wade takes *Hamlet* as the text for a mid-Victorian temperance lecture, appealing to his proletarian audience by debunking the noble Hamlet, satirizing the "high places of idealism and romance" with which he apparently assumed his rude mechanicals would have little sympathy.

The devil can quote Shakespeare for his own exegetic purposes, of course, but every generation has its own Hamlet, suited to the temper of the times. Look, for instance, at the Victorian mixture of science and moral earnestness in E. Vale Blake's 1880 reading of the text, which explains Hamlet's lack of moral fiber as the result of his physique. Hamlet's spirit is "*imprisoned in walls of adipose*," an obesity that leads to feckless procrastination. His "bulk" (Ophelia's word) makes for "a non-executive or lymphatic temperament," and, worse still, causes "fatty degeneration"—as indicated in his complaint, "How ill's all here about my heart."[5] Given Blake's diagnosis, the wonder is not that Hamlet is slow to effect his revenge but that he does not expire from a heart attack long before act 5.

Before asking what it is about the image of a fat Prince that so tickles the critics' funny bones, we may profitably glance at a few representations of Hamlet on the stage. The New Variorum, in tracing the history of the "fat" controversy, quotes Steevens's conjecture that, as the actor who played Hamlet also played Falstaff and Henry VIII, two men of substantial girth, Shakespeare wrote Gertrude's remark "to apologize for the want of such elegance of person as an audience might expect to meet with in the representative of the youthful Prince of Denmark. . . ."[6] John Payne Collier, having demonstrated that Richard Burbage originally played Hamlet, cites an elegy on the actor that quotes Gertrude's line: "No more young Hamlet, though but scant of breath, shall cry 'Revenge!' for his dear father's death." Burbage, says Collier, "would seem [by 1601] to have become rather corpulent."[7] The precision of the reference is somewhat undercut by the fact that Hamlet nowhere in Shakespeare's play "cries 'Revenge!' "; the elegist may be conflating Shakespeare's play with another *Hamlet*. Moreover, as John Dover Wilson points out, the argument is illogical: "if Burbage in 1601 was getting over-stout for the part of a young student, Shakespeare would hardly deliberately call attention to the fact. . . ."[8] Such attention to the actor rather than the character would irreparably disrupt the audience's suspension of disbelief. At any rate, Burbage's putative obesity should not prove Hamlet's.

Modern audiences are most familiar with Lawrence Olivier's Hamlet, which he has explained was conceived as "a hero with none of the usual excursions of heroism."[9] Olivier's filmic Hamlet, a substantial (but hardly *fat*) Nordic youth with blonde hair, clearly plays against romantic expectations of a dark and saturnine Prince. It is a view anticipated by Allardyce Nicoll, who defends the "fat" reading as demonstrating Shakespeare's dramaturgical acumen: Shakespeare's Hamlet "is a robust soldier, accustomed to manly exercise, but a trifle out of form owing to his sojourn at the Danish court, and hence stout, like the bearded Burbage. Too much cannot be said against the popular conception of Hamlet as a thin, emaciated figure, immaculately garbed in black and discoursing more like a medieval saint than an Elizabethan gentleman or a Danish prince."[10] One may note a certain critical sleight of hand here: to be thin is to be "emaciated," while to be "fat" is "robust" and "manly."

The conception Nicoll so disparages dates back critically at least to the romantic poet Samuel Taylor Coleridge, who confessed or bragged of having "a smack of Hamlet" himself, and theatrically to the nineteenth-century American actor Edwin Booth, whose "spare and almost attenuated frame," "hollow, low-pitched voice," "splendid dark eye," and "jetty, disheveled locks" embodied a Prince who went beyond melancholy to morbidity. Contemporary audiences preferred this anorexic Hamlet to the "sunny blue eyes" and golden hair of Charles Fechter, a Teutonic giant much more capable of portraying the Prince as fat and scant of breath.[11]

Booth had the good fortune to inherit and the good sense to augment a conception of Hamlet as a romantic—an intellectual brooder, too fine for a world of political intrigue and personal infidelity. Tommaso Salvini, reviewing his own acting career in 1893, complained about that popular conception of Hamlet:

> In the eyes of the public my form seemed too colossal for Hamlet. The adipose, lymphatic, and asthmatic thinker of Shakespeare must change himself, according to the popular imagination, into a slender, romantic, and nervous figure. . . .[12]

William Winter, who saw Salvini's performance, said disparagingly that he "looked like a gladiator" playing Hamlet. "His massive frame, his leonine demeanor, his iron firmness, and his aspect of resolute, overwhelmingly executive faculty combined to make him the literal opposite of everything that *Hamlet* is or means." Even worse, in Winter's opinion, was Edwin Forrest: "Being a resolute, formidable, athletic man, of combative disposition and truculent aspect, he was as little like Hamlet as it would be possible for any person to be. . . . [H]is demeanor was that of menace, not of melancholy, and it was evident that if any 'clouds' hung upon him they were thunder clouds."[13] Winter, reflecting and shaping public opinion of the nineteenth century, preferred Booth's slender, saturnine Hamlet.

Fiction has looped oddly on itself when a *de casibus* tragedy becomes the tragedy of Everyman, but Booth's heritage of romantic individualism enabled him to conceive the Prince as in part "poor waif"—the self-pitying child within each of us whose mother is suddenly a stranger and whose father, in the name of love, binds him to an unconscionable act. Long before Sigmund Freud and Ernst Jones explained the play's power as the residue of an infantile agon, viewers and readers and actors were identifying Hamlet with the selves they wished to be. Though his ego was clearly as colossal as his stature, was Forrest any more hubristic in thinking that Hamlet was a man rather like Edwin Forrest? Certainly an actor need not look heroic to play Hamlet well: Thomas Betterton, whom Samuel Pepys praises for his Hamlet, reputedly was a man with "a little pock-marked, corpulent body, thick legs, and large feet."[14] It is actors' talent, not their tonnage, that makes them good Hamlets.

In many instances, though, Gertrude's troublesome line never reaches the stage at all. Critics who reject the notion that Hamlet might be fat merely amend the text. Elmer Edgar Stoll suggests that the Queen actually says not "fat" but "hot," the word Claudius had used in describing his plot to Laertes, who is to ensure that Hamlet is "hot and dry" so that he will drink from the poisoned cup (4.7.157).[15] An ingenious German suggests "fatigate," a participial form of *fatigue*,[16] for which Shakespeare's use in *Coriolanus* 2.2.121 is the last OED citation. Beerbolm Tree, who was quite slender when he first played the part, altered "fat" to "faint,"[17] a change that had been suggested as an emendation at least as early as 1865, when J. Dixon suggested that "fat" might be a misprint for "faint."[18]

Another critical contingent accepts the reading "fat" but objects that Gertrude means not that Hamlet is obese but that he is sweaty. M. P. Tilley points out that "a popular physiological misconception of Shakespeare's day" held that sweat was melted human fat oozing through the pores of the skin.[19] That Gertrude immediately afterward offers Hamlet her napkin to wipe his brow confirms Hamlet's sweaty condition, which may (Tilley says) result simply from the exertion of fencing, not from a constitutional unfitness for violent exercise.

Unfortunately, understanding "fat" as "sweaty," though it rescues Hamlet from the charge of obesity, renders ludicrously explicit his earlier wish that his "too too solid flesh would melt, / Thaw, and resolve itself into a dew" (1.2.129–30). H. A. Kennedy relates the tale of a Hamlet who came to grief through this line: having stuffed himself for the part until "artificially swollen to the proportions of a Falstaff," he was laughed off the stage when, "reposing his hands upon his temporary paunch," he essayed those all too graphic lines.[20] An element of unintentional humor in the line undoubtedly has influenced scholars who prefer the reading "sullied," an adjective that does not prompt the mental image that "solid" does.

"Sallied" is the reading of the quartos, and Fredson Bowers has claimed that it is a legitimate variant of "sullied."[21] Tennyson, though he preferred "solid," noted that "sullied" is appropriate in its suggestion that Hamlet has been contaminated by the sin of his mother.[22] Samuel Tannenbaum, who frivolously traces the cause of Hamlet's "sullied flesh" to his failure to bathe, still points to the word's connection to a thematic concern of the play—sin and guilt—that is bodied forth in images of dirt, disease, and contagion.[23]

The argument for "solid" may be stronger, however. Samuel A. Weiss examines "solid" as part of an image cluster figuring mutability,[24] and Sidney Warhaft defends "solid flesh" as a recognized sign of melancholy and grief in Elizabethan times. The blood of a melancholic "was considered to contain a surfeit or surplus of the earth or lowest element, and even to tend itself to degenerate into heavy dregs or excrement."[25] Treatment by heat would first melt that earthy solidity and then evaporate it into "a dew."

Since "solid" accords with the play's images of mutability and physical decomposition while "sullied" expresses Hamlet's concern with moral and sexual impurity and even "sallied" may suggest a terror implicit in the play—that things (murder, murdered kings, lust) will break forth from restraint into sudden destructive activity, perhaps the best solution is to keep in mind all the possible solutions of this textual crux. But to say that wordplay makes Hamlet's meaning polyvalent does not settle the question of Hamlet's physical appearance. Although the Prince does seem to mature, in the course of the play, from a witty young graduate student, as I imagine him, to a thoughtful and experienced moralist, it is highly unlikely that Shakespeare instructed his actor to mature from a thin and melancholic scholar in act 1 to a fat and asthmatic swordsman in act 5—even though Claudius reports midway that "nor th' exterior nor the inward man / Resembles what it was" (2.2.6–7).

Scholars of Elizabethan physiology have suggested that Hamlet's obesity may be tied to his melancholy. Since breath keeps the heart from overheating, lack of air may lead to the typical behavior of melancholy, a sad solitariness that lends itself to soliloquies and—depending upon the mixture of melancholy with blood or choler—madness "merye" or "starke."[26] Hamlet's jeering claim to "eat the air, promisecramm'd" (3.2.94), coupled with his reference to his "windy" sighs and the little incident during the dueling scene in which Claudius toasts Hamlet's "better breath," may indicate that he was "scant of breath," either constitutionally or because of breathing the poisoned air of Elsinore ("this foul and pestilent congregation of vapors" [2.2.302–3]). Such impeded respiration might also lead to fatness, for fat is blood settled into cold parts of the body. A man suffering loss of blood from fatness, sighing, and melancholy would be extremely susceptible to illness and sudden death.[27] His heart, overheating, might indeed "break" under the "thousand natural shocks that flesh is heir to" (3.1.61–62).

Such an elegant but involved explanation of Hamlet's fatness may satisfy scholars in their studies, but students and actors are likely to protest that they do not believe in Elizabethan physiology and cannot make it relevant to their own situations. How are we, in light of a Hamlet whose silhouette has been called into question, to deal with the accidental humor in Hamlet's references to his "distracted globe" (1.5.97)—reminiscent of Nell, the fat kitchen wench in *The Comedy of Errors*, who was "spherical, like a globe" (3.2.114); his complaint that he must "grunt and sweat under a weary life" (3.1.76); or his prayer that his heart "hold" and his sinews "grow not instant old, / But bear [him] stiffly up" (1.5.94–95)? Since in a well-crafted play (as in a paranoiac universe) everything is significant, one begins, shortly, to see cryptic references to obesity and perspiration everywhere: in the name itself, Ham-let; in "My fat[e] cries out" (1.4.81); in the Ghost's "I scent the mourning heir [morning air]" (1.5.58); in Laertes' warning to Ophelia that "Nature crescent does not grow alone / In thews and bulk, but as this temple waxes / The inward service of the mind and soul / Grows wide withal" (1.3.11–14). Why does Shakespeare give us such mixed signals, and why does he interlard the text with words and images that so lend themselves to humor? Is he, in the midst of the pathetic splendors of the last act, positively *daring* us to laugh at his hero?

A fat Hamlet seems risible in part for Bergsonian reasons: the observer perceives a contradiction between the outward man, disproportionately swelled, and the inward soul, that weightless freight "like an angel in apprehension" (2.2.306). Such a contrast is appropriate in a play so full of "seeming"—for even we do not know whether the Ghost is "an honest ghost" or merely seems so, and Claudius at his most "sincere"—in prayer—proves not to have engaged in true prayer; while these acts are all mere fictions, portrayed by actors who mirror their own falseness in the play within the play.

Though beauty of soul and beauty of body traditionally belong together in fiction, Shakespeare, having endued Hamlet with the contradictory complexity of a real person, may have intended to keep audiences guessing along with Claudius, Polonius, and the rest about Hamlet's real motivation, intent, and complicity in the tragedy that overtakes Denmark. David Javitch reminds us of the importance to the courtier of *sprezzatura*, a graceful dissimulation of the difficulty of some onerous task accompanied by a painstaking attention to the trivial.[28] Perhaps Hamlet's cunning lies in part in his use of the contrast between his outward appearance and his inward character: he is most serious in his wordplay and most murderous in his swordplay. Is the role he eventually claims for himself—Hamlet the Dane—hidden not just under a scholar's gown but layers of fat as well? Today, at least, when the possibility of heroism in the realm of politics is often denied, it may be that Hamlet should be a hero who does not look heroic.

Within *Hamlet's* universe of antagonistic doubles, a fat Hamlet *can* make poetic and dramatic sense. First, being overweight correlates well with Hamlet's lethargy, irresolution, and passivity. If the revenger's delay is the central question of *Hamlet*, then its hero's physical bulk may explain that delay. Obesity could, moreover, explain the revenger's inability to be successfully devious: few physical traits are so difficult to disguise as fat. (*Hamlet* never attempts to hide behind an arras!)

Second, inasmuch as fatness may mirror an identification with women—who normally have more fat than men—a fat Hamlet could be acting out his conflicted identification with his mother and his unwillingness to assume his macho father's throne and power. W. H. Auden, in discussing Falstaff, asserts that "fatness in the male is the physical expression of a psychological wish to withdraw from sexual competition and, by combining mother and child in his own person, to become emotionally self-sufficient."[29] Thus obesity might be Hamlet's defense against the sex nausea he feels at his mother's marriage to Claudius. Feminists in the classroom might like to follow up the implication that Shakespeare, trying to portray a hero who was manly without the machismo of King Hamlet or Coriolanus, foundered on his society's preconceptions about what constitutes a hero and his own unconscious assumption that such a man would be corrupted by his feminine elements.

Finally, fatness fits several of the play's image patterns: disease; violation of boundaries—natural, political, sexual, and familial; food as poison and the human body as food; and sacrifice, for which one is "fatted." It is this fitness to the play's images and themes that seems to me the strongest argument for a fat Hamlet.

Hamlet's putative fatness is appropriate to a society that so conspicuously lacks a *via media*. In Elsinore, evil cannot be contained, and even "Goodness, growing to a plurisy, / Dies in his own too-much"

(4.7.116). As Maurice Charney points out, the play abounds in words beginning with "o'er" or "over," words that indicate excess, "departures from the ideal of temperance or moderation."[30] The disease that infects the body politic is not private but public, and it spreads like a stench, like the infectious vapors that rise from graves.[31] One "noses" the stench of Polonius's rotting flesh as one goes up the stair, and undoubtedly the closer one approaches the throne the more one smells the "rank" offense of Claudius's fratricide.

Gertrude's assertion may be simply the effusion of a doting mother. Yet sometimes the Queen's images portray Hamlet more accurately than she knows. For instance, at Ophelia's grave, she compares Hamlet—in the calmer moods of his manic depression—to a mother dove:

> Anon, as patient as the female dove
> When that her golden couplets are disclosed,
> His silence will sit drooping.
>
> (5.1.286–88)

That Hamlet should be metaphorized as a brooding mother bird foreshadows his sacrifice in the last scene. Shakespeare had noticed the self-sacrificing attempts of the lapwing to draw the predator's attention from her eggs; the "natural" mother, for him, is one who would die for her chicks. Hamlet enacts Laertes' image of the "kind, life-rend'ring pelican" (4.5.147), which was believed to feed her young with blood from her own breast, when he sheds his blood for the good of the nation. "Life-rend'ring": like the pelican, Hamlet surrenders his own life to render life to others; for Denmark his blood is a generative medium. He becomes feminine in a nurturing, maternal sense for which Gertrude is the play's inadequate representative.

Gertrude's word echoes Hamlet's gloomy pronouncement that "We fat all creatures else to fat us, and we fat ourselves for maggots" (4.3.23)—his elegy upon the "calf" Polonius (3.2.105). The image is of a beast raised in plenty and sacrificed for the good of the community. In *Hamlet*, the sacrifice is human. As Paul Jorgensen has argued, Hamlet's function as "scourge and minister" of God's will is to cleanse the corrupt center of Danish life, the court, lest it fall into a worse evil—the war for which everything is being readied in the first act of the play.[32] Hamlet's internecine sacrifices are therapeutic for the nation, a "bloodletting" that prevents worse bloodshed.

The metaphors used for the cleansing of Elsinore partake of the practicality of the sickroom. The patient, the sick country, must be "purged." These are metaphors of phlebotomy and sudorification, bloodletting and sweating conceived as medicinal processes. Gertrude's words cue us to the way in which Hamlet's body is to be representative of the body politic, the sick society that can be cured only by the most extreme of measures. In act 5, Hamlet the Dane provides a physical representation of the purification he provides as Denmark's scourge and minister: he is sweaty, and he bleeds.

Although earlier Hamlet had fractiously refused to "purge" Claudius, since "for me to put him to his purgation would perhaps plunge him into more choler" (3.2.305–7), still he is not just the "scourge" but the medicinal purger of the diseased state. The purification of Denmark keeps pace with the Ghost's purification in purgatory, which he foretells in these words:

> My hour is almost come,
> When I to sulf'rous and tormenting flames
> Must render up myself.
>
> (1.5.2–4)

If King Hamlet's words do contain the "odd cooking image" that Charney sees,[33] the fat of foul crimes clarified by melting in the flames of the place of punishment, then the Ghost metaphorically presents the afterlife as a place of spiritual purging through sweating. Robert F. Fleissner's argument for "sullied" in the first soliloquy because it suggests an alchemical metaphor of purification by melting[34] would fit this simultaneous transformation of soul and body—into worm's meat or into "something rich and strange" (*The Tempest*, 1.2.402). The reappearance of the word "render" further suggests that Hamlet has indeed succeeded his father, for King Hamlet's purgation in Purgatory takes place—in theater time—simultaneously with Hamlet's sacrificial and redemptive death.

Hamlet is sacrificed to cure Denmark's ills, a conventional enough tragic ending. Yet the fatness that fits him for slaughter encourages an unsympathetic laughter among critics. This has its own appropriateness, since while the scapegoat must be enough like the sacrificers who will survive him to serve as a suitable substitute, he must also be alien, "other," so that he may be sacrificed. If he is of royal blood, he must be reduced by ridicule and mistreatment to the status of a victim. The progress of *Hamlet* may be seen as a fitting of the Prince for sacrifice, and Gertrude's epithet marks Hamlet's assumption of the role of scapegoat. Indeed, so corrupted is the Dane by his acclimation to the saprogenic air of Denmark that he begins to decay even before he is dead; he is breathless, his heart aches, and his "too solid" flesh melts into "a dew" of perspiration. Hamlet, bloody, guilty, dying, and fat, is a microcosm of Denmark's ills.

"Our son," Claudius calls Hamlet (5.2.287), and although Hamlet would reject that possessive pronoun, Gertrude and Hamlet and

Claudius and the dead king are metaphorically joined and conflated in the last scene around the "union" that Claudius has promised Hamlet (5.2.272). Gertrude, always the victim of her sensuality, drinks the poison intended for her son, while Claudius is murdered by his intended victim. At last, the Prince becomes "Hamlet the Dane," his parents' child.

"Fat," Hamlet resembles his mother. This resemblance between mother and son—even if it exists only in Gertrude's mind—suggests that Hamlet has admitted that he *is* his mother's child, even though in his eyes she is so corrupted by sensuality that he has tried to root out the same susceptibility in himself.

Hamlet, fat and sweaty, takes on even the sins of the "bloat" king (3.4.182), committed in "the rank sweat of an enseamèd bed" (3.4.92). Only then, when they are alike, can he kill Claudius. For the theory of "the king's two bodies," some version of which informed Shakespeare's thinking about the nature of kingship, held that once Claudius had been crowned, Hamlet could not legally punish him, even if his regicide were revealed. Sir Francis Bacon explains that even if a king "were attainted before, the very assumption of the crown purgeth it. . . ."[35] Hamlet cannot kill his uncle without killing the king, thus offending the ideal of divinely appointed succession. As Claudius's Switzers know, to offer violence to the king is an act of treason.

Hamlet can touch Claudius only when they become in some sense identical—a kinship that he has repeatedly scorned. While Claudius had shot off cannons and drunk rouses, the Prince had refused the "funeral baked meats" and walked the lonely battlements of the castle. While, in Dr. Johnson's words, "every thing that happens to him gives [Claudius] occasion to drink,"[36] Hamlet refuses to drink even the cup with which Claudius pledges him, an act that represents an insulting refusal of Claudius's apparent generosity and good will.[37] Whatever his natural inclination, Hamlet consciously rejects the appetitive lust that characterizes the "bloat king" (3.4.182) in "the fatness of these pursy times" (3.4.153). His disassociation of himself from identification with his father's brother is persuasive, but Gertrude's little adjective hints that the revenge King Hamlet ordered could transform Hamlet into another Claudius, a traitor, a regicide, and the murderer of his nearest kinsman. The act of murder, however justified, leaves its perpetuator sullied. Fatness is this play's mark of Cain.

Hamlet's reconciliation with his mother paves the way to his "uncle-mother" and resolves this moral dilemma. Having acknowledged his kinship with Gertrude and Claudius, Hamlet can refuse to be their judge and executioner and leave revenge to Providence instead. Then, within Hamlet's providentially ordered world and Shakespeare's aesthetically ordered play, Hamlet's death accomplishes both the long-desired, long-delayed regicide and the suicide for which his first soliloquy had prayed. Claudius ironically achieves the relief he has sought, the elimination of the man who rages "like the hectic in [his] blood" (4.3.66), but he himself must die, too, a rottenness cut out of the heart of Denmark.

Hamlet has resisted accomplishing his revenge not only because he is loathe to identify himself with his sensual mother and the bloat king but also because he hesitates to emulate his father, a man ignominiously cuckolded and poisoned while snoozing through an after-dinner nap. Hamlet defers his revenge partly because he hopes not to die thus "full of bread" (3.3.80). The phrase seems to refer to a state of sinfulness: the prophet Ezekiel numbered among the sins of Sodom "pride, fulness of bread, and abundance of idleness."[38] Moreover, King Hamlet died without receiving the eucharist and extreme unction, sacraments that the church instructed should be received fasting.[39] Now he—poor ghost—must "render" himself to the flames of Purgatory, which will "purge" his sins. Prince Hamlet finally accedes to identification with his parents only after a long struggle: only after Ophelia is dead and his sensuality is in the grave with her, only after he is willing to follow his father into the freezing and fiery metamorphoses of the grave, can Hamlet accept the task to which he was born.

Claudius's adulterated wine and King Hamlet's untransubstantiated bread make for an unholy eucharist, appropriate in a kingdom of moral androphagists. The progress of *Hamlet's* plot is like the unfolding of Samson's riddle, when "Out of the eater came forth meat" (Judges 14:14). Indeed, Samson's riddle and Hamlet's have the same answer: the mutability of flesh, the eternally turning wheel of fate that ensures that beggar and king and worm will be interchangeable in a metamorphosis from dust to dust. We are inevitably cannibals, eating of the worm that hath eaten of a king or, indeed, though Malvolio was not philosopher enough to see it, of the chicken that has eaten of the worm that ate our grandmother (*Twelfth Night*, 4.2.50–60). *Hamlet* metaphorizes human relationship as a parasitical feeding—in Hamlet's language, Gertrude left feeding on the fair mountain that was her husband to batten on the moor that is Claudius (3.4.66–67), and Rosencrantz and Guildenstern speak to Claudius of the "many many bodies . . . / That live and feed upon your majesty" (3.3.10). The great chain of being is a food cycle, and in the end, Hamlet too must be consumed.

When Hamlet scornfully referred to the "fat weed that roots itself in ease on Lethe wharf," he did not remember that fatness is not just the antithesis of starvation but a step back to health. "Fat" land is fertile land; Cotgrave speaks of "The manuring, or dunging of land, whereby it growes the fatter, and fitter for any use."[40] The process of decomposition that destroys the mortal frame makes the land more fertile. "Fat" Hamlet, then, is a worthy sacrifice, one that cures the land of its malaise and promotes a new health. In a pun that Hamlet himself might have made, he is a "capon of greace"—*fat*, but homonymically *grace*,[41] the "fowl of season" that is fatted and fit for death (*Measure for Measure*, 2.2.85).

Fortinbras, surveying the littered stage of act 5, recognizes it for the shambles it is. He imagines death as a gourmet: "What feast is forward in thine eternal cell / That thou so many princes at a shot / So bloodily hast struck?" (5.2.365–67). The Player's speech, too, employed culinary imagery for what war does: Pyrrhus, "mincing" his victim's limbs (2.2.514), is himself a dish for the gods of death—"Bak'd and impasted" with blood (2.2.459). Now cormorant death has the "sweet prince" (5.2.359), and the "ponderous and marble jaws" of the grave will not open to vomit him back among the living (1.4.50). "Fat" Hamlet—the hero fatted as a sacrificial scapegoat—will, in his death, both purge his nation of the dross of regicide and "fat" his country's land.

Clearly, then, textual scholarship can justify Hamlet's fatness as a signifier of his readiness for a redemptive tragic sacrifice in the classical or Christian mode. When all is said and done, however, most of us do not picture Hamlet as fat. Although Hamlets in the theater have been "as fat as Falstaff and as meager as Romeo's Apothecary,"[42] nowadays, perhaps because of the influence of the "fattening" camera lens, actors and the heroes they portray are more likely to be anorexic than portly, plump, stout, fleshy, or fat. In truth, *any* actor who attempts to provide in his own flesh an "objective correlative" for Hamlet is likely to discover that the Prince is an embodiment of cultural and idiosyncratic expectations about heroism that no actor can hope to match. No actor can embody the expectations of more than a fraction of his audience. He can only hope to expand their preconceptions, so that in seeing a Hamlet who is more than they had imagined they become able to imagine themselves as more than they are.

Shakespeare himself was not ignorant of the processes of psychic projection: Claudius, defining Hamlet as his antithesis, calls him "free from all contriving" (4.7.135), while Gertrude, believing herself reconciled with Hamlet, sees him as "fat"—her chubby, playful, dependent baby. If drama holds a mirror up to nature, then this play holds up the shattered glass of *Richard II*, an emblem of perception refracted by emotional projection and a reflector of multiple personalities . . . and its universal appeal stems in large part from the immediacy with which viewers find themselves in Hamlet and must ask with him the questions of human identity and existential meaning.

In the classroom, students should learn that various interpretative perspectives need not preclude or simply contradict each other but can add to the play's psychological verisimilitude by providing a stereoscopic view of the Prince. "The observed of all observers" necessarily seems inconsistent, since he is a different man to each critic, and each critic in turn may interpret him as a twin (as Coleridge and Gertrude did) or an opposite (as Goethe and Claudius did). As the Ghost is both the devil and the spirit of Hamlet's loving father, as revenge is both an act of love and an act of hatred, as Ophelia is both chaste and corrupted, so Hamlet is both "the glass of fashion" and a fat and breathless scholar attempting, at thirty, to be a swordsman. He is all those things and more, since each of us creates him in a new melding of ourselves and Shakespeare understood through Hamlet.[43] Shakespeare's method in *Hamlet*—his use of inimical doubles and thesaurian speech and self-conscious histrionics—instructs us not to choose between such opposites but to see their reconcilement in the greater work—the play, or the world, or a regressive dream in which ambivalence is resolved and wholeness restored.

Those of us who can love, admire, and identify with Hamlet are responding to a fiction that matches our individual ego ideals, a Hamlet partly Shakespeare's, partly our culture's, and partly idiosyncratic. We reject evidence contrary to the flattering reflection we see—and that such evidence is plentiful only adds to our stubborn hero-worship of the Prince, since in the Oedipal psychomachia we too have been misunderstood and wronged.

Since fat is not heroic in the modern world, however, perhaps Gertrude's deflating description of her son could be used to warn us, the witnesses who survive him, that we must disengage our sympathies from Hamlet. The critics' derisive laughter at padded Hamlets and their uneasy modifications of Gertrude's adjective hint that a Hamlet dedicated to death must be understood not as a twin but as an opposite. We draw back then, glad not to be Hamlet, content to suffer ordinary rather than tragic fates.

In a theater—or a world—that has grown more cynical and mundane, perhaps we actually despise the scapegoat hero for his failure to survive. Many of us comprehend Hamlet's fear of dying more readily than his desire to act heroically, and the rituals of our culture teach us neither classical stoicism nor Christian belief. So with Prufrock, that quintessential twentieth-century urban man, we say, "I am not Prince

Hamlet." We will be observers, "attendant lord[s]," supernumeraries and survivors, not tragic heroes.[44] In the end, perhaps we are all a little more than kin and less than kind to Hamlet.

Notes

1. William Shakespeare, *The Tragedy of Hamlet*, 5.2.287. Quotations from Shakespeare follow the Riverside text, ed. G. Blakemore Evans (Boston: Houghton Mifflin, 1974). Subsequent citations will appear in parentheses in the essay.

2. J. Wolfgang von Goethe, *Wilhelm Meister's Lehrjahre*, quoted in *The Footnote* 1 (1949):9.

3. "An Eye-Witness," "Byron and Shelley on the Character of Hamlet," in Claude C. H. Williamson, *Readings on the Character of Hamlet, 1661–1947* (London: Allen, 1950), p. 55. Edward P. Vining uses the passage as evidence for his assertion that Hamlet is a woman in disguise (*The Mystery of Hamlet: An Attempt to Solve an Old Problem* [Philadelphia: Lippincott, 1881]). Karl Elze thinks Hamlet's fatness is a good objective correlative for his personality (*Shakespeare's Tragedy of Hamlet* [London: Sampson, 1882]).

4. Thomas Wade, "What Does 'Hamlet' Mean?: A Lecture Delivered before the President and Members of the Jersey Mechanics' Institute" (London: J. Miller, n.d. [1855?]), p. 32.

5. E. Vale Blake, "The Impediment of Adipose: A Celebrated Case," *Popular Science Monthly* 17 (1880):60–71.

6. George Steevens, *The Plays of William Shakespeare*, vol. 10: *Hamlet* [1778], quoted in the New Variorum *Hamlet*, ed. Horace Howard Furness, 13th ed., vol. 1 (Philadelphia: J. B. Lippincott and Co., 1871 [1905]), p. 446.

7. John Payne Collier, *Memoirs of the Principal Actors in the Plays of Shakespeare* (London: Shakespeare Society, 1846), pp. 52, 21.

8. John Dover Wilson, ed., *Hamlet*, rev. ed. (Cambridge: at the University Press, 1961), p. 255. See also Martin Holmes, *Shakespeare and Burbage* (Totowa, NJ: Rowman, 1978), p. 188.

9. Brenda Cross, ed., *The Film Hamlet: A Record of Its Production* (London: Saturn, 1948), p. 15.

10. Allardyce Nicoll, *Studies in Shakespeare*, in Williamson, *Readings*, pp. 477–78.

11. Charles Shattuck, *The Hamlet of Edwin Booth* (Urbana: University of Illinois Press, 1969), p. 90, quoting a contemporary review of Booth's Hamlet.

12. William Ackerman Buell, *The Hamlets of the Theatre* (New York: Astor-Honor, 1968), p. 102.

13. William Winter, *Shakespeare on the Stage*, series 1 (New York: Moffat, 1911), pp. 411–12, 334–35.

14. Henry P. Phelps, *Hamlet from the Actors' Standpoint* (New York: Werner, 1890), pp. 5–6.

15. Elmer Edgar Stoll, "Not Fat or Thirty," *Shakespeare Quarterly* 2 (1951): 295–301.

16. Westenholz, as summarized (disparagingly) by Anton Aldoph Raven, *A Hamlet Bibliography and Reference Guide, 1877–1935* (Chicago: University of Chicago Press, 1936), p. 215.

17. H. C. Newton, *Cues and Curtain Calls*, in Williamson, *Readings*, p. 471.

18. J. Dixon, "Line in *Hamlet*: 'He is Fat and Scant of Breath,'" *Notes and Queries*, 3d series, 7 (1865): 52.

19. M. P. Tilley, "Two Shakespearean Notes," *Journal of English and Germanic Philology* 24 (1925): 315–16.

20. H. A. Kennedy, "Was Hamlet Fat?" *Notes and Queries*, 5th series, 1 (1874): 484–85. See also J. C. Maxwell, "'Fat and Scant of Breath' Again," *English Studies* 32 (1951): 30; and Waldo H. Dunn, "Hamlet's Fatness," *Times Literary Supplement*, 26 May 1927, p. 375.

21. Fredson Bowers, "Hamlet's 'Sullied' or 'Solid' Flesh: A Bibliographical Case-History," *Shakespeare Studies* 9 (1956): 44–48.

22. Malcolm Ware, "Hamlet's *Sullied/Solid* Flesh," *Shakespeare Quarterly* 11 (1960): 490. See also Helge Kökeritz, "This Sullied Solid Flesh," *Studia Neophilologica* 30 (1958): 3–10; and Richard Flatter, "'Solid' or 'Sullied', and Another Query," *Shakespeare Quarterly* 11 (1960): 490–93.

23. Samuel A. Tannenbaum, "Editorial Notes," *The Shakespeare Association Bulletin* 9 (1934): 217.

24. Samuel A. Weiss, "'Solid,' 'Sullied,' and Mutability: A Study in Imagery," *Shakespeare Quarterly* 10 (1959): 219–27.

25. Sidney Warhaft, "Hamlet's Solid Flesh Resolved," *English Literary History* 28 (1961): 21–22. See also Roland J. McCaig, "Further Speculation on 'Solid' in *Hamlet*," *Shakespeare Newsletter* 16 (1966): 32.

26. Jane O'Hara-May, *Elizabethan Dyetary of Health* (Lawrence, Kans.: Coronado, 1977), p. 57. See also Andrewe Boorde, *A Compendyous Regyment or a Dyetary of Helth*, ed. F. J. Furnivall (1592; London: Kegan Paul, 1870 [1893]), p. 289; James Hart, *KΛinikh, or the Diet of the Diseased* (London, 1633), p. 103; and Thomas Becon, *A Fruitful Treatise of Fasting* (London, [1551?]).

27. O'Hara-May, *Elizabethan Dyetary*, pp. 128–29.

28. David Javitch, *Poetry and Courtliness in Renaissance England* (Princeton: Princeton University Press, 1978), p. 36.

29. W. H. Auden, *The Dyer's Hand* (New York: Random House, 1948), p. 196.

30. Maurice Charney, *Style in Hamlet* (Princeton: Princeton University Press, 1969), pp. 133–34n.

31. Richard D. Altick, "Hamlet and the Odour of Mortality," *Shakespeare Quarterly* 5 (1954): 167–68.

32. Paul Jorgensen, *Shakespeare's Military World* (Berkeley: University of California Press, 1956), p. 190.

33. Charney, *Style*, p. 98. According to the OED, however, "render" meaning "to melt like fat" is a rare usage before 1700.

34. Robert F. Fleissner, "Hamlet's Flesh Alchemically Considered," *English Studies* 59 (1978): 508–9.

35. Francis Bacon, *The Case of the Post-Nati of Scotland*, in *The Works of Francis Bacon*, vol. 7, ed. James Spedding, Robert Leslie Ellis, and Douglas Denton Heath (1609; London: Longman, 1879), p. 668. See also Ernst Hartwig Kantorowicz, *The King's Two Bodies: A Study in Medieval Political Theology* (Princeton: Princeton University Press, 1957).

36. Samuel Johnson, *Annotations by Samuel Johnson and Geo. Steevens and the Various Commentators upon "Hamlet," Written by Will. Shakspere* (London: John Bell, 1787), p. 20.

37. Martin Holmes, *The Guns of Elsinore* (London: Chatto and Windus, 1964), p. 174.

38. William W. Heist, "Fulness of Bread," *Shakespeare Quarterly* 3 (1952): 140. See also Leslie Hotson, who understands "fat" as "sated" or "stuffed," and notes Hamlet Jr.'s dying resemblance to his father in "Hamlet Fat?" *The Spectator* 188 (1952): 701.

39. T. M. Parrott, "Fulness of Bread," *Shakespeare Quarterly* 3 (1952): 380.

40. Randle Cotgrave, *A Dictionarie of the French and English Tongues* (1611; New York: Da Capo, 1971).

41. Madge Lorwin, *Dining with William Shakespeare* (New York: Atheneum, 1976), p. 309.

42. William Ackerman Buell, *The Hamlets*, Foreword.

43. Norman N. Holland, "Hamlet, My Greatest Creation," *Journal of the American Academy of Psychoanalysis* 3 (1975): 419–27.

44. T. S. Eliot, "The Love Song of J. Alfred Prufrock," in *Prufrock and Other Observations* (1917), reprinted in *The Complete Poems and Plays* (New York: Harcourt, 1952), p. 7.

Part II
The Stage

6
Notes on Playing Prospero

SHERMAN HAWKINS

CRITICISM OF SHAKESPEARE'S PLAYS HAS, I THINK, REACHED A POINT WHERE it is no longer necessary to insist on the complementarity of stage and page, poetry and performance. Just as in Plato's republic kings are also philosophers, so in the ideal or platonic university, Shakespearean scholars would have the experience of acting or directing the plays they teach. Even the most regular theatergoing is no substitute for this direct involvement in production. So when one of my students, a gifted young director named Amy Seham, asked me to play Prospero in her production of *The Tempest*, I eagerly agreed. I think I half expected the literary meaning of the play-as-poem to change completely in performance. Let me say at once that I have no such magical transformation, no miracle of new interpretation to report.

What I discovered instead was the extraordinary, almost symbiotic interplay between critical and theatrical interpretation: how "literary" meaning can be embodied in minute details of performance—a gesture, a bit of blocking, the inflection of a line, a single word—how these, often the results of spontaneous intuition or acccidental conditions of performance, generate new reaches of meaning.[1] This process continues when the performance is over: only now in retrospect do I as critic begin to understand some of the things we as actors did.

Let me give a simple example of the way performance "embodies" symbolic or thematic meaning. Prospero's magic island is a fiction, a poetic fantasy, grounded in fact. Every stage, every theater is just such an island, where for a time illusion comes to seem reality. And if the audience experiences this reality in performance, it is because the actors have come to experience it through long weeks of rehearsal. Certainly this was so for me: that imaginary island became as important, as "real," as my home or classroom, and I lived surrounded by enchanted beings whose true names were not Mark and Josh and Laura but Ariel, Caliban, and Miranda. The interpenetration of reality and dream, one of *The Tempest's* central literary themes, is thus directly apprehended by actors and audience in any good production of the play. But our director contrived a further "realization" of it, for this was an environmental staging, with audience seated among the acting areas and actors moving around and behind members of the audience. The result was that *The Tempest* was not a remote and gorgeous pageant, viewed across the felt division of a proscenium or platform stage. The worlds of audience and play literally interpenetrated: the spectators, like the characters, found themselves shipwrecked on Prospero's island, held captive or enchanted, as the case may be, before being released back into that lesser dream we call reality.

Another literary motif that became very real for me in performance was Wilson Knight's polar opposition of storm and music. In *The Tempest*, of course, these symbols become facts, direct sensory experience: the stormy clamor of the opening scene, the heavenly music Prospero calls for in the final one. Such sound effects, contrived with a thunderscreen and "twangling instruments," blend into the voices of the actors: the terrified cries of the mariners, Ariel's enchanting songs. And these voices in turn express or evoke inner states of disorder or of concord. In these terms, Prospero as well as the play moves from storm to music, and he must find vocal equivalents for both, so that his wrath echoes the storm and the "solemn air" he calls for becomes mere background to the music of his words. The whole play centers on this change from an isolating and disruptive fury that Prospero can hardly control to a tempered harmony that extends itself to the other characters, turning chaos to community. The two moods are balanced very symmetrically. At our first reading, I looked ahead after the second scene of the play—as actors will—to see when Prospero speaks again. I was astonished to find that his next big speeches do not occur until the beginning of act 4, after which he is on stage almost continuously. The speaking part, in other words, breaks into two halves, one near the beginning and the other at the end. These are literally halves. Counting lines during a particularly dull faculty meeting, I discovered that in our text[2] act 1, scene 2 contains exactly as many lines for Prospero as the whole rest of the play: when he finishes this scene, Prospero's speaking part is half done.

As anyone who has played the scene will tell you, its great problem is monotony. The reason is not just the quantity of exposition it contains but also the fact that Prospero is angry throughout. He threatens Ariel, Caliban, and Ferdinand in turn; even his affectionate dialogue with Miranda is interrupted by harsh rebukes: "Dost thou hear?" "Thou attend'st not!" Each of these rebukes, I noticed, occurs directly after a reference to Antonio: the mere mention of his "false brother" arouses in Prospero a fury that threatens to engulf him. The actor readily finds nuance and variety in the differing kinds of anger—real or pretended—

that Prospero directs at Antonio and Ferdinand, Ariel and Caliban. My present point is that this first half of his part is mainly "storm" as the latter half is mainly "music." Of course I am simplifying: storm can erupt in the midst of music, as when a hollow and confused noise interrupts the wedding masque, or Caliban and his fellows are hunted down with cries and shrieks and baying hounds. Conversely, Prospero's tenderness to Miranda in their first scene provides musical contrast and counterpoint to his fury against Antonio. Nevertheless the main movement from storm to music seems clear, and we find it repeated in smaller structural units: in the two contrasted masques Prospero stages for the three "men of sin" and the young lovers, or the long narration of his shipwreck, or the great speech in which he renounces his magic. In performance, the same motif can inform a gesture or the reading of a line. Consider how Prospero's first movement in our production—a slow turn from the shipwreck and the storm toward Miranda—can epitomize his inner movement through the rest of the play: the forbidding figure of the hooded mage turns to reveal the father's loving face. Or consider Prospero's answer when Ariel, reduced to submission by his angry threats, promises to obey: "Do so; and after two days / I will discharge thee." The actor can of course speak all this in a tone of benevolent promise—music after storm. But he is better advised to extend that caesura into a tense pause, marking a change in mood, making the first two words all threat and the rest all promise—a change from storm to music that releases Ariel into ecstasy. Thus in performance even two lines can become a mirror or microcosm of the whole.

Prospero is, of course, the central figure in the play. Shakespeare establishes his centrality in the text, the play-as-poem, by surrounding him with analogies to the playwright and to God. But in performance the actor playing Prospero must earn this centrality for himself. Shakespeare uses the instinctive rivalry of actors as they maneuver to occupy center stage or cap each other vocally and emotionally as a tacit, running metaphor for the play's political struggle: everyone wants to rule Prospero's island or escape his control. If he is to dominate the world of the play, Prospero must "outdo" Ariel and Caliban, must center the audience's imaginative response upon himself. He is not funny like the clowns; he lacks the immediate appeal of Ariel's music or Caliban's grotesque appearance. He has only the power of the word and the vocal and intellectual force it articulates. Thus the long second scene is a struggle for mastery, and Prospero first appears to us as a figure of numinous and frightening power.

Yet he seeks to impose his vision as well as his will on Ariel. We played Prospero as a "visualizer": his mind creates images so vivid that they exist for him—and sometimes others—on the borderline between fantasy and reality, where the play itself exists. Thus when Prospero speaks of the boat in which he and Miranda were cast adrift, he traces its outlines with his staff, and Miranda, huddled at his feet, begins to shiver with fear and cold. So when Prospero reminds Ariel how Sycorax tormented him, the spirit writhes and struggles: he is once more imprisoned in the cloven pine. Prospero can enter Ariel's mind as he cannot Caliban's, or even perhaps Miranda's: the border between the two is singularly fluid. Prospero is not just torturing Ariel, but educating him, forcing him to remember, to connect past and present, to see the difference between evil and good, Sycorax and himself.[3] Of course what he is doing to Ariel parallels what he is doing to the audience: he has access to our consciousness and we, increasingly, to his. But what the magician does as he works on Ariel's memories and feelings is also typical of the way one actor helps another, creating a mood or image the other can play. This cooperation in fantasy is the reverse of the rivalry I spoke of a moment ago, and it is crucial to the developing relation between Ariel and Prospero. Ariel increasingly comes to understand what Prospero feels, to see as he sees.

At our very first rehearsal I remember Ariel, sitting on a bookcase, watching Antonio tempt Sebastian. This has no basis in the text: Ariel is off-stage during the temptation scene. Still, it brought home to me how much Ariel—who has hitherto known only Prospero and Sycorax and their contrasted offspring—learns of human nature from observing the courtiers and clowns. By the time he plays the harpy who denounces the sins of Alonso, Sebastian, and Antonio, he knows them as Prospero does: "You are three men of sin. . . ." The voice he uses here comes as a surprise from the delicate Ariel: it is storm, not music, sounding to Alonso like thunder, wind, and sea. It is, I think, Ariel's magically enlarged imitation of Prospero; he speaks in his master's voice what his master taught him to say. Yet this is not mere ventriloquism: Ariel is *acting* Prospero—or acting one side of him—discovering how moral indignation and moral judgment feel. In the contrasted masque that follows, Ariel "presents" Ceres, changing from harpy to goddess. Again he is enacting his master's "present fancies," but we sense that here Prospero is less playwright, more audience: the spirits are improvising freely on themes of chastity and temperance he wants to teach. And in Ceres, the goddess who mourns a daughter lost to another love, Ariel seems to touch on Prospero's inmost feelings, feelings of which he is himself perhaps not yet entirely conscious. It is almost as if the spirit were consoling him. So we are not surprised when Prospero summons Ariel to meet with Caliban and his conspirators, only to find that Ariel has already disposed of them on his own initiative. Thus is prepared the climactic moment in which Ariel provides the final impulse that moves Prospero from vengeance to virtue, storm to music. Like an actor, Ariel uses the recollection of his own experience of confinement to color his description of the prisoners. His "were I human" thus expresses as a condition contrary to fact what seems a possibility almost accomplished. The striking indecorum of his comparison of Gonzalo's tears to "winter's drops / From eaves of reeds"—what does Ariel know of winter or thatched roofs?—suggest how far he is domesticated. And now he must humanize his master. He works on Prospero's memories of Gonzalo as Prospero worked on his own memories of Sycorax. This is in fact a reversal of their first scene together: Ariel is using Prospero's own methods, invading his imagination, teaching him to see and feel. Once again the symbolic interplay is grounded in theatrical reality, the way one actor catches emotion from another. I was lucky in my Ariel, a young black actor named Mark Wade who in each performance gave me the sense of pity I needed to transform Prospero from a magican to a man like other men.

Prospero here experiences wonder: "Hast thou, which are but air, a touch, a feeling / Of their afflictions?" The point deserves emphasis, for in a play which—as Miranda's very name suggests—turns on the sense of wonder, Prospero, whose magic creates wonder for others, seems himself almost untouched by it. What is miracle for them is only art for him. Those resurrections from the dead, those touching recoveries of the loved and lost which regularly come to the hero in other late romances, are in *The Tempest* reserved for secondary characters, for Alonso and Ferdinand. Prospero, who speaks of losing his daughter "In this last tempest," has—in the sense he means—lost her forever. The nearest equivalent for him to Leontes' amazed discovery that Hermione is alive is the amazing fact that Ariel can feel.

This fits the play's progression from wonders that are in whole or part illusory to those which are real. The opening storm is an illusion that both audience and characters take to be reality: only afterward do we discover that we have been deceived, mistaking art for nature. The great paired masques of judgment and blessing are miracles of art, illusions whose supernatural aura create wonder in the audience as well as those who watch them on stage. But when at the end Prospero reveals Ferdinand and Miranda playing chess, what seems a "most high miracle" to Alonso and the rest is simple fact for us. This revelation is clearly the completion of the interrupted wedding masque, yet the goddess who appears to Alonso is not a spirit who will melt into thin air but a mortal maiden who will become his daughter and Ferdinand's bride. The continuity between the two "shows" is marked by dramatic business, by the theatrical flourish with which Prospero draws the curtain of the cave to disclose the lovers. We played the scene with Prospero facing the courtiers: I never saw how Ferdinand and Miranda appeared. But for Prospero, what is magical here is the effect on Alonso and the rest.

Only in rehearsal did I realize that the other masque of judgment is likewise continued in this final scene. It was the blocking that helped me recognize this also as a scene of judgment, a little apocalypse. Gonzalo and Alonso, Sebastian and Antonio entered in the order Prospero addresses them, ranging themselves, by happy accident, on his right hand and his left. The sequence of address moves symbolically from good to evil, but psychologically from what is easy—Prospero's reunion with Gonzalo—to what is hard—the confrontation with Antonio. This judgment is not the final one, and Prospero is not God to punish sinners: he must forgive his brother even though Antonio does not repent. It is an exercise of will, an act of deliberate virtue. Once again the theatrical business as Prospero "discases" himself and dons his hat and rapier emphasizes that this too is a "show," another epiphany. Only this time the "three men of sin" are confronted not with a supernatural harpy but with the real and human figure of the "wrongèd Duke of Milan." The forgiveness Prospero offers them is as potentially miraculous—and as humanly real—as the love of Ferdinand and Miranda. But once more what makes the miracle is the response to it. And as Prospero presents himself to Antonio and Alonso, he does not know how they will respond.

Hitherto I have analyzed Prospero's role as if it were only speeches. However, any actor would remind us that acting is not all talking and doing: even as wordy a character as Prospero must sometimes listen and watch. Mark Rose's analysis of the chiasmic structure of *The Tempest* makes its center and turning point a scene in which Prospero does nothing: his only acting is reacting as Ferdinand and Miranda declare their love.[4] And this brought home to me an equally central truth about the play. Prospero's "so potent art" controls the action and the other characters only up to a point: other forces are at work more magical than his. Though he can bring Ferdinand and Miranda face to face and confront Alonso with the knowledge of his offense, he cannot make the prince and princess fall in love or the sinner repent. Love is clearly a form of enchantment: "They are both in either's pow'rs," murmurs Prospero as the lovers gaze on each other in wonder. But this is not his magic, and like all magic it may be white or black. Lust is to love as Sycorax to Prospero, and he does not know which Ferdinand feels. Indeed of all the characters, Ferdinand is the one most unknown to Prospero and most vital to his plan. Hence the tests and ordeals; hence, in this central scene, his anxiety as Ferdinand speaks of all those other ladies he had "eyed with best regard." The prince sounds like an erotic epicure: if so, Miranda's enchantment is enslavement. But then as

Prospero listens, the direction of the speech changes: "But you, O *you*. . . ." Shakespeare has more than one means of marking the importance of the moment. The literary critic will find that Ferdinand's speech and Miranda's exactly equal reply are the central speeches in this central scene; the forty-eighth line out of ninety-six is one they share between them. Yet in the theater the audience will see the play's shift from storm to music reflected in Prospero as anxious jealousy gives way to delight and wonder. This is a miracle not of his making: "Heavens rain grace / On that which breeds between 'em!"

So too in the last scene Prospero's plan depends on a change in Alonso that his magic cannot bring about. Indeed, as we played the scene, Prospero when he turns to confront Alonso no longer possesses any supernatural power. As he abjures his rough magic and calls for heavenly music, he lays down his staff, never—in our production—to take it up again. So, as with Ferdinand, Prospero must wait in expectation to see what Alonso will say and do. Again, forces other than his—grace, heaven, providence divine—are at work. But Prospero here acts as well as reacts. Having laid aside his magic powers, my director told me, Prospero must exert his human power. And this is a power he finds in weakness. It is not enough to present himself as the wronged Duke of Milan or even to embrace his wronger: these prompt Alonso to a formal repentance and restoration which correct the past without creating a new future. Prospero must change enmity to affection, must find in Alonso the brother he has been denied in Antonio. It is in their common sense of loss that he sees the chance for new community between them: Prospero turns from Antonio to Alonso when the King speaks of the death of his son to reveal that he himself has suffered a "like loss." This fiction is very real for Prospero: it is quite possible that when he and Miranda return to live and rule in different cities, these two who for a dozen years have shared the magic isle will not see each other any more. In early rehearsals, I was inclined to let Prospero indulge his feelings here. But this is sentimental: Prospero is using his own emotion to reach and touch Alonso. We sense his success as Alonso, drawn from his own grief and self-absorption, echoes him: "A daughter?" And then the miraculous occurs. "O heavens!"—surely not here a random exclamation—"O heavens! that they were living both in Naples / To be the king and queen there!" It is everything Prospero might wish and more than he could contrive. His delight and wonder are expressed in the almost prattling excitement of the speech with which he discloses Ferdinand and Miranda. It is enough for him to watch the effect in Alonso: "giving up" is different from "giving to."

Yet there is a deep sense of giving up in Prospero's final speeches. The son he finds in Ferdinand, the brother he wins in Alonso, cannot really substitute for the primary objects of the father's and brother's love. He must leave his magic and his island realm, must release Ariel and admit failure with Caliban. I found a yearning sadness in acting the last lines I had not suspected in reading them. Prospero talks of bringing the others to their ship as if he were not accompanying them, of his "hope" to see the bridal of Ferdinand and Miranda as if he might not be there, of "retiring" to Milan—and here Prospero's slow turn brought him face to face with Antonio, whom his magic cannot change, who will be there with him. He returns to rule his dukedom, but Prospero knows what we have also learned, that power, whether political or magical, is a form of service, not self-fulfilling but self-emptying. He speaks of the story of his life as if it were already over: clearly his every third thought is of the sleep that rounds the dream of life.

Then the movement ends on an "up-beat" as Prospero promises fair seas and prosperous gales, summoning his magic the last time: "My Ariel, chick, / That is thy charge." In our production, however, Prospero has given up his magic; he no longer has power over Ariel. I marked the change by a shameless "double-take": as Prospero raises his hands in the familiar gesture of command, he finds that his hand is empty: the magic staff lies behind him on the ground. The imperative becomes almost a question, the caressing monosyllable, "chick," almost an appeal: has Prospero succeeded in creating any human ties of gratitude or loyalty in this free spirit? There is a final hovering moment of choice—then Ariel nods and smiles. Thus Prospero's last magic is achieved through Ariel's free assent, an assent that springs from something that is almost love. The farewell that follows can be said with affectionate regret, even with yearning, but I had invested these feelings earlier in the simple confession, "I shall miss thee." I spoke the lines with elation: as he dismisses Ariel—"Then to the elements / Be free"—the old visualizer is able for a moment to imagine what such absolute liberty would be.

Thus by surrendering power, Prospero attains it in a different kind. This may be the point of the epilogue. In our production, "Please you draw near" was addressed not to the other characters but to the audience who surround Prospero's acting space. And so they do, for at this point the boundary between dream and waking, play world and real world, almost dissolves. Though Prospero declares that his magic is "overthrown," I think that both for actor and audience, no moment in the play is more magical than this. And surely never is Prospero's power over the audience stronger than now, as he asks their pardon. He speaks for the actor and the playwright, but he also speaks in character. The magician who first appeared to us as a "god of power," evoking awe and admiration, is now the weary and very human Prospero whose failings we have come to know so well. Garrulous, testy, domineering, he is one of us. But he is also something more, and now as he speaks with a new humility of the need for forgiveness that is both his and ours, we become aware of the magical transformation which is the real subject of *The Tempest*, and which is nowhere more evident than in Prospero himself.

Notes

1. I found John Russell Brown, *Shakespeare in Performance: An Introduction Through Six Major Plays* (New York: Harcourt Brace Jovanich, 1976), helpful in preparing the part. His annotations to *The Tempest* are sometimes echoed in the interpretation that follows—see, e.g., pp. 552–53 on the first scene between Prospero and Ariel.

2. Our text was the Pelican *Tempest*, ed. Northrop Frye (Baltimore: Penguin, 1959), from which the quotations in this essay are taken.

3. Cicero's definition of *prudentia* in *De Inventione* (2.53.160) as a knowledge of good and bad whose parts are memory of the past, understanding of the present, and foresight of the future is a Renaissance commonplace surely familiar to Shakespeare.

4. *Shakespearean Design* (Cambridge: Harvard University Press, 1972), p. 173.

7

The Merry Wives of Windsor in the People's Republic of China: A Director's Notebook

SIDNEY HOMAN

FOUR WEEKS BEFORE I WAS TO LEAVE FOR THE PEOPLE'S REPUBLIC OF CHINA, where I would teach at Jilin University and direct the actors of the Jilin Art College and the Changchun Modern Drama Theater in a production of Shakespeare's *The Comedy of Errors*, I received a message from my hosts asking if I would consider, instead, directing *The Merry Wives of Windsor*. I decided not to inquire about this change of heart. Perhaps the managers of the two companies thought *Comedy* with its two sets of identical twins would be too complex, or, conversely, that *Wives* would be more appealing since the story of a community acting in concert outside the law to reform a decadent aristocrat threatening their values parallels that country's own system of provincial justice. There had been a spectacular Shakespeare festival in Beijing in April; possibly some members of the cast had been impressed with the production there of *Wives*. Since I would be directing an all-Chinese cast, in a Chinese translation of Shakespeare, albeit with a translator at my side, I resolved not to argue that we stay with *Errors* but rather to go along with whatever play the actors felt comfortable doing. *Wives* itself was relatively new to me. I had accorded it what, in a very different (and sad) context, Daniel Moynihan had once termed "benign neglect," never bothering to examine my fellow Shakespeareans' dismissal of it as a slight work from the playwright's hand, perhaps written to satisfy a Queen wanting to see Falstaff in love, an occasional piece whose Falstaff was a pale imitation of that colossal figure, that aging Life-Force in *Henry IV*.

As things turned out, my schedule of teaching and working with acting companies in Changchun City was so crowded that I never did have enough rehearsal time to see *Wives* through to opening night. I did manage to get the actors into the early stages of rehearsals, besides outlining for both companies my general concept of the play and the specifics for the production. When I returned to the United States in last August, I sent my detailed director's notes to the companies, and so even if I cannot take up their generous offer to return this spring to complete rehearsals, my Chinese codirector, complementing these notes with his own imaginative and technical grasp of the play, will finish what I started. Content with a video tape of a play that I have, in essence, codirected, I will also be content in another way, for my absence from the final weeks of rehearsals, when coupled with my "presence" in the form of what I could accomplish while there as well as those notes, will make the production a "collaborative effort" in a very literal and, I hope, meaningful sense of the phrase.

Here I offer, then, a digest of my thoughts as the play's codirector, as a way of showing how, in this volume on *Shakespere and the Triple Play*, my own understanding of *Wives* as a scholar and teacher will be enacted onstage. Not all stage directors keep such detailed notes, of course; some of my colleagues in the theater settle—or *claim* they settle—the concept and the particulars of the staging only during rehearsals. By disposition I am more methodical: months before the first rehearsal, I make such notes, attending to all the light cues, the style of costuming, every business of the blocking. To be sure, things are more fluid in actual practice. In rehearsals one finds that this particular downstage cross is impossible because what seemed attractive in theory looks awkward when seen onstage. And the actor you had thought perfect for Falstaff gives you something else, often as good or better, than the character as conceived in the study. Rehearsals are properly an expansion of the literary text, a time when new possibilities of interpretation, not to mention limitations, present themselves. Still, for me, the difference between those director's notes born of my solitary self and the play as it emerges in the communal efforts of rehearsals is not that radical.

I offer below, therefore, these compressed director's notes that will, with such alterations as I have just suggested, control the production of *The Merry Wives of Windsor* to be staged this spring in Changchun City, with or without my being present. They are divided into the very sequence I follow from the moment I first begin to think of a play: the "concept" as it is called in the theater (the statement the production is designed to make, the philosophical tone, the mood to be established that influences everything from blocking to acting style), the set and its lighting, the costumes and music, the characters and the style or styles of acting to be employed, some general thoughts on blocking for the first two scenes only (a microcosm, in effect, for a much larger text), and miscellaneous thoughts, ranging from suggestions for the props to cuts in the text.

Concept

Is Falstaff's punishment excessive? Do the numerous interlocking stories involving deception—indeed a plot second only to that of *Cymbeline* in its intricacy—point to a larger view of humankind, of Windsor society? Or how literally is the play to be taken, given the fact that while scholars tend to accord it short attention, *Wives* itself is the fourth most produced play of Shakespeare? *Wives* is the playwright's only full-fledged citizen comedy, the only one set in a rural town. Should this fact influence the "look" of the production? Since I had staged *The Comedy of Errors* the year before as something more than a "farce" (in the the more limited sense of that term), should *Wives*, which also has elements of farce, be given that same serious psychological and metadramatic dimensions I found in that earlier comedy, where deception is the product of circumstance rather than the will of the characters? And—simply or not so simply—what about Falstaff? What is his role in the play and—inevitably—in the context of his appearances in the two histories? I reached my concept of *Wives* by raising these very questions.

It was my feminist reading of the text that provided some answers—though hardly THE answer—to such problems, or challenges—depending upon one's perspective. For me the "fault" in *Wives* lies with the men, and, no less, the solution with the women. Ford and Slender set the boundaries for the general malaise affecting their gender. The former is too imaginatively aggressive, reading his society and his wife, in particular, from his own idiosyncratic and, as a consequence, neurotic scenario. Ford anticipates Othello, of course, nor is he a mere caricature of the jealous husband. His lack of trust in his wife's fidelity—in contrast to his neighbor Page's confidence in his—suggests his own insecurity, perhaps a sense of unworthiness that has impotence, literal or imagined, at its root. It is revealing that when Ford speculates that if he and Page were dead their wives would marry again, Mistress Page retorts that he can "be sure of that—two other husbands" (3.2.16–17). Slender, in contrast, is a literalist, without a touch of the poet, so aloof from society that there is, correspondingly, little danger of his imposing a Ford-like scenario on the people he meets. Slender is incapable of jealousy because he is incapable of establishing any relationships, even with Anne Page, the woman he professes to love, or must be instructed to love by Evans and Shallow. Neither man can function as a husband, though for opposite reasons; in this comedy whose "hero" is society both are therefore sterile.

The other males, with Page and Fenton the sole exceptions, fall between the limits set by Ford and Slender, though, for me, they are not just "types" but rather men temporarily arrested, distorted by a self-induced sense of inadequacy—and one that is most often sexual. Shallow desperately seeks his youth, and is eager to establish for whatever audience surrounds him the image of a hot-tempered swordsman denying his present role as an aging country justice. Evans is a curious combination of the cowardly cleric and the adviser who attempts to live vicariously through Slender as he urges his unwilling pupil to pursue Anne Page for her money. As with Falstaff, for these patriarchs fiscal has displaced sexual conquest; even the good, contrastive aristocrat Fenton confess to Anne that it was her money that first attracted him. Caius is, of course, aggressive to the extreme, but his only sexual conquest is the pliant Dame Quickly whose official role as "his nurse—or his dry nurse—or his cook—or his laundry—his washer and his wringer" (1.2.3–5) is a crude but revealing euphemism for that relationship. The Host is drowned in his own boozy male comaraderie, while Falstaff's three companions, Bardolph, Pistol, and Nym, are simultaneously chips off the old block and rebellious servant/sons to their father figure. Like the drifting, purposeless Venetian males in the opening scene of *The Merchant of Venice*, their rural counterparts here are waiting for liberation at the hand of a female like Portia or, before that, exploitation by the scheming of an outsider: *Merchant*'s religious outcast Shylock is in *Wives* that aristocratic outcast Falstaff.

Certainly not the energetic geriatric figure of *Henry IV*, down and almost out both in his money and his wit, his world of male companions threatening to abandon him no less than Mistress Ford *seems* to be abandoning her husband, perhaps even impotent now in his decline, Falstaff is a sorry figure, but less so, or no more so within the context provided by his fellow males. To raise his self-esteem, now at a very low ebb, he needs a conquest, a prey. Given the malaise affecting the males of Windsor, that half of society is ripe for such preying. Like the villain and his corrupt victims in *Richard III*, Falstaff and the men of Windsor in a sense *deserve* each other, are made for each other. For me, then, Falstaff is the aging lion, no longer fleet of foot, reduced to attacking the sick or infirm animals in a herd. Or attacking the herd's *supposedly* weaker sex. Both Falstaff and Ford are afflicted with this male chauvinism. The former assumes that his amorous success at court, albeit in decline, will still prove attractive to *mere* country women; the latter that women are by nature weak-willed and prime for seduction. In his excellent *The Metamorphoses of Shakespearean Comedy*, William Carroll suggests further that Falstaff is invoked by Ford, that the lecherous knight projects the husband's own insecurities; an absurd womanizer, Falstaff thereby echoes Ford's own sexual problems.[1]

Dame Quickly is the bridge here between the afflicted men and the three stable women of the play. She boasts of an authority she does not have, particularly over Anne Page, even as she is the seemingly vital go-between for the men. Perhaps past her sexual prime, Quickly is now something of a linguistic bawd, ferrying messages back and forth for insecure men who conduct their affairs, sexual and social, through such intermediaries. With Quickly as their servant and the other women relegated to the background, the males engage in various personal and social brawls for which the woman is the victor's prize, from Slender's and Caius's suits for Anne's hand, to Falstaff's attempted seduction of Mistresses Ford and Page, to Ford's insane impersonation of "Brook" in order to test—or vicariously seduce through Falstaff—his own wife. But just as clearly the authority in the play gravitates to the women, first in the two tricks played on Falstaff, then with the third trick in Windsor forest when a repentant Ford joins his wife, and finally in the lovers' trick on the entire community when Anne elopes with Fenton. Dame Quickly in turn metamorphoses from the male's intermediary to the women's helpmate to—however bizarre the casting—the Faerie Queene who leads the spirits in exorcizing Falstaff.

The wives are not without shortcomings or distractions, but these prove minor: Mistress Page does back Caius for her daughter's hand, and Mistress Ford shows the inevitable nervous irritation of someone who must endure marriage to Ford. Still, they remain confident of their sexuality, of their relation to their husbands, and hence of their role in the Windsor community. For me, Anne Page, no shallow romantic heroine, is something of a Cordelia or a Desdemona, no less sure of herself, able, after first testing him, to see the liberated man in Fenton, a woman waiting at the end of the play to appear, as a bride, before a community now harmonized and, in particular, before its male members who have recognized the Falstaff in their midst, in themselves, and have accordingly dealt with him. A community, after all, is a matter of trusting, a social contract, like a marriage, like the proper relation between men and women. That relationship cannot be bought, nor measured by money. It is a matter of the spirit, and properly, Falstaff's ultimate punishment will be fiscal: he must pay back twenty pounds to "Brook." I note on my prop list that there are some four moments when characters pay others to aid them in disreputable amatory conquests.

The play then moves from unproductive male to productive female control, to a literal joining of hands as men and women reestablish the community, as one marriage is reaffirmed and another celebrated. This suggests a parallel movement in *The Comedy of Errors* when Aemilia appears for the first time in the final scene, bringing with her the two Syracusian twins whose presence explains the mad happenings of the day and then leads to marriages reaffirmed or anticipated. As Barbara Freedman argues, *Wives* is, more accurately, a "farcial comedy," one where the male inbalance manifested in the farcial subplots of deception is resolved by the comedy of a reunited Windsor community.[2] Falstaff symbolizes the problem—indeed is more symbol than actual since there is little possibility, in fact no possibility of his success. Once this symbol of Ford's diseased imagination is exposed, Ford himself suddenly recovers. In act 4, scene 2 he beats the aunt of Brainford when Falstaff—revealingly—takes the form of a hideous old woman whose addiction to magic infuriates Ford who is himself no less addicted to his imagination's own black magic. Eleven lines later in act 4, scene 4 we see the Fords and Pages reunited, men and women now plotting the final play-within-a-play to be perpetrated on Falstaff.

As some have suggested, Falstaff is a scapegoat invested with the sins of the community.[3] Nor is the curative role played by this scapegoat without cost to Windsor. The tone in the final scene, I think, is practical rather than idyllic: it is necessary to project the problems of male inadequancy onto a single character, Falstaff, so as to provide a mirror image of the problem. Yet eradicating the problem thus symbolized by that individual is a compromise, perhaps even a temporary solution. When Slender and then Caius rush onstage, frantic that they have almost been deceived into marrying boys dressed as girls, we will remember that both Pages, husband and wife, now witness the humiliations of their personal candidates for marrying their daughter. Still, the marriage of the Pages has made them impervious to Falstaff, and the final deception played on the knight and his punishment, both physical and fiscal, reflect the efforts of a reconciled Master and Mistress Ford and a harmonious community.

In effect, the play moves from selfish to communal deception, in a medium that is by definition communal. Shakespeare's own audience is "deceived" by the accomplished boy actor into thinking Anne Page a young woman, but, again, that deception is for larger, positive ends. Central to my concept of the play, then, is this issue of perspective: do we see the world, do the inhabitants of Windsor see their fellows, idiosyncratically or communally?

Set and Lighting

For me, this issue of perspective determined the set. Like Blanche in *Streetcar*, I prefer magic to realism or, rather, think of realism as a contradiction in a medium where, as Bert States persuasively argues, our pleasure in the actor's skill and our coequal role in sustaining the illusion is no less a factor than the theater's realistic imitation—that phrase itself gives me trouble—of the world offstage.[4] For these reasons, I prefer my set for *Wives* to be open, suggestive, even minimal. Upstage-right and upstage-left would be two door frames, just frames, certainly not realistic, perhaps exaggerated or distorted like those Salvador Dali watches. For outside scenes the upstage-right frame would suggest the entrance to the Fords', the upstage-left the Pages' house. Upstage-center is a square (6′ by 6′), raised (1′) platform, at the back of which is a third door frame, with a slitted curtain; during outdoor scenes this door serves as the entrance to the Inn. Balancing the upstage platform is a circular (5′ in diameter), 1′-high platform downstage, serving in outdoor scenes as a "dry" fountain or circular park bench on which characters can sit.

I have asked my Chinese companies, whose theater is the more conventional one, to consider converting the auditorium so that the audience can sit on stage-right and stage-left as well as downstage, and to allow for exits downstage-right and downstage-left through the three sections of that divided audience. Thus, for outdoor scenes the two downstage exits would suggest streets of Windsor. This same set, with the audience's perspective reversed, would also serve for indoor scenes. For example, in act 3, scene 3 set inside the Ford house, the upstage-right door would be the inside of the front door, leading to the street, the upstage-left door an interior one opening to another room in the house. When Falstaff hides at Ford's approach, he would do so behind the curtain of the upstage-center door. Even this outside-inside arrangement would need to be flexible, for the outside street scene of act 1, scene 1 would become in act 2, scene 3 the area near the town center where Caius waits to meet Evans. Similarly, the indoor arrangement would also serve for Falstaff's tavern scene in act 1, scene 3, or Caius's house in act 1, scene 4. Shakespeare, as always, provides enough identification at the start of each scene for the audience to know just what external or internal location is at hand. However, to aid my audience in moving from general outdoor to general indoor scenes I would have a full-stage white light, with some green gells, for outdoor scenes, and white light with yellow gells for indoor scenes. Surely by the fourth scene in the play this convention could be sufficiently established.

This outdoor-indoor set would remain until the final three scenes of *Wives* (5.2–3, 5.5—I have cut 5.4), where the action moves to Windsor forest. My plans here are to have the three characters in act 5, scene 2 (Page, Shallow, and Slender), while delivering dialogue, bring in and drape over the three upstage doors a large, green hanging (with three slits for entrances upstage-right, -center, and -left), thereby obscuring the doors and, in turn, suggesting a grassy knoll upstage. When Mistress Page, Mistress Ford, and Caius enter in act 5, scene 3, they would bring in the oak tree, centering it on the down side of the upstage platform, as well as making sure that the hanging was firmly in place and relatively free of folds. I should note that for these three scenes the full illumination for outdoor or indoor scenes now changes to twilight, and I plan to keep this twilight effect until the appearance of Anne and Fenton on the upstage platform (they enter through the middle slit in the hanging). Once these young lovers, who have performed the final deception after deceiving Slender and Caius, take the stage, I—throwing realism to the winds—would bring the lights to full illumination, with those green gells used earlier in the outdoor scenes. The lighting change thus suggests the health of the community, the possibility of a new generation born of this marriage between an ethically responsible aristocrat and a virtuous middle-class woman. When the house lights go on for the curtain calls—indeed I would raise the house lights before then, as the characters make their final exits—this same "unrealistic" change also allows both halves of the performance, actor-characters and the audience, to be seen and to see each other. That is, the now solid community of Windsor males and females here parallels that united community of performer and spectator who together have sustained the stage's illusory world.

This sense of collaboration is why I use actors as stage hands in act 5, scenes 2 and 3, for, by this time in the production, and at this stage of the plot, characters and audience are at the same level of awareness (with the exception that the onstage characters know nothing of the tricks to be played on Slender and Caius). We are witnessing actors playing characters staging a play to trap Falstaff's conscience: thematics and metadramatics overlap here. By simultaneously being in character and functioning as stage hands, the reconciled Windsor community can thereby draw even closer to the audience otherwise "hidden" from them by that "fourth wall" of stage etiquette.

Costuming and Music

If the men are distorted, not as caricatures but rather in their current state as asocial individuals obsessed with the self, then I would have them, with the exceptions of Page and Fenton, be dressed in rather stark, simple, most certainly not elaborate costumes, each made from a material of a single color or, at most, shades of a single basic color. My instructions to our costumer at the Hippodrome Theater would probably call for something like "those sterile, a bit-too-functional uniforms from *Star Trek.*" The limitation of each man, the exclusive nature of his personality, would thereby be matched by both the costume's design and its single, unchanging color. The fiery Caius in a too-brilliant red (or what we would call a "glow suit" in the 1950s); Shallow in a dullish brown, at one with his own faded physicality; Slender—obviously—in a "sickly" yellow; Falstaff perhaps distinguished by three colors, albeit close on the spectrum, to be distributed one each to his three followers; Ford, to be sure, in a bright, "jealous" green. In the last three Shakespeare plays I have directed (*Errors*, *A Midsummer Night's Dream*, and *Romeo and Juliet*), I have preferred the costumes to be suggestive, open to interpretation, and most certainly not historical or realistic: in *Errors*, for example, we established an Elizabethan base, but covered it with a style that ran from modern chic to lightly punk; in *Romeo and Juliet* the costumes were purposely timeless, classic, no more indicative of 1595 than of 1986. I would want the same for *Wives*, especially given its open set. A stage floor painted white, by the way, could highlight the single color of the male costumes and, in scenes involving several of the males, provide a revealing background to the several distinct colors onstage. This singularity in design and color would, appropritely, be muted in the three twilight scenes in Windsor forest, for there the switch to, say, 40 percent illumination would sustain the audience's impression that the men—Ford in particular—were now less distinct, less self-centered, blending in more, both visually and socially, with the community.

The four women, in contrast, would be clothed in full dresses, modest yet supportive of their figures, a complex of layers of material, "full" in contrast to the sterile, overly functional male costumes, and most certainly not confined to a single color. As I did with Aemilia's costume in *Errors* or Hippolyta's and Titania's costumes in *A Midsummer Night's Dream* (and here those parts were doubled), I envision the women's costumes as disclosing a more open, complex personality, nuturing, caring, very unlike the exclusive, anal (if you will) suits of the men. Quickly's dress, of course, needs to be a bit garish, even tawdry, a parody of the more handsome matronly dresses of Mistress Ford and Mistress Page.

Given the stress on artifice in the Windsor scenes, as evidenced by my use of actors as stagehands, I would confine the fairies to masks, with tapers in their hands, but otherwise not require costume changes. By this point in the play, as well, Falstaff is easily tricked; the deception is more symbolic than technical. I use, by the way, only six fairies (Quickly, Pistol, Evans, Anne, and the servants John and Robert dressed as girls), whereas in act 4, scene 4 Mistress Page suggests using her son and daughter, along with "three or four more of their growth" (48–49). If that fat woman of Brainford represents Ford's own diseased imagination, a hideous fortune-teller given to magic and thereby flaunting reality in much the same way that Ford imposes his own Othello-like fiction on the truth, then Falstaff's female disguise here should be a basic, bulky green, matching Ford's own color. Likewise, if the impersonation of "Brook," allowing one man to pay other man to seduce his wife, albeit unawares, also represents an unintended image of how Ford sees himself, then no elaborate new costume is called for. My director's instinct is to give Brook nothing more than a pair of hideous dark-rim glasses and a mustache—not unlike those Groucho Marx props one buys for party jokes. Stage convention or the knight's own avarice are enough to explain Falstaff's not recognizing Brook as Ford; the issue here, as I see it, is more psychological than practical.

I (otherwise) curiously link costumes and music here because, for me, both establish the "tone" of the staging, though no less than the set does. Over the last several years I have experimented with a more pronounced use of music in Shakespearean productions. In the above-mentioned *Romeo and Juliet*, for example, I had a talented musician friend write a cool, 1950s Dave Brubeck–like jazz score for the production, a jazz suite, in effect, with three distinct themes centered on the feud, love, and death. We played the appropriate theme, or variations on it, not just during scene changes but at times with the dialogue, not as background but rather as something of a coequal with the dialogue. As a result, the Shakespearean text gave a specific meaning to the music while, conversely, the music, in both its tone and rhythm, influenced the actors' delivery. For *Wives* I commissioned a suite in five parts, one progressing from a dense, fugal score whose countermelodies threaten to erase each other, music, in essence, that like overtufted grass seems to choke on itself; to a third movement of breezy, highly playful comic melodies—high-jinks music as I describe it to my composer friend; to a fifth movement that is more romantic, sustained, broad in its sound. Each movement would be played between the scenes of a single act. And while I have only allowed for a single intermission (between act three, scenes 3 and 4) and otherwise make no distinctions between acts, each musical movement, matched with its appropriate act, would establish, more subtly, Shakespeare's textual, if not theatrical five-act structure. Thematically, the music would suggest the play's change from that initial male-dominated world threatening to cave in by virtue of its own quarreling and absurdity; to the increasingly productive theatrics, the comic deceptions enacted by the women; to that very comic, but also very profound, final scene, where communities, illusive and real, onstage and off-, begin to act in concert. My habit, also, is to start music sometime during the final lines of a particular scene, and to continue it, with a fade-out, into the opening lines of the next.

Characters and Acting Styles

If I slighted *Wives* before being asked to direct it by my Chinese hosts, I feel very differently now about the play. In fact, if Shakespeare, overwhelmed as he must have been with responsibilities as actor, director, member of the company, and full shareholder, could write profound plays under such circumstances, would he do anything less in this case? I think it no less reductive on the director's part to do *The Comedy of Errors* as a "farce" in the more limited sense of that term. My attitude toward *Wives* most certainly extends to the characters. As a director, my practice is to write, early in rehearsals, letters to my actors in which I speak as the character they have been assigned. This way I establish the particular character's subtext on which the actor can then collaborate with me.

A very concise version of such subtextual letters would, for example, reveal Shallow as someone embarrassed by his age, by his loss of physical abilities. Nor does his current status as a Justice compensate for this self-induced deficiency. Insanely, he tries to relive his youth through that zero, Slender, an anemic soul who can boast only youth and precious little else. Caius's belligerence is a patently obvious and, no less, unsuccessful compensation for some flaw; perhaps he is ugly, marked, like Cyrano, by an ill-shaped nose. Wishing to be married to an exquisite creature such as Anne Page, he finds himself stigmatized by a parody of a family: his "wife" a former prostitute, his son the servant Rugby whom he mistreats, usually without cause. In constrast, Fenton carries his aristocratic heritage with grace, but perhaps—and with some cause—he feels himself superior to the suitors about him, and is incredulous that the otherwise rational Page prefers Caius. Evans lacks courage and would conceal this fault in his pose as a peace-loving cleric, yet, like Shallow, he tries to rekindle a former or an imagined aggressive image through Slender. The latter's name is well taken; not only does he slip through life, through any significant relationships with others, but is himself an inadequate "ground" for the two older men who would experience life vicariously through him.

Other characters play off each other psychologically. Tiring of Falstaff, seeing through him, Pistol and Nyn—unlike Barolph who is fortunate enough to enter the Host's service as an apprentice tapster—still cannot abandon him, and so, like Genet's *Maids*, they torture Falstaff, in a sense torture themselves, by being disloyal servants. If Ford is an early draft for Othello, might they not be a crude, comic sketch of his Iago? Simple, in contrast, has even more reason for revolting from his master Slender's service, but is checked, as his name suggests, by his lack of wit and initiative. Falstaff, as I have argued, tries to rebuild a fallen self-esteem with what he mistakenly perceives to be an easy economic, if not sexual—does his "fall" include sexual ability as well?—victory over women and the weak men of Windsor. With only dim memories of those happy tavern days spent with young Hal, and now barred from the political realm of his former tutee, here in the successor to the history plays he is landlocked in Windsor, reduced to living by himself, isolated, trying pathetically to establish a community amid women, trying to hide from a prying male world under their skirts, as manifest both in the laundry basket and in the costume of the aunt of Brainford. If Falstaff is a projection of Ford's own neurosis, it seems no less true that Ford as Brook provides Falstaff with a reason to live, a position, albeit ridiculous, as a would-be seducer's would-be seducer. Ford, as I have already remarked, has all the qualilties, the insecurities, of an Othello, and the fact that Mistress Ford is not defenseless like Desdemona alone establishes him as a comic figure, and one therefore capable of reformation. If the women, like playwrights or surrogates for Shakespeare, celebrate those controlling figures we also see in Portia or Rosalind, Ford parodies Shakespeare's own craft, as, like Othello or Leontes, he tries to impose a self-disclosing fiction on reality.

Quickly, for me, has affinities with Falstaff's character. Because of her past reputation—and deservedly so—she is, like him, an outsider, yet trying not so much to victimize others as to carve a place for herself, a role, in this middle-class community. Her attempt is tenuous, however, for at best she is a go-between—and everybody's go-between, indiscriminately so, as it turns out—a messenger whose role evaporates when such relationships as she has tried to foster are either canceled or established. Not a tragic, nor even a pathetic figure, to be sure, she epitomizes the—I use the cliché shamelessly here—problems of communication that beset Windsor. In contrast, Mistress Page and Mistress Ford complement each other, the way good friends do. I would draw the former's character close to that of her husband; like happily married people they have grown to resemble each other, to sound like and to think like each other. In the best sense of the phrase, they are one, even, I might add, in their excessive concern that their daughter marry well. Mistress Ford is the more high-strung of the two friends, more energetic on the surface, and this energy seems a product of her ongoing struggle to keep her sanity, saddled as she is with Ford as her mate, or at least the Ford before his conversion in act 4, scene 4. For me, Anne Page, though her part is relatively small after the opening scene, is not the slight heroine, but a full-blooded, confident young woman, the "reward" waiting at the end of the play, someone marking time until this community, so given to deceptions and self-deception, can right itself.

These, then, would be some possible psychological bases for the major characters, and if psychology and reality are complementary entities, then this would be, no less, the "realistic" motivation for the actors. Still, the characters are part of an artifice, an illusion confirmed by a real-life audience present for the production. In point of fact, that audience offstage is the ultimate reality of the play, its destination. As has been my custom when directing Shakespeare, I would stress, as coequal with such psychological realism, the presence of this audience, and its role in seeing the stage's two hours' traffic as just that, an illusion that, however significant or relevant to life offstage, is made possible by the actor's craft and spectator's presence. This is why I prefer the audience to surround three sides of the stage; each spectator simultaneously observes both actors and fellow spectators, both the performance and the reaction to that performance. If the actors, most of the time, "play" to the world onstage, without directly acknowledging the area offstage, I would also have them at select moments play to the audience, thereby affirming their presence, their creative role during the performance.

Some examples. In act 2, scene 1, after Mistress Page, sitting on the downstage platform, reads Falstaff's love letter, she rises and then, alone onstage, shares with the audience her contempt for this arrogant would-be lover. In act 3, scene 3, when Ford rushes back onstage (in my blocking, from the upstage-left door), having failed to find Falstaff in the house, I would have him deliver to the audience his "I cannot find him. May be the knave bragged of that he could not compass" (199–200) as if he needed having to share with us the possibility that Falstaff has lacked courage to enter the house, that his wife, if only through the knight's cowardice, is still faithful. Through this remark delivered to us, he pleads that someone in the audience will comfort him that his doubts about himself, as manifest through this projection in Falstaff, are only that. He may not believe what he says, yet he hopes the all-knowing audience will. I would have Falstaff seek a parallel confirmation from the audience in act 3, scene 5 when, having sent Bardolph offstage to fetch wine, he reviews his humiliation in the river, prefacing his speech with the rhetorical question "Have I liv'd to be carried in a basket like a barrow of butcher's offal?" (4–5). In the two scenes (3.3 and 4.2) where the ladies trick Falstaff, surely they can talk at times to the audience, sharing their plans and their pleasure with them, suggesting that everyone in the theater, with the exception of their victim, is in on the joke. When Mistress Page takes stage-center in act 4, scene 4 to unveil her "Herne the Hunter" scheme (ll. 29ff), her audience is, equally, the husbands, her comrade Mistress Page, and the spectators offstage.

Indeed, as the characters onstage draw closer to the audience's level of awareness, and as two now-united groups mirror each other on both sides of the stage, such direct contact should, I think, increase. Rather than "breaking the illusion," this literal playing to the house only celebrates in Brechtian fashion the artifice, reminding us all of the collaborative factors allowing for the onstage enactment. The aside, of course, is a "natural" moment for such direct address. If delivered to the audience, Quickly's line "That's my master, Master Doctor" (3.4.85), said in response to Mistress Page's reassurance that she seeks a better husband for her daughter than Slender, has the double effect of revealing Quickly's need, her eagerness to be in the know, as well as a mania to confirm her status in the play: she isn't just another faded character, but the mistress/servant of a man whom Mistress Page seeks for her son-in-law. I should note that in the production of *The Comedy of Errors* we established an "aside spot" (downstage-left, near the audience, indeed at the entrance to the vomitory, or the "vom" in stage parlance, leading to the house exit door) to which the character would cross, speaking there directly to the audience and illuminated with a special spot, while the other onstage characters, now in 20 percent light, would freeze in position.

I also like to use the downstage area, no less than that upstage, for exits and entrances. In fact, in direct correlation with the addresses to the audience, such use of the downstage grows, as if—increasingly—the characters came from the audience, were at one with the audience, and, their particular passage finished, exited through the house. At the Hippodrome State Theater, the actor who exits downstage and then needs to make an upstage entrance in the next scene must rush upstairs, cross to the back of the building, and descend the backstage stairs. I have suggested to my Chinese hosts that if even this "circumlocution" proves impossible or if exits through the audience are impractical, then it would be fine to have two screens downstage-left and -right, behind which an actor, having exited, could wait before reentering downstage. If his next entrance were upstage, then he could merely—however obviously—cross in front of the first row of the stage-right or stage-left audience to make his way backstage. This is to say, I prefer to show the play "working," rather than hiding its mechanics from the audience. Here in *Wives*, rife with deception, impersonation, and illusion, with numerous plays-within-plays where characters play actors aware and unaware, by design this disclosing to the audience of how the play is done avoids as much as possible that presentational style dictated by taking the stage as a self-contained "world." In my view, it thereby parallels the theatrical metaphor, or what I have called elsewhere the "theater's turning to itself,"[5] that here dominates Shakespeare's play.

Generally, the two platforms have a practical function, the downstage one as an area on which characters can sit for dialogue (as in the conversation between Anne and Fenton in act 3, scene 4), the upper one as both a sitting area and the "steps" leading to Falstaff's room at the tavern. However, at times even these platforms can become playing areas, small stages within the larger stage. This is particularly true at the end of scenes, as when Pistol and Nym, upon Falstaff's exit, mount the downstage platform to announce to us their plans to inform on their master (1.3), or at the end of act 2, scene 2 when Ford, in a monologue, condemns Falstaff as a "damned Epicurean rascal" and then informs us of his scheme to detect his wife in a compromising situation.

A Suggested Staging of Act 1, Scenes 1 and 2

Even here, of course, I offer only a digest of the more detailed director's notes now in the hands of my Chinese colleagues. Still, in this suggested staging for the play's first two scenes, my intent is to show "in action" the various issues, from concept to acting style to blocking, that have been the focus so far.

Shallow and Evans enter from downstage-left, the actors improvising dialogue as they make their way through the vom to the audience. Slender enters, and characteristically so, a second later. While he is one of "them"—they are, after all, his uncle and spiritual advisor—he is still not "with" them. As they cross right-center, Slender goes left-center, staying there as they review the Falstaff situation. He crosses to them, as if automatically, only when he hears Evans mention "Anne Page . . . which is pretty virginity" (45–46). The issue here is "male business"—suits, countersuits, insults, the community's patriarchs, its judicial and spiritual pillars who deal with emergent problems, in particular with their perceived enemy in the fat knight. Yet in the minds of these decrepit males, legalities and marriage are interchangeable. Evans crosses to left-center, leaving uncle and nephew, as he describes the "seven hundred pounds of moneys" (50–51) defining Anne Page. This section, the first of five large "beats" (or distinct dramatic entities) in these opening scenes, ends with Shallow first pointing upstage-center, to establish Falstaff's door, and then upstage-left, to which he crosses when he knocks on Page's door. The characters, that is, enter from the audience, but as the scene progresses and as they move upstage, they begin as actors to disclose the set to us, in particular the fradulent tavern "home" of Falstaff and the Pages' solid middle-class residence.

When Page enters—the play's second beat—this masculine shop-talk, this effort of the men to establish an aggressive image, only intensifies. Shallow harps on the ill-killed venison, and Slender, as if taking the cue, turns to sports talk as he chides Page for his dog's poor performance at Cotsall. Such strutting is suddenly punctured with Falstaff's entrance, through the upstage-center door, with Pistol, Bardolph, and Nym entering directly behind their master, forming, in effect, a frame of three colors for his stage debut. As Shallow crosses to him bringing the charge that he has disturbed the peace, we see for a moment a touch of the old Falstaffian wit as the knight answers with a non sequitur, "But not kiss'd your keeper's daughter" (113). Falstaff is very much the actor here, sensing his hostile audience, quickly devising strategies to "play" them. When Slender crosses to him with a complaint against his companions, the three emerge from behind their master and, threatening Slender both verbally and physically, push him toward the downstage platform, forcing him to sit, and then surrounding him as they themselves take seats. The rather simple blocking of the first beat is here more complex, more frantic. Slender manages to extricate himself from his "jailors" with the illogical question "Where's Simple?" (134), on which he rises and crosses upstage-left to Shallow. Evans then takes centerstage in an attempt to restore peace, but once again the frantic movement returns as Pistol rises and crosses right-center to respond to Evans. A second later, Nym does likewise to confront a very timorous Slender. Falstaff, upstaged by Evans in his aborted peace-keeping mission, now takes centerstage with his "You hear all these matters denied, gentlemen" (186). This second beat ends with the sudden appearance of Mistresses Ford and Page, and Anne Page, as they enter downstage-left. After Falstaff has interrupted this image of feminine harmony with a quick cross to Mistress Page, whom he kisses, the women exit just as quickly upstage-left into Page's house. My feeling is that the women, later to dominate the play, here constitute only a fleeting image. If they are the promise of the resolution to come, at present they can find no stage in the farcical, exclusive male world opening the play.

In the scene's third beat we return to the first: Shallow at right-center, Slender center, and Evans left-center. As Evans raises the issue of marriage, Slender, again characteristically, leaves his companions, crossing downstage to the platform. Accordingly, both Evans and Shallow cross to him at the start of their next two lines. Uncomfortable in being pressed to a decision, Slender leaves them on his "I will marry her, sir, at your request" (245), and takes centerstage to deliver his rather reductive comments about love: "if there be no great love in the beginning, yet heaven may decrease it upon better acquaintance" (245–47). Again, Evans and Shallow pursue him, leaving the downstage platform and crossing to the center to join Slender. I parallel here the blocking of that moment in the second beat when Falstaff's companions push Slender to the downstage platform, and then follow him again when he rises to cross to the protection of Evans. The parallel blocking itself underscores the curious way men here equate martial and amatory situations.

If we have had only a brief appearance so far from the women, we get with the scene's fourth beat a more sustained stage-time from Anne who enters from upstage-left, seconds before Shallow and Evans exit there for dinner. Now Slender is all alone with the woman he both fears and desires. As if by instinct, he crosses to downstage-right when she, in centerstage, makes the simple request that he come to dinner. She crosses to him with her "I may not go in without your worship" (277), even taking his arm with her next line, "I pray you, sir, walk in" (281). He bolts from her, and paces up and down stageright with the speech wherein he uses his bruised shin as an excuse for avoiding dinner. Slender here, as I see his character, desperately needs to assert his battered male image, as he boasts of playing "at sword and dagger," alludes with the phrase "stew'd prunes" to prostitutes he has known, and then changes the topic, but not his psychological need, by referring to bears and bear-baiting rings (282–87). Indeed, when Anne confesses her ignorance of the subject, Slender, feeling bolder, crosses to her at centerstage, as he brags of seeing "Sackerson loose twenty times" (295). As he distinguishes himself from women who cry and shriek at bears, he crosses to the downstage platform, sits decisively on it, now feeling very much at home, emboldened by the fact that this male talk—though pathetic from our perspective—allows him to dominate the conversation. When Page enters from upstage-left, to remind Slender that the dinner guests wait for him, we see in the following awkward stage business the "real" Slender return. After some strained courtesies about the proper order for exiting to dinner—even a simple stage exit proves a burden to Slender!—he leaves first, after protesting that he "will not go first; truly, la! I will not do you that wrong" (309–10). Father and daughter, exiting after him, perhaps with Page's arm about Anne, make a telling contrast to this asocial, defective male who has just charged offstage.

No sooner do they exit, than in beat five Evans and Slender's servant Simple appear upstage-left: planning to use Dame Quickly to foster Slender's suit, Evans gives Simple the first of the play's many letters, one asking Quickly "to solicit [Slender's] desires" to Anne (1.2.10). Evans then returns to dinner upstage-left, as Simple exits downstage-right, through the vom, or into the streets of Windsor to make his way to Caius's house. Within a matter of seconds, therefore, we see the socially defective Slender exit singly, followed by the wholesome union of father and daughter, followed by the first of many acts where intermediaries are employed, where a character through a letter, rather than any direct human contact—we have just seen Anne's frustrated attempts to bring Slender to dinner—tries to forge a relationship, or rather a relationship by which he himself voyeuristically redeems his own deficiencies.

The "orchestration" of these two scenes, then, is a microcosm for the larger play: beat one, the trinity of men planning battle against Falstaff and, in the same breath, a union between Slender and Anne; beat two, Falstaff's appearance and the resulting widening of conflicts among the males, capped by the fleeting appearance of the women; beat three, a return to the efforts of Slender's father-figures to marry him to Anne, with the counterpart of his resistance or, at best, cloying indifference to the match; beat four, Anne's confrontation with Slender on the simple matter of exiting to dinner, and his efforts to best her in controlling stage dialogue and business, this episode concluded with Slender's bizarre exit and the wholeome tableau of father and daughter; beat five, and something of a coda, Evan's use of Simple as an intermediary to use Quickly as an intermediary in an absurd marriage.

Miscellaneous

By my count, eight letters change hands during the play, and this relatively large number is to be expected in a society whose members deal with each other indirectly, through messages, go-betweens, and, ultimately, deception. As Barbara Freedman observes, the citizens of Windsor, obsessed as they are with language as a way of fashioning personality, expend their efforts in borrowing clever phrases from poetry, striving for just the proper vocabulary, or quoting from the latest play "as opposed to speaking for oneself, or speaking truly." In the process they displace "the dignity of the individual" with an "absurdly scripted language."[6] This lack of verbal or spoken integrity, this parody of the way real men and women speak or should speak, is inseparable, I think, from the malaise afflicting the men: verbal play has displaced real social intercourse. When the Host fools Caius by defining "mock-water" as "valor" (2.3.57–62), language becomes a means of entrapment, however comic the situation or deserving Caius is of such trickery. Surely, Falstaff's generic love letters to the women epitomize the insincerity of this culture aping refined speech, or imagining that words alone can gloss over a tawdry, or diseased, fact. I would, therefore, use exaggerated letters, oversized, the paper perhaps a garish color, a surreal prop that when held by the character would seem to overshadow him, taking our attention from the bearer to the letter that its author believes represents his real self. And if a problem of perceived sexual inadequacy, or foolishly unconscious chauvinism, characterizes the males, then the several swords and rapiers called for might be similarly exaggerated, not ordered from a props catalogue, but handmade and looking suspiciously like parodies of the phallus, "play" swords more potent as symbols than as practical military weapons.

Now to the matter that will perhaps raise the ire of fellow Shakespeareans. I work at a commercial, Equity regional theater, the Hippodrome State Theater, and our audience, although a sophisticated college audience, has demonstrated to us that a two-hour production approaches the maximum period in which they can or will give full attention. Any performance over two hours, no matter how skillfully done, risks losing that attention. Shakespeare himself in the Prologue to *Romeo and Juliet* speaks of the "two hours" traffic of the stage," but quite probably his actors delivered lines at a speed too great for the conventions of modern acting styles. To be blunt, 2,000 lines of Shakespeare takes roughly two hours in performance; *Wives* has 2,728 lines. Though as a scholar I feel as if I were pulling flesh from my own breast, still, as a director concerned with such practical and vital matters as the mood of my audience, I look for ways to cut the play, to get it closer to that "magical" 2,000 lines. I am doubly sensitive, of course, about the audience's mood when that audience is Chinese, and hearing *Wives* in translation. Therefore, the text of *Wives* that I have sent with those director's notes to the two companies in Changchun City is a cut one. Those cuts are various, and have various justifications; some are easier to make, and more obvious, than others.

Since I reduced the number of fairies in the final scene from the ten or so proposed by Mistress Page to six, then I also deleted act 5, scene 4, that short scene where Evans instructs the little children in the roles they are about to play. I also cut the first ninety-two lines of act 4, scene 5, in part because some of the dialogue, the account of the fat woman of Brainford, seems a bit repetitious. Yet I also made cuts here because I had earlier decided to eliminate the subplot about the Germans' tricking of the Host. This plot is perhaps the most topical in the play but it also occupies the smallest space: in 3.1.115–26 Caius and Evans first vow to take revenge on the Host for embarrassing them with the aborted duel; in act 4, scene 3 Bardolph brings the Host the Germans' request for three horses; and then we learn of the results of the tricking, and see the Host's reaction in act 4, scene 5. This may be funny business, and it is central to the play's theme of a deception by which the victim turns the tables on his former deceiver. Nevertheless, something had to go, especially in a play almost overwhelmed with these plots involving trickery. I also wanted the second act (which I tried to make two-thirds the length of the first act) to move quickly so that I could give more prominence to the final scene. Finally, I cut act 4, scene 1, William's Latin lesson. Surely inserted by Shakespeare for a court performance, it is a hilariously bawdy scene, as Dame Quickly makes her unintentional double-entendres on the boy's Latin drill. Besides, the issue of misunderstanding words, the problem of translation, is at the center of this play where characters speak through others or through letters whose text is read differently than intended. Still, the scene stops the dramatic action, and with a two-hour limit staring me in the face, I had to sacrifice this oasis, however funny. Then, too, imagine the problems of translating into Chinese a scene involving the punning interplay of English and Latin!

Did Shakespeare intend the play as conceived in these director's notes? Have I been faithful to his text? Though inevitable, surely such questions are either unanswerable or not fully relevant—or both. The several ways enumerated by June Schlueter and James Lusardi of understanding Gertrude's character or Hamlet's behavior in the closet scene, or Philip McGuire's argument that the playwright's script itself invites the director to choose among options, assuages my sense of guilt here. I am also aware that my concept for *Wives* reflects in part my feminist politics, and, no less, the bias of a metadramatic critic. Nor can I expect my Chinese codirector to be absolutely faithful to my own text.

Actually, in my notes I have tried to anticipate, indeed to capitalize on, the cultural metamorphosis that will, and should, occur. While in Changchun City I saw a production of a prize-winning play, *The Green Corn Return*, whose political theme, centering on the individual's responsibilities to the state, and the definition of a good leader, only reminded me of how in this country we usually force such political content to the peripheries of the drama. I think here of the guerrilla theater of the 1960s or, conversely, of such innocent pieces as *Mr. Smith Goes to Washington* or the musical *Mr. President*. *Wives* should be received in a more overtly political fashion in the People's Republic, and this is why my concept underscores the individual's responsibility to Windsor society. And, in the fashion of modern Chinese plays I witnessed, where communal dancing and singing signaled the society's resolution of a problem, this is why, for me, the united assemblages of actors and audience are so essential during the play-within-a-play perpetrated on Falstaff.

Some aspects of my concept should blend easily with the current practices of Chinese theater. For example, even their most traditional drama had an exhilarating mixture of realistic and nonrealistic stagings. In one production, while characters downstage were speaking in a very colloquial style about a country fellow who, returning from Beijing as a prosperous businessman, was showing them his Honda motocycle, upstage there was an elderly man sitting motionless before an altar, thereby establishing a purely symbolic tableau of the community's more profound values. In similar fashion, my blocking adheres, with some clear exceptions, to the realistic demands of the characters' psychologies, their motivations, while, conversely, the male costumes are purposely symbolic and interpretative.

Other aspects of my notes will, instead, ask my codirector to make adjustments, especially the notion of the character's inner life or subtext. That latter phrase was fairly new to the actors, accustomed as they were to a more ritualistic theater, or one where the individual was defined by his role in the community—the "other," if you will. On this issue, it was little wonder that my actors were fascinated with Beckett's plays. On one occasion, I recall their struggling with his dramaticule *Come and Go* before giving a brilliant performance. Yet they could do this only after taking my word that here the details of the tragic life of a character who had just exited, whispered by one of the two remaining onstage characters to the other but unheard by the audience, was the play's central issue, one so profound, so buried in the psyche, that Beckett had denied his audience its customary right to be privy to everything said onstage. In other instances they will probably expand on my notes. I suggested earlier that the five-part musical score, echoing the play's own movement from a too exclusive community, to one loosened by the women's sense of play, to a more inclusive community at the end, be played between scene changes. But in the Chinese theater the director can underscore important moments in the dialogue or stage movement with percussive instruments played from the side of the stage, within view of the audience. Thus, my experiments with a jazz score performed simultaneously with the dialogue in *Romeo and Juliet* can be expanded in the production of *Wives*.

I have been invited to return this spring to see *Wives* through its final rehearsals to opening night. However, if practical matters prevent my returning, I know that this prodigious child of Shakespeare that I have adopted as my own will, halfway around the world, continue to grow—and in good and friendly hands.

Notes

1. I am very indebted to William C. Carroll for this notion of Falstaff's being a projection of Ford's phobia. And to his observation that in taking a boy actor as

Anne Page, the audience is tricked no less than the onstage characters (*The Metamorphoses of Shakespearean Comedy* [Princeton: Princeton University Press, 1985], pp. 178–202 ["Falstaff and Ford"]). Jeanne Roberts also offers a complex view of Falstaff in her *Shakespeare's English Comedy: "The Merry Wives of Windsor" in Context* (Lincoln: University of Nebraska Press, 1979). My text for *The Merry Wives of Windsor* is *The Riverside Shakespeare*, gen. ed. G. Blakemore Evans (Boston: Houghton Mifflin Co., 1974).

2. Barbara Freedman explores this play in "Falstaff's Punishment: Buffonery as Defensive Posture in *The Merry Wives of Windsor*," *Shakespeare Studies* 14 (1981): 163–74. I have also been fortunate to have read the manuscript chapter ("Borrowed Selves and Buffonery: Self-Debasing Strategies in *The Merry Wives of Windsor*") from her forthcoming book on Shakespeare.

3. On this issue of Falstaff as a scapegoat, see J. A. Bryant, "Falstaff and the Renewal of Windsor," *PMLA* 89 (1974): 296–301.

4. Bert O. States, *Great Reckonings in Little Rooms: On the Phenomenology of Theater* (Berkeley and Los Angeles: University of California Press, 1985), pp. 157–206 ("Actor/Audience") in particular.

5. *When the Theater Turns to Itself: The Aesthetic Metaphor in Shakespeare* (Lewisburg, Pa.: Bucknell University Press, 1981).

6. Again, Freedman in the manuscript of "Borrowed Selves."

8

Culture, Character, and Conscience in Shakespeare

MARVIN ROSENBERG

ONE OF THE MARVELS OF SHAKESPEARE'S WORK IS HIS COMPACTING, IN single characters, of the best and worst of human qualities, of high wisdom and low impulse, of noble purposes and ignoble means, of love and hate, of hope and despair. A further marvel is the fluidity of these character configurations, never fixed, insistently changing and developing.

I have elsewhere proposed the metaphor "polyphony" to suggest how the many, sometimes conflicting notes in the character-structures flow or jerk into different combinations, harmonious and dissonant.[1] I am interested here in how major forces, internal and external, are made to form and malform these polyphonies.

Shakespeare seemed to be aware, long before Freud, of how the human organism is impelled by erotic and aggressive drives. His plays demonstrate his understanding of how society and family construct a "superego" to restrict and tame these drives: we can call this control the "culture." Shakespeare saw it as very powerful; but he knew another at least equally powerful control, a private one: conscience.

Conscience is commonly regarded as an innate moral force. It has been called only another-directed, culturally installed phenomenon. But what if it has a biological base, fixed in the tissue as a kind of self-protective, society-protective reflex, an inbuilt corrective to the more destructive native human energies? Shakespeare evidently sensed such a humanizing force.

So I will here enlarge the implications of conscience to suggest what is humane in the human condition; that which, for instance, leavens aggressive ambition to rule with a care for the welfare of the ruled; which leavens the erotic impulses with the love and tenderness that can illuminate the interpersonal experience. This conscience sets value on giving as well as getting; on sacrifice as well as success. Even in our own very learned time we know that not simply a combination of heredity and environment makes a personality: now, as in Shakespeare, seemingly identical products of such combinations manifest widely different quotients of compassion and constructiveness, wildly different mixes of destructive energies and what is here called conscience.

Whatever we call it, we surely recognize in Shakespeare's world view such a humanizing component: and what results when the stupendous surge of his characters' aggressive and erotic energies beats against the constraints of this conscience as well as the culture. Frustrated, the current recoils; and under insistent, sometimes intolerable pressure, elements in the deeps rise toward the surface, and alter the texture of tragic personality. We will see that the ratio in Shakespeare's tragic characters of inner resistance, as well as outer, to violent impulse can be one measure of their complexities—and of the playwright's.

To go so deeply with them into the pain of human experience can be daunting. Some whole cultures have not been able to endure the full measure of Shakespeare's mirroring of what it is to be torn between impulse and culture-conscience. I would like to consider how this has happened in historic interpretations of Macbeth and his Lady, as one way of discerning the deep outlines of Shakespeare's character sculpture.

The first useful information we have is from the eighteenth century. Then both criticism and the theater refused to share Shakespeare's immense vision of the resistances in the two roles.

Early in the century Charles Gildon said of them:

> the characters of Macbeth and his Lady are too monstrous for the stage.

As the years wore on, differences began to be seen. Lady Macbeth, in the theater, became a victim of the Restoration "improvement" of the play, which drained the characters of Shakespeare's complexity. When Davenant turned *Macbeth* into a semimusical, the witches were transformed from the dangerous, death-contriving sisters of Shakespeare's text into harmless, broomsticked girls of the chorus. But the plot structure of the play somehow survived: Macbeth still had to be tempted to murder. Only Lady Macbeth was left for his outer motivation: she had to shoulder virtually all responsibility. She would be seen as vile; Dr. Johnson would call her merely detestable; and Lord Kames:

> I hope there is no such wretch to be found as is here represented.

In the theater, two actresses in particular became famous for justifying such critical strictures by the uninhibited power with which they made a killer out of Macbeth—and by the hollowness they made of his inner life.

Hannah Pritchard, David Garrick's famous Lady, was described in the role as having

> a mind insensible to compunction, bent inflexibly to gain her purpose.

She manifested "apathy"—that is conscienceless unfeeling, a "horrible force of implacable cruelty." When Macbeth, his aggressiveness diminished, offered his faint resistance to her urging to murder, she turned on him scornfully:

> Her whole ambitious soul came forth in fury to her face, and sat in terror there.

Cuts in Shakespeare's text accommodated this Lady's halved image: thus she did not "faint" in act 2 when Macbeth told of murdering the grooms—Garrick assumed that audiences would laugh at the evident "hypocrisy" of such a monster. She was remorseless.

After Pritchard came Sarah Siddons. Siddons's own comments, and her admirers', tell how, in her dark, majestic way, she played "the female fiend of Scotland." She wrote that she would have preferred, in corrupting the now brave, honorable Macbeth, to appear as an innocent-looking, fair-haired woman, with

> all the charms and graces of personal beauty . . . fair, feminine, nay, even fragile.

Siddons was not allowed her vision. Her audiences wanted, not the seeming dove, but, as her biographer said, the hawk:

> Her idea of a delicate and blonde beauty . . . the public would have ill-exchanged for her dark locks and eagle eyes.

Hazlitt described her unrelieved image:

> Her turbulent and inhuman strength of spirit, her unrelieved fierceness yielding no intercourse with human sensation or human weakness. Vice was never so solitary and so grand. The step, look, voice of the Royal Murdress forces our eye after them as if of a being from a darker world, full of evil, but full of power—unconnected with life, but come to do its deeds of darkness, and then pass away.

What had happened to these eighteenth century Ladies was an accentuation in them of aggressive impulses and images—id images—that

Shakespeare had discerned deep in our—his—subconscious. Here was the incarnation of what society found fierce and frightening in the female: the first adored, terrible, powerful woman of childhood with whom the male child spends so much time, who can give or deny love, who can punish and—in nightmare imagination—destroy, even by smashing the brains out. Here was the figure of Medusa, the Amazon, Omphale, Medea, the Bad Mother, the matriarchal monitor, who would wean the son from pity, and conspire with him to destroy the father, and assume all power. Norman Holland has suggested that this fantasy encloses the fearful, buried implication that for a man to submit to a woman is in itself dangerous.[2] This female will refuse the nourishing tenderness of woman that men have felt comfortable with, in lieu of the kind of fearless force that men—especially Shakespearean men—assumed belonged to man. In this the terrible Lady Macbeth would echo, but without Shakespeare's modulation, the sinister, tempting, destructive energy of the three male-featured Sisters.

In a century ostensibly restrained, this Lady loosed aggression unbridled, unconstrained by the social and moral inhibitions Shakespeare designed. She would ask to be unsexed, meaning relieved of all her intended nutritive conscience—though, as was observed of Pritchard, she seemed to have no sex to lose: the culture would indulge stage violence, but the erotic had to hide in it. This Terrible Woman had no compunction about invoking the spirits of darkness: she commanded them to her service. Nor was the inhumanity of her femaleness ameliorated, as in Shakespeare, by the warm, familial aura radiated by Lady Macduff, whose appearance was cut. The Terrible image alone survived.

What kind of Macbeth could stand up to so terrible a Lady? The century had the answer: the bloody but conscience-troubled tyrant was transformed fashionably into an honorable murderer—Shakespeare's inner dialectic almost gone. Macbeth became a man of sensibility, who grieved to do wrong, did it almost in spite of himself, in handsome anguish, and died repenting.

Subdued by such a wife as Pritchard's, Garrick's Macbeth could hardly be blamed for submitting to her commands. His aggression was sharply modified: besides the social code which the text stipulates as inhibiting the murder of his king, his conscience was enlarged, his impulse to aggression weakened. Guilt and remorse hollowed him—so much so that he ended not as Shakespeare's giant, inwardly divided criminal, but as a craven.

Garrick was the century's greatest actor and hence a model for its enfeeblement of Macbeth. His own conception of the role is revealing:

> An experienced general crown'd with conquest, innately ambitious and religiously humane, spurr'd on by metaphysical prophecies and

> the unconquerable pride of his wife, to a deed horrible in itself, and repugnant to his nature.

Grief and shame—the outriders of conscience and culture—would harry this Macbeth through the play. One of Garrick's correspondents complained to the actor about his absence of inner aggression:

> You almost everywhere discovered dejectedness of mind . . . more grief than horror . . . heart heavings, melancholy countenance and slack carriage of body . . . The sorrowful face and lowly gestures of a penitent which have ever a wan and pitiful look . . . quite incompatible with the character.

But the characterization was popular; Garrick won praise for his Macbeth's "humane" side—his sensibility, his sufferings:

> His pensively preparatory attitudes . . . the propriety and gracefulness wherewith he touches the soft falls of sorrow, terror, and compassion.

Accommodating Garrick's "defence" of Macbeth went textual cuts, that softened his aggression while by contrast enlarging his conscience. In the crucial act 1, scene 7 speech ("If it were done when 'tis done . . ."), Garrick simply cut "If th'assassination could trammel up the consequence . . .," to avoid speaking the murder thought. Scenes were eliminated to prettify Macbeth: so goodbye Lady Macduff and her babes, and the killing of young Seyward. A mealy "poetic justice" was grafted onto Macbeth's death scene, transforming Macbeth's giant passion into puny self-pity:

> 'Tis done. The scene of life will quickly close. Ambition's vain, delusive dreams are fled, and now I wake to darkness, guilt and horror. I cannot bear it. Let me shake it off—'T wo' not be; my soul is clogg'd with blood—and cannot rise. I dare not ask for mercy. It is too late, hell drags me down. Forever . . . O, I sink . . . Oh! . . . my soul is lost forever . . . O!

Inevitably, by the end of the century, and the beginning of the nineteenth, the Garrick/Pritchard pattern slowly lost favor as actors and actresses searched further into the polyphony of the characters. Meanwhile the prototypes of the Terrible Lady and her driven Thane had also found homes elsewhere in Europe, especially in Germany; but before 1800 a German actress, Rosalie Nouseul, had begun to discover—generally to the dismay of the conventional German critics—two modulations by which Shakespeare countered Lady Macbeth's aggressiveness:

first, her conscience; and second, her love for her husband. Thus a German journal, in 1779:

> In an ecstasy of mind—caused by flattering visions of royal grandeur, Nouseul tries to realize a plan from which normally she would have shrunk. Thus she was able to seize our sympathy as well as our interest.

An outraged conservative critic insisted that the actress pleased audiences so much because she played the Lady wrong:

> People ask, how could a spectator's heart have been moved, when the Lady had fallen into madness? How could such an abnormal villain, such a female image of Richard, acquire our sympathy? If the actress had performed the Lady's part according to Shakespeare's portrayal, she would unquestionably never have gained our sympathy. *That* Lady is a superhuman monster . . . Mrs. Nousuel humanized this character.

It would be many years before Shakespeare's multiple tones could be widely heard in Germany, in England, in America, or elsewhere in Europe. Still, a gradual admission of the erotic as well as the aggressive impulses in the Lady led to some interesting variation in actresses' methods of overcoming Macbeth. One such was by the Italian actress Adelaide Ristori. For the power Pritchard and Siddons had used to overwhelm Macbeth, Ristori used corruption. In her portrayal English observers discerned

> a bloody-minded virago, without heart, without sensibility . . . a Lucretia Borgia, an adept at crime . . . the most unscrupulous of all our Lady Macbeths . . . an Italian intriguante, such a woman as Catherine Medici was . . . she enjoys her power over Macbeth more than English actresses.

The comments reflect a kind of English outrage that Ristori was so masked, so underhanded in her persuasion of Macbeth, that she drew the erotic into her attack, and used it to half-seduce Macbeth into murder, reflecting the archetype of Circe, of the sirens, la belle dame, who lured men to their doom. Similarly, she did not command the murdering ministers, as the fierce Ladies did. She armed herself with supernatural powers, she said, speaking as if a spirit herself, from out of some abyss: she was invoking her sisters.

Outwardly, Ristori's Lady was a very attractive woman, and her physical sensuality—what she called the Lady's "extraordinary personal fascination"—hypnotized her Macbeths. They yielded with little struggle, their compunctions visitings of conscience and constraints of culture offering little resistance.

Slowly in Europe a groundswell was building up to recognize a more complex polyphony in both Macbeth and his Lady. Actresses learned that she might only temporarily smother conscience because of erotic love for her husband, as well as by ambitious impulses for herself and for him. Actors would find that he had his own impulses to kill. Both would be dogged by deep-lying conscience.

Edmund Kean, the first English star after Kemble, found the murder in Macbeth that Shakespeare designed, and also the polyphony that restrained him, as his biographer observed:

> A marvellous compound of daring and irresolution, ambition and submissiveness, treachery and affection.

Kean's half-murderous characterization made it easier for his Ladies to discover conscience. Reviewers at first were not pleased:

> We have . . . but one Lady Macbeth [i.e., Siddons] . . . . [Miss Campbell] had none of the dignity, none of the masculine energy, none of the unrelenting cruelty, none of the devouring ambition which belongs to the cool murderess. She seemed to coax and wheedle her husband to the commission of the crime, instead of pouring her bold spirit into his milky nature.

This womanly Lady was one of the first in England who *had* to be unsexed. Gradually, some of the romantic critics in Germany, perhaps influenced by Nouseul's conception of Lady Macbeth, began to champion the possibility that countering forces were meant by Shakespeare to complicate the character. Most notable was Tieck, who knew the theater as practitioner as well as observer. He would irritate colleagues like Goethe, now grown conservative, by his perceptions of the Lady:

> It is an old custom to exaggerate this role and to present it as a fury. Many actresses have gained fame in this way; and thus the poet's quiet, subtle hints, which he often provides, have remained unnoticed. Basically Macbeth and his spouse are noble, wise characters . . . What happens is that both she and he are torn from their proper place . . . She has to mobilize all her greatness of heart, all the anger and mockery her eyes and face are capable of. Thus the audience perceives her metamorphosis into an enigmatic creature, which is the more deeply moving, the more the loving woman shows through at times.

Tieck's interpretation first puzzled and then angered Goethe, who, a great artist himself, might have been expected to share Shakespeare's creative vision. In 1826 he suggested that perhaps Tieck didn't really mean it, was being paradoxical. Two years later Goethe was sardonic:

> We good Germans cannot rid ourselves of Shakespeare the conqueror. . . ; we happily attribute every value and depth to [his work]. . . . Recently even we have been so retrograde as to allow ourselves to be misled into constituting Lady Macbeth a loving wife. We have become so sick and tired of the truth, it doesn't seem desirable any more, and we prefer to indulge in nonsense.

Soon after, when the actress Auguste Stich-Crelinger (1834), more in tune with the Shakespearean mirror, dared to mix her "demonic forces of passion" with the tender notes of an "honest and fervent love," again audiences were pleased, again a critic scolded her and her mentor, Tieck, in Goethe's fashion:

> It is a shocking phenomenon, that a very famous critic and dramaturg has revealed all sorts of new findings concerning this character, which can only be perceived with greatest surprise. One of these [is] that love and only love is the motive of all the activity of Lady Macbeth. Unfortunately even celebrated actresses accepted this interpretation, [and] this grandiose tragedy becomes crooked and foolish.

Another German actress of the later nineteenth century helped lead the way toward enlarging, with a ripe sensuality, the Lady's "loving" side, as implied in Shakespeare's text. Fanny Janauschek channeled much of her force into the warmth of her relationship with her husband. An observer noted:

> She loved him passionately, and, in her own tigress fashion, tenderly.

She was pointing the way toward an emphasis on the physicality of erotic love between the Macbeths that would come slowly in the world's theaters, that were used almost until this century to polite hints of sexual desire; Janauschek's Lady foreshadowed a frankness that would lead to modern Lady Macbeths fusing their erotic and aggressive forces, even rolling on floor or bed with their husbands, to seduce them physically as well as psychically.

Meanwhile, critics in England, prompted perhaps by creative stage interpretations, began to discover the Lady's conscience. Thus Maginn:

> With the blindness of affection she persuades herself that he is full of the milk of human kindness, and that he would reject false and unholy ways of attaining the object of his desires. She deems it, therefore, her duty to spirit him to the task. . . . Her sex, her woman's breasts, her very nature, oppose the task she has prescribed herself;

> but she prays to the ministers of murder. . . . and she succeeds in mustering the desperate courage that bears her through.

The critic George Fletcher was evidently *directly* influenced by an actress. In his essay, he mentioned Helena Faucit. A transitional figure between the Siddons and post-Siddons characterizations, Faucit had injected the love of a wife into her portrayal, though she still insisted on Lady Macbeth's power as well. Even so she was too mild for *The Lady's Newspaper:*

> She expresses care, anguish, and a fiendish vindictiveness with force. This, however, does not accord with our notion of the character, which requires the subtle hardihood and terrible immobility that the greatest actresses have hitherto given . . . She is an odious as well as a criminal woman, who could hardly be personated by the most feminine and delicate of our actresses, and the effort to throw tenderness into the part seems to us absurd.

But Faucit continued to plumb Shakespeare's perception of the Lady's disabling subtextual conscience. Significantly, she would "faint" after Macbeth told of the dead grooms, without seeming hypocritical.

Fletcher partly vindicated Lady Macbeth's "femininity" by shifting the essential criminal intent to Macbeth—who became the killer, bloodthirsty, selfish and callous, "poetically whining," "morbidly irritable." Lady Macbeth only for him so desperately invoked the murdering ministers. She tried to suppress her "human and feminine conscience."

Kean had helped restore Macbeth's semiautonomy, by calling up not only the deep aggressiveness of the character, but also the antisocial impulses symbolized in the Weird Sisters: he eliminated their "broomstick rubbish" and added their sinister equivocation to Macbeth's inner capacity for violence. Macready's Macbeth, particularly, let the supernatural intervene between his conscience and his impulse. He seemed to

> reel through a visionary region where he must stumble on, urged by a mysterious power which he cannot resist and cannot fathom, through a dark, unriddled, portent-laden future.

So far had the pendulum swung by late in the century that Macbeth and his Lady had changed places. He was now the almost conscienceless murderer; she grew in feeling, fought her conscience, even forced herself to help kill. Among the remarkable new Ladies emerging was, in France, Sarah Bernhardt:

> We have for the first time a womanly Lady Macbeth, a terrible creature, but still a woman. . . . She is usually remorseless and brutal, but Madame Bernhardt has changed all that. There is human nature in all its strength and weakness.

In Poland the actress Modrejewska (who would be called Modjeska in the West) similarly found a vulnerability in her Lady. She

> stressed that Lady Macbeth really faints. Of course that would weaken our repulsion for her. But besides that, there was no scene in which she did not emphasize that there was a trace of humanity inside that monster.

An American counterpart, Clara Morris, by turns coaxing and clever, wrote:

> There is something appalling in [Lady Macbeth's] ready faith and eager summoning of the spirits of evil to her aid; and right in the invocation I find my proof that [she] was naturally womanly, pitiful, capable of repentance for wrong done.

The most famous English exemplar of the new Lady, who led her husband astray partly because she loved him so, was Ellen Terry. Hers was a most "feminine" wife, loving and tender: but she learned to yield to a murderous potential when she joined in collusion with her husband. She could both coax and drive him:

> feminine [her characterization] is; wifely it is; powerful it is; [she] seizes Macbeth in a vice, and uses it and him by sheer force . . . We observe for the first time the stormy, dominant woman of the eleventh century equipped with the capricious emotional subtlety of a woman of the nineteenth century. . . . We can readily accept this clinging, and cajoling enchantress, whose enkindled ambition affects her with a temporary paralysis of conscience.

Terry's Macbeth, Henry Irving, following Fletcher's interpretation, now portrayed Macbeth as the primary villain, nervous, fearful, plausible, murderous—and still incomplete. By his time, in the later nineteenth century, when Freud was beginning, psychologists were learning to perceive character formations that the artist-actors had intuited—as Freud said must be the case. The theater began to recognize the traumas that Shakespeare knew would come when conscience and culture resisted impulses, erotic and hostile, toward father figures, mother figures, sibling figures; from the alliances, holy and unholy, between sexuality and power; from the craving for magic omnipotence; from the images of horror and degradation that lie behind rationality. The Continental theater was beginning to externalize some of these phenomena of felt life in expressionist drama. In more traditional theater, some German actors of Macbeth particularly began personating him so shaken in his single state of man by forbidden thoughts and urgings as to appear what was then called "neurasthenic"—we would say neurotic.

Irving, almost conscienceless as a villain-Macbeth, overcorrected. But he had a share in leading the stage and criticism to a more balanced view of the complexity of Shakespeare's two great figures. The humanity of each was to be recognized, and the criminality: that the Lady, in the terrible act of summoning the murdering ministers, might fearfully as well as daringly be calling on the magic powers that the children in all of us imagine, in spite of the conscience that would surface later; and that Macbeth, moved to repress his conscience and resist cultural restraints, might try to abolish them once and for all—and fail. The two figures need not be locked into gender; each touched with the androgyne Shakespeare felt, is endowed with ambiguous "male" and "female" tones. And so they could be portrayed as recognizable individuals, transcending the archetypal images lying in them. Then their inward struggles could seem so nearly balanced that, until their first killing—the point of no return—conscience and culture might still stop them, and negotiate a sublimation. But of course most tragedy is, almost by definition, a failure of sublimation. Shakespeare made Macbeth and his Lady our surrogates—and his: they are doomed to kill—and die—for us all.

Every new staging of the play brings us an opportunity to search out, from the insights of the actor-artists, new tones, new chords, that Shakespeare heard within himself so long ago. In stagings, the depth, intensity, and interrelation of the tones must depend on the actor's sense of the inward struggles shaping the character structures: how the Lady is roused—and how much she needs to be—to her frightening, antisocial aggression; how inhibited by humane conscience—and by the strangers at the door; how her personality shifts under intensifying pressures of conscience—and by the strangers at her table. Macbeth's many notes will be composed in the furnace of his aggressive and erotic drives as modulated by the pressures wrought on him by the Sisters, by a structured—but competitive—society, and by a wife more or less obsessed, sensual, loving; and ultimately by his conscience and the cultural forces that seek to restrict him from within, and, as these are repressed, from without. The more intense the resistances, the harsher, and sadder, and deeper the range of tones, the closer do they bring us to the full experience of the complexity and depth in Shakespeare's characters.

Notes

1. See my *Masks of Macbeth* (Berkeley and Los Angeles: University of California Press, 1978), p. 1. In that study I discuss the various commentators on *Macbeth* mentioned in the present essay, as well as provide bibliographic citations.

2. Norman Holland, *Psychoanalysis and Shakespeare* (New York: McGraw-Hill, 1964), pp. 219ff., 227.

9

The Camera in Gertrude's Closet

JUNE SCHLUETER and JAMES P. LUSARDI

MAURICE CHARNEY, IN "*HAMLET* WITHOUT WORDS," POINTS OUT THAT TO AN Elizabethan "closet" meant a private apartment, not a bedchamber. Yet modern stagings of the closet scene in *Hamlet* have included a conspicuous bed, inviting audiences to look upon the exchange between Gertrude and her son within the intimacy of the bedroom. Charney argues that the "ponderous marriage bed that usually dominates this scene is entirely out of place."[1] Literary purists, and even those with a stage orientation, might also feel that a television or film camera in Gertrude's closet, or in any part of a Shakespeare play, is similarly out of place. Yet in this century there have been a sizable number of television and film productions of Shakespeare. Moreover, the ready availability of videocassettes has not only directed unprecedented attention to the plays as theater but provided scholars with the luxury of repeated viewings and opportunities for comparative analyses.

Our own interest in camera-ready Shakespeare has guided us through the sequences and scenes of Shakespeare's plays in three stages: first through the consideration of problems inherent in a literary understanding of the scene, then through an identification of the signals the text provides for staging, and, finally, through a close look at the ways in which film and television productions have staged—and hence interpreted—the scene. Following is a literary and theatrical look at act 3, scene 4 of *Hamlet*, with the 1948 Olivier film camera and then the 1980 BBC television camera in Gertrude's closet.

The Enigmatic Text

The closet scene in *Hamlet* is a drama of conflicting motives and frustrated intent. Gertrude has summoned Hamlet to the interview "in most great affliction of spirit,"[2] according to Guildenstern, and she assures the eavesdropping Polonius that she intends to be "round" with her son. If maternal concern could previously accommodate collaboration with the King and Polonius, it has now been compounded with "amazement" at Hamlet's insulting behavior on the occasion of the play-within and with distress at her threatened husband's distress. Gertrude means to confront her son with his offense and to get to the bottom of it. She means also to reassert her claim on Hamlet's obedience. After all, the last time she did so, in act 1, scene 2, he had assented: "I shall in all my best obey you, madam." For Hamlet, of course, the "matter" of the meeting is not his own offense against Claudius but his mother's offense against his father and himself. He goes to Gertrude's chamber not to be probed but to probe, not to be instructed but to instruct. This is the first private moment Hamlet has had with his mother in the play, and, having just tested the Ghost and the King through the play-within, he is determined to expose her sin. As A. C. Bradley describes Hamlet's disposition in the closet scene, his "whole heart is in his horror at his mother's fall and in his longing to raise her."[3]

Neither Gertrude nor Hamlet intends that the closet be a place of death, but within moments of Hamlet's entrance, Gertrude cries out for help, fearing her son will murder her, and Polonius lies slain by an impulsive thrust of the sword that was earlier paralyzed. With the eavesdropper dead, Gertrude is without protection; condemning the "rash and bloody deed," she defends herself by twice challenging Hamlet to explain why he has treated her so unkindly. Hamlet's first response, an eloquent indictment of her infidelity, brings only her second defensive question; but his next reply, a comparison of the two husbands, humbles her, leaving her thrice begging that he speak no more. Her motive frustrated, Gertrude yields any claim to her position of dominance in the exchange. Hamlet's intention prevails.

But Hamlet's intention, to shame his mother into reform, becomes either too insistent or too elaborate for the Ghost to endure. Having counseled Hamlet to "Leave her to heaven," it reappears when Hamlet persists in his reproaches, even in the face of Gertrude's pleading. Hamlet immediately thinks it has come to chide a tardy son, which it does do, but it has come as well to protect a wife for whom love still urges kindness: "O, step between her and her fighting soul! / Conceit in weakest bodies strongest works." Whether the Ghost's intervention is prompted by Hamlet's growing excitement or, as J. Dover Wilson proposes, by Hamlet's imminent disclosure of the particulars of the murder,[4] the Ghost succeeds in altering Hamlet's behavior and Gertrude's perception of it. Once the Ghost departs, Hamlet's counsel is that Gertrude confess herself to heaven, that she "Assume a virtue," avoiding Claudius's bed until use changes "the stamp of nature." Clearly Hamlet *has* cleft his mother's heart in twain, and she has acknowledged her fault.

But just as clearly Gertrude is prepared to yield to Hamlet's demands before the Ghost appears. Gertrude's original admission of the "black and grained spots" in her soul comes as the consequence of a drama as purposefully staged as Hamlet's more famous play-within-the-play. Early in the closet scene, Hamlet instructs his mother to sit down and remain seated. As in *The Murder of Gonzago*, he plans to hold a mirror up to nature, this time to catch the conscience of the Queen. In this drama, Hamlet presents his mother with the "counterfeit presentment of two brothers" that she may see the difference between them. Even as he inserted a speech of "some dozen or sixteen lines" in the Gonzago play and interrupted the Players with explanatory notes, now he accompanies the images with an interpretive monologue, drawing the moral conclusion he wants his mother to draw. Acting on Hamlet's direction, Gertrude studies the godlike man who was her husband and the "mildew'd ear, / Blasting the wholesome brother," then pleads, "O Hamlet, speak no more! / Thou turn'st mine eyes into my very soul."

Despite the success of his second play-within, Hamlet is not content. The emotional intensity of this intimate scene in his mother's chamber once again urges him into overreaction. Earlier, hearing Polonius's echo of Gertrude's cry for help, Hamlet had run his sword through the curtain and the anonymous torso behind it. Now, though Gertrude admits she has seen her sinful soul and enjoins her son to speak no more, Hamlet elaborates his catalog of reproaches, forcing her to beg him to be silent—and forcing the ghost to intervene.

On the one hand, the Ghost's appearance seems itself tardy, since Hamlet has already indicated his mother for her poor judgment in men and mentioned the murder. If the Ghost's injunction to leave Gertrude to heaven was intended to secure Hamlet's silence about her "o'erhasty marriage," Hamlet's "Such an act / That blurs the grace and blush of modesty" should have been sufficient cue for it to intrude. If the warning was meant to exclude her from implication in or knowledge of the murder, then the Ghost should have materialized even earlier, at Hamlet's pronouncement on Polonius's death: "A bloody deed—almost as bad, good mother, / As kill a king, and marry with his brother." On the other hand, the Ghost's appearance could not be more timely. For its intrusion deflects Hamlet from his headlong course, substituting a distraction that his unseeing mother thinks "the very coinage of [his] brain." Its appearance offers Hamlet a more acceptable tack: urging Gertrude not to excuse her own trespass as his madness but to confess herself to heaven. In effect, the Ghost saves both Gertrude and her son from Hamlet's excess and renews its injunction as well.

Ironically, Gertrude is left to implement her program of abstinence alone, for Hamlet, at Claudius's order, "must to England." The Ghost's reappearance may well have served to restore its injunction about Gertrude, but Hamlet's departure neutralizes its more potent command: Hamlet can hardly avenge the death of his father if Claudius has sent him from court. The final appearance of the Ghost signals the end of the long sequence of fits and starts that has defined Hamlet's reaction to the mandate for revenge. The visitations of act 1, scene 5 and act 3, scene 4 create a frame for the inaction and bungled action that have compromised the avenger and frustrated the Ghost's intent. Now Hamlet's threats are directed not at Claudius but at his schoolfellows, "Whom I will trust as I will adders fang'd, / . . . And blow them at the moon."

The Ghost's sudden entrance is, of course, a highly theatrical event, providing Hamlet with a terrifying reminder of his charge and the audience with a fourth encounter with the supernatural. But the presence of the Ghost in Gertrude's chamber also provides a stage image of a family that has been fragmented by lust and murder. Though Gertrude does not see the Ghost, the audience does, and the tableau of husband, wife, and son in Gertrude's chamber, the Ghost (at least in Q1) in his nightgown, gives corporal form to the domestic trinity that for thirty years was Denmark's royal center. The audience has been presented with several stage images of the now prevailing three, with Hamlet sulking off to the side, as in act 1, scene 2, or scheming to undo the King, as in the play-within. But with Claudius wearing the crown, the audience does not see the compassion or the "piteous action" that, despite distraction and amazement, it sees in Gertrude's room. In a sense, the image of old Hamlet's family is being held up against the image of Claudius's family, in much the same way that Hamlet held up the "counterfeit presentment of two brothers" to Gertrude.

But the image of husband, wife, and son is for the audience's eyes, not Gertrude's, for, when the Queen looks upon the ghostly form, she sees only "th' incorporal air." Assuming the Ghost does have physical presence, as entrance and exit lines urge, why does Gertrude not see it? Most critics accept or offer variations on the standard moral perspectives that the Ghost is sparing the Queen's feelings, Bradley's view, or that Gertrude is not worthy of the vision, Dover Wilson's view. Some endorse W. W. Greg's speculation that the Ghost is indeed the coinage of Hamlet's brain.[5] In act 1, though, the Ghost is visible not only to Hamlet but to Horatio and the sentries as well, suggesting that there are no moral—or psychological—prerequisites for the vision and that the

Ghost is not simply Hamlet's invention. Still, the Ghost has not always assumed an individual corporal form or identity in production. In Tony Richardson's 1969 version, with Nicol Williamson, the presence of the Ghost was manifested by bright light and a disembodied voice. In the 1986 New York University production, in which five actors simultaneously played Hamlet, the entire supporting cast became the Ghost in act 1, positioning themselves in a grid formation before the frightened Hamlet to chant its admonitory lines, while the Hamlets themselves became the Ghost in the closet. In the 1985 American Shakespeare Repertory adaptation, Douglas Overtoom's Hamlet fell to the floor, contorting his body in a shaft of red light, and spoke the Ghost's part with a gravelly, unearthly voice, in a spectacular display of demon possession. Though exciting and imaginative theater, the commitment to any of these renderings in act 1—or to the position that, while the Ghost has physical presence in act 1, Hamlet hallucinates in act 3, scene 4, as in the 1964 Kozintsev film—neutralizes this domestic stage image in the closet scene and the corollary that Gertrude's failure to see is part of that image.

Gertrude, by Hamlet's account in his first soliloquy (1.2), was a devoted wife, and yet before "the salt of most unrighteous tears / Had left the flushing in her galled eyes," she married her husband's brother. Hamlet imputes this appalling reversal to "Frailty," by which he evidently means a failure not only in virtue but in judgment and even simple perception: "My father's brother, but no more like my father / Than I to Hercules. . . ." The shocked Hamlet's early reflections anticipate both the "counterfeit presentment of two brothers" and the stage image created by the appearance of the Ghost in the intimate atmosphere of the closet. Gertrude's inability to see that her devotion to this "Hyperion" should have kept her from the "incestuous sheets" of a "satyr" now finds a physical correlative in her inability to see the apparition of her husband at all. As Harley Granville-Barker points out, the visitation of the Ghost in act 3, scene 4, seen by Hamlet, unseen by Gertrude, presents a "picture of mother, father and son, united but divided, together, but in understanding curelessly apart,"[6] implying that Gertrude's inability to see the Ghost is emblematic of her spiritual blindness.

Certainly Gertrude is no moral giant. But, because Shakespeare is kinder to her than his sources are to her counterpart, the actual extent of her guilt remains in doubt. Interestingly, the Q1 version of the play is more generous and less elusive in its treatment of the Queen than the received version derived from Q2 and F.[7] In the Q1 closet scene, Hamlet is explicit in identifying Claudius as the murderer of old Hamlet: comparing the portraits of the two brothers, he asks, "can you looke on him / That slew my father, and your deere husband, / To live in the incentuous pleasure of his bed?" (p. 602). And Gertrude, following the exit of the Ghost, is explicit in disavowing the deed: "I swear by heaven, / I never knew of this most horride murder" (p. 602). Moreover, she promises to support her son in his quest for revenge:

Hamlet. And mother, but assist me in revenge,
And in his death your infamy shall die.
Queene. Hamlet, I vow by that majesty,
That knowes our thoughts, and lookes into our hearts,
I will conceale, consent, and doe my best,
What stratagem soe're thou shalt devise.

(P. 602)

In the received text, there is no such clarification or confirmation of Gertrude's position. She remains a morally ambiguous figure. She may be merely obtuse and self-indulgent. She may be a servant of time and circumstance as shaped by Claudius. Or she may be worse.

The narrative of the Ghost, in making the revelations of act 1, scene 5, is so structured as to suggest that Gertrude's infidelity preceded her husband's death. Moreover, the specific language of the text reinforces that impression. The Ghost styles Claudius "that incestuous, that adulterate beast," and Hamlet reviles both his mother ("O most pernicious woman!") and his uncle ("O villain") in his response to the Ghost's story.[8] Hamlet's charge that Gertrude's behavior "makes marriage-vows / As false as dicers' oaths" may likewise be taken as evidence of her adultery. And yet the case against her is never really clinched. Hamlet's penchant for generalizing about his mother's betrayal of his father blurs distinctions among kinds of infidelity. And Gertrude herself proves to be an enigmatic commentator on her own guilt, admitting the "dark and grained spots" that infect and, in act 4, scene 5, the anxiety that afflicts her "sick soul" but never specifying the nature of her sins. Similarly, her reactions on other occasions fail to resolve the issue. Speaking to Claudius alone in act 2, scene 2 on the cause of Hamlet's distemper, she makes no apparent reference to an illicit liaison between them: "I doubt it is no other but the main, / His father's death, and our o'erhasty marriage." Her response to Hamlet's interruption of the play-within—"The lady doth protest too much, methinks"—seems simplicity itself: the Queen may be objecting to the redundancy of the dialogue, to the strident assertions of the Player Queen, or, perhaps embarrassed by her own recent history, to the devotion that death, she has learned, negates. When Claudius rises, calling for lights, she expresses interest only in the welfare of the King.

Nonetheless, as Hamlet prepares for the interview with his mother, he is in a violent mood. Pausing to soliloquize, he articulates his wrath: "Now could I drink hot blood, / And do such bitter business as the day / Would quake to look on." Though he fails to kill Claudius when he discovers him at prayer, his savage anger persists, expressed now in imaginings of Claudius in hell. Once in Gertrude's closet, he suggests what neither the Ghost nor Claudius nor Hamlet himself has spoken before: that Gertrude was an accomplice in the murder of the king. The killing of Polonius is "A bloody deed—almost as bad, good mother, / As kill a king, and marry with his brother." In interpreting this line, critics have assumed, with Dover Wilson, that Hamlet is putting Gertrude to the test and that her "astonished" response "As kill a king!" "acquits" her.[9] It is, of course, also possible, as Harold Jenkins urges, that the testing is not deliberate but rather incident to Hamlet's "not distinguish[ing] the elements of killing and marrying in what he apparently regards as one composite crime."[10]

As the closet scene progresses, it is clear that Gertrude has seen her fault in Hamlet's mirror. Imploring Hamlet to be silent, she anguishes in shame—until the Ghost intervenes. Before the visitation, Hamlet had labored at getting Gertrude to see what he saw, and he was successful. Now, despite his excited descriptions of the apparition, Gertrude is unable to see what her son sees, and she concludes that Hamlet is mad. Whether she retains that opinion until the end of the scene or permits Hamlet to persuade her that "It is not madness / That I have utt'red" remains unclear. Hamlet closes the closet scene with three long speeches of counsel before his parting lines. The first of these, a defense of his sanity, ends with his urging his mother to repent. Gertrude's single line response is "O Hamlet, thou hast cleft my heart in twain." Are these the words of a still repentant Queen acknowledging the trespass shown her by one whose "pulse, as [hers], doth temperately keep time, / And makes as healthful music"? Or is this the expression of a deeply saddened mother who has witnessed the "ecstasy" of her son? Hamlet's second speech, which importunes Gertrude to repudiate Claudius's bed, is punctuated by three of Hamlet's four good nights and, finally, by "One word more, good lady." Gertrude's response to Hamlet's guidance in moral remediation and to his erratic attempts to leave is, simply, "What shall I do?" Is she so humbled at having provoked such a schooling from her son that she can say no more? Or is she protecting her own person by lending a seeming ear to Hamlet's preposterous counsel, daring to say no more? Hamlet's third speech is a tauntingly ironic injunction to secrecy, lest his mother reveal to the "bloat king" that "I essentially am not in madness, / But mad in craft." It secures Gertrude's cryptic promise: "Be thou assur'd, if words be made of breath, / And breath of life, I have no life to breathe / What thou hast said to me." Whether she follows Hamlet's instructions in reporting the interview remains questionable in act 4, scene 1, where she tells Claudius that Polonius is slain and that her son is mad. She may be keeping Hamlet's secret, or she may herself believe in Hamlet's distraction.

Nor is it certain after the encounter in the closet is over and Hamlet has departed for England that Gertrude no longer goes to Claudius's bed. The signals she gives are mixed. In act 4, scene 5, just before the entrance of Ophelia, she professes the chastened consciousness of sin that Hamlet has inspired, but, in the same scene, at the entrance of the incensed Laertes, she becomes the determined protector of Claudius, putting herself in danger to shield him from assault. When Laertes makes the demand for his father and the King replies that he is dead, Gertrude quickly adds, "But not by him." Such solicitous concern hardly seems the mark of a wife who has alienated herself from her husband. When Hamlet appears at Ophelia's grave, challenging Laertes to match his love for the dead girl, Gertrude speaks of her son's ranting as one privileged to know what it imports and what its course will be:

> This is mere madness,
> And thus awhile the fit will work on him;
> Anon, as patient as the female dove
> When that her golden couplets are disclos'd,
> His silence will sit drooping.
>
> (5.1.284–88)

Does Gertrude believe her son mad, which would neutralize his earlier counsel to her, or is she playing the protector once more?

Textually, Gertrude remains a mystery. She will appear one more time, in the final scene, to drink from the poisoned cup, knowingly or accidentally, and so die, leaving unanswered the questions concerning the extent of her guilt and the extent of her repentance. Yet these are questions that must be addressed in production and in some measure answered. Gertrude will become a compelling theatrical reality only when a coherent sequence of theatrical signals is associated with her presence on the stage, particularly in the pivotal closet scene.

Theatrical Cues

Before we turn to see how the Olivier and the BBC productions handle the character of Gertrude as well as other opportunities for interpretation, it is worth looking at some of the signals the text itself provides for playing the scene. The closet scene, like so much of Shakespeare's dramatic writing, is chary of stage direction, recording entrances and exits and an occasional action. But this scene (again, like so many others) is rich in verbal clues and cues that variously guide and prescribe the action that supplements, prompts, and validates words.

There is, for example, no stage direction that says Gertrude neither sees nor hears the Ghost. Yet Gertrude's language leaves no doubt that she does not. In response to Hamlet's sighting, she cries, "Alas, he's mad!" When, at the direction of the Ghost, Hamlet inquires after his mother's welfare, she replies, "Alas, how is 't with you, / That you do bend your eye on vacancy, / And with th' incorporal air do hold discourse?" Convinced of her son's distemper, she asks, "Whereon do you look?," then "To whom do you speak this?," and, finally, she confirms she sees "Nothing at all; yet all that is I see" and hears "nothing but ourselves."

The encounter with the Ghost is otherwise prescriptive in its language. Hamlet's words reflect fear and excitement and offer a description of the Ghost's appearance and behavior: "look you how pale he glares? . . . Look, where he goes, even now, out at the portal!" Even without reference to the Q1 specification of a "night gowne," we still know from Hamlet that the Ghost is dressed "in his habit as he lived." While Hamlet is describing the Ghost to his mother, his mother is describing Hamlet, whose eyes are wild ("Forth at your eyes your spirits wildly peep") and whose hair "like life in excrements, / Start up and stand an end," the second a bit difficult to play.[11]

There are other moments in the scene in which dialogue clearly specifies action but any number of stagings could be managed. Hamlet's presentation to this mother of the two "counterfeit presentments," for example, must find its shape in production. On the New York University stage, one of the five Hamlets held up the palms of his hands in turn, providing no picture but verbal description. In the 1984–85 Royal Shakespeare Company's *Hamlet*, Roger Rees pointed to two imaginary paintings on the wall. Ian McKellen's Hamlet compared an oval framed picture of Claudius from a side table with one of his father that he pulled from his shirt. Nicol Williamson wore a locket containing the miniature portraiture of his father around his neck, which he held next to the likeness of Claudius around Gertrude's. How forcibly Hamlet imposes his lesson upon his mother remains a directorial decision as well. In the NYU production, Hamlet stood threateningly over his seated mother, forcing her head back so that her long red hair cascaded in the air. In ASR's contemporary staging, Hamlet held a pistol to Gertrude's forehead as he spoke of the act that "takes off the rose / From the fair forehead of an innocent love / And sets a blister there. . . ." As Gertrude pleaded with him to speak no more, Hamlet pinioned his mother, pressing his fingers into her neck.

Similarly, how Hamlet discovers that it is Polonius he has slain may also be variously staged. At line 27, Hamlet asks whether he has killed the King. By line 32, he knows it is Polonius: "Thou wretched, rash, intruding fool, farewell! / I took thee for thy better." Does Hamlet lift up the arras and see Polonius, as the editorial direction in several modern editions suggests, or does the falling body brush the curtain aside to lie within view as soon as Hamlet turns to discover it?

Throughout the closet scene, Shakespeare provides verbal cues for physical action, ranging from the prescriptive (Hamlet, about to wring his mother's heart, notices she is wringing her hands) to the suggestive (might Gertrude press her hands to her ears at "O, speak to me no more! / These words, like daggers, enter in my ears. / No more, sweet Hamlet!," preventing her from hearing Hamlet's condemnation of Claudius as "A murderer and a villain"?). There is one moment in the closet scene, however, in which action prompts language and Shakespeare's text provides neither stage direction nor apparent cue. We are referring to Gertrude's cry early in act 3, scene 4: "What wilt thou do? Thou wilt not murder me? / Help, ho!" Textually, there seems to be little motivation for Gertrude's unfortunate presumption, the consequence of which is Polonius's death. But the Queen must have had cause to be afraid, and, in the absence of language signaling that cause, it is only in production that an audience can know why.

The sequence begins with the quick exchange between Hamlet and his mother, Hamlet challenging Gertrude's charges with barbed accusations of his own. Exhausted by her son's caustic cleverness and dismayed by his wish to deny her maternity, the Queen concludes, "Nay, then, I'll set those to you that can speak," to which Hamlet retorts, "Come, come, and sit you down; you shall not budge. / You go not till I set you up a glass / Where you may see the inmost part of you."

Action is clearly demanded here: Gertrude, moving away from Hamlet, either to recall Polonius or to fetch her husband and his attendants, is prevented from doing so by Hamlet, who insists she sit down and not budge until she has recognized her fault. His "Come, come" might at first appear to be merely an invitation to sit, albeit a firm one. But the Queen's extraordinary reponse demands that it be more. Q1 offers guidance. In her account to Claudius of Hamlet's behavior in her closet, Gertrude reports: "Whenas he came, I first bespake him faire, / But then he throwes and tosses me about, / As one forgetting that I was his mother" (p. 603).

That Hamlet is in a violent mood has already been established by his readiness to "drink hot blood" and by his wish to secure Claudius's damnation. Moreover, his swift slaying of Polonius immediately after Gertrude's cry at least confirms that mood and may even be taken to indicate that killing was on his mind. Traditionally, in production, Hamlet is rough, even brutal with his mother, pushing her down and restricting her movements with force, the assumption being that a sufficient show of Hamlet's physical superiority and of his intemperance will leave Gertrude fearing for her life.

Production may even provide a more tangible cue for Gertrude's cry. Hamlet tells his mother he plans to "set you up a glass" wherein she may see her fault. While no property is mandatory here since Hamlet's mirror is metaphorical, he might hold up an actual mirror or, in the absence of one, the reflective edge of a sword. Though offered as the glass that will expose her soul, the sword may terrify the Queen, who concludes that Hamlet has drawn it to slay her. Or Hamlet may draw his sword or rapier to restrain his mother from leaving. Either reading provides the ancillary benefit of an already drawn weapon with which to slay Polonius.

But even without the menacing weapon or the throwing and tossing that did not find its way into Q2 or F, Gertrude's cry might be explained in either of two ways. The first brings us back to the question of Gertrude's guilt. Her "What wilt thou do? Thou wilt not murder me?" may be prompted not by Hamlet's behavior but by his plan to undress his mother's soul. If the Queen knows the blackness within and fears that Hamlet knows or will soon know as well, her frightened cry may be the culmination of a mental drama in which she recalls her deeds and anticipates Hamlet's response. In such a reading, her readiness to conclude that Hamlet will murder her may be presumptive evidence of the enormity of her guilt. Her "As kill a king!" need not be so astonished—nor exonerating—an exclamation as Dover Wilson assumes but, rather, a tentative expression of what she most fears Hamlet knows: that she was accomplice in her husband's murder. Her ensuing questions, imploring Hamlet to identify her deed, become a test of the extent of her son's knowledge. That Gertrude is not satisfied by Hamlet's reference to false marriage vows in his first response lends credibility to such a reading, for though she should now know what Hamlet accuses her of, she still seeks more: "Ay me, what act, / That roars so loud and thunders in the index?" In such a reading, Gertrude's response to Hamlet's comparison of the two brothers would leave her contrite but relieved that Hamlet was claiming no more.

But even if Gertrude is not guilty of the terrible crime Hamlet is about to suggest, her cry and the ensuing action have an arresting effect on an audience that previously did not associate Gertrude with her husband's death. The small but suggestive patch of drama begins with Gertrude's "Thou wilt not murder me?" and ends with her "As kill a king!" In between these outcries, the audience is provided with a stage image of death, in the form of the slain Polonius, whom Hamlet first thought the King. The drama would seem to be urging the audience into considering the possibility of Gertrude's complicity, a possibility that, while never made patent, invites more careful scrutiny of the Queen.

The second approach in effect renders gratuitous the psychological paradigm inherent in the first. But demanding psychological accountability or consistency in Shakespeare's characters may not always be warranted. Alan C. Dessen makes this point in his excellent book *Elizabethan Drama and the Viewer's Eye*. Taking care not to repudiate our traditional sense of dramatic character, he argues that our sense of character may at times be "superseded by some other principle we may not take into account." More specifically, he proposes that characters "can for a moment cease to be important as individuals but instead can participate in some larger, shared effect. . . ."[12] Gertrude's cry in act 3, scene 4 may well be a moment that is unjustifiable within a psychological matrix. Connecting as it does with the pent-up fury of Hamlet's soliloquy on his way to his mother's room, it may find its most reasonant validation as one of Dessen's larger, shared effects. For an audience carrying the verbal images of Hamlet's self-appraisal with them into the closet, Gertrude's cry prompts and articulates its own astonishment and fear.

Hamlet, we know, has emotional warrant to kill as he approaches Gertrude's room. In his present mood, he is capable, by his own account, of terrifyingly "bitter business." Yet, in a prayer as potent as Lady Macbeth's plea that the spirits unsex her, he prays that the soul of Nero not enter his bosom, that he be "cruel, not unnatural," that he "speak daggers to her, but use none." This is the Hamlet who had advised the Players in act 3, scene 2 to "Suit the action to the word, the word to the action." Now he urges on himself a hypocritical division between "tongue and soul": "How in my words somever she be shent, / To give them seals never, my soul, consent!" An audience recognizing the pattern would, when it hears Gertrude's cry, fear that Hamlet's action will, after all, match his word; he will speak daggers to her and use one.

In Dessen's own analysis of the closet scene, he concentrates on Hamlet's rash and bloody frame of mind and on the way theatrical images may reflect on the state of Hamlet's soul rather than Gertrude's. The larger pattern he identifies consists of visual analogues linking the First Player as Pyrrhus brandishing his sword over the doomed Priam, Hamlet lifting his sword over the praying Claudius, and Hamlet thrusting his sword into the shrieking Polonius. Here the use and abuse of the revenging sword, as a symbolic stage property, becomes the focus of interest. "What would be the effect on an audience," asks Dessen, "if the director left Polonius's body, covered with blood, in full view and left the sword, also bloodied, in the hero's hand throughout much if not all of the scene?"[13] The suggested answer is that much of Hamlet's commentary on Gertrude's corruption would apply ironically to the commentator, for he "has himself been tainted with the disease and disorder of the world he has sought to cure, and the blood on the sword becomes an apt visual symbol for that stain or implication."[14] Dessen's recommended staging is, of course, a reading of the play, and that is just the point. An actor who lets the curtain fall on the dead Polonius and casts aside his weapon to turn his attention to Gertrude will create a different and probably more favorable impression of Hamlet, at Gertrude's expense. The given in the text is the stage property and its bloody use. How a director reads this textual signal will determine how the closet scene takes shape.

Productions

Since the Laurence Olivier film version of *Hamlet*[15] features the director in the role of the protagonist, the production is to an unusual degree under the control of a single creative personality. Olivier chose to film in black and white, for example, "to achieve through depth of focus a more majestic, more poetic image, in keeping with the stature of the verse."[16] While he managed to recruit a remarkable cast, including Eileen Herlie as Gertrude and Felix Aylmer as Polonius, he was still "prepared to take on the entire responsibility"[17] for the result.

It is an active camera that introduces us to the scene. The opening moments show Hamlet's shadow ascending a winding stairwell, Gertrude and Polonius conversing in the spacious chamber, Hamlet himself on the stair calling "Mother, mother, mother," and Gertrude rising to conceal Polonius in a curtained archway stage-right, then moving left to face the entranceway and the camera. With the frame fixed, Hamlet suddenly appears in it. In deep focus, we see Hamlet's back in the foreground as he enters the room and Gertrude in the distance standing in front of her bed. Having established the authority of the camera, Olivier makes bold use of it to shape the scene and to regulate both the perspective and the responses of the audience.

Thus, though Hamlet on the stairs calls quietly, even tentatively, to his mother, he moves steadily, inexorably toward the camera. When he enters the room for the first exchange with a self-possessed Gertrude, bareheaded but regal-looking in her elegant *robe de chambre*, the camera remains on his back as he pauses in the entranceway and then slowly bears down on her, reaching her on his wish that she were not his mother. When Gertrude attempts to come forward to get those that "can speak," Hamlet seizes her by the arm and throws her backward on the bed. The camera now makes a series of suggestive switches and movements. From behind the bed, it shows Hamlet in the act of throwing Gertrude down, follows her as she lands, her robe parting in the violence of the fall, and lifts to reveal Hamlet standing over her with his sword drawn. The angle is then reversed, with the camera looking at Gertrude over Hamlet's shoulder, the point of his sword poised at her naked throat, while he expresses his determination to expose her "inmost part." It is this gesture that motivates Gertrude's terrified "Thou wilt not murder me?" and Polonius's echoing "Help!" Viewed again from the front, Hamlet is exhilarated at the cry of the outsider who, he thinks, is the King. As he turns to Polonius's archway, the camera switches to that perspective for Hamlet's onrush, eyes wide and glaring, and his lunge with the sword almost into the camera's eye.

The manipulation of the camera in this opening sequence is clearly meant to dramatize the progressive violence of Hamlet's demeanor and his quick seizure, by force and terror, of the dominant position in the scene. For an audience primed by Hamlet's reflections in soliloquy in the two previous scenes, he is obviously yielding to his rash and bloody mood and seems ready to give it full scope. The camera invites the audience to share the shock of Gertrude and Polonius at Hamlet's towering excitement and precipitate actions.

When Hamlet stabs through the curtain and Gertrude screams behind him, his face is a mask of manic glee. Turning slowly toward the distraught Queen, he shouts defiantly, "Is it the King?" The camera switches angles, holding the weeping Gertrude in the foreground and her son, with head thrown back, by the archway. As Hamlet delivers his comment on the "bloody deed," he stands in his murderous pose, right arm outstretched, the sword in the curtain and in the body, now carefully watching his mother's startled reaction to "As kill a king. . . ." On "Ay, lady, it was my word," he withdraws the weapon and pulls the curtain, and Polonius topples into view. Casting his sword upon the body, Hamlet leans forward over the camera to utter a disappointed and contemptuous farewell to the "busy" old man. Though the body remains exposed, the camera will not return to it until late in the scene. Attention is fixed on Hamlet and Gertrude.

An unarmed Hamlet, but still a violent one, turns back to his sobbing mother, now in the center of the frame, her writhing hands folded as though in hysterical prayer. When Hamlet seizes her by the shoulders as she tries to rise, abruptly sitting her down again, she recovers from her weeping to shout angrily, "What have I done, that thou dar'st wag thy tongue / In noise so rude against me?" During Hamlet's indictment, she looks appalled, stifling sobs as she stares into his face; she starts her second question, "What act . . .?," only to have it cut short when

Hamlet grabs at the picture of his father hanging from his neck and that of Claudius hanging from hers to begin his comparison. Gertrude studies the image of old Hamlet as the son celebrates the virtues of his father. But, when Hamlet speaks of "An eye like Mars, to threaten and command," she raises her own languid eyes to gaze fixedly, lovingly on Hamlet's face. The spell is broken only when his disgust at his stepfather's image becomes disgust at her. This Hamlet's obsession and the sexuality of the woman who inspires it are made visually evident by the appearance of Gertrude as she sits on the bed, her robe open wide to reveal a full, firm body in a thin, clinging shift. In his pain and fury, Hamlet tears Claudius's picture from his mother's neck and stalks away, rounding on her with "O shame, where is thy blush?" Gertrude herself turns away at this reproach, into a closeup camera that frames her in a crouched position, the bottom portion of Hamlet's torso in the distance. Her contrite acknowledgment of her soul's "dark and grained spots" seems to solicit a tender response, but her son becomes only more incensed. Leaning forward on her bed, he assails his mother with images of corrupt sensuality. Holding her hand to her cheek, the beleaguered Queen turns back to Hamlet and throws her arms about his neck to beg "no more." His response is to grab her by the wrists and to deliver another verbal assault, which leaves her sobbing uncontrollably and screaming in anguish for relief. As a climax to the sequence, Hamlet seizes the panting Gertrude by the throat, but he is arrested in his physical assault by the ominous sounds of a drum.

With the drum pounding like a heartbeat, the camera rests on Hamlet's paralyzed face, then on the pleading face of Gertrude, whose lips move inaudibly. We are locked during an extended pause in the traumatized consciousness of Hamlet. Then, as abruptly as it stopped, the action resumes, with Hamlet roughly pushing his mother backward on the bed. She lies there mute, her arms outstretched, watching in amazement as her son turns away, looks upward, and prays to "heavenly guards" for protection, even as the sounds of the swelling winds accompany the ominous drum to signal the visitation of the Ghost.

This Ghost, however, does not assume corporal form. Though old Hamlet had appeared in his armor on the battlements, now he remains a disembodied voice. Here, as in act 1, Hamlet drops to the floor at its presence, as though felled by a blow, twisting his body and craning his neck to behold and address the apparition. Gertrude, sitting up to observe the spectacle of her son, concludes sadly, "Alas, he's mad!" The failure of the Ghost to materialize lends credibility to her judgment and eliminates the symbolic stage image of family reunion. But Olivier compensates for the loss of the Ghost as a physical presence and secures comparable effects by means of the camera. During most of the visitation, the camera becomes the Ghost. Hence, Gertrude no sooner reaches her conclusion than the prone Hamlet appears in a long shot, speaking and reaching toward the camera. When the father reminds the son of his "almost blunted purpose," the camera is fixed on the chastened Hamlet; but then it swings slowly stage-left to fix on Gertrude and returns to Hamlet for the Ghost's admonition, "But, look, amazement on thy mother sits." Never taking his eyes from the camera, Hamlet reaches toward Gertrude to ask, "How is it with you, lady?" When she counsels patience and questions him, "Whereon do you look?," Hamlet urgently points at the camera—"On him, on him!"—and describes the figure he sees. Finally, as Gertrude bows her head in weary conviction, he stretches toward the camera on his elbows to plead, "Do not look upon me, / Lest with this piteous action you convert / My stern [intents]."

As Olivier contrives the scene, it is difficult to disbelieve in the Ghost just because we don't actually see it. And Gertrude's perception of nothing but "vacancy" remains as fully a comment on her moral disability as it is on Hamlet's distress. Similarly, though the domestic stage image is sacrificed, the audience is invited to share the perspective of the dead father in his last encounter with the two people he loved most in life. The impact of this cinematic device, in contrast to the stage image, is psychological rather than symbolic, a poignant expression of alienation and loss. In the final moments of the visitation, the camera separates itself from the Ghost's perspective and then adopts it again to reassert the effect. In closeup, Gertrude asks, "To whom do you speak this?" We next see Hamlet and Gertrude in turn, now from behind the bed, each on the margin of the space where the Ghost presumably stands, Gertrude descrying nothing and Hamlet pointing at the archway. When woodwinds signal the departure of the Ghost, Hamlet, now in closeup, looks and lunges to his right, calling, "Why, look you there, look how it steals away!" The camera is already moving away from Hamlet as he lunges and crawls after it, pulling himself with one arm and reaching out with the other. The Ghost/camera retreats, holding the writhing Hamlet in sight until the darkness of the corridor closes it in.

In the aftermath of this extraordinary episode, Gertrude walks alone through the spacious chamber toward its empty archways, looking for "nothing." As she pauses to peer in the direction of the corridor, a peal of chimes indicates the return of ordinary reality, much as the knocking at the gate does in *Macbeth*. Coming back downstage, she looks and crosses left, where Hamlet is discovered sitting on the floor at the foot of the bed. "This," she comforts him, "is the very coinage of your brain."

At the imputation of madness, Hamlet rises to insist calmly on his own sanity and firmly on his mother's trespass. But this Gertrude is no longer interested in what Hamlet has to say. Consistent with this interpretation, Hamlet says a good deal less; Olivier makes his heaviest cuts here in the final panel of the scene, reducing Hamlet's lines by more than half (from nearly ninety to forty). Refusing to meet her son's eyes, she turns her head to the side and looks downward, then walks slowly away, saddened and resigned. As she reaches the bed, she sits down and weeps, not in terror as earlier and not for herself. These tears are for her distracted son, whose madness, not counsel, has cleft her heart. In the meantime, Hamlet comes up behind her, but the touching between mother and son is no longer cruel: Hamlet holds her tenderly at the shoulders, and she reaches her hand back to touch his. As he tells his mother to throw away the "worser part" of her divided heart, he rests his head on hers, then gently touches his lips to her forehead. Though his voice takes on an edge when he asks that she not return to Claudius's bed, Gertrude shows no resistance, turning to him afterward to hold his face and kiss him on the lips. This pair are like lovers making up rather than mother and son. Hamlet's "I must be cruel only to be kind" is gently said. It occasions a full embrace, after which Hamlet rests his head in Gertrude's lap, receiving her caresses. When he announces his imminent departure for England and his intention to remove Polonius's body, they once again face each other for a long meaningful look and a truly passionate kiss. For all that has happened in this remarkable encounter, the end of the scene recalls the beginning. In deep focus, we see Hamlet's back in the foreground as he drags out the body of Polonius and Gertrude in the distance standing by the richly draped bed. At last alone, she sits down for the fade-out.

The Oedipal suggestions in Olivier's rendering of this scene endorse the position popularized by Ernest Jones in *Hamlet and Oedipus.*[18] In 1937, ten years before he made the film, Olivier, in the company of Tyrone Guthrie and Peggy Ashcroft, went to visit Jones. According to Olivier:

> I have never ceased to think about Hamlet at odd moments, and ever since that meeting I have believed that Hamlet was a prime sufferer from the Oedipus complex—quite unconsciously, of course, as the professor was anxious to stress.[19]

It is the Oedipal premise that provides a coherent sequence of stage images. Even if this production were a *Hamlet* without words, the premise would be apparent. We could clearly discern the sexual energy in the closing embraces and kisses of mother and son, consummated on Gertrude's bed. Moreover, we could also see the external expression of the matricidal impulse, first examined in detail by Frederic Wertham[20] and accommodated in Jones's analysis: it is signaled in the escalation of

Hamlet's violence when he grasps his mother's throat. The Ghost's intervention thwarts it. The Ghost may thus be taken as the correlative of a self-imposed restraint, appearing just as Hamlet is about to yield to his murderous urge and become "passion's slave."

Perhaps because the Oedipal pattern makes it clear that Gertrude will be guided by a son who has established his tacit right to demand the fidelity that she has betrayed, Hamlet's instructions to his mother about what she should tell Claudius are cut, as is the scene (4.1) in which Gertrude makes her report. Also cut is her anguished aside in act 4, scene 5 ("To my sick soul . . .") and her protection of Claudius from Laertes' wrath later in that scene. Yet here in act 4, scene 5, Gertrude twice rejects Claudius's touch, the second time poised at the base of a flight of stairs as the King laments, "O Gertrude, Gertrude, / When sorrows come, they come not single spies, / But in battalions. . . ." The messenger from act 4, scene 7 appears in a coda to act 4, scene 5, presenting separate letters from Hamlet to the King and to the Queen. As the Queen reads hers, she begins her ascent up one staircase; Claudius, pausing to look at the absorbed Queen, reads his as he ascends another. Olivier has extended the division suggested by Hamlet's separate letters to a potent theatrical image of the division between the pair engendered by Hamlet as Oedipal son.

The effect of Hamlet's lesson in the closet becomes fatally apparent in the final scene when Gertrude knowingly drinks the poisoned wine intended for her son. Starting at Claudius's dropping of the pearl into the drink, she sits in silence, the camera holding her and the hand that holds the cup in its frame. She looks to the cup repeatedly, as though planning her course. Then, before Claudius has a chance to intervene, she drinks. Olivier moves the Queen's toast—"The Queen carouses to thy fortune, Hamlet"—to a position following her apology to Claudius—"I will, my lord; I pray you pardon me"—diminishing further the possibility that Claudius's "Gertrude, do not drink" can come in time. Her farewell to Hamlet, abbreviated to "No, no, the drink, the drink! O my dear Hamlet," spoken gently and with a fragile smile, ignores the exclamation points of modern editions. This Gertrude knows what she has done and sees her own death as a gesture of atonement, of protection, and of love.

As in the Olivier film, the "ponderous marriage bed" that draws Charney's wry objection is a feature of the closet scene in Rodney Bennett's BBC *Hamlet.*[21] There is some difference, however, since the apartment of Claire Bloom's Gertrude is divided into two chambers, her closet and her bedroom, joined by a curtained opening. In the course of the scene, she moves between these spaces, first with Eric Porter as Polonius and then with Derek Jacobi as Hamlet. The movement is suggestive. Gertrude intends to conduct her interview with Hamlet in the closet, yet before long she finds herself being dragged into the bedroom, the more appropriate place for Hamlet's recriminations. Like Olivier's, Jacobi's Hamlet, in attempting to expose his mother's inner part, at the same time exposes his own; his moral disgust is also informed by sexual outrage. Still, despite this similarity and the presence of the marriage bed in both productions, there are important differences in the portrayal of this mother-son pair.

Bloom's Gertrude begins the scene by primping before an unseen mirror, removing her rings and touching her loose auburn hair, while Polonius in the doorway behind her adjures her to be firm with Hamlet. Turning, she sweeps past Polonius, from bedroom into closet, and sits in a chair facing the curtain at stage-right, where Polonius conceals himself at Hamlet's offstage cries of "Mother." Dressed in a copper-colored robe over a white nightdress, she seems composed, though she breathes rapidly. When Hamlet enters, from far upstage, he is disheveled. In contrast to the sober dignity of Olivier's mourning habit, even without his doublet, Jacobi's costume manifests neglect; with an open shirt tucked loosely into rust breeches and one boot drooping to his ankle, his appearance recalls Ophelia's account of his visit to her closet in act 2, scene 1. On this occasion, he carries under his left arm both sword and dagger.

Hamlet's first line cues the camera to begin the sequence of alternate closeups that accompanies the mother-son exchange. Hamlet is swift in his retorts, Gertrude sure but a bit hesitant in hers. At "Have you forgot me?," she stands to face her son, who responds with withering sarcasm: "You are the Queen, your husband's brother's wife." Stung by the insult, she angrily slaps Hamlet on the face and provokes him to a snarling conclusion, "And—would it were not so!—*you* are my mother." Gertrude immediately heads upstage to fetch assistance, but Hamlet crosses her path with his sword, preventing her progress. Backing away fearfully, she cries out, "Thou wilt not murder me?," and calls for help. Her astonished son, who despite his meanacing manner had no such intention, throws down his dagger on the instant and looks with bewilderment at his drawn sword. When he responds to Polonius's voice, he shouts "A rat?" as though he is frightened also and stabs frantically, then furiously thrice into the curtain. As Gertrude screams at him, he stands hugging the curtained form, asking doubtfully, "Is it the King?" There is no note of triumph in the question, as there was in Olivier's. Clearly, both Hamlets are dangerous, but they are so in different ways. While Olivier's Hamlet is actuated by a determined fury, which may overmaster him, Jacobi's acts on impulse and seems completely unpredictable. He responds, literally, to the moment, and if he terrifies Gertrude, he also terrifies himself.

Still hugging the unseen body, Hamlet becomes truculant again in response to Gertrude's condemnation of the deed—"almost as bad, good mother, / As kill a king"—yet he casts his eyes downward instead of studying Gertrude as she meekly repeats the charge. At "Ay, lady, it was my word," he pulls out the sword, stepping back, and when the dying Polonius falls out, he drops the sword and practically sings his surprise, "Thou wretched, rash, in-truu-ding fool. . . ." Then, kneeling over the body, he caps a gentle "farewell" with a contemptuous "too busy," while Gertrude stands behind him whimpering and clasping her hands before her face. So mercurial a Hamlet makes for a very uneasy audience.

To set up the "counterfeit presentment of two brothers," Hamlet backs his mother into the chair, leans over her, and inveighs against her fault. "What have I done?," she demands, and "Ay me, what act . . .?" Both protests are vigorously spoken, with an angry sob, the camera singling her out for the second, but they represent the last vestige of defiance in Gertrude. When Hamlet kneels to show her the images, worn about their necks as in the Olivier production, his voice softens, and Gertrude breaks down, breathing painfully and weeping quietly. Unlike Herlie's Gertrude, this one does not look at the image of her dead husband or at her son; she closes her eyes and turns away toward the camera. Similarly, when Hamlet becomes vicious again, battering her with his words and moving behind her to shove the picture of Claudius in her face, she doesn't want to see it and throws back her head in agony. Finally, as her son rounds on her to display both images—"what judgment / Would step from this to this?"—she wails, leaps up, and runs from him out of the frame. Shouting reproaches, Hamlet pursues her, first as she stands fretfully and next as she paces erratically around the room, cupping her hands over her ears, trying to escape the wounding diatribe. There is no escape for Gertrude. At length, Hamlet catches her by the wrists, staring into her face for "O shame, where is thy blush?," then strides left dragging her to the inner chamber, where he throws her on the bed. The camera follows the pair through the opening, before it switches frames for Gertrude's rough landing.

On her back in the foreground, Hamlet standing over her, the rumpled Gertrude is especially vulnerable now, and Hamlet is intolerably cruel. In a sudden movement, he mounts the bed and his mother, his hips jerking in mock intercourse as he chides her "compulsive ardor." When he falls by her side, he is only apparently exhausted. For, when Gertrude begs that he speak no more and, wracked by sobs, confesses her fault, he resumes in near frenzy his verbal and physical pummeling of the thrashing woman for her corrupt sexuality. At her second plea for mercy—"These words, like daggers, enter in my ears"—he pulls himself up over her head and shouts directly into her ear, "A murderer and a villain." As he continues, he yanks her from behind into a sitting position, her skirts around her thighs, and pinions her arms at her back, her long hair spread over her weeping face and wrenched shoulders. Had Gertrude concluded here that her son was about to kill her, she could not be accused of overreacting. An audience is as relieved as Hamlet is amazed and shaken at the Ghost's intervention.

The figure of the Ghost, framed by the open curtains at the entrance to the bedroom, seems nearly translucent in sharp blue light, shimmering as though in an aura. In this manifestation, played by Patrick Allen, the Ghost's "habit as he lived" is not a nightgown but the armor of the earlier visitations, only now it bears helmet in hand. A strain of music in muted monotone accompanies its appearance. The camera, as it did early in the scene, again alternates shots, switching between the Ghost and the mother-son pair, never showing all three in tableau. Pushing away his mother with a gasp, Hamlet comes to the foot of the bed and drops to his knees to address the apparition. Seated behind him, Gertrude witnesses her son's distress and, frowning in her pity for him, concludes that he is mad. Meanwhile, reacting to Gertrude's concern, the Ghost steps farther into the room to admonish Hamlet to speak to her. Still looking up, eyes fixed on the shade of his father, Hamlet does so quietly and draws an affectionate but incredulous response. Though the camera documents Hamlet's insistent claims with shots of the Ghost looking down at him, Gertrude perceives nothing. Then a curious thing happens. In a long shot, the kneeling Hamlet turns from the Ghost to his mother and, imploring her to see and hear, points to vacancy. It is just enough to create an ambiguity about the Ghost. A moment later, as Gertrude rises to comfort her son and Hamlet turns back to the Ghost with "Why, look you there," the camera shows the steel blue form backing away. When the frantic Hamlet finally identifies "My father," the effect on Gertrude is stunning: she screams in horror, pressing her hand to her mouth, and collapses in tears. A final glimpse of the Ghost's retreating figure leaves Hamlet downstage staring after it and his mother on the floor behind him sobbing hysterically, "This is the very coinage of your brain."

Just as Bloom's convulsive outcry contrasts with Herlie's tender reading of the line, so the reconciliation of mother and son proceeds on rather different terms. It is a seemingly pensive Hamlet who swings on his knees toward the distraught Gertrude to confute the charge of madness. Alerted by the change in tone, she looks up with a quizzical expression. Calmly and deliberately, Hamlet remonstrates with her, slowly closing the distance between them. When he brings his face up to hers, the camera focuses on Gertrude as he counsels her to confess and repent. Looking searchingly into her son's eyes, for the first time, she shows pain and sadly tells him that he has cleft her heart. Then, with Hamlet in closeup, he clenches her hands and, for the first time in the scene, speaks lovingly to his mother, joyfully urging her to throw away the "worser part." The moment ends with the camera on Gertrude, winding her arms around her son and clasping him tightly, her head cradled in the recess of his shoulder.

The reconciliation is interrupted, however, when Hamlet enjoins Gertrude to avoid Claudius's bed. Her expression sobers, and she draws back, looking hurt. Although Hamlet becomes openly persuasive, she looks away, at which he becomes vehement: "And when you are desirous to be bless'd, / I'll blessing beg of you." Ironically, it is Hamlet's reaction, on reentering the closet, to the sight of Polonius that wins her over. Starting, his hand to his mouth, he turns back to his mother, repentent but also resigned to his role as "scourge." Explaining that he "must be cruel only to be kind," he reaches out his hands to her; responding eagerly, she cries out softly when he suddenly withdraws them from her grasp. Returning to the closet to retrieve his sword and dagger, Hamlet pauses as Gertrude follows him in, and, dropping the weapons on the body, he remarks, "One word more, good lady," and sits in the chair. Her "What shall I do?" is unresisting. Indeed, throughout his bitterly snide injunctions to secrecy and his conspiratorial revelation of his plans for Rosencrantz and Guildenstern, she kneels by his side, stroking, embracing, and caressing him. She firmly assures him of her silence and shows distress when reminded of his departure for England. Only at the end of his discourse, when Hamlet seems strangely exhilarated by his uncertain prospects, does her face cloud; but even this may be expressive of tender concern. As Hamlet pronounces his benediction over Polonius, trying to be clever but stifling a sob, and drags the body off, uttering his final good nights, Gertrude stands silently, touching his chair.

At the end of the closet scene, this Gertrude does not know for certain whether her Hamlet "essentially [is] not in madness, / But mad in craft." Still, she has been powerfully moved to accept her marital shame and to reaffirm her maternal love. If emotionally exhausted, she remains morally resolved to abide by the lesson of Hamlet's "mirror" and to act in the interest of her son. Hence, in act 4, scene 1, her voice is strained near weeping yet controlled when she tells the King of Polonius's death at the hand of the maddened Hamlet. When Claudius speaks of his own danger, she is noncommittal, and when he touches her shoulder, she brushes past him to sit in the chair. Although at the end of the scene Claudius appeals to her, "O, come away! / My soul is full of discord and dismay," she remains seated in the place where she sealed her submission to Hamlet.

In the case of this Gertrude, however, the lesson does not hold. While she speaks her guilty aside in act 4, scene 5, later in the scene, when the mad Ophelia enters, Gertrude embraces Claudius and then clings to him as the Messenger reports that the mob is backing the returned Laertes. Her fierce comment on "false Danish dogs" is prelude to her defense of Claudius from Laertes' assault. Though Laertes' weapon is drawn when he enters, she approaches him directly, placing a hand on his shoulder in an effort to pacify him. Claudius must twice tell her to let the furious young man go before she tentatively steps away, to interject firmly that it was not Claudius who killed his father. For Ophelia's second mad scene, Gertrude stands by Claudius again, showing no signs of the separation her son had advised.

Bloom sits on the throne next to Patrick Stewart in the final scene, holding onto his arm as Hamlet and Laertes duel. When Claudius drops the poisoned pearl into the cup, her face shows no suspicion. It is in the spirit of a toast that she picks up the cup and drinks, wanting to celebrate the prowess of her son, and it is in this same spirit that she ignores as inconsequential Claudius's instruction not to drink. Having wiped Hamlet's face, she even offers the cup to him, although he refuses it. In fact, this Claudius might have made a gesture to save his Queen; instead, he stands idly by. Only when the drugged Queen slumps to the floor does she realize that the drink was poisoned. She leaves this life clinging to Hamlet, aware of the treachery of her husband, but unreformed.

In the Olivier production, Gertrude seems incapable of the perfidy attached to the killing of a king. Hamlet may not have been far from the truth when he cynically told Horatio in act 1, scene 2 that it was "thrift" that seduced his mother into a hasty remarriage. This Gertrude is a weak, yielding woman who, as the consequence of Hamlet's traumatizing counsel in the closet, alters the poor judgment that allowed her to move with apparent ease from a Hyperion to a satyr. Though her final fatal tribute to Hamlet risks sentimentality, it completes the sequence of theatrical images—the intimate closet scene, the separate letters, the drinking of the poisoned cup—that together endorse the psychological paradigm of a morally unstructured woman whose Oedipal love for her son reconstructs her. For this Gertrude, Malcolm's epitaph for Cawdor might serve: "Nothing in his life / Became him like the leaving it."

The BBC Gertrude, by contrast, might well have assented to the killing of a king, not because she was in the habit of initiating evil but because, with Edmund in *King Lear*, she believed "that men / Are as the time is." The chief quality of this Gertrude is malleability: she adjusts readily to circumstance, assuming the virtue or the vice appropriate to the occasion. In the Queen's closet, Gertrude is emotionally involved in her son's anguish and in the recognition of her sin. But virtue readily abandoned is cheaply earned. With Hamlet away from court, Gertrude's fawning on Claudius continues. Amid the carnage of the final scene, her death, like Edmund's, is "but a trifle here."

Notes

1. Maurice Charney, "*Hamlet* without Words," in *Shakespeare's More Than Words Can Witness: Essays on Visual and Nonverbal Enactment in the Plays*, ed. Sidney Homan (Lewisburg, Pa.: Bucknell University Press, 1980), p. 33.

2. Quotations are from *The Complete Works of Shakespeare*, 3d ed., ed. David Bevington (Glenview, Ill.: Scott, Foresman, 1980).

3. A. C. Bradley, *Shakespearean Tragedy: Lectures on Hamlet, Othello, King Lear, Macbeth* (London: Macmillan, 1929), p. 138.

4. J. Dover Wilson, *What Happens in Hamlet*, 3d ed. (Cambridge: At the University Press, 1960), p. 252.

5. See Bradley, *Shakespearean Tragedy*, pp. 139–40; Dover Wilson, *What Happens*, pp. 353–55; W. W. Greg, "Hamlet's Hallucination," *Modern Language Review*, 12 (1917): 393–421.

6. Harley Granville-Barker, *Prefaces to Shakespeare: Hamlet* (Princeton: Princeton University Press, 1946), p. 230.

7. Quotations from the first quarto (referred to as Q1) are from *Shakespeare's Plays in Quarto: A Facsimile Edition of Copies Primarily from the Henry E. Huntington Library*, ed. Michael J. B. Allen and Kenneth Muir (Berkeley: University of California Press, 1981). Quotations from the first folio (referred to as F) are from *The First Folio of Shakespeare: The Norton Facsimile*, ed. Charlton Hinman (New York: Norton, 1968).

8. It is worth noting that in Q1 the Ghost omits the epithet "adulterate" from its imprecation and Hamlet expresses contempt only for Claudius: "Yes, yes, by heaven, a damnd pernitious villaine, / Murderous, bawdy, smiling damned villaine" (p. 588). The implication that Q1 absolves Claudius and Gertrude of the blot of adultery is contravened, however, by Claudius's admission in the prayer scene (3.3) of "the adulterous fault I have committed" (p. 601).

9. Dover Wilson, *What Happens*, p. 248.

10. Harold Jenkins, ed., *The Arden Shakespeare: Hamlet* (London: Methuen, 1982), p. 320n. Jenkins invites comparison with the Player Queen's lines: "A second time I kill my husband dead, / When second husband kisses me in bed" (3.2.182–83).

11. Charney, in "*Hamlet* without Words," is amused by the prospect of staging the biological feature of the pilomotor response, the same reaction predicted by the Ghost in act 1, scene 5, when it warns Hamlet that a description of its postdeath experiences would make part his "knotted and combined locks," causing "each particular hair to stand on end." Charney notes that the one literal rendering, reported by Arthur Colby Sprague (*Shakespeare and the*

Actors: The Stage Business in His Plays (1660–1905) [Cambridge: Harvard University Press, 1944], p. 382), was Garrick's: the famous eighteenth-century actor accomplished the effect with a mechnical wig (pp. 40–41).

12. Alan C. Dessen, *Elizabethan Drama and the Viewer's Eye* (Chapel Hill: University of North Carolina Press, 1977), p. 163.

13. Ibid., p. 98.

14. Ibid., p. 100.

15. *Hamlet* (1948), produced and directed by Laurence Olivier. With Laurence Olivier (Hamlet), Basil Sydney (Claudius), Eileen Herlie (Gertrude), Jean Simmons (Ophelia), Felix Aylmer (Polonius), Terence Morgan (Laertes), Norman Wooland (Horatio), Peter Cushing (Osric), Anthony Quayle (Marcellus), Esmond Knight (Bernardo), John Laurie (Francisco), Harcourt Williams (First Player), Patrick Troughton (Second Player), Tony Tarver (Third Player), Stanley Holloway (Gravedigger), Russel Thorndike (Priest).

16. Laurence Olivier, *Confessions of an Actor: An Autobiography* (New York: Penguin, 1984), p. 151.

17. Ibid., p. 183.

18. Ernest Jones, *Hamlet and Oedipus* (Garden City, N.Y.: Doubleday, 1949).

19. Olivier, *Confessions*, p. 102.

20. Frederic Wertham, "The Matricidal Impulse: Critique of Freud's Interpretation of Hamlet," *Journal of Criminal Psychopathology* (April 1944): 455–64.

21. *Hamlet* (1980), produced by Cedric Messina, directed by Rodney Bennett. With Derek Jacobi (Hamlet), Claire Bloom (Gertrude), Eric Porter (Polonius), Patrick Stewart (Claudius), Patrick Allen (Ghost), Emrys James (First Player), Lalla Ward (Ophelia), Robert Swann (Horatio), David Robb (Laertes), Christopher Baines (Francisco), Niall Padden (Bernardo), Paul Humpoletz (Marcellus), John Humphry (Voltemand), John Sterland (Cornelius), Raymond Mason (Reynaldo), Jonathan Hyde (Rosencrantz), Geoffrey Bateman (Guildenstern), Jason Kemp (Second Player), Geoffrey Beevers (Third Player), Bill Homewood (Prologue and Mime King), Peter Richards (Mime Queen), Terence McGinity (Mime Murderer), Peter Burroughs, Styart Fell (Other Players), Ian Charleson (Fortinbras), Dan Meaden (Norwegian Captain), Iain Blair (Sailor), Reginald Jessup (Messenger), Tim Wylton (First Gravedigger), Peter Benson (Second Gravedigger), Michael Poole (Priest), Peter Gale (Osric), David Henry (English Ambassador).

Part III
The Classroom

10

Intentions, Options, and Greatness: An Example from *A Midsummer Night's Dream*

PHILIP C. McGUIRE

PEOPLE COME TO SHAKESPEARE'S PLAYS—WHETHER VIEWING THEM IN PERformance, reading them in private, or studying them in courses—either convinced of their greatness or willing to be convinced. For those who teach (as well as those who perform) the plays that is a considerable advantage, but built into it are significant liabilities. Our ingrained tendency is to equate greatness with permanence, with fixity, with immutability. In effect, we reflexively attribute to Shakespeare's plays a capacity to withstand time and change equivalent to that his sonnets claim for themselves—as when the speaker of Sonnet 55 insists, "Not marble nor the gilded monuments / Of princes shall outlive this pow'rful rime. . . ."[1]

One consequence of such a conception of greatness is that we think of Shakespeare's plays as works that he himself completed in all important detail and thus fixed in permanence, forever monolithically impervious to the vicissitudes of time. A further consequence is that we routinely expect, perhaps even demand, that those who teach, those who study, and especially those who perform Shakespeare's plays will honor and conform to Shakespeare's intentions as manifested in the words he wrote. I'd like to plumb a moment of silence that occurs within *A Midsummer Night's Dream* in order to begin to show the limitations of such patterns of thinking and to suggest the need for an alternative conception of greatness that, because it acknowledges the play's capacity to change in and with time, is, I believe, more attuned to the collective and contingent character of drama.

In act 4, scene 1, Duke Th seus and his hunting party come upon the four young lovers sleeping on the forest ground after their baffling experiences of the night. Lysander, "Half sleep, half waking" (4.1.146), begins to explain that he and Hermia were fleeing "the peril of the Athenian law" (l. 152) that sentences Hermia to death or to a life of perpetual chastity if she persists in refusing to marry the man her father has chosen to be her husband. Hermia's father, Egeus, interrupts Lysander, shrilly calling upon Theseus to apply the law in its full rigor: "Enough, enough, my lord! You have enough. / I beg the law, the law, upon his head" (ll. 153–54).

The Duke to whom Egeus addresses his appeal is the very man who had earlier cautioned Hermia that "the law of Athens" is something "Which by no means we may extenuate" (1.1.119–20). Now, however, after hearing Demetrius, Egeus's choice to be Hermia's husband, declare that his love for Hermia has "melted" (4.1.165) away, Theseus proceeds to set aside the very law upholding an Athenian father's right to "dispose" (1.1.42) of his daughter that Theseus had earlier declared himself powerless to "extenuate." The Duke announces that he will not only allow the marriage between Hermia and Lysander but will also endorse it by combining their wedding with his to Hippolyta:

> Egeus, I will overbear your will,
> For in the temple, by and by, with us,
> These couples shall eternally be knit. . . .
>
> (4.1.178–80)

How does Egeus respond to Theseus's decision? In both the Quarto of 1600 and the Folio of 1623—the two versions of *A Midsummer Night's Dream* that are considered authoritative[2]—Egeus says nothing in reply to Theseus's words setting aside not only his "will" but also the Athenian law that enshrines his right as an Athenian father to exercise that will. The agreement between Quarto and Folio suggests that Egeus's silence is not an accident or oversight.

The standard tactic for determining the meanings and effects generated by a specific moment in a play by Shakespeare is to scrutinize the words of the play in order to determine his intentions. When we turn to the words of the Quarto and the Folio, however, we discover that neither gives us information of the caliber we need to clarify Egeus's silence. Because both the Quarto and the Folio impose silence upon Egeus after Theseus overbears his will, there are no words spoken by Egeus for us to scrutinize. Both the Quarto and the Folio provide stage directions; however, those directions not only fail to clarify Egeus's silence but also reveal just how little what other characters say illuminates his silence.

The Folio specifically requires that Egeus enter with Theseus: "*Enter Theseus, Egeus, Hippolita, and all his traine*."[2] The stage direction for the exit to be made after Theseus overrules Egeus is less precise: "*Exit Duke and Lords*." Note that there is no specific mention of Egeus. Egeus could be one those "*Lords*" who exit with Theseus—as happened in Elijah Moshinsky's 1981 production that was part of the BBC-TV/Times-Life series entitled "The Shakespeare Plays." In such a case, Egeus remains a member of Theseus's entourage and of Athenian society, whether or not he accepts his daughter's marriage to Lysander. However, nothing in the Folio *requires* that Egeus depart with Theseus. By first specifically including Egeus among those who enter with Theseus and by then not specifically listing him as one of those who exit with Theseus, the Folio allows the possibility—enacted in Peter Brook's famous production of the early 1970s—that Egeus makes an exit separate from Theseus and those who go with him. Such an exit, which—I want to emphasize—the Folio permits but does not mandate, would establish that Egeus's response to Theseus's exercise of ducal authority is to withdraw from Athens.

The corresponding stage directions in the Quarto are, if anything, open to possibilities even more diverse. The Quarto reads: "*Enter* Theseus *and all his traine*"—a phrasing that does not single out Egeus and Hippolyta as the Folio does. For the exit the Quarto provides no stage directions beyond what is implicit in Theseus's final words in the scene: "Away, with us, to *Athens*. Three and three, / Weele holde a feast, in great solemnitie. Come *Hyppolita*." As stage directions, Theseus's words are inconclusive. "Away, with us, to *Athens*," for example, may be delivered as words of reassurance spoken to Egeus—an effort to include him that Egeus may either accept or refuse. Spoken sternly, the same words could be an order from the Duke to Egeus, a command that Egeus may or may not obey. Theseus need not address those words specifically to Egeus, however. Spoken to Hermia after Egeus has already departed in anger, they could be Theseus's effort to ease whatever anguish Hermia feels at the loss of her embittered father: "Away, with US[3], to *Athens*." In such a context, "Three and three" can function as a phrase that implies who is (and who is not) included among the "us" who will return to Athens to participate in a "feast" to be held "in great solemnitie." Thus, like the Folio, the Quarto allows the option that Egeus exits with Theseus and his "*traine*" but does not require it. It is equally true, however, that, again like the Folio, the Quarto does not require that Egeus exit apart from them either.

Should we try to clarify the meanings and effects of Egeus's silence in act 4 by looking at the wedding festivities of act 5, we come upon differences between the Quarto and the Folio that compound rather than reduce our uncertainties.[4] The Folio, which begins act 5 with the stage direction "*Enter Theseus, Hippolita, Egeus and his Lords*," specifies that Egeus is present at the nuptial festivities. The corresponding stage direction in the Quarto is significantly different: "*Enter* Theseus,

Hyppolita, *and* Philostrate." There is no specific identification of Egeus as there is in the Folio, and there is no term equivalent to the "*Lords*" of the Folio that could be taken to include Egeus.

Having Egeus absent from festivities that (in part) celebrate his daughter's wedding is fully compatible with taking Egeus's silence when he is last onstage as a refusal to accept the marriage between Hermia and Lysander. The Quarto, then, offers justification for a production such as Brook's in which Egeus, embittered at Theseus's decision to "overbear" his will, withdraws from Athenian society rather than countenance his daughter's marriage to Lysander.

Egeus's absence from the wedding festivities poses what might be called a dramaturgical problem: what means does Shakespeare provide to give that absence theatrical impact, to make it register on those watching a performance? One way to appreciate the problem is to try to remember whether Egeus was absent from the wedding festivities in the last performance of *A Midsummer Night's Dream* you saw. There are no explicit references to the absent Egeus in act 5 of the Quarto. Twice, however, what a character says might refer to Egeus. Early in act 5, Theseus asks, "Where is our usuall manager / Of mirth?" The possibility that Egeus is the *usual* manager of mirth cannot be ruled out conclusively, but even if Theseus's question does refer to the absent Egeus, a reference so oblique is unlikely to register with much force on a theater audience. A second possible reference to the absent father comes after the end of the play-within-the play, when Snug, stepping out of his role as Lion, explains why Wall is not one of those "left to bury the dead." "No, I assure you," he tells Demetrius and others in the Athenian audience, "the wall is downe, that parted their fathers." Again, however, if this is a reference to Egeus, it is indirect and its theatrical impact is questionable.

Words, however, are not the only means at a dramatist's disposal. Doubling Egeus with another character is a tactic available to Shakespeare that would use the visual dimension of drama in order to draw attention to Egeus's absence.[5] One option that the Quarto permits is to double Egeus and Philostrate, which would create a theatrical situation in which seeing Philostrate, whom Theseus calls upon to provide the wedding entertainment, would make the audience conscious that Egeus has chosen to absent himself from his daughter's wedding and the ensuing merriment. Another option is the one enacted in Brook's production: to double Egeus and Peter Quince. The presence during act 5 of the novice director struggling to bring theatrical order out of the impulses and imaginings of the rude mechanicals was a visual reminder of the absent father who had tried to make his daughter's fancy and sexual energy fit his will. Whomever Egeus is doubled with, the visual parallels generated by the doubling would enhance the theatrical effectiveness of what are otherwise very indirect verbal references to him in act 5 of the Quarto.

The Folio, in sharp contrast to the Quarto, not only requires that Egeus be present during act 5 but also provides a means for directing attention to him by giving him words to speak that in the Quarto are assigned to Philostrate.[6] For example, the Folio has Egeus, rather than Philostrate, explain how the play of Pyramus and Thisby can be both "tragicall" and "merrie" as well as "tedious" and "breefe."

By requiring the presence of Egeus,[7] the Folio rules out the possibility that his response after Theseus overrides his will is to withdraw *permanently* from Athens. Even if the silent Egeus stalks off along when he exits in act 4, the Folio does not allow his isolation to endure. It requires that he be present and speak in act 5 and thereby heightens the possibility that he is, or comes to be, fully accepting of the marriage between Hermia and Lysander—a possibility more difficult to envision if, as the Quarto allows, Egeus is absent from the festivities. In the Folio it is Egeus, rather than Philostrate, who provides the list of available entertainments. "There," he tells Theseus, "is a breefe how many sports are rife [*sic*]: / Make choise of which your Highnesse will see first." The Folio also has Egeus reveal that watching a rehearsal of "Pyramus and Thisby" made "mine eyes water: / But more merrie teares, the passion of loud laughter / Never shed."

Although act 5 of the Folio allows us to think of Egeus as a father now genuinely pleased by his daughter's marriage, it does not rule out at least one other option. The first words Egeus is given to speak in act 5 of the Folio explicitly acknowledge Theseus's power and authority. "Heere mighty *Theseus*," Egeus says in response to the ducal command to "Call *Egeus*." And the actor playing Egeus can deliver Egeus's words about his eyes watering with "merrie teares" so that they register the fact that Egeus has also recently shed tears that were not merry. Note, too, that while "more" can serve as an adverb of comparison, it can equally well function as an adjective meaning "additional." When it does, the sentence of which it is a part says that Egeus had not shed any *merry* tears since the rehearsal. Another point worth noting is that Theseus calls upon Egeus to "Say" what entertainment is available to "beguile / The lazie time," but Theseus never does "Say" what he is called upon to say. Instead he presents "a breefe," and it is Lysander, not Egeus, who actually *says* what "sports" are available.[8]

Perhaps the most telling evidence for the possibility that Egeus's presence at the nuptial festivities signifies no more than obedience to his "mighty" duke is that nothing he says during act 5 is addressed to his daughter or to her new husband. A point of equal importance is that neither Hermia nor Lysander speaks to Egeus.[9] Thus, Egeus's acts of speaking during act 5 of the Folio may help to establish and draw attention to the silence that persists between him on the one hand and his daughter and her husband on the other. Consequently, even though the Folio requires the presence in act 5 of an Egeus who is no longer silent, we remain uncertain whether he participates in the festivities as a jubilant father or as a dutiful courtier.

Thus, we find ourselves in a situation in which neither the Quarto nor the Folio provides information that enables us to decide how Shakespeare wanted Egeus to respond to Theseus's decision authorizing Hermia's marriage to Lysander and (in the Folio) to the marriage itself once it has been performed. Even if we could convince ourselves that we had divined Shakespeare's intentions, the differences between the Quarto and the Folio suggest that those intentions did not remain fixed and constant but were fluid and changing. The Folio may be a revision of the Quarto, but if it is, the revising process was not one that worked toward clearer definition and greater specificity of intention. The aim of any revision that may have occured seems to have been to give Egeus's response to Hermia's wedding—whatever that response is—greater theatrical effectiveness by requiring that, after his silence in act 4, he be present and speak during act 5.[10]

We can, of course, respond to the difficulties posed by Egeus's silence and the differences between the Quarto and the Folio by dismissing them as trivial. Egeus is a minor character, such a line of reasoning would run, and his response to the wedding that Theseus declares will take place is a peripheral matter of no major significance.

One way to establish the inadequacy of such reasoning is to examine the process of reincorporation with which *A Midsummer Night's Dream* concludes.[11] Lysander and Hermia enter the woods as the result of a deliberate decision to withdraw from Athens. Once in the woods, they, as well as Helena and Demetrius, undergo experiences that ultimately permit the four young lovers to pair off as male and female: each "Jill" ends up with a "Jack," When Theseus overrules Egeus and sanctions Hermia's marriage to Lysander, he makes possible the reincorporation of Lysander and Hermia into an Athens from which they had fled. The postnuptial festivities of act 5, which is set in Athens, make manifest that reincorporation, but its precise nature and quality vary according to how Egeus responds to his daughter's marriage.

If Egeus's silence and (in the Quarto) his absence from the wedding celebrations signify his permanent withdrawal from Athens, *A Midsummer Night's Dream* is a play in which marriage and the movement toward it occasion an irreparable break between father and daughter. The family composed of father and daughter fragments as the more inclusive social unit of the city accepts and validates the formation of a new family through marriage. The beginning of the process of reincorporation triggers Egeus's withdrawal. Athens loses a citizen in the process of acquiring a new couple whose (potential) offspring will be part of the next generation of Athenians. Renewal of the city becomes possible through a process of change that exacts a lasting cost.

The reincorporation that occurs is radically different, however, if Egeus and Hermia are reconciled and he wholeheartedly accepts her marriage. In such a case, the family unit into which Hermia was born survives her entry into the marital family that she and Lysander form. The social unit of the family—in both its natal and its marital embodiments—and the social unit of the city emerge from the process of reincorporation intact and regenerated.

Should Egeus, withholding heartfelt acceptance of Hermia's marriage, do no more than obediently submit to Theseus's ducal power, a third variety of reincorporation takes place. The continuing estrangement of father and daughter testifies to the shattering of the natal family, but the city itself remains capable of including both the embittered but dutiful father and the marital family that Hermia's union with Lysander brings into being. Egeus loses Hermia, and Hermia loses Egeus, but Athens loses no one. The city itself benefits as the result of a process that sees one family break apart even as a new family that will help to ensure the city's future comes into existence.[12]

Egeus's response to Theseus's decision to "overbear" his will and his response (in the Folio) to the fact of Hermia's marriage are not peripheral details but essential components of the play's vision, yet the very words mandating that such responses must occur do not give us information adequate to determine what Shakespeare wanted them to be. In cases such as this one, the notion of obedience to Shakespeare's intentions is profoundly inadequate. Perhaps because of Shakespeare's own dramaturgical design, perhaps because of the accidents of textual transmission, the Quarto and the Folio establish a situation in which those who perform *A Midsummer Night's Dream* are empowered to decide what Egeus's responses will be. They are called upon to endow the play with details that Shakespeare's words establish are crucial but do not themselves furnish. Each time actors and directors do, they in effect bring to fulfillment a process of creation that Shakespeare initiated but did not himself complete. Thus, they become more than agents implementing Shakespeare's intentions; they become virtual cocreators with him, and *A Midsummer Night's Dream* becomes their play as well as his.

The only way to know with precision what Egeus's responses are is to see the play performed. From production to production, perhaps even from performance to performance, those responses will vary—I would even say must and should vary. As they do, the play reveals itself to be an entity capable of changing in essential ways yet retaining its identity. That capability—far more than the immutability we customarily attribute to Shakespeare's dramatic works—is a fundamental component of the greatness of the play and of his greatness as a dramatist. It is what makes his plays *live* rather than merely recur.

In baseball, a triple play is a rarity, but the question of Egeus's silence and (in the Folio) his response to Hermia's marriage demonstrates why the triple play referrred to in the title of this volume is one that we who are privileged to teach Shakespeare's plays must strive to make routinely. We need to make our students aware of the essential function of actors and directors, of how the process of performance completes the play. We also need to challenge the myth of immutability by calling upon our students to ponder such matters as how variations between Quarto and Folio versions of a play establish different, sometimes conflicting, yet equally valid options for performance. Above all, we need to affirm that the greatness of Shakespeare's plays flows from their capacity to change. Each time we do not try to make that triple play, we distort Shakespeare's plays and improverish ourselves and our students.

Notes

1. All quotations from Shakespeare's works that are not from either a Quarto or a Folio version are according to William Shakespeare, *The Complete Works*, Pelican text rev., gen ed. Alfred Harbage (New York: Viking Press, 1977).

2. Quotations from the Folio follow *The Norton Facsimile: The First Folio of Shakespeare*, ed. Charlton Hinman (New York: Norton, 1968; London: Paul Hamlyn, 1968). Quotations from the Quarto of 1600 follow *Shakespeare's Plays in Quarto: A Facsimile Edition of Copies Primarily from the Henry E. Huntington Library*, ed. Michael J. B. Allen and Kenneth Muir (Berkeley and Los Angeles: University of California Press, 1981). A second quarto of *A Midsummer Night's Dream* was printed in 1619 with the false date of 1600 on the title page. The second Quarto was based on the first and therefore has no independent authority. When quoting, I have changed the Renaissance long "s" to modern "s" and normalized u/v and i/j.

3. Rather than italicize words that I emphasize when quoting from either the Quarto or the Folio, I have resorted to capitalizing all letters in them. This enables me to preserve the italicization present in the Folio and Quarto. It should be noted, however, that we cannot be certain that in Shakespeare's time italiciation was an indication of emphasis.

4. Barbara Hodgdon's essay "Gaining a Father: The Role of Egeus in the Quarto and Folio," *Review of English Studies* n.s. 38 (1986): 534–42, has enriched my understanding of Egeus's role in act 5 of the Folio.

5. For a discussion of doubling in various plays by Shakespeare, including *A Midsummer Night's Dream*, see Stephen Booth's "Speculations on Doubling

in Shakespeare's Plays," in *Shakespeare: The Theatrical Dimension*, ed. Philip C. McGuire and David A. Samuelson (New York: AMS Press, 1979), pp. 103–31. An expanded version of that essay was published as appendix 2 of Booth's book *"King Lear," "Macbeth," Indefinition, and Tragedy* (New Haven: Yale University Press, 1983), pp. 129–55.

6. It is important to note that the Folio does not give all of Philostrate's lines to Egeus. In the Folio, as in the Quarto, it is Philostrate who tries to persuade Theseus to reverse his selection of the play of Pyramus and Thisby as the nuptial entertainment: "No, my noble Lord, it is not for you. I have heard / It over, and it is nothing, nothing in the world. . . ." It is conceivable that the lines remain Philostrate's in the Folio only because someone was not thorough in changing the speech heading "Philostrate" in the Quarto to "Egeus" in the Folio. There is, however, no way to prove or disprove such a conjecture, but before we accept it, should we not at least consider the equally plausible possibility that there has been no carelessness and proceed to ponder the implications of having both Egeus and Philostrate present during act 5? Consider, for example, the sequence of questions Theseus asks to learn what entertainment is available:

> Come now, what maskes, what dances shall we have
> To weare away this long age of three houres,
> Between our after supper, and bed-time?
> Where is our usuall manager of mirth?
> What Revels are in hand? Is there no play,
> To ease the anguish of a torturing houre?
> Call Egeus.

If Philostrate is present, then the possibility exists that he steps forward when Theseus asks, "Where is our usuall manager of mirth." His silence in response to the questions Theseus then puts to him may indicate that he suggests by an appropriate gesture that Egeus is the one to answer such questions. In such a context, the "you" in the question (or command) Theseus then directs to Egeus takes on particular weight, especially if Egeus's silence in act 4 indicated his displeasure: "Say, what abridgement have YOU [as disgruntled father of one of these brides] for this evening?" In effect, by deferring to Egeus and thus giving him an opportunity to have a role in managing the evening's mirth, Philostrate can function as an agent of his inclusion (on whatever terms) in the festivites.

7. One effect of Egeus's presence from the start of act 5 is that it gives Theseus's speech about "The Lunaticke, the Lover, and the Poet" a potential theatrical impact in the Folio that it does not have in the Quarto. The Folio establishes the opportunity for an audience to watch Egeus's reaction as he hears Theseus declare that he "never may believe" the four young lovers' account of their experiences during the night in the woods. From those experiences emerged the erotic pairings that prompted Theseus to "overbear" Egeus's will.

8. Lysander's reading of the "breefe" is presented as a dialogue in which Theseus responds to each entertainment after Lysander describes it. The corresponding passage in the Quarto is a single speech by Theseus in which he both reads the "breefe" and responds to each entertainment. By having Lysander read the "breefe," the Folio allows for several options, each of which establishes a different relationship between Hermia's father and her husband. Egeus may give the "breefe" to Lysander, in effect allowing his son-in-law to speak for him;

Egeus could give the "breefe" to Theseus, who in turn could give it to Lysander, thus indicating his new status; Lysander could take the "breefe" from Egeus, and by so doing substitute his voice for Egeus's. A fourth option is that Egeus does not have the "breefe" in his hand but points to it "there," and Lysander, by picking it up and reading it, fulfills a role Egeus chooses not to carry out.

9. In fact, Hermia, like Helena, says nothing at all during act 5. In both the Quarto and the Folio we have a situation in which two of the brides remain silent throughout festivities celebrating their weddings. Hermia's silence is particularly intriguing when set against her insistence on speaking at other moments in the play. In act 1, for example, she first asks Theseus's pardon, then "made bold" by "I know not" "what power," she goes on "In such presence here to plead my thoughts" (11.59, 61). The silence of Hermia and Helena accentuates the fact that Hippolyta, who remained silent during Hermia's trial in act 1, is the only bride who does speak during the festivities. For a discussion of Hippolyta's silence in act 1, see my *Speechless Dialect: Shakespeare's Open Silences* (Berkeley and Los Angeles: University of California Press, 1985), pp. 1–18.

10. In "Gaining a Father . . .," Barbara Hodgdon points out that by requiring Egeus's presence in act 5, the Folio raises the issue of when and how he makes his last exit. She perceptively describes several options, and the point I wish to emphasize is that his final exit, whenever and however it is made, is—like his exit in act 4—made in silence and is therefore open to various, even conflicting alternatives.

11. As Lynda E. Boose explains in her excellent "The Father and the Bride in Shakespeare," *PMLA* 97 (1982): 325, separation, transition, and reincorporation are the three phases that the anthropologist Arnold van Gennep has identified as the components of all rites of passage. Boose goes on to comment: "Hence in *A Midsummer Night's Dream*, a play centered on marriage, the intransigent father Egeus, supported by the king-father figure Theseus, poses a threat that must be converted to a blessing to ensure the comic solution" (327). While it is clear that Theseus's opposition is "converted to a blessing," it is by no means certain that Egeus's intransigence is similarly converted.

12. Another way of establishing the importance of Egeus is by reference to the issue of authority. At the beginning of the play, the authority of the father and the authority of the duke are in perfect alignment. Egeus's response to Theseus's decision to "overbear" his will and (in the Folio) his response to Hermia's marriage will determine whether that alignment endures or breaks. For a discussion of the issue of authority in the play, see Leonard Tennenhouse, "Strategies of State and Political Plays: *A Midsummer Night's Dream*, *Henry IV*, *Henry V*, *Henry VIII*," in *Political Shakespeare: New Essays in Cultural Materialism*, ed. Jonathan Dollimore and Alan Sinfield (Ithaca: Cornell University Press, 1985) pp. 109–28.

11

Actualizing the Metaphor: Image and Act in *Twelfth Night* and *King Lear*

BARBARA ROSEN

IN A 1985 LECTURE AT THE UNIVERSITY OF CONNECTICUT ON "THE POETICAL Character of *Twelfth Night*" Professor Geoffrey Hartman contended that Shakespeare's drama is distinguished from that of other playwrights by the continuous unfolding of a rhetoric full of options, in which the figures are at any moment open to change and fresh interpretation. In the case of comedy, he suggested, the skein of dialogue unwinds as a rhetoric almost unaffected by connection with the role of the actor who speaks it; the language has the negative capability that Keats ascribed to the poet.

Part of the mysteriousness of Shakespeare's dialogue is without doubt due to the loss of understanding of his topical references; for instance, the jokes about Malvolio's "possession" and the Fool's disguise as a Puritan preacher who comes to visit him in jail are much clearer when we recognize allusions to the case of the possessed Starkey children and Darrell, their would-be exorcist.[1] But the recognition that the mysteries may have an anchor in fact does not contradict a sense of connotations free-floating in the language, as well as arising from subconscious associations in the mind of the poet or the viewer.

Yet certainly Professor Hartman, like many other modern critics, underestimates the visual impact that is crucial to drama. The words are seen to be spoken onstage by a human being in a certain posture, with a certain modulation guided by either an actor's sense of his character or fidelity to a director's controlling concept of sound and gesture for the play as a whole. The actor can scarcely avoid underscoring some of the implications of the language by his speech or movement, however much he may wish to leave Shakespeare free; and there are innumerable occasions when the figurative language comes to a full close in a visual statement.

Part of the difficulty of teaching Shakespeare is to teach students to be sensitive to the possibility of visual comment on the spoken word, and to the open-ended nature of performance. Students seldom realize that any stage or screen production presents only one set of choices. It is fairly easy to make people aware of the cues for staging, movement, and modern lighting that are built into Shakespeare's lines, but the translation of metaphor or simile to action is not so simple. At Stratford-on-Avon in England I once saw Orsino presented with a hunting dog when he spoke of "my desires, like fell and cruel hounds";[2] this is literalizing, something quite different and capable of its own ironies. More often, in Shakespeare's plays, literal images take on by repetition or usage metaphoric connotations, which remain associated with the image when it is actualized on stage.

For example: Malvolio's dreams of ambition are summed up by himself and others in descriptions of clothing. In his first unprompted dreams of being "Count Malvolio" (2.5.35) he skips over the encounter on the daybed which has left Olivia "sleeping" (49), and pictures himself wearing a gold-embroidered velvet gown instead of a dark suit, a rich jewel instead of his steward's chain; in such rich garb he will exercise control over his servants and his cousin Toby. Still, these clothes show no essential change in Malvolio's dignified self-image; they do not draw attention to body.

Maria, Toby, Andrew, and the Fool have already devised and planned to thrust upon him a much cruder metaphor of his misplaced and ambitious love; they or he refer four times[3] to Malvolio clad in cross-gartered yellow stockings and smiling, before he finally appears onstage in the costume, his behavior disastrously adapted to its sexual connotations and to Olivia's supposed praise of his leg (an imaginary event that he eagerly adopts as fact).

Both sets of clothing image of course play off against the clothes that Malvolio is actually wearing. We do not know what these are, as Shakespeare obviously assumed that everyone knew what the valued steward of a great house would wear. But references to Malvolio as "sad and civil/ And suits well for a servant with my fortunes" (3.4.4–5), and the suggestion that "sometimes he is a kind of puritan" (2.3.140) do seem to indicate dark clothes. Most directors show him dressed in the self-effacing but well-cut garb of an important employee who is not required to wear livery, yet shows his knowledge of "place" by restrained rather than fashionable sartorial taste. Paradoxically, this restraint in garment and behavior is much more in accord with true upper-class fashion of the time than the garb he is led to be believe that Olivia favors.

Geoffrey Squire and Jane Ashelford[4] have shown that during the middle years of the sixteenth century there was a remarkable proliferation of bizarre and colorful leg fashions for men, all designed to draw attention to that area of the body. Doublets, jerkins, and trunk-hose stiffened at times into geometric forms, codpieces were hidden, but extraordinary care was devoted to the tight, smooth fit of wrinkle-free hose. Fully displayed and well-shaped male legs became a prime focus of sexual attention, and this attention was only gradually diverted as other areas of male costume became more body-conscious.

By the late 1590s, brilliant colors and violent contrasts were giving way to subtle shades and a more natural, coordinated look. In 1602, when John Manningham records a production of *Twelfth Night*, the elegant Sir Walter Raleigh was painted in a costume of brown, buff, silver, and white.[5] Four years earlier, I. Oliver painted the three Browne brothers and their page; the young brothers wear black, easily cut, with soft lace collars focusing attention on the face, and subdued matching stockings and shoes. Their page's clothes, doubtless cast-offs, are dated—a stiff and gaudy doublet with differently colored trunk-hose, canions, and netherstocks of a different color again.[6] Yellow, always a different color to match (and perhaps partly for that reason the color of jealousy), had had its moment of high fashion and passed; by 1600 it was, as the Fool said of Malvolio's would-be trendy word "element," already "overworn" (3.1.58–60). Like a décolleté red gown among little black dresses, it would have been perceived as vulgarly sexual and self-assertive.

Cross-gartering did not mean what we usually see presented—ankle to knee criss-crossing, a fashion confined to peasants who wore baggy trousers or straw leggings for warmth—but a garter starting under the knee in front, crossing behind the knee and fastening above it. At the date of the play, when the all-important garters maintaining the fit were often soft silk scarves, tied with apparent carelessness, the suggestion of cross-gartering was that the wearer had bought cheap hose and lacked confidence in their fit (like today's type who wears both belt and suspenders). So the garb suggested by Maria and accepted with such self-deluding joy is a lethal combination of dated sexual signal, self-asssertion, and general insecurity. Malvolio's gauchely self-conscious comment—"This does make some obstruction in the blood, this cross-gartering" (3.4.19–20)— is rich in suggestions of the ill fit of his ambition. The smiling, hand-kissing, and elephantine flirtation put on with the costume show that it is, astoundingly, a truer reflection of Malvolio's parvenu self than the chosen dignity of the long robe. Malvolio has been cruelly lured from the reserve proper to a gentleman as well as the servant's practiced muting of personality; the clothing metaphor is activated onstage and the absolute, physical impossibility of the dream is made clear.

In tragedy, the actualization of images in the rhetoric of a scene is much more insistent, and frequently much more horrifying. For it is in the power of the villains of Shakespearean tragedy to take the hidden implications of speech from the heroes, to recognize them as the heroes, blinded by their good intentions, do not, and to turn their worst connotations against the speakers. *King Lear*[7] is of all plays the one in which the ability of the villains to wrest the Shakespearean rhetoric to their own purposes is the most explicit and terrifying. For in this play the good are by definition inarticulate; their true speeches are only actions, to which what they say is often irrelevant or inadequate—and vulnerable.

The play is rich in paradoxical ideas—the man who cannot see till he is blind, the man who cannot know till he is mad. Yet onstage, the physical horrors of mutilation and exposure (represented horrors that are, apart from *Titus Andronicus*, rare in Shakespeare) fix audience attention upon immediate suffering rather than possible enlightenment. What appears to be deliberate revision in the Folio version of the play continually removes the diversion provided by minor characters,[8] or the rationalization of events in moral terms, to emphasize the arbitrary nature of suffering and the essential purposelessness of the torturer. Caroline Spurgeon has pointed out how many of the figures of speech themselves keep us focused upon the vision of a body in pain.[9]

The most terrible example of the evil giving physical life to submerged elements of the rhetoric of *Lear* is the scene of Gloucester's blinding. Responding to the "treachery" of Gloucester, Regan hisses "Hang him instantly" (3.7.4) and Goneril replies "Pluck out his eyes" (3.7.5); accepting these as nonspecific expressions of rage, Cornwall answers grimly and generally "Leave him to my displeasure" (3.7.6). Tied to a chair and questioned mercilessly, Gloucester says that he has helped Lear to get away

> Because I would not see thy cruel nails
> Pluck out his poor old eyes. . . .
> But I shall see
> The winged vengeance overtake such children
> (3.7.55–56,64–65)

Gloucester also is not speaking literally but Cornwall picks up the echoing images of sight and activates them on stage:

> See't shalt thou never. Fellows, hold the chair.
> Upon these eyes of thine I'll set my foot. . . .
> If you see vengeance. . . .
> (3.7.66–67, 71)

Interrupted by the servant who challenges him, he receives his own deathwound, though Regan instantly stabs the servant from behind. As the servant dies, his sense of achievement is, with a terrible irony, expressed through the destructive image:

> O, I am slain! My lord, you have one eye left
> To see some mischief on him. O!
>
> (3.7.80–81)

And Cornwall, enraged and bleeding, picks up the cue as a new challenge:

> Lest it see more, prevent it. Out, vile jelly!
> Where is thy lustre now?
>
> (3.7.82–83)
>
> *Gloucester.* All dark and comfortless. Where's my son Edmund?
> Edmund, enkindle all the sparks of nature
> To quit this horrid act.
> *Regan.* Out, treacherous villain. . . .
>
> (3.7.84–86)

The last reach toward the light dies in the revelation of Edmund's treachery.

The speech of the villains in *Lear* is less vulnerable to this kind of attack because it is both more guarded and more procedural; it tends to be fixed on the business at hand. Almost all the emotional purposes of Edmund and the sisters are expressed in body language, or in the network of letters which are found, planted, forged, forwarded, passed on or undelivered (there are over thirty references to letters in this play). It is very easy to overlook these crucial properties in the classroom, as it is easy to ignore the silent and "strange oeilliads" (4.5.25) through which the affairs of Edmund and the sisters are carried on. In the pursuit of power Edmund, initially a rather likable and talkative tough, becomes a servile gigolo and time-pleaser, his relationships with the sisters and their husbands parodying the ideal of silent "service" embodied in Kent [10] (here as elsewhere, the villains consistently embody in action the worst connotations of the terms they share with the good).

Edmund's transformation begins with the punning assurance to Cornwall and the lustfully attentive Regan:

> I shall serve you, Sir,
> Truly, however else.
>
> (2.1.116–17)

The emphasis on service as sexual as well as servantlike is maintained and elaborated in speech and manner in Edmund's scenes with Regan and Goneril; and it is embodied again in the insolence and sexual presumption of Oswald's behavior to the sisters. Regan does not give orders to Oswald, but approaches him seductively in order to win a look at Goneril's letter to Edmund. She accuses him, in suggestive imagery, of being "of her bosom" (4.5.26) as she will accuse Edmund of being "conjunct and bosomed" (5.1.12–13) with her; an ugly little network of corrupt and disordered relationships builds itself, by the actor's art, around the images and between the lines.

Yet the consistent twisting of images and ideas to their worst possibilities by the villains is also linked with self-destruction. Edmund, leaving Goneril for the war, assures her that he is "Yours, in the ranks of death" (4.2.25). The context supports the usual double entendre of sexual "death"; later, he coolly balances the two deaths as he calculates of the sisters that "Neither can be enjoyed / If both remain alive" (5.2.58–59). When Regan offers herself and all her possessions to Edmund her "lord and master" (5.3.79), she is visibly dying of Goneril's poison. When "a Gentleman with a bloody knife" (5.3.221) brings news of the sisters' deaths, the dying Edmund muses:

> I was contracted to them both. All three
> Now marry in an instant.
>
> (5.3.228–29)

As part of his plan—and, according to many directors, spurred by envious rage at the happiness of the captured Lear and Cordelia—he had ordered the deaths of the king and his daughter; now the sudden conviction "Yet Edmund was beloved" (5.3.239) enables him to desire to save them. However, the immediate cue for that speech is the stage direction "The bodies of Goneril and Regan are brought in" (5.3.238), one poisoned, one, like Edmund, bleeding. The images of commitment, love, and marriage are actualized in death and horror, a "dark and vicious place" (5.3.172) worse than that of Edmund's conception. The issue of such love cannot be other than the entry of a crazed old man carrying a dead child.

Such a relationship between image and action is consistent with Shakespearean tragic patterns, where the wicked flourish because of their pure devotion to self, and self-destruct for the same reason. The roles of the heroes are far more puzzling. The disguised Kent's refusal to change his bluntness of speech almost negates his ability to help Lear, while Edgar changes roles so often that we scarcely know what he is like until the last scene. Edgar begins as an almost mute victim in his brother's "old comedy" (1.2.141–42) of revenge. Fear of death energizes him into a spectacular disguise, which, as far as we know, protects him only against friends; care for his suicidal father takes him through four additional roles,[11] three of them indistinguishable by the audience, and only one of them for the benefit of an outsider (Oswald). Belated offstage revelation of his true self kills his father, he fights incognito to defeat his brother in a technically illegal trial by combat, and he emerges finally in his own name and unpleasing personality. Feebly throughout the play he keeps trying to "recuperate" the images of a providential world; yet he ends the play with a naked antirhetoric beyond any other in its despair.

To start simply, we might say that his disguise as Poor Tom represents visually his social and emotional state as a son disinherited and falsely convicted of an attempt at parricide. He is never able to express those feelings verbally. The rhetoric of possession, closely borrowed from Samuel Harsnett's attack on the Catholic exorcists,[12] is oddly superimposed upon the image of mad Tom when we meet him on the heath. Elizabethans distinguished quite clearly between mental disturbance, such as that of the Abram men described by Edgar in his "disguise" speech (2.3), and the bizarre behavior of those possessed or obsessed by demons; the two states were not necessarily connected with each other. Harsnett attacked both Catholic and Puritan exorcists, stressing the elements of showmanship and propaganda in their dealings with those supposedly possessed, and the frequent faking of the latter; his books are full of images of "production" and "performance" and "theater." Surely, in having Tom "act out" possession, putting onstage Harsnett's metaphors of drama, Shakespeare is aiming at topical reference, and probably at laughter. By contrast with the real madness of Lear and the Fool, Edgar's double pretence both distances the audience and puts an edge on the grotesquerie.

Edgar's startling rhetoric as Tom is biblical in cadence, erotic and confessional in substance, and yet detached from anything we know to be true of Edgar himself. Its hallucinatory images of courtly clothes, dead dogs, and named demons become signs for whole categories of experience fragmenting under the world's injustice, under nakedness, cold, and hunger; ultimately the topical satire drowns in represented pain, the fake becomes part of the pity for "the poor creature of earth"(3.4.122).

Yet if in this scene Edgar's language appears to have been overtaken by the wind and the rain, audiences are made acutely uncomfortable by that scene in which, in full control of his rhetoric, he invents a series of religious metaphors for his suicidal father and presents them to the blind man as literal truth. (Precisely what Harsnett accused the Jesuits of doing was inventing a drama of possession and exorcism of their cowed and hysterical patients, for the edification of the ignorant.) We know that Gloucester is given to belief in signs and miracles, but ultimately he is deceived into life only because he is blind; and we watch the deception as collaborators. Edgar withholds his own identity—knowledge of which would certainly have kept his father from suicide—in favor of playing both God and devil in his own morality play, a drama that finds no echo in the macrocosmic world of *Lear* (4.6).

Like Cordelia, Edgar cannot speak his love; he offers a moral lesson instead.[13] We see the suicidal old man persuaded that he climbs a hill, when he walks flat boards, we see him pray on the edge of an imaginary cliff, created with all the impersonal brilliance of a Chorus. Then we watch Gloucester fall flat on his face, unconscious or dead indeed. Edgar's adjuration to him to "look up" (4.6.58) and see the comically childish devil who led Gloucester to "the edge" is a kind of exorcism of Poor Tom and his theology. But humor and irony die as the old man accepts the picture literally, with a child's gravity; because of his salvation from its temptation, he will live. (Harsnett would have been less concerned with his exorcists if they had not created believers.) Such salvation seems a flat and demeaning thing, divorced from the more dignified images of religious belief; in this scene man's image-making powers are both affirmed and discredited.

In the final scene, the figures of Shakespeare's rhetoric, already brought into question by such brutal or puzzling uses, are finally overwhelmed by staged situations that, at every point, break with the ideas that they are supposed to embody. The drums and colors of the Folio stage directions in act 5 show us Lear and Cordelia on the enemy side; the victorious English enter in two bands, one led by Edmund, one by Albany, and a quarrel about leadership at once breaks out. We have been shown no climactic battle, such as serves in many plays to sum up and contain the suffering of political change. Instead, the duel between Edmund and Edgar seems to initiate suffering that spreads itself over the period between "victory" and the play's end. Regan stands before us, visibly poisoned, for several minutes; Edmund is not killed cleanly, but lies dying onstage until he is carried off to clear the stage for Lear; the dead sisters are brought on and apparently remain; a stricken Kent strives unsuccessfully to win recognition of his services from Lear; and Lear's inconsolable mourning over Cordelia only flickers into temporary silence as Albany begins his conventional victory speech.[14]

Yet both actors and audience hear everything in that image-ridden speech as a contrast to what they see—the dying Lear, the hanged Cordelia, poisoned Regan, stabbed Goneril:

All friends shall taste
The wages of their virtue, and all foes
The cup of their deservings. . . .

The ironies multiply till Albany breaks off in despair and simply cries

Oh, see, see!

(5.3.302–4)

After Lear's death, he can say nothing but order the removal of the bodies and give control of the kingdom to Kent and Edgar. Even this gesture fails to bring closure, as Kent rejects the offer in the face of approaching death. If it is indeed Edgar who brings the play to an end by accepting the leadership of the country, he stands before us without followers, without banners, in an armor without insignia, and associates himself, not with a new beginning, but with the tableau of the dead, both young and old:

The weight of this sad time we must obey;
Speak what we feel, not what we ought to say.
The oldest hath borne most: we that are young
Shall never see so much, nor live so long.

(5.3.323–26)

His is an almost figure-less speech of bare monosyllables that leaves no place for ironic contradiction by the visible dead. Rhetoric has moved to its own negation and precipitated itself in a final silence:

I would not take this from report; it is,
And my heart breaks at it.[15]

(4.6.162–63)

Notes

1. For a brief account, see D. P. Walker, *Unclean Spirits* (Philadelphia: University of Pennsylvania Press, 1975).
2. William Shakespeare, *Twelfth Night, or, What You Will,* ed. Herschel Baker (New York: New American Library, 1965), 1.1.23. All quotations from *Twelfth Night* come from this edition.
3. 2.5.152–54; 2.5.166–67; 2.5.171, 179; 2.5.200–203; 3.2.73–80.
4. Geoffrey Squire, *Dress and Society 1560–1970* (New York: Viking Press, 1974), esp. pp. 45–50. Jane Ashelford, *A Visual History of Costume: The Sixteenth Century* (London: B. T. Batsford, Ltd., 1983).
5. Ashelford, *Visual History,* p. 140
6. Ibid, p. 134
7. William Shakespeare: *King Lear,* ed. Kenneth Muir, rev. ed., repr. (1952; Cambridge: Harvard University Press, 1959). All quotations from *King Lear* are taken from this edition.
8. For an illuminating discussion of the textual problems, see *The Division of the Kingdoms: Shakespeare's Two Versions of King Lear,* ed. Gary Taylor and Michael Warren (Oxford: Clarendon Press, 1983).

9. Caroline Spurgeon, *Shakespeare's Imagery and What It Tells Us* (Cambridge: At the University Press, 1935).

10. See John Reibetanz, *The Lear World: A Study of King Lear in Its Dramatic Context* (Toronto: University of Toronto Press, 1977), pp. 88, 136

11. 4.6.6–10; 4.6.46–79; 4.6.220–24; 4.6.236–46; (5.1.40–49).

12. Samuel Harsnett, *A Discovery of the Fraudulent Practises of John Darrell* (London: John Wolfe, 1599).

13. See Stanley Cavell, "The Avoidance of Love," in *Twentieth Century Interpretations of King Lear*, ed. Janet Adelman (Englewood Cliffs, N.J.: Prentice-Hall, Inc., 1978), pp. 70–87.

14. See Philip C. McGuire, *Speechless Dialect: Shakespeare's Open Silences* (Berkeley: University of California Press, 1985), pp. 97–122.

15. In his *Shakespeare's Theater of Presence: Language, Spectacle, and the Audience* (Lewisburg, Pa.: Bucknell University Press, 1986), Sidney Homan also comments on the inadequacy of language in *King Lear* to accommodate the play's reality, or what "is," as that verb is used in the lines quoted. His book, however, was still in press when I wrote this essay.

12
Hamlet's First Soliloquy: An Exercise

ROBERT HAPGOOD

I SHOULD LIKE TO DESCRIBE AN EXERCISE WITH HAMLET'S FIRST SOLILOQUY, the one that begins "O that this too too sallied flesh would melt, /Thaw, and resolve itself into a dew!" The exercise is designed to enable students to make their own triple play between script, classroom, and performance.

I have used it for many years in the upper-division introduction-to-Shakespeare course. It works best in the latter part of the semester, when students have built some confidence in their ability to read Shakespeare. This takes some doing. Many students have to get past a fear (and consequent hatred) toward Shakespeare that they brought from high school, and many do have serious problems with Elizabethan English. At this first stage, I have found performances—whether live, on film, or videotape—invaluable as a way of getting around the language-barrier to the human interest of the characters and stories. With that interest awakened, and with a great deal of encouragement from me, almost all of the students find that, after studying a few plays and really putting their minds to it, they can handle Shakespeare's language on their own, and even enjoy it. They are now ready to use performances as if they were a particularly vivid form of interpretive analysis.

Before coming to the soliloquy exercise, the students will have read *Hamlet* through and will have had a class-meeting surveying the whole play. The assignment for the exercise asked them to read the soliloquy very closely, to be able to specify the emotions that Hamlet expresses in it, and to single out one or two of them that are especially dominant.

In the time before class I am busy setting up the equipment I'll be using: the film projector, audiocassette player, and VCR. As the students come into the classroom they go immediately to the blackboard. For their row they put in one column one of the emotions Hamlet expresses in the soliloquy, each emotion different from any other in the column (this task gets harder and harder!). When completed, the column might read: despair, anger, sorrow, frustration, helplessness, disillusionment, disgust, world-weariness, desire to escape, desire to kill himself, admiration. In another place on the board, students have also indicated the emotion that seems, to them, dominant. When it is time for the class to begin, we thus have before us a survey of the range of Hamlet's emotions in the soliloquy and a vote as to which ones are dominant.

Naturally, our first activity is to look over the variety of emotions surveyed. I ask if anyone would like to have an item on the board clarified or illustrated. (Students these days are not inclined to *challenge* one another directly.) Let us say someone wonders why "admiration" is on the board. Whoever put it there might point to Hamlet's feeling for his father, comparing him to Hyperion. Once in a while, there will be an item for which there is no evident basis. Someone may think that Hamlet is feeling bad because he was refused permission to return to Wittenberg or resentful that he has not succeeded his father to the throne. I will say that it is true that Shakespeare might well have put such matters in the speech. And they may be somewhere in its implicit background—is Hamlet's desire to go to Wittenberg an aspect of his general desire to escape? But I conclude that I don't see evidence that Shakespeare in fact chose to have Hamlet put these matters into words. I will then give the better students a chance to shine and ask for emotions that our survey has omitted. Perhaps someone will point out that Hamlet is feeling sorry for himself and—in his self-pity—inclined to dwell "too, too" much on his own plight.

This far is easy going. Students have typically identified only two or three emotions on their own and are pleasantly surprised at the variety our mutual effort has found. The next step is harder, as we go on to debate which of the emotions are dominant. Usually, three or four emotions will attract the most votes, and I try to get advocates to support each. My purpose is not to arrive at a single definitive reading but to ventilate the pros and cons of alternative choices. This students today are very disinclined to do. Discrimination of any sort (however legitimate) is taboo. When I started teaching thirty years ago, students expected to be told the One Right Reading for a play or passage, and the teaching challenge was to open their minds to alternative readings. Now I find my students all-too-ready to credit multiple options—to the point of thinking that anything goes. The teaching challenge now is to encourage judgments among interpretations, to rule out certain impossibilities, see some of the possibilities as more central or profound or well-balanced than others. In the soliloquy, for instance, one may observe that certain emotions are expressed primarily in one place, such as suicidal tendencies at the beginning or a sense of frustration at the end: "But break my heart for I must hold my tongue." Other emotions run through the speech, such as disillusionment, and thus have relatively more importance.

It is now time for some performances. I did not use them earlier because experience has taught me the irresistible power of a persuasive performance to make itself seem forever after the One Right Reading. The only cure for that is to see several other persuasive performances of the same text, which I can rarely make possible. If, however, the students have made their own initial response to the text and, in class, enlightened it by discussion with their peers and me, even the spell of an Olivier or a Richard Burton will not be permanent.

Before the advent of videotape, I used this as an exercise in "Hearing Shakespeare" on recordings. It was helpful to contrast Paul Scofield's broken and grieving prince with Tony White's Angry Young Man on the Marlowe Society recording. Or John Gielgud's architecture, carefully mounting to a climax at "married with mine uncle," with Burton's fireworks, which went all-out for effect on every line. If one does not have audiovisual aids available, students can do "oral interpretation" readings. They are more willing to participate in that way than they used to be. Some are quite good. Yet in such sessions, I cannot get out of my mind a remark that Jan Kott once made to me: "Whatever goes on in the front of the classroom should be *professional*."

These days I revel in having film and videotape versions for this exercise. As time permits in an eighty-minute class, we watch the soliloquy as delivered by Derek Jacobi in the Shakespeare Plays tape, Olivier in a taped version of his film, Nicol Williamson on film. I still use Richard Burton on record because, even unseen, he is generally the class favorite.

Often classes will find that the performers have added an emotion to our survey. Williamson's self-torment—he pounds his knuckle on his temple toward the end of the speech—often surprises the students. I may need to be the one who shows the textual basis for this self-torment, that Hamlet progressively makes the time elapsed between his father's funeral and his mother's wedding shorter and shorter, thus making the enormity even worse than it is in order to feel it the more.

The performances raise considerations that often have not come up before, particularly questions of degree. How strongly does Hamlet feel the various emotions? And beyond that, how strong does Hamlet himself seem at this point? Jacobi, for instance, lacks energy. When he wearily sighs "O god, god," it is almost as if he were saying "Dear me, dear me." He says "but break my heart" with a wistful half-laugh. One doubts that he would have the gumption ever to get the job done. Burton, on the other hand, has a superabundance of energy. One wonders why he wouldn't finish his work by the end of the first act. Both performances help one to see that Hamlet's feelings must not be so strong as to demand that he do something immediately, yet they must be strong enough to make him (and the audience) feel heart-breaking frustration.

The exercise is designed to help students to arrive at such awarenesses as this. It is meant to project, and make immediately available to students, a way of looking at Shakespeare's artistry, one that rejoices in the fact that his text leaves generous room for more than one valid interpretation yet holds that the text is not open to just any rendering—that some interpretations are not valid and that some valid ones are, in various respects, to be preferred to others. It is a lesson that I wish many of my professional colleagues would learn.

13

Shakespeare Live—on Videotape

ROGER GEIMER

IN ATTEMPTING TO EXPAND STUDENTS' EXPERIENCES OF SHAKESPEARE BEyond the printed page we now have the rich resources of videotape, which, by judicious editing, can be used to illustrate differing interpretations of the plays as well as the influence on productions of Shakespeare by the various media. Here I will try to illustrate how three separate renditions of the play present completely different views of the central action of Shakespeare's *The Taming of the Shrew*. Readily available to the public through videocassette recordings, they represent a filmed, a televised, and a stage production: Franco Zeffirelli's film version starring Richard Burton and Elizabeth Taylor; Jonathan Miller's BBC television production with John Cleese as Petruchio; and the stage performance directed for Joseph Papp's Shakespeare in the Park by Wilford Leach and starring Raul Julia and Meryl Streep, as televised in a one-hour program entitled *Kiss Me Petruchio*.

I focus on Petuchio's first scene (1.2) where the farcical elements establish his character and control the interpretation of the larger play. Though to many critics the scene is an obvious piece of farce, I believe the audience's sympathy here is directed toward or against Petruchio according to the way it is played. This fact would confirm Irving Ribner's notion that in Shakespeare's comedies moral attitudes are presented not so much in didactic speeches, but rather in the "larger dramatic context."[1] In my own classroom I prefer to show each version of this scene (approximately five minutes for each) before commenting on the action.

At issue here is how the audience perceives the characters of Petruchio and Katherine within the context of the play's farcical elements. Many modern revisionist and feminist critics, in their attempt to interpret Katherine sympathetically, apparently share H. J. Oliver's dictum that "characterization and farce are, finally, incompatible,"[2] as well as Robert Heilman's argument that farce oversimplifies life "by selective anaesthetizing of the whole person," portraying only "limited personality that acts and responds in a mechanical way and hence moves toward a given end with a perfection not likely if all the elements in human nature were really at work."[3] For E. M. W. Tillyard, if a "lesser" literary type, such as farce, achieves a certain excellence the work transcends that form.[4]

By comparing the three versions, students can appreciate how the three elements generally associated with farce—"an absurd situation, normally unacceptable libidinal actions, and flat, surrealistic characters"[5]—can coalesce to reveal a deeper significance to the action. By not perceiving such characters as capable of real feelings and emotions, we can accept the farcical action, but deny its resultant suffering. As Eric Bentley suggests, we are "permitted the outrage but spared the consequence."[6] To take the recipient of the farce's unwarranted aggressive behavior as a real sentient person capable of suffering would impose a seriousness incompatible with the genre or, as some feel, would raise the work to a higher level than farce. But, as Barbara Freedman insists, it is the "denial" of meaning, rather than its absence that makes farce work.[7]

To see *The Taming of the Shrew* as both farce and as a romance involving a genuine relationship between its two main characters may seem to demand conflicting principles of characterization. While farce normally depicts single-dimensional characters, all characters in the play need not be so. My feeling is that Petruchio and Kate transcend the conventional farcical characters of the subplot: Bianca, Lucentio, Hortensio, Gremio, and the servants, Grumio and Tranio. In his introduction to the Oxford edition of the play, H. J. Oliver suggests that Shakespeare intended to write a farce, but in seeking answers to why Kate is a shrew found himself portraying her sympathetically to the audience.[8]

Petruchio's first appearance establishes the audience's expectations for the future relationship between Petruchio and Kate. While all three versions stress the scene's obvious farce, one manages, at the same time, to portray Katherine and Patruchio in a sympathetic light, suggesting that their relationship can become loving and fulfilling.

As Grumio deliberately misconstrues Petruchio's words "knock me here" and his master refuses to clarify his meaning, Petruchio's "Faith, sirrah, an you'll not knock, I'll ring it" is accompanied with the stage direction "*he wrings him by the ears.*" What is important here, I believe, is that the audience recognize the easy familiarity and playfulness allowed the servant by his master. If Petruchio were the type who, almost by instinct, beats his servant, Grumio would be more hesitant to pun. The comedy in all three productions is slapstick, yet crucial to the audience's response are two factors: how the director interprets Petruchio and whether the farce does or does not project a denial of the effects of the aggressive action perpetrated.

In the Zeffirelli version, the director adds some stage business just before Petruchio and Grumio enter. As Lucentio and Tranio switch clothes so that Tranio can masquerade as his master, the servant dressed like an aristocrat haughtily removes Lucentio's hand from the clothing and brushes off the cape as if the former master turned servant has somehow defiled it with his touch. Joining in the joke Lucentio rushes after the presumptuous Tranio, playfully kicking at him. Throughout all this horseplay, the audience is keenly aware of the camaraderie between master and servant, one that will contrast ironically with that between Petruchio and Grumio.

When Burton's Petruchio says "Knock me here," he delivers the line less as a farceur and more like a tragedian demanding something of a menial. When the servant quibbles over his choice of words, he takes gusto in beating the hapless Grumio who then cowers in fear of further blows. Zeffirelli thereby underscores the violence in Petruchio's nature and its consequence to the servant. He further delineates this Petruchio in two other scenes. In one, Petruchio sits at the table with the effete Hortensio, picking fleas from a dog and presenting the insects for the perusal of his squeamish companion. Then, after imbibing freely of wine, the drunken Petruchio falls asleep. Later, when he awakens, the servants timorously pour water for his bath. We see at such moments a hero who is brash, boorish—thoroughly unlikeable. His later treatment of the shrew Katherine is no different. By emphasizing the consequences of Petruchio's violence, Zeffirelli seems insistent on producing a "realistic" apprehension of the farcical behavior.

In the BBC production, John Cleese offers a Petruchio with the deadly seriousness of a Puritan. Instead of slapstick antics between him and Grumio, we see him grab Grumio and, wringing his ear, force the writhing servant to the ground. Later, as he swings his arm around Hortensio's shoulder, Petruchio gratuitously slaps Grumio in the face. At such moments the principle of farce should deny the consequences of the actions: Grumio should emerge unscathed and undaunted, but here Grumio appears instead to be genuinely discomfited.

Later, as the servant is explaining Petruchio's situation to Hortensio, Petruchio stares malevolently and then, circling Hortensio, angrily paces after Grumio who deftly keeps Hortensio between himself and his master. These actions somehow lack the spirit of true farce. The "unacceptable libidinal action"[9] of farce is certainly here, yet there is something present beyond a flat characterization that would deny any profound consequences of Petruchio's action. With an overbearing master who gives him no peace, Grumio's position seems intolerable. How could this servant be so foolishly bold as to pun on his master's words "knock me here"! Possibly Petruchio is incapable of understanding the pun.

This puritanical Petruchio affects no less the other characters and, in the process, alters our perception of them. As he distractedly points his finger, poking at Petruchio's chest, the foppish Hortensio seems even more ridiculous than he is. Petruchio coldly eyes him and gingerly steps back, leaving Hortensio obliviously gesticulating into the empty air. Cleese's Petruchio barely seems to fit into the spirit of farce. Rather than fulfilling that concept of denial of cause and effect of "unacceptable libidinal actions" of aggression, his actions are made to seem more realistic as he soberly metes out punishment as a way of ridiculing others who, in his mind, richly deserve the consequence of being beneath his contempt. This portrait later influences our response to Petruchio's taming of Katherine. There his treatment of her seems a righteous act, and the punishment dealt her genuine.

Perhaps these two productions undermine the vitality of farce because of the nature of the media of film and television: both lack the immediacy of audience reaction. And while the two media can establish a level of realism impossible on the stage, such realism runs counter to farce. Because of the technical virtuosity of these predominantly visual media, directors usually feel the need to accelerate the pace, substituting for the dialogue those visual aspects of staging and lighting so lacking in Shakespeare's theater. Zeffirelli adds much visual footage to create lusty Italian Renaissance scenes of revelry, a kind of feast-of-fools carnival atmosphere. Still, he also omits great amounts of dialogue that cannot be replaced by anything visual. And the televised production, by focusing on closeups and more intimate shots, perhaps overemphasizes the seriousness of the action; the audience need to be at a distance to maintain a comic overview. Most of all, both media lack the essential interplay between live actors and an audience present and sharing in the experience.

Wilford Leach's version was filmed before a live audience whose responses to the farce is a factor in our own experience as an audience. Still, the main virtue of this performance is the interpretation of the characters of Petruchio and Kate. Although the role of Petruchio is made farcical in the opening "knock me here" scene by adding the physical action of his grappling Grumio to the floor and then applying a wrestling clamp to his leg, the audience feels their relationship is one of, in Irene G. Dash's words, "mutual enjoyment in words, of robustness, and of horseplay."[10]

Later, Petruchio begins to walk off the stage while Hortensio is describing Kate, only to turn on his heels when her wealth is mentioned. Although Bernard Shaw praised Petruchio's mercenary attitude as a redeeming realistic touch, Petruchio's action here is pure farce—he is making clear that his intentions are for money only, that he is unconcerned with any bad or good qualities of the yet unseen Katherine. However, through his easy and playful relationship with his servant earlier, the audience realizes that Petruchio can love Kate for more than her dowery, that he is capable of genuine human relationships.

In this televised production, the lead actors also comment on their roles. Raul Julia perceived Petruchio's original intent as purely mercenary, but after seeing Katherine and verbally sparring with her, Petruchio—for Julia—comes to realize that she is an attractive person intellectually as well as physically. In this version the later scenes develop a meaningful relationship between the two despite the farcical elements abounding in the play. Here the farce coexists with deeper psychological characterization and serious intent.

Before these three versions are shown in the classroom, it is essential that the entire play be thoroughly studied. I also try not to comment on the interpretations beforehand and find, in addition, it best to have the students discuss each version immediately after seeing it. With little or no prompting, they develop their own critical insights: that any given production is not the only one possible; that more than just dialogue constitutes the meaning of a play; that they can disagree with a director's decisions; that the medium itself affects the production.

I have always shown the scenes in the sequence presented here; yet it would be revealing, I think, to rearrange that sequence so as to compare the differences in the class's reception. So far, I have not encountered the problem of the initial version's becoming the exclusive way the students read the play. A poll of the students in my last Shakespeare class indicated that the majority felt it more helpful seeing several versions of the same scene than a single production of an entire play. I myself like the "economy" of focusing on a single scene and then sharing with my students the immediate dramatic experience.

Notes

1. Irving Ribner, "The Morality of Farce: *The Taming of the Shrew*," in *Essays in American and English Literature Presented to Bruce Robert McElderry, Jr.*, ed. Max F. Schulz et al. (Athens: Ohio University Press, 1968), p. 166.
2. William Shakespeare *The Taming of the Shrew*, ed. H. J. Oliver (Oxford: Oxford University Press, 1984), p. 52. All references to the play are based on this edition.
3. Robert B. Heilman, "The Taming Untamed, or, The Return of the Shrew," *Modern Language Quarterly* 27 (1966): 152, 160.
4. E. M. W. Tillyard, *Shakespeare's Early Comedies* (London: Chatto & Windus, 1965), p. 69.
5. Barbara Freedman, "Errors in Comedy: A Psychoanalytic Theory of Farce," in *Shakespearean Comedy*, ed. Maurice Charney, *New York Literary Forum* 5–6 (1980): 235.

6. Eric Bentley. *The Life of the Drama* (New York: Atheneum, 1970), p. 222.
7. Freedman, "Errors," p. 236.
8. Oliver, *Shrew*, p. 51.
9. Freedman, "Errors," p. 235.
10. Irene G. Dash, *Wooing, Wedding, and Power: Women in Shakespeare's Plays* (New York: Columbia University Press, 1981), p. 38.

14

Students Write about Shakespeare: The "Triple Play" in the College Classroom

SUZANNE BURR

IN HIS 1977 WORK, *THE SHAKESPEARE REVOLUTION*, J. L. STYAN MAKES A number of assertions regarding the need for a stage-centered study of Shakespeare, assertions that are only beginning to be answered at the present time. Styan notes the chasm that exists between the practice of theater and the activity of theater criticism, remarking that the real advances in Shakespeare scholarship have come from studying the practical business of staging a play rather than from analyses of verbal or thematic patterns. He praises the work done on the history of performance, including research by Arthur Colby Sprague and Marvin Rosenberg, and notes that the pioneering efforts of Poel and Granville-Barker have not yet found complete fulfillment in the theater of today. Yet, Styan asserts that a knowledge of the living theater has enriched scholarship, and is optimistic for the future, mentioning in this light such critics as Bernard Grebanier, Stanley Wells, Maurice Charney, and John Russell Brown, all of whom have worked to bring theater experience into the dialogue and practice of academic criticism.[1] Brown himself has stressed the need for "theater criticism" (rather than literary criticism) of Shakespeare, and has argued that theater research can extend the critic's response to the visual and temporal elements in a play.[2] Similarly, Norman Rabkin writes in the foreword to *Reinterpretations of Elizabethan Drama* that there has been a shift in the approach to the criticism of Shakespeare and his contemporaries: the writers in this collection of essays, he says, discuss drama in terms of "the play as it impinges on its audience, as it is experienced."[3] For critics such as Styan, Brown, and Rabkin, the world of academic criticism is not wide enough to capture the complex reality of the theater event.

I am also concerned with the same issue—the importance of contact between the living theater and the language of criticism—but from another angle, approaching Shakespeare through the eyes of twenty-two University of Michigan undergraduates, mostly first-year students, all of whom came to my class on Shakespeare and Composition with a heavy load of assumptions that it became my job to whittle down, launch assaults at, and otherwise challenge, while simultaneously attempting to encourage an active, participatory engagement with Shakespeare's texts. The essence of my argument here is that, as Styan and others have urged, the time has come to bring our knowledge of stage practice and performance into the college classroom. The "double play" that can emerge for the student of Shakespeare is especially rich, for the integration of literary and theater criticism allows the student to "see" the text with new eyes. In my discussion I do not, of course, assume that such an approach is not already being practiced by teachers of English, but I do hope that by offering my experience as an example of the successful enjoining of theater and academia, of art and the study of art, I will lend support to the growing number of teachers and critics who see the need for more than a truce between two hitherto opposed camps—for a reconciliation that brings together the best of both worlds.

Our "experiment" began one autumn day when I wrote the word "Shakespeare" on the board and asked my students to "free-associate." "Don't censor anything," I said. "Say whatever comes into your mind." I looked at them, they looked at me. Some blank faces, some furtive smiles, a few giggles. "Boring!" someone shouted from the back of the room. Ouch. I tried to keep a frown from undermining my teacherly pose of neutrality, that mask we try to maintain, as if we had no assumptions of our own. Shakespeare? Boring? Unheard of. But instead I replied, "All right. Boring. Let's hear more. What else?" Now poured forth a stream of varied associations, including "the greatest poet who ever lived," "tragic flaw," and other reasonable and fairly predictable responses. We began a discussion of what they felt and thought about Shakespeare, about what they had experienced in previous classes. For the most part, they had enjoyed reading Shakespeare in high school English classes, though they had found him "difficult." Some reported their enjoyment had been forced, affected—the kind of response one has when to express dislike bars one from entrance into the circle of civilized, cultured human beings. Many had felt bored, even alienated, forced as they were to learn monologues, to memorize set speeches, to infix Great Poetry in their minds and hearts. More than that, however, many had felt a perfunctory appreciation without the sense, somehow, of mastery; thus they clung to the pieces of knowledge they did have, antagonistic at times to rediscoveries and reappraisals.

Once, when I distributed a drawing of the Globe playhouse (what we know of it from reconstructions), a student responded by saying disdainfully, "We *did* that in high school," as if one could "do" Shakespeare, or "have" him, once studied. In truth, this attitude seems widespread in college classrooms, where to "do" a writer means taking a one-semester course, taking notes, taking an exam. An author is "surveyed," "covered," and subsequently buried. What fuels this attitude, I believe, is not simply the necessity of moving quickly through a semester's work (a dilemma we all face and make the best of), but student anxiety. Let's "do" Shakespeare, they seem to say, and thus get it over with. One finds students approaching the Bard with reverence and trepidation, as they would a monument erected to the ennoblement of Western culture. Shakespeare has become, for many, a word so loaded with cultural appropriations it is difficult to elicit anything but the same tired generalizations. Most of these students had read Monarch notes and other quick-study guides, but not, I believe, out of laziness; rather, they did so in order to master what seems like an overwhelming cultural presence. Students *have* to like Shakespeare, so they do; but I wanted to find a way to get at more authentic responses, to find out how students could appropriate Shakespeare for themselves.

I believe that contact with performance is an essential way to bring this about. The easiest way for most college classes to have such exposure is through the viewing of videos; in our case, the excellent BBC Shakespeare productions were available at the University of Michigan libraries. These videos gave students the opportunity to step beyond a literal reading of Shakespeare's texts, to see what a difference performance can make in the interpretation of a play. Viewing the *Romeo and Juliet* video, for example, students immediately picked up on visual and spatial elements. They noticed that during the scene of the Capulet ball the camera moved back and forth between Capulet and his cronies (the "old folks") sitting on the sidelines, commenting philosophically about life, and the young people enacting the vital pageant of life in the dance, a dance that sets the scene for, and is an emblem of, the passion that Romeo and Juliet will play out, to the horror of their parents. Only the camera could reveal so emphatically in visual terms the thematic schism between youth and old age that Shakespeare emphasizes throughout the play. What formerly had been a "difficult" passage now becomes full of meaning.

Similarly, seeing the actors in the flesh (so to speak) helps a great deal to solidify the characters in the students' imaginations. Before viewing the *Romeo and Juliet* video, we discussed the physical appearance of each character. How should Romeo look? What actor would you cast to play him? What about Juliet? Mercutio? Responses were original and often amusing: that Romeo be the typical "hero" type, thus modeled on

Robert Redford's boyish good looks; that he indicate a "smolderingly passionate" quality—like Warren Beatty or the late Richard Burton; or that he look more "refined," like the young Laurence Olivier. Playing casting director, fantasizing over choices, students formed judgments that immediately called into question thematic and literary issues.[4] Many students disliked the actress who played Juliet in the BBC video, for example, because they felt Juliet must convey a sense of emerging sexuality, that we must see the woman in the girl in order to believe the lovers' passion for each other. This particular Juliet, students argued, was badly cast: her innocent appearance and soft-spoken manner undermined the forcefulness they felt she needed in the role. Bad casting, they said, does have an effect on the interpretation of a drama; a character is not simply a verbal construct, a nexus of words, images; a character is not "real" until embodied on stage—or, in this case, on videotape.

As we were viewing the BBC videos, I asked students to be especially aware of other choices the director and actors had made in the interpretation of the text. We isolated details of costume, set design, stage movement or blocking, facial expression, gesture, and delivery as among the most important variables manipulated by director and cast. Meanwhile, our class discussions focused on Elizabethan performance conditions as well as the conditions under which Shakespeare composed most of his plays—particularly those written at the Globe. Initially, I stressed facts that Bernard Beckerman and other researchers have uncovered—namely, that performance schedules were rushed, with a new play mounted every couple of weeks; that revision, if any, was a hasty matter; that Shakespeare, as a shareholder in the company as well as an actor himself, was preeminently a man of the theater; that performance was a more direct, visceral experience than the kind of productions students were likely to have seen.[5] Thus I tried to place Shakespeare the man in the context within which he worked, the real hurly-burly world of the London theater, a world of quick decisions and spontaneous action, a world in which his genius found expression before his "canonization," where his works seem to have become dead relics in an English teacher's library instead of the living, vital, and sometimes even flawed creations that they are.

One issue we dealt with was the bawdy side of Shakespeare's plays—a side I quickly learned had been minimized in the students' past classroom experiences. Midway through the semester, I asked these students to justify this bawdiness, and to explain how it was different from, say, profanities one might find in a film or a paperback novel. Was there any way in which the vulgar puns and suggestive language could be called "gratuitous"? What were the standards we might use to form such judgments? Some students were offended that I might suggest there could be a negative element, a mistake even, in Shakespeare; most were simply struck, at first, by the juxtaposition of Shakespeare's name with names familiar from popular culture. Clearly, to them, Shakespeare was not just another writer, but one whom they were expected to approach with religious sobriety. I then asked them to write an essay that I generically called "A Defense of Shakespeare," in which they were to defend his work to an imaginary Board of Supervisors seeking to eliminate this "obscene" material from high school and college libraries. Because censorship for them was a very "hot" issue, extending not only to books but now to music lyrics, the censorship of Shakespeare did not seem so far-fetched, and they tackled the assignment with gusto. Arguments for the defense ranged from somewhat predictable responses (Shakespeare's works make moral judgments on the characters that mitigate the damaging effects of obscene material on young minds) to fresher apologies ("It's better to hear it from Shakespeare than to learn it on the street," said one student). In general, the assignment enabled students to probe some of their assumptions about Shakespeare, and to formulate for themselves the importance of his work in the "canon."

Such assignments would have been meaningless, however, without the actual experience of Shakespeare in the theater. Fortunately, that semester we were able to see two productions: *Macbeth* and *As You Like It*. While *As You Like It* was the more successful of the two plays in terms of local critical reception and wholeness of presentation, it was *Macbeth*, an undeniable "flop" by academic and theater standards, that was the true "success" of that semester, for it produced in these students a sense of outrage that got them thinking like theater critics rather than students in a classroom.

The Old Vic Company, a prestigious and highly competent group of individuals, chose to stage the play against a backdrop that students called "new wave," "postholocaust," and even, "like the set of *West Side Story*." The structure was formed by three movable panels that served both as a medieval background and as an abstract, neutral territory. Painted steel gray, with rods forming geometric angles and footholds upon which the actors could climb, the set created two distinct worlds—one realistic, in period, the other metaphoric, suggestive of the psychic devastation in the play. Such dissonance was carried through every level of the production, and was immediately noticed by the students. The three witches, for example, were clothed as modern-day bag ladies, right down to their glow-in-the-dark sneakers and their plastic shopping bags; in general they seemed less frightening than pitiful. A similarly incongruent element was Lady Macbeth's nightgown, which appeared to be a very modern silk negligee; like her terry-cloth bathrobe, the nightgown heightened her contemporaneity but undermined her impact.

Students objected strongly to the problems they perceived in costume choices, such as the clash between Duncan's medieval garb of gold and silver and the black leather outfit squired by Macbeth, a costume that suggested sadomasochism in the bedroom and totalitarian authority in the political world. But more serious than mistakes of costume were matters of acting style and authenticity of gesture. The declamatory style practiced by the actors playing the lead roles seemed out of place in their intimate scenes, and there was a pronounced lack of horror at moments where the full force of the tragedy should emerge. The appearance of Banquo's ghost, in particular, sparked animated class discussions about realism, the use of the supernatural, and the importance of theatrical technique. Students knew that Banquo's appearance should be horrifying to an audience, or at least should produce suspense mingled with fear for Macbeth's sanity. When this Banquo appeared, however, intruding himself into a nicely orchestrated dining scene like a late guest rather than a specter, he was met with laughter, grunts of amusement, but no horror whatsoever. Students found ample occasion to attack this violation of an important moment in the play. The reviews they wrote inveighed against "cheap shots" and staging that wasn't fully thought out.

Two final events in the play also furnished fuel for energetic denouncements of the production. The first came when the invading army entered bearing the "woods," which in this case were armfuls of leafy branches, and which were unceremoniously dropped upstage with an embarrassing noise. The literalism of this bit of business obstructed what should have been a highly intense passage in the drama. Instead, for the students it seemed a parody of Shakespeare's intention. A second example occurred when Macduff dropped Macbeth's head on the stage, and again the audience was greeted with a resounding "thud" when the head hit the boards. Since most of the audience began to laugh at this point, the mood of horror that should accompany Macbeth's bloody end was ruined. Students noticed that though these bits of business were minor, in the magnifying arena of the theater they became major impediments.

The students' reviews combined insightful analyses of the play with trenchant attacks on the "production values," a phrase I heard often after that event. These students were developing more critical insights into, and sharper perceptions about, the nature of Shakespearean drama, and more generally, about the difficulty of staging a text, any text. They discussed ways in which the production could have been altered to maintain some of the same values without violating the spirit of the play, as this production seemed to do. They found ways to describe the performance based on their own judgments and perceptions, on their likes and dislikes, on their responses as members of an audience. Jerzy Grotowski has written that the essential theater experience is the relationship between the actor and audience;[6] there is an equality among individual audience members that is not available to students within the hierarchically structured world of the classroom. I believe that the authenticity of these students' reviews derived from the direct perception of the theater event. Students were able to trust their own instincts as theatergoers, rather than fearing to assert themselves because of their "outsider" status in the world of literary criticism. Uninhibited by a teacher's assumptions or authoritative interpretation, they were able to come up with fresh complaints and fresh solutions. They became, in fact, literary and theatrical critics.

An outgrowth of this experience, though secondary, was not unimportant. The students saw that Shakespeare's work was not sacred, was not fixed in some teacher's mind, but was fluid, capable of many interpretations, of distortion even, although essentially indestructible because of its integrity. Students saw risks taken, and saw failure, but this, I believe, inspired some of them to a fresher outlook, a perception that drama must be made new to be kept alive, that what separates "deadly" from "holy" theater, to use Peter Brook's terminology,[7] is the willingness to experiment, to take risks, to fail, and to see where failure can lead you. I think this is an important experience for anyone engaged in an educational process, but especially so for students in college, where success is at a premium, measured in grades. For them, the "hidden message" of the *Macbeth* production was that one can fail and yet still succeed; the production was a "flop," but the text was still there, ready to be reinvented anew. The element of live theater that encourages risk-taking, the very liveliness of it all, is what is so often lacking in academic discourse; it is this liveness and liveliness that can allow a student to reinterpret Shakespeare on her or his own terms.

Recently, the New York Shakespeare Festival formed a multiracial acting company that will present Shakespeare on Broadway for school audiences; at present they are trying to obtain funding for year-round operation. The plays will be limited to students, their families, and teachers. As Joseph Papp, the producer, remarked in the *New York Times*, "We're not saying that Shakespeare is easy. We don't want to oversimplify. But we do think it can be taught in a way that's exciting and compelling."[8] While Papp's project is aimed at younger audiences, the essential point here—exposure to the living theater—holds true for college students as well. We do not want to oversimplify, yet we need to provide more opportunities for student contact with taped, filmed, and live performances. In this way, students will be able to supplant their teachers some day, and to make Shakespeare their own.

Notes

1. J. L.Styan, *The Shakespeare Revolution: Criticism and Performance in the Twentieth Century* (Cambridge: At the University Press, 1977). See pp. 3–9 for his discussion of the gap between theater practice and academic criticism. See p. 6, n. 14, for his reference to Sprague, Rosenberg, et al., and p. 8 for his citations of works by Grebanier, Wells, Charney, and Brown.

2. John Russell Brown, *Shakespeare's Plays in Performance* (New York: St. Martin's Press, 1967), pp. 223–31. See also pp. 233–37 for four suggestions on how literary critics can develop a fully theatrical criticism.

3. Norman Rabkin, *Reinterpretations of Elizabethan Drama*, Selected Papers from the English Institute (New York: Columbia University Press, 1969), p. vii. Quoted by Styan, *Shakespeare Revolution*, p. 9.

4. The "casting" idea was suggested to me by Dr. Bruce Mann, who currently teaches at Oakland University in Michigan.

5. Bernard Beckerman's *Shakespeare at the Globe 1599–1609* (New York: Macmillan, 1962) continues to be highly useful, as do more recent studies, such as Andrew Gurr's *The Shakespearean Stage 1574–1642* (Cambridge: At the University Press, 1970) and Michael Hattaway's *Elizabethan Popular Theatre: Plays in Performance*, Theatre Production Studies, ed. John Russell Brown (London: Routledge & Kegan Paul, 1982).

6. Jerzy Grotowski, *Towards a Poor Theatre* (New York: Simon and Schuster, 1968). Grotowski writes: "We can thus define the theatre as 'what takes place between spectator and actor'. All the other things are supplementary—perhaps necessary, but nevertheless supplementary" (pp. 32–33).

7. Peter Brook, *The Empty Space* (New York: Atheneum, 1968). See his chapters on "The Deadly Theatre," pp. 9–41, and "The Holy Theatre," pp. 42–64. Brook suggests that the holy theater, in which we experience our aliveness, has a responsibility to remind us of our spiritual selves. "A holy theatre not only presents the invisible but also offers conditions that make its perception possible" (p. 56).

8. See Samuel G. Freedman, "Students to Meet Bard on Broadway," *The New York Times*, 6 January 1986, sec. C, p. 11. It's cheering to note that Shakespeare is also being shared with younger audiences, as another recent *New York Times* article indicates. In "Romeo Rated by Youths," 2 January 1986, sec. B (see "New York by Day"), p. 2, the *Times* reports that two members of the Royal Shakespeare Company held workshops for hundreds of public-school students in the city, engaging them in the acting and speaking of Shakespeare's plays. One of the goals of the workshop, according to Tony Hill, is to teach students " 'that Shakespeare won't be made accessible if they come to it with too much reverence.' " He adds, " 'It's good enough to be pummeled. It was written for the people.' "

15

The Triple Stage and the National Endowment Shakespeare Institute

RONALD SHAFER

A SHAKESPEARE INSTITUTE, SPONSORED BY THE NATIONAL ENDOWMENT FOR the Humanities and held at our campus in 1986, parallels in remarkable detail the triad focus of this volume. The entire thrust of this institute for high school teachers was the progression of insights into Shakespeare that results when one amalgamates scholarly perspectives on the plays with the experience of seeing those plays enacted and, in turn, blends these combined findings with workable strategies for classroom teaching. The institute involved a host of intricately related ancillary programs—exhibits, excursions, workshops, guest lectures, live productions, backstage work, films (historical, educational, and Shakespearean), and more—all of which were synthesized into a program that encouraged a total immersion in the Elizabethan milieu.

The institute first attempted to help teachers assess their current insights into the plays most commonly taught in the high schools: what are the themes, are there mutations of those themes in other Shakespearean plays, how unique is Shakespeare's use of metaphor? The intent here was to have the teachers examine in a fresh light those insights they share with their students, so that interpretations are not taken for granted, so that they do not become institutionalized or even reductive. It is fine, for example, to concentrate on the display of unbridled ambition in *Macbeth*, but the play need not be limited to this approach alone. By talking among themselves, the teachers realized that interpretations may calcify after years of teaching. The teachers also concluded that their teaching of the plays can become simplistic if it is severed too completely from performance and ongoing scholarship, both of which can help check a tendency toward stagnation.

One example will illustrate the point. When asked about the delivery of the opening lines of *Macbeth*—"When shall we three meet again?/ In thunder, lightning, or in rain?"—the teachers had not given much thought to how these lines might be delivered, or about the actors' blocking and stage movement. Years of classroom instruction had never offered them occasion to consider such issues. But when three of the teachers read the opening lines "on stage" in the front of the classroom, we all came to see how they might be chanted, how the lines lend themselves to dancing, and how the witches' movement casts a spell over the entire stage, establishing concentric circles of evil, grinding into and engulfing everything in their path. Who could escape that ubiquitous incantation and its dance of death? The experiment showed what classroom teaching, even background reading in the scholarship on the play (for those who do stay current in the literature), had failed to do: that the stage elements—voice, the silences, the sound effects, music, the actors' movements and gestures, the uses of space—greatly affect our interpretations of *Macbeth*.

For us, this beginning experiment, albeit a simple one, defined our intent and justified our approach. We now wanted to learn more about the plays and the age, to address the three stages of the study, the theater, the classroom separately, and then to combine our findings at the end of our four-week institute. Attention was turned, then, to the first stage, the study; the intent here was to become the scholar, to forget temporarily the plays as drama. A variety of strategies was used. My own lectures on the plays—the product of research, teaching, assistance in editing *The Shakespeare Newsletter*, lecturing abroad, teaching Shakespeare on television—and occasional lectures by other members of the teaching staff were supplemented by films dealing with the history of Elizabethan England and the theater of Shakespeare's day, as well as by exhibits of rare books and a specially created display in the University Museum consisting of paintings, prints, furniture, costumes, and books. Perhaps most important, however, was the teachers' actual research into designated areas of scholarship. Each was required to write a paper on one of the plays considered during the institute: *A Midsummer Night's Dream, Twelfth Night, Measure for Measure, Richard II, Romeo and Juliet, Julius Caesar, Hamlet*, and *Macbeth*. We emphasized traditional scholarship, divorced from both the experience of teaching and exposure to live performance, so that such insights from the study might later be compared to interpretations generated from live productions and classroom teaching.

A wealth of facts were presented that many of the teachers had not known, and such facts colored their interpretations of the plays. A girl named Katherine Hamlett drowned near Stratford when Shakespeare was sixteen years old. Did he recollect the incident in Ophelia's drowning? We learned as well that Shakespeare's daughter was written out of the will after he wrote *King Lear*. The fact that *Richard II* was restaged the day before the foiled Essex uprising of 7 February 1601 encouraged the teachers to examine that play's political overtones in light of the court upheaval of the time.

During the four weeks of the institute the teachers kept a reader-response journal in which they recorded their feelings about the lectures, the teaching units, and the live productions. Here we encouraged them to monitor their evolving views of the plays, and to note the basis of their perceptions. In these early days of the institute the approach was mainly analytical, the text our major concern. The diaries provided a fascinating barometer, enabling all of us to appreciate to what extent readings of the plays evolved in proportion to the new scholarship gained.

If their immersion in phase 1, the study part, was fast and furious, immersion in phase 2, the theater part, was slow and systematic. Phase 1 was revelation and analysis; phase 2, process and synthesis. Armed with an array of new facts that had perhaps modified earlier interpretations, we then experienced the transformation that occurs when those plays are experienced in the theater. The private moments of contemplation, the cloistered hours of library reading, the hours of writing, research, and discussion gave way to performance. What happens when those theories, born in the study, are applied to the bedrock reality of a theatrical production? If dissection, a tearing apart of the whole to analyze its components, was the task during those opening days of the institute, our presence in the theater saturated us with the play's totality—the music, the elocution of the lines, the studied gestures, the barrage of color, the costumes, the tonal modulations, the effects of stage lighting. In a sense, the intellect was emancipated; now examination was upon the whole rather than the part. Conclusions arrived at in the study were qualified, enhanced, modified. For example, during the study part of the institute we had considered Hamlet's "To be or not to be," yet our discussion yielded little. Now, when the attention was upon theater, we reconsidered the line with the help of John Styan: how might it be delivered on the stage? As some of the teachers said Hamlet's words, we noted that it is a "hearing" rather than a "seeing" line, indeed one almost totally lacking a visual dimension, an abstract line suggesting passivity and stasis. Hamlet's "be" suggested to the teachers a man barely eking out a living—*being* as opposed to living, or thriving or prevailing. Does the abstractness of the line suggest how removed Hamlet is from life, even how unreal the notion of suicide is for him?

This experiment of comparing a scholarly and then a theatrical analysis of a single line sensitized us to those various signals in the text more readily discerned by the actor than the teacher. The teachers began to realize how interpretations that do not take into account the props

Shakespeare requires or the implied stage directions can be incomplete, perhaps even shallow. Our next task was to heighten awareness of the actor's point of view, a challenging task for those teachers who had acted or directed little. We held three workshops, the first conducted by John Styan, the others by the directors of the Shakespearean plays we would attend later. *Twelfth Night,* seen at the Folger Shakespeare Theater, provided a graphic example of the differing interpretations yielded by the study and stage. During the reading of the play, the teachers had not considered how out of place Sebastian first appears in Illyria, since his reason and sanity contrast so greatly with the deluded characters about him. The extent of the Duke's and Olivia's delusion and surfeiting could not be adequately gauged until Sebastian stands next to them on stage.

Richard II provided another example. We had talked at length about how we would stage the opening scene—a resplendent King Richard with his entourage, jewel-bedecked, brightly lit, Richard in a white gown atop his throne high on stage. In act 5, scene 5, however, he appears in a dimly lit dungeon, stripped of his gown and jewels, isolated, sitting on the floor. This discussion of a potential staging enabled us to appreciate the seeming wreck Richard has become by the end of the play, but also to note how, despite his loss of the world, he had ironically begun to attain an exquisite moral vision. Still, it was the enactment that led us to appreciate firsthand that commonplace of criticism—namely, that Richard does obtain a moral vision proportionate to his loss of the world.

Seeing the plays as theater—through the workshops, film adaptations, live productions, and the group acting by members of our institute—led to one overriding conclusion: that as we teach *Hamlet* or *Macbeth* year in and year out, we can freeze the characters, the scenes, the lines into interpretations that only harden as time goes by. Such rigidity in turn inhibits our entertaining alternate viewpoints. Thus, we vowed to disinter the text from the fiction of right or wrong views. While this indeterminacy or ambiguity may be difficult to acknowledge, especially for students geared to television caricatures, surely it is far superior to our unconscious, unintended efforts to control the text. The distinction between text and stage, never before so marked for the teachers, was especially obvious when they selected a scene to rehearse and then stage for all the institute enrollees, as well as the university community. First, they formulated interpretations of that scene based upon scholarship and study. Then our teacher-actors turned the attention to its staging—blocking, rehearsing, and, finally, performance.

Our experience with the opening line of Antony's "Friends, Romans, countrymen" is illustrative. Prior to the staging we had only been hearing words; now we were hearing a voice, the actor's tonal modulation and inflection, and seeing Antony's effect on his audience in their actions and gestures. Earlier we had tried to imagine the importance of a stage prop, say, the will or Caesar's bloody mantle; now we noted in the theater how eyes were riveted to such props and how powerful was the actor's manipulation of them. Antony's three terms, "Friends, Romans, countrymen," may suggest that he is having difficulty quieting the large crowd gathering for his oration. Would he need to repeat himself if that crowd were small, tightly banded together, and thus easily controlled? Perhaps the physical distance between him and his audience accounts for his having to win their attention. The line could even be shouted, with lengthy pauses between the first three words. This acquisition of the actor's or director's view was attained slowly, but at least we initiated the process. Our efforts were substantially aided in a workshop with the directors and actors, whose productions of *The Taming of the Shrew* and *All's Well That Ends Well* we attended later in the institute.

Although we had accomplished much, we still had one remaining objective: to take these interpretations, born of the study and the stage, and bring them into the classroom. How could we adapt our experience for our students? Thus, the final days of our institute were devoted to the practical. This move to the classroom was, no less, a paradoxical challenge. To this point, the teachers had essentially been audience members (except for the enactment of brief scenes), as they listened to lectures, watched movies, viewed exhibits, attended concerts, and saw plays. Now they had to prepare for their own entrance on the stage. Knowledge acquired while a student at an institute is one thing; that knowledge discovered while teaching is altogether different. The first is, to a degree, passive, since for us teachers it is not totally felt in the soul until we are in the classroom; that experience of teaching others is, paradoxically, active learning. Besides, we had offered a barrage of intellectual and cultural experiences so kaleidoscopic that adequate reflection was difficult. For this reason, we asked in the final, quiet days of the institute that the teachers shape that newly acquired mountain of data into manageable group-designed teaching units. We felt that by working with colleagues, the individual teacher, thus presented with a variety of viewpoints, could avoid being locked into a single, idiosyncratic interpretation of a given play. Emphasis during this period of the institute was upon integration.

One of the several conclusions the teachers arrived at during these final days of the institute was that to comprehend Shakespeare's genius and the age that helped fashion it, moderns need to disassociate themselves from the particulars of time and place in twentieth-century life.

The teachers also realized that, prior to the institute, they had often been victims of spotty knowledge and factual inaccuracies. Eight plays were considered in detail, but another eight had been seen either on stage or in film versions. This exposure significantly increased the teachers' confidence, for it enabled them to trace the mutations of themes, and the evolution of characters, images, and Shakespeare's dramatic technique. Individually, the teachers benefited much from the institute, yet there was also a feeling that they had absorbed too much of the new too quickly. In this regard the group discussions were singularly important as the teachers thrashed out the findings and hammered those into classroom strategies.

One might have concluded that this stage emphasizing the classroom would be anticlimactic, that the teachers had already considered every new interpretation that the stages of the study and theater could afford. This was not the case. Discussing how to teach *Romeo and Juliet* in their classrooms, several of the teachers decided to emphasize the conformity-nonconformity theme as a way of making the play relevant to their students. This mutual decision made them reconsider Romeo's fight with Tybalt: in a frenzied moment when hate overcomes love, Romeo decides to heed the ancestral Montague voice and slay a Capulet. They had assumed that Romeo killed Tybalt because he was expected to; his retaliation was dictated by honor, and by his friendship with Mercutio. Now, the preparation of the classroom lesson-plan forced them to a new insight. Who was to say that Shakespeare felt Romeo should retaliate? Why be puppet to an ethic that did not make sense? Shakespeare was known to have mocked gentlemen in other plays—witness Osric et al—so why might he not be condemning their code here? This discussion made them consider staging that scene so as to reveal great anguish on Romeo's part as he looks offstage to consider Juliet, his vows, his recent affirmation of love, then looks back to the Montagues surrounding him onstage. He wavers, and then decides that conformity is the easier path—drift is always easier than decision.

By the time the teaching units were complete, the results were evident: teacher burnout had been checked; familiarity with available resources for teaching Shakespeare had been gained; classroom strategies, formerly stale and stock, had been fortified, even replaced, by more creative ones; interdisciplinary, multimedia, and culturally related approaches could now be employed in the classroom; philosophies of life extolling the present and denigrating a historical perspective had been exchanged for more historically sensitive ones. Teachers had learned to confront and audit their own reactions to the plays. They now returned to their classrooms immeasurably reinvigorated. Questionnaires, distributed shortly after the completion of the institute and again after the group-designed teaching unit had been used, told us this. The enrollees also returned to campus for a one-day workshop, during which discussions were held about the successes and failures of presenting the teaching units. Lastly, the teachers themselves offered a detailed report to their colleagues about the Shakespeare Institute, its format, and findings.

Perhaps for too many of us our research and writing, preparation and teaching has been insular because we have viewed the world of the theater from one stage only. Once we have traversed the triple stage, I believe that our thinking, our writing, and our teaching coalesce into a fuller understanding, a deeper appreciation of its finest practitioner.

Afterword

Afterword

NORMAN N. HOLLAND

"ANOTHER BOOK ON SHAKESPEARE!"—I CAN HEAR SOME GRUMPY CIVILIAN grumbling that as Sid Homan's collection makes its way through the book catalogues and retailers. Indeed, recently, I even caught myself making the familiar mock-horrified complaint.

It was at a Ph.D. preliminary exam. The candidate was going to do a dissertation on staging *King Lear.* Under our new, enlightened Ph.D. structure, the candidate can put forward, as the subject-matter on which to be examined, a span of work directly related to the proposed dissertation. Accordingly, Ron Boling offered an astutely annotated bibliography of some 151 articles and books relating to *King Lear.*

I was appalled, not at Ron's work, which was copious and intelligent, but at my fellow critics. In article after article and book after book, a critic would stress a line differently from other critics, weigh the importance of an episode in a new way, or find a different meaning for a word, a line, or a scene, and proudly hale forth a new theme or "angle" on Shakespeare, new, however, only in the nuance. How can a single tragedy, even one as magnificent as *King Lear,* bear such an intolerable weight of human lucubration? And I do not exclude myself. I wrote the same way, at least when I was a proper Shakespearean, before I became interested in readers' and audiences' responses. Suddenly I felt overrun by a wave of antlike busyness.

I brought my melancholy and despair to Ron's Ph.D. exam. "Look at all these neat little abstracts," I said to him and, or course, obliquely to my colleagues. "Look at them and ask yourself if it would make any difference in the total sum of human endeavor if number 37 had not written or number 122 or number 138. Surely not. And perhaps it would make no difference if the whole crew had not written. How do you propose," I asked Ron, "to write something that will matter or, at the very least, will be different from the 151 who have written before you?"

I was hoping Ron would say that he would do something experimental or creative, something frankly personal. I was hoping he would say he planned to write an essay whose claim on its readers would be not so much the matter of Shakespeare as the matter of a human being confronting *King Lear* in all the humanness of both—that would be one way reader-response theory points us toward a criticism of Shakespeare that matters. Ron is no reader-response critic, though, and my question, my wondering, really, accomplished nothing more than disconcerting him.

A wise colleague, Sid Homan in fact, came to his rescue. "That's a question you ask at his age, not at yours," he said to Ron, and laughed. "Look out for him, he's just had a birthday." A touch, a touch, I do confess it, birthday and all. All true. One does, at a certain age, look round oneself and ask, grimly playing with that expansion of tenses our English admits, What is it all for? What was it all for? What will it all have been for? And Ron was most assuredly not at an age or stage where one asks that of one's profession.

Nevertheless, I thought Sid's defense a bit of a dodge, sage under the circumstances of the exam, perhaps under any circumstances, but no answer to the question Ron's collection seemed to me to shout out. At the time I had not read this collection of essays. I did not know that Sid was proceeding from an altogether different model of the critical process.

That is, just about all of Ron's 151 critics shared a certain model of what they were doing, a model I might add, shared by the birthday boy as well, when he was behaving more like a Shakespearean and less like a reader-response critic. We tended to assume that there was the play, the poem, or, most rigorously and portentously, the Text. The business of the critic is to read that text and to report on what one finds there, like an explorer coming back from Terra Incognita with wondrous stories or a miner coming triumphantly up from underground caverns with a nugget of purest, shiniest gold. The critic is merely a skilled Everyman. Anyone would have seen the same, found the same, and reported the same, had they gone to the same place and looked with the same perspicacity that *this* critic has demonstrated by these findings.

To be sure, all of the 151 did demonstrate perspicacity—well, nearly all of them—and paradoxically, that is a big part of the trouble. One by one, the 151 almost without exception make convincing cases for their "new" points of view. I can believe just about all of them, but they all compete and conflict with their different readings so that to believe all is by that very token to believe none. Hence the feeling of futility.

Sid Homan imagines here, and through his various contributors realizes, an altogether different model of Shakespearean criticism. Sid's collection does not deal in "the" answers, perhaps because so many of his writers draw on backgrounds in the theater, psychoanalytic criticism, reader-response, or experiment in teaching Shakespeare. Their essays move naturally toward a different kind of criticism.

I would call it, in a much-used and much-abused term, postmodern.

For me, the word indicates a shift from the modernist idea of a work of art as a self-contained structure of intrinsic richness and complexity—think of the work of such great twentieth-century artists as Picasso, T. S. Eliot, Brecht, or Stravinsky. The postmodernist treats a work of art as *the relation between* such a structure and its audience (or its author, its historical context, its society, or other works of art). We have changed from the structures of a *Guernica, The Waste Land*, or the Guggenheim Museum, to the questioning of conceptual sculpture, the ricochet of performance art, or the parodies of postmodern architecture. The same shift applies to the postmodern critic. For the critic as for the artist, the work of art exists in relation to audience, readers, critics, author, and other works of art, and the business of the critic is to enter into that relationship, deepening and complicating it.

So far postmodern art and criticism seem to me thinner, more hellenistic, less magisterial than high modernism, but interesting and valid in their own right. The postmodern is hard to judge, however, because it is hard to fix in permanent form. (By that very aim, of course, I reveal my modernist roots. As Philip McGuire remarks at the opening of his essay, "Our ingrained tendency is to equate greatness with permanence, with fixity, with immutability," and it is just that tendency which our postmodern era questions.) "Relation between" can be just as rich and complex as the "structure" of an earlier era, although we have not yet had enough time to know (or, to be postmodern, believe) what will prove rich and lasting, if indeed that is a criterion any more. (I think a hallmark of postmodern writing, mine anyway, is too many parenthetical remarks like that one—or this.) At any rate, it is in this postmodern mode that Homan's *Triple Play* plays, while Ron Boling's 151 critics mostly imagined themselves in the permanences and self-containedness of high modern.

This kind of criticism bears a close relationship to what, in another context, we would call systems thinking. It is widespread in the natural and social sciences. Thomas Kuhn and other philosophers of science have shown that science is not as we once imagined it, simply "objective," a sturdy Paul Muni battling the microbes with scientific Truth (like a New Critic digging out the True Meaning of a text). Science is a complex social phenomenon. A new idea in science enters a preexisting system of ideas and persons, and it is the system that determines its fate. Even in a science, ideas rise and fall as they do or do not accord with the social institutions of a science: promotions, prestige, scholarships, grants, or contracts. Less crassly and more importantly, the fate of a scientific idea depends as much upon whether other scientists can fit it into their own conceptual frameworks as upon the truth of the idea itself.[1]

In the same vein, recent psychological work by Howard Gardner and

Mihalyi Csikszentmihalyi on "creativity" in the arts as well as the sciences suggest we can only understand that most individual of traits as no trait at all. "Creativity" does not simply exist in the creative person's head. Rather, it consists of interactions between three foci: an individual talent, a domain of works and ideas, and a field that organizes that domain socially. As the work of some persons bulks larger and larger in that system, that individual is, we say, "creative."[2]

In my own recent book, *The I*, I argue that the recent explosion of work in the architecture of the brain or the psychology of perception or symbolization breaks down the old boundary between subject and object. The I is a system constantly interacting with its environment in feedbacks by which a personal style interacts with the world "out there."[3] The distinguished biologist Stephen Jay Gould argued, in a lecture I heard not so long ago, that Darwin's original picture of natural selection as operating on individual bodies is too narrow.[4] What is "an individual"? A field of grass is "an individual," for example. A swarm of bees may be. We have to imagine individuals, in a biological sense, as not just bodies bounded by skin, scales, or fur. "An individual"—the I, in my sense—can include whole species that battle and adapt to survive. At the other end of the scale, "an individual" can mean viruses and genes that cannot survive by themselves but even so take over the bodies that host them in the interests of their own survival, not the bodies'.

The reason I have invited these scientific texts into an afterword to an anthology of essays on Shakespeare is to say that the shift these essays embody pervades current thinking about all the arts and sciences. The individual artist or scientist—and their subject matter, and their audience—exist only in systems of interaction. Whether we call this mode of talking about the world postmodernism or systems thinking, we deal, in these latter days of the twentieth century, not so much in things as in relationships. Shining, youthful faces look up to us in our classrooms for an understanding of Shakespeare. The Shakespeare they seek is not "the" but their Shakespeare. They may never have heard of Marshall McLuhan, but they are his heirs.

Literary historians have long noted that criticism of Shakespeare mirrors and indeed often provides a curiously pointed example of an era's core ideas. The seventeenth century rewrote him, a testimony to the profound intellectual changes between Shakespeare's lifetime and 1700. The neoclassic period concerned itself with how "right" he was, that is, whether he matched the laws that century so proudly displayed—of the stage, music, clockwork, the planets, or human psychology. The nineteenth and early twentieth centuries regarded him as the portrayer of "character" or, in a larger sense, of changing historical realities "out there," separable from the "in here," Our own century has moved from close verbal analysis (in criticism and performance) of a defined text, to the sixties' breaking down of the boundaries around that text, to, most recently, a more careful working with the boundary between audience and text, both in performance and, as these essays show, criticism.

It would be superfluous of me to comment on them individually. Sid Homan has already done that. Simply, I would like to call to your attention how they build on three poles of a system: Shakespeare in the study, the classroom, and the theater. In study and classroom, Shakespeare is provisional. We can have him both ways, indeed, we can imagine him any way we want, because we can change our minds. Theater and film require the director, actors, and therefore the audience, to make a choice, but a choice that the next production can undo. The Shakespeare of these essays is not locked in the fixity of the Text.

What these essays propose and what they work with is a Shakespeare-system: the plays and poems move constantly from critic to teacher to performer, each drawing from the other as each constantly changes. What these essays recount is the way this group of contemporary critics have made that relationship explicit, indeed the subject of their work, as postmodern artists make the relationship of text and audience theirs.

Hence I find it characteristic of these essays that they move easily—joyously—from criticism to teaching to performance, with Shakespeare's text all the time circulating around a ring like the circulation of gold James Calderwood points to in *The Merchant of Venice*. Marvin Rosenberg's work has long shown us how different ages imagine the characters and plays differently—to use the psychological term, how in performance we *project* ourselves upon the text. Laura Keyes shows that, despite the disconcerting "fat" of the text, we can imagine Hamlet from skinny to obese and it's simply a part of the reader's normal projection. Or the director's, as Philip McGuire instances, from Egeus's silence in the final boy-gets-girl of *Midsummer Night's Dream*. Sid Homan's essay shows how a director uses the projections of his coworkers, especially in so different a culture from Shakespeare's as the People's Republic of China. Closer to home, the Birenbaum and Rosen essays show us how the plays use their own status as symbols and rhetoric to call into question the relation between play and audience. Back in the study, Sherman Hawkins finds in his Prospero a professor, as many of us have long suspected—and projected. The professors, in turn, invite actors and directors via videotape into their classrooms. In teaching they and their students read text and criticism against performance and vice versa to see, for example, in Schleuter and Lusardi's essay, how subtly the psychology of the closet scene varies in different stagings and filmings. This group of essays linking teaching and performance demonstrates perhaps most strikingly Csikszentmihalyi and Gardner's model of creativity. "Shakespeare" involves an entire system of himself as creator and person, an intellectual "domain" in which he is taught, performed, and studied, and a social field in which all the people involved in these activities interact with one another—and that is, of course, this book

In other words, "another book on Shakespeare" is only appalling if you believe a critic is to find *the* answer, and there are 151 of them claiming to have it, and they all differ as to what it is. You should not be—*I* should not be—appalled at all if we imagine literary criticism, classroom teaching, and performance on a stage as all parts of an interacting system, that is, if we visualize "Shakespeare" as a continuing process. "Another book on Shakespeare" simply demonstrates—you could call it, and I intend no pejorative whatsoever here, just the opposite—the Shakespeare industry. That is exactly what "Shakespeare" is, must be, and *ought* to be: various people's industry at analyzing, teaching, and performing his extraordinary plays and poems, making them work on our imaginary forces. Because of Homan's method, his collection shows us that "another book on Shakespeare" is precisely what we need in order to make Shakespeare's works work. It is something—especially with this collection—to rejoice in.

Notes

1. Thomas S. Kuhn, *The Structure of Scientific Revolutions* (Chicago: University of Chicago Press, 1962). For other philosophers of science, see Imre Lacatos and Alan Musgrave, eds., *Criticism and the Growth of Knowledge*, Proceedings of the International Colloquium in the Philosophy of Science, London, 1965, vol. 4 (Cambridge: At the University Press, 1970).

2. Mihaly Csikszentmilhalyi, "Society, Culture, and Person: A Systems View of Creativity," unpub. paper, September 1986 (Department of Psychology, University of Chicago). Howard Gardner, "Freud in Three Frames: A Cognitive-Scientific Approach to Creativity," *Daedalus* 115 (1986): 106–34.

3. Norman N. Holland, *The I* (New Haven: Yale University Press, 1985).

4. Stephen Jay Gould, "Dinosaurs, Nuclear Winter . . .," Chautauqua Institution, Chautauqua, N.Y. 14712, 23 August 1985 (audiotape available).

Notes on the Contributors

HARVEY BIRENBAUM: Harvey Birenbaum has taught at San Jose State University since 1965. In 1984–85, he held an NEH Fellowship. His *Tragedy and Innocence* was published in 1983. A new book on the philosophy of myth, *Myth and Mind*, will be out in the fall of 1987. It will be followed by *The Art of Our Necessities: Form and Consciousness in Shakespeare*.

SUZANNE BURR: After training at the American Academy of Dramatic Arts in New York City, Suzanne Burr is now in the graduate program at the University of Michigan, where she recently completed a doctoral dissertation on ghosts in modern drama. Her focus is on Ibsen, Strindberg, and O'Neill, and their legacy to contemporary playwrights.

JAMES L. CALDERWOOD: James L. Calderwood is professor of English and associate dean of the humanities at the University of California, Irvine. Along with numerous articles, texts, and poems, he has published *Shakespearean Metadrama*, *Metadrama in Shakespeare's Histories*, *To Be and Not To Be*, and *If It Were Done*. His *Shakespeare and the Denial of Death* is forthcoming.

ROGER GEIMER: Associate professor of English at Purdue University Calumet, Roger Geimer has published widely in both scholarly journals and books designed to support students in their study of literature. A contributor to the Shakespeare Data Bank, he is currently working on a book on Shakespearean comedy.

ROBERT HAPGOOD: Besides his "role" as professor of English at the University of New Hampshire, Robert Hapgood is the director of that university's London Program. He has published numerous articles and theater reviews, and won the English Institute Prize in 1968 for his influential essay "Shakespeare and the Included Spectator."

SHERMAN HAWKINS: Sherman Hawkins taught at Princeton and Rochester before coming to Wesleyan University, where he is professor of English and highly respected as a dynamic teacher. He has published widely quoted essays on Chaucer, Spenser, Shakespeare, and Milton, and is currently working on a book about Shakespeare's history plays.

NORMAN N. HOLLAND: Milbauer Eminent Scholar at the University of Florida, Norman N. Holland writes and teaches psychoanalytic criticism, particularly as applied to the interpretations of text by readers. The author of eight books, he is best known for his studies of readers' responses: *Poems in Person* (1973), *5 Readers Reading* (1975), and *Laughing* (1982), and the more theoretical *The I* (1985). His afterword in this volume represents a return to his *Psychoanalysis and Shakespeare* (1966).

SIDNEY HOMAN: At home on both the campus and the stage, Sidney Homan is a professor of English at the University of Florida and a visiting professor of Jilin University in the People's Republic of China. He has edited *Shakespeare's "More Than Words Can Witness,"* and is the author of *When the Theater Turns to Itself: The Aesthetic Metaphor in Shakespeare*, the prize-winning *Beckett's Theaters*, and *Shakespeare's Theater of Presence: Language, Spectacle, and the Audience*. Most recently, he coedited, with Norman Holland and Bernard Paris, a collection of essays entitled *Shakespeare's Personality*.

LAURA KEYES: After receiving her Ph.D. from the State University of New York at Buffalo, Laura Keyes taught at the College of Wooster, Mankato State University, and Birmingham Southern College. Her major interest is in the psychological dimensions of literature and, in particular, children's literature and Shakespeare. She is a member of the English Department at DePauw University.

JAMES P. LUSARDI: Professor of English at Lafayette College, James P. Lusardi is an editor of the Yale edition of *The Complete Works of St. Thomas More* (1973). Along with publishing articles on Shakespeare and reviews of productions, he coedits *Shakespeare Bulletin* and serves as an associate editor of *Stages*. He and June Schlueter are collaborating on a book-length study of Shakespeare in performance.

PHILIP C. MCGUIRE: Professor of English at Michigan State University, Philip McGuire is the author of *Speechless Dialect: Shakespeare's Open Silences* (University of California Press, 1985). He is also the coeditor of *Shakespeare: The Theatrical Dimension*. He has published articles on Shakespeare's plays and sonnets, and on Renaissance poetry. He is currently writing a book on Shakespeare's Jacobean plays for Macmillan (United Kingdom).

MICHAEL PAYNE: Chairman of the Department of English at Bucknell University, Michael Payne is the author of numerous articles and of *Irony in Shakespeare's Roman Plays*. He is presently at work on a book on *The Tempest* in the context of changing critical tastes. Besides having served as editor of *Bucknell Review*, he is the editor of the two journals of the College English Association: *CEA Critic* and *CEA Forum*.

BARBARA ROSEN: Barbara Rosen teaches English at the University of Connecticut. A coeditor of the critical journal *Children's Literature* published by the Yale University Press, she has also coedited Shakespeare's *Julius Caesar* and edited sixteenth-century accounts of witch trials.

MARVIN ROSENBERG: A playwright and actor, Marvin Rosenberg is a Professor of Dramatic Art at the University of California, Berkeley. Scholars as well as people in the theater are familiar with his three studies—each prefaced with *The Masks of*—of *King Lear, Othello,* and *Macbeth,* published by the University of California Press. He is currently finishing *The Masks of Hamlet*. He asks that if readers recall seeing any illuminating moments of stage action in productions of *Hamlet,* he would like to hear from them.

JUNE SCHLUETER: Associate professor of English at Lafayette College, June Schlueter has published *Metafictional Characters in Modern Drama, The Plays and Novels of Peter Handke,* and, with James Flanagan, *Arthur Miller*. Along with coediting two volumes with her husband, Paul Schlueter, and being the coauthor, with James Lusardi, of the forthcoming *Reading Shakespeare in Performance,* she is the coeditor of the journal *Shakespeare Bulletin*.

RONALD SHAFER: An award-winning teacher at Indiana University of Pennsylvania, Ronald Shafer is the founder and president of the Friends of Milton's Cottage, and has directed the International Milton Symposia in London and later at Cambridge University. In 1986 and 1987 he was the project director for the National Endowment for the Humanities Summer Shakespeare Institute. Author of numerous articles, he has edited a collection of essays called *Shakespeare and English History: Interdisciplinary Perspectives*. He was a semifinalist in a professor-of-the-year national search in 1986.

MASON Y. H. WANG: Professor of English at Saginaw Valley State College in Michigan, Mason Wang has edited *Perspectives in Contemporary Chinese Literature* (1983) and is a contributor to the Annotated Shakespeare Bibliography in *Shakespeare Quarterly*.

ZHANG HUAIQING: Zhang Huaiqing teaches at Jilin University in Changchun City, in the People's Republic of China. He is a well-known scholar and poet.

ZHANG SIYANG: Zhang Siyang is professor of Chinese at Jilin University in the People's Republic of China. Author of numerous books and articles on Shakespeare and modern Chinese literature, he was the first president of the Shakespeare Society of Jilin Province. His two-volume study, *Shakespeare: A Survey*, is scheduled for publication in 1987.

ZHANG XIAOYANG: At once the son and the student of Zhang Siyang, Zhang Xiaoyang is lecturer in English at the Beijing Language Institute. He is the author of many articles in Chinese scholarly journals on Shakespeare and aesthetics.

Index